# Just Friends

# Just Friends

ROBYN SISMAN

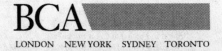

LONDON  NEW YORK  SYDNEY  TORONTO

This edition published 2000
by BCA
by arrangement with Michael Josephs
The Penguin Group

First Reprint 2000

CN 3476 HB
CN 7611 PB

First published in Great Britain by Michael Joseph 2000

Set in Monotype Garamond
Typeset by Intype London Ltd
Printed and bound in Great Britain by
Mackays of Chatham plc, Chatham, Kent

For my mother

# I

Freya peeled off her clothes and stood in her underwear, contemplating her reflection. She wanted to
look her best for Michael tonight. There had been no
time to go home to change; she must make do with
this cramped ladies' room beneath her office, with its
unforgiving light and damp basement smell. Her new
dress hung from the cubicle door: not classic black,
not vampish leopardskin, but a cool thousand dollars'
worth of palest pink that shimmered with a tracery of
opalescent beads – a Cinderella dress chosen to make
her as feminine and delicate as a porcelain doll. That
was the look she was aiming for, less *femme fatale*, more
. . . *femme*, plain and simple.

*Let's go somewhere special*, he had said over breakfast
on Monday morning, *somewhere we can talk*. Questions
had exploded in her head, like popcorn in a hot pan.
Talk about what? Why not right here in the apartment?
Freya had choked them back. Instead, she'd done a
lot of shopping.

But all week long she had carried his words around
with her, a time-bomb in the pit of her stomach, tick-
tick-ticking as the days passed. Was this It? Was
she about to become Mrs Normal, grouching about
schools and the state of her suburban lawn?

With a hand that was not quite steady, Freya twisted the tap and splashed her cheeks with cold water. On with the war paint. She began to make up her face – a pencil to darken the pale arches of her eyebrows, mascara to bring her light-blue eyes into focus. Which lipstick? Scarlet Woman was out, obviously. So, frankly, was Vestal Virgin, a relic of her infatuation with an artist who had left her for a seventeen-year-old. Ah-hah, Crimson Kiss, that was more like it. She slid the colour back and forth over her lips, then bared her teeth, satisfactorily white against the red. I floss, you floss, we all floss. God bless American dentistry.

But what if she was wrong? Maybe Michael just wanted to discuss the new service charge for the apartment, or to finalize plans for their trip to England. Freya cocked her head to fix an earring, considering this possibility. No, she decided. Michael was a lawyer, and a man: habit was his middle name. Every January he bought his suits in the sales, always two, always Armani, either navy or charcoal. He called his mother on Sunday evenings (allowing for the time change to Minneapolis), got his annual hay fever shot right after Groundhog Day, and always tipped ten per cent on the nose. There was nothing unpredictable about Michael, thank God. If he wanted to 'talk', he must have something important to say.

Balancing precariously on one flamingo leg, then the other, Freya slid on sheer stockings, then stepped carefully into the precious dress and drew it up her body, shivering at its silky opulence. A hidden side zip pulled it snug around her small breasts, miraculously creating a discreet cleavage. She slotted her feet into flat shoes, with the faintest sigh of regret for those strappy four-inch heels she'd seen in a Fifth Avenue store. It was too bad that Michael wasn't taller. She reminded herself sternly that successful relationships were founded on compromise.

A few adjustments, a mist of perfume and she was finished. Did she look the part? Freya found her brain flooding with words she had never associated with herself: *fiancée, engagement, honeymoon, Mr and Mrs ... Daddy and Mummy.* She grabbed the washbasin with both hands and peered close. Narrow pointed face, skin pale as buttermilk, collarbones you could beat a tattoo on, long arms and legs – too long? She was as tall as many men: 'giraffe' they had called her at school. Could somebody really *love* this person – for ever and ever, amen? She picked at her newly cropped hair (another hundred bucks), so fair it looked almost colourless in this light. 'Freya the beautiful', her mother used to call her, named after the warm-hearted goddess of the icy north who was loved by all men. But that was when she was six years old. It was impossible to know what her mother would make of her now.

As she turned this way and that, assessing this unfamiliar self, Freya was reminded of one of those ballerinas that twirled mechanically on one leg whenever someone opened a musical box. She gave an experimental twirl herself, laughing a little as her legs tangled and she almost lost her balance. The movement had dislodged a lock of hair, and as she smoothed it back she caught sight of her left hand, with its bare ring finger. Her expression sobered. It was nice to be wanted, she told her twin in the mirror. It was wonderful to be loved. She wasn't twenty-nine any more.

Yes, Michael was the one, she was almost sure.

The restaurant Michael had chosen was a new and very expensive place on the edge of the Village, so confident of its must-go status that Freya walked past it twice before spotting the tiny engraved entry phone. She leant on the buzzer, and immediately the door was opened by an angelic young man with a peroxide crop. She found herself in a waiting area furnished according to the latest style edict to look 'just like your own home' – if you were a millionaire. Voluptuous sofas flanked a faux fireplace. There were Georgian-style urns on the mantelpiece, magazines and 'real' books artfully disarranged on low tables, even a chess set apparently abandoned in mid-game. Shallow steps led down into the dining room. From it wafted up fashionable smells, and the uninhibited chatter of people utterly at ease with their own tremendous success. The name of the restaurant, she remembered, was Phood.

As the young man led the way, Freya scanned the crowded tables. On one of the plump banquettes, perched somewhat stiffly between lime-green bolsters, was Michael. Sober-suited and serious, frowning slightly as he checked some document with a hovering pen – perhaps, knowing Michael, a checklist of their compatible qualities – he looked so out of place among the flashy media poseurs and Wall Street dudes that Freya's face melted into a tender, teasing smile. Her anxieties retreated. She realized that his choice of restaurant was a compliment to her, and vowed to keep any sardonic comments to herself. She would be amusing, charming, attentive: the perfect partner. She made her way down the steps, waiting for him to notice her. When he did, he looked startled, almost shocked: very gratifying. Cramming his papers into a side pocket, he leapt up from his chair to greet her with a kiss on each cheek.

'Freya, you look wonderful!'

'I know.' She put her hands on his shoulders and laughed into his eyes, then stepped back so that he could admire her properly. 'It's the new me. Don't tell me, you thought I was *born* wearing trousers.'

'No, no.' Her exuberance seemed to disconcert him. 'I mean, you always look fabulous.' He pulled the table out so she could sit down opposite him, and resumed his position. How adorably lawyerly he looked, with his square, handsome face, serious brown eyes, and wavy hair clipped close. They would love him in England. She wondered if he'd already bought her a ring, and if so where he was hiding it.

A waiter brought them menus, and drew a bottle from a cooler by the table.

'Champagne?'

'Absolutely.' Freya shot Michael a sparkling smile. 'Are we celebrating?'

'Well . . .' He looked bashful. 'It *is* Friday night.'

Freya held her tongue. After five months of living with him, she knew perfectly well that Michael's favourite Friday-night routine consisted of gourmet take-out, a video and early bed. But then he did work very hard.

As the waiter filled her glass, Freya was surprised to see that the bottle was already half empty. It was unlike Michael to drink alone. He must be gathering his courage.

'So how was your day?' she heard herself ask. Holey moley, she was turning into the perfect little housewife already!

'Fine. They're holding a meeting next month to vote on the new senior partners. Fred thinks I have a good chance.'

'Fred always says that.' Freya popped a couple of char-grilled pistachios into her mouth. Then she saw Michael's lips purse and quickly added, 'But I'm sure you do. King of the divorce courts, that's you. Hey, look at this.' She pointed to the menu, hoping to distract him from her lapse in tact. 'Beggar's Purse, *seventy dollars*. What can it be? Molten Deutschmarks?'

'Some kind of pancake, I think, with caviar inside. Seems a lot to pay for fish eggs, doesn't it?'

'Not if it's beluga. My father took me to St Petersburg once, when he was working at the Hermitage, and we went to this special dinner. I was about twelve, and it was the first time I'd ever tasted caviar, but I've never forgotten it. Total heaven. Go on, try it.'

'Fish gives me a bad reaction, you know that. I think I'll go for the soup.'

'Good choice.' Michael always had soup.

There was an awkward pause. Freya felt suddenly artificial in her expensive dress amid the chic absurdities of this place, smiling at this man who was smiling back at her. It was if they were in a play and had both forgotten their lines. To prod the scene into life, she launched into a girly pantomime of choosing what to eat. Was this too fattening? (Of course not, she could never be fat.) Was that too garlicky? (It didn't matter; he positively liked garlic.) She exclaimed over the restaurant. How had he succeeded in getting a reservation? Wasn't it original to have feathers in the vases instead of flowers? Michael responded distractedly and blew his nose, saying he thought he might be allergic to feathers. Freya suppressed a twinge of irritation. Michael had always been shy; she must let him go at his own pace.

It was his shyness that had caught her attention in the first place, that evening at an uptown gallery. Michael had come to the opening with his boss and the boss's ghastly wife, one of those pampered Manhattan ice-queens who liked to think of themselves as a patroness of the arts when they weren't having their nails done. Freya was supposed to be checking out the competition, but it was as much as she could do to stay upright. Still recovering from a bad relationship with the evil Todd, she felt shaky and listless. No one spoke to her; she knew she exuded misery and defeat. From her vantage point in a corner, the cold concrete wall at her back for support, a glass in her hand for cover, she had watched the pantomime of Michael's super-polite behaviour as he was alternately patronized and snubbed, dispatched to fetch wine or to deposit a fur coat. She was impressed by his good humour. She liked the way he bent carefully to read the titles and descriptions beside each painting, then stood back to give them his serious, slightly perplexed consideration. Romance was the last thing on her mind; she was done with all that. But observing his open, masculine face, free of cynicism, the thought had occurred to her: *Why can't I fall for a nice man like that?*

Later Michael confided that he had dared approach her only because she looked as lost and alone as he felt. Galleries were not his scene; he had no talent for social chatter. When it turned out that the boss's hospitality did not extend to dinner, Michael had asked Freya out instead. She couldn't remember what she'd replied – nothing perhaps. But he had found her coat and drawn her out into the snowy street, then into a steamy restaurant. She was too thin, he said, and he'd made her eat pasta and drink red wine until he could see the colour return to her cheeks. He'd asked nothing of her, just told her about his home and his family and his job – soothing, undemanding talk about normal people and normal lives. Afterwards, he had taken her home in a cab, wheels hissing through the slush, and made it wait while he accompanied her right to the door of that miserable walk-up off Lexington Avenue. He hadn't pounced on her, hadn't even asked to come in, just made sure she had her key and said goodnight.

It had been a slow, old-fashioned courtship, especially by Manhattan standards – flowers, exhibitions, walks in the park, tea and muffins at Bendels. Michael treated her almost like an invalid, and she had liked the attention. Fifteen years in New York had taught her the art of detachment – from the drunks and crazies, from filth and noise, from the loneliness that came in the small hours and the men who said they'd call and never did. It was nice to feel attached. Michael's apartment on the Upper West Side was blissfully warm and comfortable. Freya spent more and more time there until one day – and it was shaming to admit that she couldn't remember the exact details – they became lovers. Soon afterwards Michael persuaded her to move in altogether. And she had liked that too. The simple domestic pleasures of shopping and cooking, that relaxed moment at the end of the day when they would exchange news of what had happened since they parted in the morning, made her feel that she was at last having a grown-up, normal relationship. It was comforting to have someone who wanted to listen to this sort of personal trivia, and it felt special to be entrusted with someone else's, even if it wasn't always that interesting. Michael was patient and kind, and in due course she had bounced back, as she always did. They bickered, of course – once she'd accused him of preferring that pathetic wreck he'd picked up at the gallery to her real self – but bickering was normal, wasn't it? Now they were almost like a married couple. Very like a married couple, Freya realised, for Michael had been talking to her for some time and she hadn't heard a word.

'. . . so I said, "Okay, we'll shut you down." That shut him up.' Michael looked up triumphantly; Freya wanted to ruffle his hair. He was so sweet and straight-forward. He would make a wonderful father. Not that she wanted children right now, of course. But it would be reassuring to have some quality sperm on tap, as it were.

'But that's enough about me. How about you? How's Lola?'

'In Milan, thank God. At least the time difference means the phone calls peter out by the afternoon.'

Lola Preiss was Freya's boss, a woman of unspeci-fied Central European origins and legendary repu-tation, whose gallery on 57th Street attracted punters with a million or so to spend on big-hitters like Warhol, Lichtenstein and Stella. Three years ago, after years of dogged drudgery in half the museums and galleries in New York, learning about everything from framing and lighting to printing techniques, publicity and US Customs forms – while simultaneously developing her own 'eye' – Freya had been rewarded by an offer to set up Lola Preiss Downtown, a brand-new gallery in a beautiful space in SoHo. Her brief was to seek out and develop younger artists who might one day feed into Lola's megabucks machine. Freya loved the work, and it would have been a dream job but for Lola's monstrous ego, which made her interrogate Freya over every decision she made, castigate her for her failures, and publicly claim Freya's successes as her own. Fortunately, now that Lola was nearing seventy she spent increasingly more time visiting the homes of her wealthiest clients (known uniformly as 'dahlink') along the seaboards of America and throughout the moneyed cities of Europe. But her influence was never very far away.

'So has it been a good week?' Michael persisted. 'Sell any big ones?'

Freya rolled her eyes. 'Michael, you don't measure art by the square yard.'

'I know that. You've told me often enough. I was just taking an interest.'

'Sorry.' Freya bit her lip.

The waiter brought wine and food. Over her truffle salad, Freya told Michael about her appointment this afternoon with a client sent by Lola, one of 'my dear old friends', who had arrived an hour late and turned out to be a complete time-waster. 'All he did was give me a pompous lecture on the inner meaning of each canvas – total art catalogue crapspeak. In the end I had to throw him out so I could get dressed. Otherwise I'd be here looking like a grunge.'

She paused, in case Michael wanted to comment on how un-grungy she was. He didn't.

'I hate that type, don't you?' she burbled on. 'All Rolex watches and phony European accents, and leering at you as they talk about the role of art in breaking sexual taboos.'

'Not a lot of leering goes on at Reinertson & Klang, I'm afraid.'

'Glad to hear it! I wouldn't want you running off with Mrs Ingwerson.'

'Mrs Ingwerson is fifty-four years old.' Michael's tone was cool. 'And the best secretary I've ever had.'

'Joke, Michael!' Freya gave her fork a humorous little flourish. He certainly was slow on the uptake tonight.

'Oh. Sorry.'

'Anyway,' she continued brightly, trying to smooth things over, 'we don't want to talk about work, do we?'

'No,' he said uncertainly. 'Here, have some more bread.' He grabbed a basket in front of him and held it out to her. 'You never eat enough.'

To please him, Freya took a piece and crumbled it on to her plate. Over his shoulder she caught sight of a couple leaning close to smile into each other's eyes, their faces lit by a glow of candlelight, their legs entwined under the table. Wasn't that how it was supposed to be? She felt a tremor of disquiet. Why didn't Michael get to the point? She was beginning to lose her nerve.

The waiter cleared their plates and brought the main courses while Michael began telling her, at some length, about some article he'd read in *The Times* about the mayor's controversial policy on under-age crime. Freya nodded at appropriate moments while her mind raced along its own track. Romance wasn't everything, she told herself. By Monday morning that couple probably wouldn't even be on speaking terms. Or he'd say he'd call, but he wouldn't, and she'd wait by the phone for a while, then go out and buy a new dress and start again. Freya knew the routine well. It was juvenile to expect to be swept away by passion. Mature relationships were founded on companionship and mutual respect, not to mention cash flow and a nice place to live. You had to take the long view.

Michael rambled on. It was almost as if he was marking time before – before what? Freya pushed her fish nervously round her plate. One man – *this* man – for the rest of her life, 'till death us do part': it was a scary idea. She told herself she was lucky to have the option, in a city where a single woman was ten times more likely to receive a dirty phone call than a proposal of marriage. And people changed when they got married . . . didn't they?

But when Michael finally finished his steak and laid down his knife and fork neatly, Freya's heart began to hammer. He cleared his throat. Uh-oh, was this it? What was she going to say?

Michael cleared his throat. 'Freya. I've brought you

here tonight for a special reason. I have something to say, and something to give you.'

'Really?' She gave an inane laugh.

'Please. I'm serious. I want you to listen.'

'I will, I will.' Freya felt herself flapping helplessly like a fish in a net. 'But, you know what, I'm still hungry. Isn't that amazing?' she gabbled. 'I've just got to have one of those irresistible-looking chocolate things.'

'Okay,' Michael said curtly. He waved over a waiter.

'What about you? The berry pie sounds good. Or the sorbet. I always think sorbet is so – '

'I don't want to eat. I want to talk.'

'Oh. Right.' Freya grabbed her wine glass and drained it.

Michael smoothed his tie down his shirt-front. 'These last few months we've been together have been some of the best of my life,' he began. 'You've opened my eyes to so many new things – art, and interesting food, and parts of the city I never knew existed. I want you to know that I think you're a terrific person.'

'You're a terrific person too,' Freya responded chirpily.

He ploughed on as if he hadn't heard. She realized that he'd rehearsed this speech. 'I've been thinking about the future. I'm thirty-six now, and I know what I want. I'm ready to settle down soon. If I get the partnership, I'll be able to afford to move. A house out of the city, Connecticut maybe, or some place upstate. Who knows, I might even take up golf.'

'Golf?' squeaked Freya, beginning to panic.

'And I want someone to share that life with me.'

Freya suddenly saw herself trapped behind a white picket fence with a frilly apron glued to her waist.

'Home. Stability. Shared interests,' Michael intoned. 'And kids, one day.'

Behind the picket fence there now appeared a scrum of yowling toddlers with jammy faces, freighted by bulging nappies. Freya could actually feel her biological clock whirling into reverse. A hand placed her dessert before her – brown goo in a creamy lake. Her stomach heaved.

'These are the things I see happening, things I'm looking forward to, things I want to share with another person.' He stared at her intently, almost fiercely.

Quick! Head him off at the pass. 'Could we order some coffee?' she croaked. 'I'm feeling kind of tired.'

'In a minute. What I'm trying to say – ' He broke off in exasperation as she gave an enormous fake yawn. 'God, you're making this so difficult. There's something I want to give you.'

Now he was patting his pockets. Any minute he was going to produce the ring!

'I don't need anything. Really. It's not my birthday.'

'Please stop interrupting. I've got something important to say to you.'

'There's no rush. Let's leave it till tomorrow.' Freya

was now giving her hair careless little flicks and grinning like a Disney chipmunk.

'You see, I think you're wonderful,' Michael continued.

'Hey, I think I'm wonderful too. So why don't we . . .' Freya cast around wildly for inspiration and caught sight of the canoodling couple. She leaned low across the table, clenching her forearms to her sides to give herself a Grand Canyon cleavage. 'Why don't we go home,' she cooed, 'and make mad, passionate love?'

'You don't understand.' Michael had now taken whatever it was out of his pocket. He held it hidden, cupped between both hands, and was looking down solemnly, like a small boy about to show her his pet toad.

Freya tried a different tack. 'It's too soon.' Her voice was redolent with untold tragedy. She nudged his hand. 'Please, put it away.'

Instead, Michael pressed the object into her fingers – a small, square box.

Freya hesitated. She might as well see what he had picked out. Did she rate diamonds? Or the predictable sapphire, 'to match your eyes'?

She opened the box. Inside was a gold signet ring engraved with the monogram MJP. The initials stood for Michael Josiah Petersen. She knew this because she had bought him the ring herself. American men liked that kind of thing. It had been a gesture, to show her gratitude to Michael when he first gave her shelter.

'Wow.' She was completely at a loss. In American high schools, girls and boys swapped 'class rings'. Maybe this was a grown-up version. 'I – I don't know what to say.' She took out the ring and turned it round in her fingers, then looked into Michael's face for guidance.

'We've had such great times together.' Michael's voice was thick with emotion.

'Yes . . .' She hung her head.

'I so much want you to be happy.'

'I know.'

'But – '

*But?* Freya's head jerked up. But what? She'd lost the script. What was going on here?

' – but I think it would be better if . . .'

'If what?'

'Well, you know . . .'

'No, Michael, I don't know.'

'If we could be . . .'

'Yes . . . ?'

'I think it would be better if we could be . . . just friends.'

'Friends,' she echoed. '*Friends?*' she repeated loudly.

There was a dull splat. It was the ring, dropping from her lifeless fingers into the chocolate torte.

# 2

*Walk. Don't walk.* Signs flashed. Headlamps dazzled. Traffic revved and roared. There was the *whoop-whoop* of a police siren, a percussive strafe of rap music from a passing car. Freya strode up Broadway, heels clacking, long legs scissoring in leather trousers. A piece of crushed material dangled from one swinging fist. From time to time she swished it angrily, like a lion-tamer with his whip. People got out of her way.

Bastard! How dare he ditch her like that? He'd led her up the garden path, then pushed her head first into the muck-heap. 'I think you're a terrific person,' she mimicked to herself, waggling her head like a crazy. So *terrific* that he'd made her spend over a thousand dollars, just so he could ask her to be 'friends' with him. So *terrific* that he'd taken her to the most fashionable restaurant in town for the pleasure of dumping her in public. Her eyes blurred, and she stepped out into the street without seeing that the lights had changed.

A clash of car horns made her jump. Automatically Freya responded with a rude gesture and kept walking. She sniffed fiercely and swiped the heel of her hand across her cheeks. She was *not* crying. She began to sing loudly in her head to drown out the voice that told her she was alone, that she would always be alone, that no one wanted to be with her if they could help it, that she'd been a vain, ridiculous fool to think Michael could want to marry her. It was always the same tune, she couldn't have said why. She didn't even know the words.

> *Land of hope and glory, mother of the free*
> *Dum dum dum-dum dum-dum dum*
> *Dum dum diddle-y dee . . .*

Sure enough, as she marched up the street in time with the music, Freya felt the steel re-enter her soul. Tough, tough, tough, she reminded herself. She hadn't cried in front of anyone since she was fifteen years old, when her little sneak of a stepsister had peeked through the keyhole of her bedroom door and then run to tell the household that Freya was a cry-baby. Well, not any more. Freya had chosen this city *because* it was the toughest in the world. Manhattan wasn't like a European city where people wandered hand in hand, stopped to kiss in the middle of pavements and bridges, and took their children and grannies to restaurants. This was a place where you walked fast and avoided eye contact, where you got your Christmas tree delivered already decorated and threw it out on Christmas afternoon, where you told your cab driver he was a fucking cretin, and developed that 'don't-mess-with-me' glint in your eye. Freya liked it; it suited her.

Okay, so she was back to square one. So what? She'd been alone before. She was used to it. It was better than staying with a man who didn't love her. She wasn't doing that, not even for one night.

For after itemizing the reasons why she wasn't right for him – psychobabble about mutual trust and compatible life goals – Michael had been insensitive enough to suggest that she stayed on in his apartment until she found a new place, and had accused her of being 'emotional' when she refused. That's when she'd got up and left the restaurant – just cut him off in mid-sentence. There was no way she was going to let anyone see her get emotional. Anyway, she didn't need Michael's charity. There were alternatives to hanging around like Little Miss Grateful, sleeping on Michael's couch and demurely passing him the skimmed milk at breakfast time. 'I have plenty of other *friends*,' she'd told him pointedly.

The bad news was, they were all out. She'd made some calls from the gallery, when she returned to take off that stupid dress and change back into her work clothes. But it was still only ten o'clock on a Friday night, when most normal people were out having a good time – even Cat, her best friend, who had complained to her this very week that she hadn't been on a date in months. So where was she? Freya shrugged. It was no big deal: she would try later from her mobile. If the worst came to the worst, she could check into a cheap hotel. Freya pictured the desk-clerk's leer as she arrived in some seedy, ill-lit foyer, a lone woman with no luggage. Her scorching pace faltered. Where was she?

Union Square opened up ahead of her. Instinctively, she crossed 14th Street to get away from the traffic, climbed the steps into the square and began to circle it aimlessly. It was a warm night, the 4th of June with the first promise of real summer, and the place was bustling. People streamed out of the subway, some pausing at the news kiosks, others heading for the trendy restaurants that ringed the square. On one of the benches a group of teenage girls rocked back and forth, helpless with giggles, while two boys on roller blades swooped around them in complicated patterns, showing off. An old man was leading his big collie from tree to tree, softly urging it to perform. By the fountain in the middle of the square some guys had set up an ad hoc band – saxophone, double-bass, guitar, a singer in a worn top hat, a cardboard box laid on the grass containing a pathetic sprinkling of coins. Behind them the city reared into the night sky, sparking like a perpetual firework display. The husky voice of the singer drifted out across the square:

> *. . . but I'm broken hearted*
> *Cos I can't get started*
> *With you.*

Freya came to a halt and wrapped her arms tight, tight across her chest. Under her fingers, she could feel the delicate beading of the pink dress. New York might *look* like the most romantic city in the world, she thought; just don't go there expecting to find love.

Abruptly she turned her back on the music and the view. Her eye fell on a large, metal garbage container on which someone had crudely painted 'Jesus loves you'. She strode over to it and in a sudden, savage gesture stuffed the dress inside, between newspapers and crushed styrofoam cups and cigarette butts, pushing it deeper until the delicate chiffon began to rip, and red goo from pizza cartons smeared across the fancy beadwork. So much for her foolish female fantasies. She brushed her palms clean and stepped back to survey the mess. It occurred to her that certain art dealers she knew would transport that garbage can straight to their gallery and display it with a five-figure price tag as 'Study With Pizza Carton No. 25'. Hmm, pizza. Now what did that remind her of . . . ?

Twenty minutes later she was in Chelsea, standing outside the basement door of one of the seedier-looking town houses, a paper bag clasped under her arm. The window overlooking the narrow front yard was barred and curtained, but a light shone from inside and she thought she could hear the hum of voices. It was the first Friday of the month, right? Some people never changed. Freya pressed the doorbell.

She heard an inner door open, a casual male shout, the sticky tread of sneakers on bare tiles. A shadow loomed behind the panel of coloured glass. Then there was the click of a lock, and light streamed on to her face. Standing in the doorway was a tall, loose-limbed man with a haystack of blond hair, holding a drink in one hand.

Freya pointed two fingers at his chest. 'Stick 'em up,' she said. 'It's a raid.'

His eyebrows rose in surprise. Had she done the wrong thing? What if he was holed up with some babe? Then he shouted, 'Freya! I don't believe it!', and drew her inside with an easy hug. He smelled of bourbon.

'Hiya, Jack.' She stepped back from his embrace. 'You're still running the game, aren't you?'

'Sure. Come on in.' He grinned at her. 'We can always use another sucker.'

'Sucker yourself!' She followed him across the chequerboard floor, squeezing past a bicycle propped against one wall. 'Who tricked you out of a full house that time with a lousy pair of nines?'

But Jack was already pushing open the door to the living room with his foot. 'Hey, everybody, look who's here!'

The scene was so familiar she didn't know whether to laugh or cry. In the centre of the room was a big round table covered with a stained cloth and littered with beer bottles, cigarette papers, pretzels, coloured poker chips, dollar bills, overflowing ashtrays, and – yes! – pizza cartons spattered with dried tomato and coagulated cheese. Smoke hung in a visible cloud below the globular ceiling lamp. And there they all were, the old crowd – Al, sitting backwards astride his chair, rolling a joint; Gus, doing his fancy double shuffle; Larry, counting his chips and totalling the amount with a pocket calculator. There was another man, too, a stranger in a black shirt, with dark eyebrows and a challenging stare. The tableau held for a split second, then jerked into life as if her entrance had broken a spell.

There was a general hubbub of greeting. Someone went to the kitchen to get more ice. A glass was pressed into her hand. Larry bounded over and gave her a bear hug, his springy hair tickling her chin. 'My, how you've grown,' he teased. Everyone asked her how she was, and where she had been all this time, and she thought of Michael with a fresh burst of resentment. How dared he try to trap her in his pernickety routines and domestic demands? These were her real friends.

'I didn't know you let women play.' A sardonic voice cut through the chatter. It was the stranger, still sitting at the table, tapping ash from his cigarette with a restless finger.

Jack gave his rich, disarming laugh and hooked a heavy arm around Freya's shoulders. '"Women", no. Freya, yes. This here's my oldest friend, Leo. Freya's one of the boys.'

'She taught us Cincinnati Spin, for chrissakes,' added Gus. 'She'll clean you out if you aren't careful.'

'But I'm always careful.' He got up to shake Freya's hand in a formal manner, introducing himself as Leo Brannigan.

'So you're the famous Freya?' He scrutinized her with interest.

'I suppose so.' She laughed.

'Jack used to talk about you. You're English, aren't you?'

'Yes.'

'But you live in New York.'

'Yes.' What was this — an inquisition? He was still holding on to her hand.

'Are you married?'

'*No!*' Freya withdrew her hand and glared. 'Are you?'

'Of course not.' He gave an amused half-smile. Freya wasn't sure if this was a put-down or a very slimy pick-up.

'And you've played poker before?'

'Since I was eight.'

'Well, well.' His eyebrows rose. 'May the best man win.'

'Okay, Al, your deal.' Jack's voice was suddenly brisk. 'Freya, you know the rules.' He brought her a chair and counted out a pile of chips at her place. 'One-dollar ante, fifty-dollar limit, dealer's choice.'

Freya knew the rules: number one was no girly chit-chat. That suited her fine. In one swift movement she reached into the paper bag, drew out a bottle of Southern Comfort and plonked it on the table. Then she tossed her handbag and jacket on to the big couch, flipped her thumbs through the straps of her singlet as though they were braces, and sat down. 'Hit me,' she said.

They started with five-card stud. As soon as Freya gathered her cards into her hand she felt focused, alive, confident. She loved this moment, when her world shrank to a pool of light and there was nothing but the clack of chips, the whisper and snap of cards, the clink of a bottle against glass. Outside, the world went about its business; everything here depended on the flip of a card and the intensity in her head. 'Poker isn't a game,' her father used to say; 'it's Greek drama: man against Fate. Never crow, and never whine.' Well, she wouldn't. She poured herself three fingers of Southern Comfort, took a deep slug, and blanked out Michael and the whole disastrous evening.

Lady Luck was with her and she played like a witch, finessing winning hands out of the air, varying her play to fox the opposition. Every time she remembered Michael's pitying eyes, or the fact that she had no place to sleep tonight, or that her life was a mess, she simply took another little drink. It worked a treat.

Male conversation washed over her – companionable, familiar, relaxing. The happiest years of her life had been spent in male company. There was none of that sly innuendo you got with women, no prying questions, no edgy competitiveness; just sport, jokes, new stories, media gossip, sex. At one point a spirited debate on whether a certain female talk-show hostess was sexy or not led to a general discussion of the kind of women they each favoured. Lots, said Jack. Big bazoomas, Al gestured widely. Loaded, said Leo. Larry didn't care, so long as they weren't taller than him.

'Quite right, Larry,' Freya agreed. 'Everybody knows the ideal woman is four foot tall with a flat head – so you have somewhere to rest your drink.'

'That's you disqualified.' Jack laughed. 'So tell us, your majesty, what's your ideal man?'

'Not afraid of spiders. See you five.' She dropped a stack of chips into the pot. 'And raise you . . . twenty.'

Gus slapped down his cards in disgust. 'Fold.'

'Me, too,' sighed Al.

'She's bluffing!' protested Jack. 'Look at her face.'

Freya arched her eyebrows at him. He was such a boy.

'Go on, Freya,' urged Larry. 'Slaughter him.'

'I'm going to.'

'Bet you don't,' challenged Jack.

'Bet I do.' Freya held his gaze. They were both grinning, enjoying this.

Jack pointed his finger at her. 'If you win this hand I'll – '

'You'll what? Fly me to the Caribbean? Give me a signed copy of your book?'

'I'll buy you dinner at Valhalla's on your birthday.'

'But that's months away!'

'So?'

'You'll forget.'

'No, I won't. November seventh, right?'

'Wrong. It's the eighth.'

'That's what I said.' His blue eyes danced. 'The

27

eighth at eight – who could forget that? It'll be a special rendezvous, like that movie – '

'Yeah, yeah, I know. Bogart and Bacall in *Key Largo*.'

'Not *Key Largo*.' Leo was emphatic.

'Wasn't it Cary Grant and whatsername?' offered Gus.

'Whatever,' Freya said impatiently. Her fingers tingled. She was on a roll and wanted to finish this hand. She nodded at Jack. 'I accept the bet.'

'If you lose, you pay,' he warned.

'Of course.'

'Okay, everyone. I want you all to bear witness.' Jack counted out his chips and placed them ceremoniously on the table. 'See you,' he told Freya.

Freya laid down her cards with an elegant ripple of the fingers. 'Three of a kind. Queens.'

'Shit!' Jack slumped over the table in mock despair and flipped his cards to show her a flush in clubs.

With a crow of triumph Freya stretched out her arms and gathered the lovely pile of chips to her. This was a great game. She felt marvellous. 'I'm going to order lobster,' she told Jack, 'and the truffle risotto. And champagne, naturally.'

Now it was her deal. 'Mississippi Hi-Lo,' she announced, spinning out the cards. 'Deuces, aces, one-eyed faces wild.'

Leo pulled disdainfully on his cigarette. 'That's a girls' game.'

She reached across to pull the cigarette out of his

mouth, and ground it into the ashtray. 'Not the way I play it.'

When they broke for coffee around midnight, Freya found she was more than a hundred dollars up. She felt great, high on adrenalin and alcohol.

'It's not fair. I'm losing,' wailed Larry, pressing the buttons of his calculator.

'Don't be so emotional,' Freya told him. 'Have a pretzel.'

She stood up, stretching her arms wide to ease her back muscles, and went to join the others in the kitchen. Everything looked the same in here, too – chipped fifties cabinets, crumb-encrusted toaster, yellowing newspapers, the framed *New Yorker* cartoon Jack loved, which showed a patrician publisher addressing a cowed author: 'It's Dostoevsky, it's Tolstoy, it's Fitzgerald – but it doesn't *dance*.' She couldn't find a cup, so she washed one up from the collection of dirty dishes in the sink. Jack was over by the stove, listening intently to Leo. They made an odd pair, the one amiably sloppy, the other as watchful and contained as a cat. She wondered what they were talking about. When the coffee was ready, Jack took the pot round, pushing through the crowd with his big shoulders, joking with everyone. He was wearing a blue shirt hanging out over frayed and faded cut-off jeans, sneakers with no socks, and he had a joint tucked behind one ear. How did he get away with it? She couldn't help smiling. It was good to see him, though she couldn't tell him so. He was far too big-headed as it was.

When he reached her, she leaned back against the work-top and held out her cup. 'You're a pig,' she told him, gesturing at the kitchen.

'I'm busy,' he countered. 'My mind is on higher things.'

'Does that mean the novel's going well?'

'A work of art can't be rushed.'

'I wouldn't call three years a rush. How many missed deadlines is it now?' She caught his eye. 'Okay, I'll shut up. Tell me about Leo. I haven't seen him here before.'

'That's because he hasn't been here. I ran into him a couple of weeks ago and told him to drop by if he wanted.'

Jack looked the tiniest bit shifty. Freya wondered what he was up to. 'So what does Leo do?'

'He started that magazine, *Word*, remember? – the one that published my story about the boy in the storm?'

Freya nodded. 'You got fifty dollars, and bought a bicycle.'

'Yeah, well now he's a literary agent, really into the big time, doing million-dollar deals.' Jack rubbed a hand backwards through his hair. 'He thinks I have talent.'

'Of course you have talent. I've been telling you that for years. You also have an agent. You're not thinking of leaving Ella after all she's done for you?'

'No . . .' Jack said uncertainly, looking put out. He set down the coffee pot and dug his hands into his pockets. 'So how's Mark?' he asked.

'Michael.'

'Whatever. Do we gather that he's let you come out to play tonight?'

'What kind of a question is that?'

'Only that we haven't seen you much since you two have been together.'

Freya folded her arms defensively and looked him in the eye, saying nothing. The humiliations of the evening flooded back. What a fool she'd been! But she wasn't about to break down and sob like a soppy girl – especially not in front of Jack.

'Everything's just "super", is it?' he persisted, standing over her with his lazy smile.

Freya gripped her elbows. 'Didn't "y'all" know that nobody in England has said "super" since about 1969?'

'You're getting awfully snappy in your old age. Poor old Martin was probably happy to get rid of you tonight, so he could settle down with some nice, restful briefs.'

'*Michael.*' Freya glared at him. 'At least he does a real job. Some people have to earn their living, you know.'

Jack grinned. 'Careful, you're flaring your nostrils. You look like a very superior camel.'

'Oh, shut up.' She pushed him out of the way, and returned to the card table. She wasn't in the mood to be teased.

When they started playing again, her luck changed abruptly. Maybe it was drink or dope, or simply a brute, masculine lust to win kicking in, but the men became more raucous and aggressive. Freya began to feel excluded. Her pile of chips dwindled to nothing; she drew some more from the float and wrote an IOU. She folded early in one hand, and took her cellphone into the hallway to telephone Cat, who would surely be home by now.

'You have reached Caterina da Fillipo. Please leave your name and number, and I'll get back to you.'

Freya groaned. 'It's me,' she announced, after the beep. 'I need you. Call me on my mobile the minute you hear this. *Please.*'

When she returned to the poker table, the men were all talking about someone she didn't know, a guy who worked on Wall Street and was fabulously successful. He was called Waverley Lions.

'Daft name,' she chipped in, reminding them she was still there.

No one took any notice. They bored on regardless about Waverley's three-bedroom apartment off Central Park, his house in East Hampton – beach-front, natch – his handmade shoes, his Lamborghini.

'I don't know when he does any work,' said Al admiringly. 'Waverley always seems to be in the Wine and Cigar bar, drinking Cristal champagne or sending couriers for designer drugs. And you know how he likes to celebrate a really big deal? He gets himself

32

some "red menace".' Al nodded conspiratorially at the other men. 'Know what that means?'

'What? What?' Larry was getting excited.

Al flicked a cautious look at Freya and lowered his voice. 'A Russian hooker. A really classy one, five hundred dollars an hour. Waverley says they have to be Russian or he can't, you know . . .'

'Capitalist machismo crap,' muttered Freya. She had tipped her chair back on two legs, distancing herself from this trivia that they batted back and forth like tennis balls.

'Five hundred dollars an *hour.*' Gus sounded envious.

'For Waverley it's like buying a candy bar. His annual salary's at least one and a half mil.'

'Jeez . . .'

'And on top of everything else, his penis is gigantic.'

Freya's chair crashed back on to four legs. These men were insufferable! 'How gigantic?' she asked boldly.

'Obscene.'

'The biggest in company history, he told me.'

'It would be vulgar to bandy exact figures.'

'I'll bet.' Freya sniggered. Men could be so childishly boastful. She turned to Al. 'I mean, how do you know for sure?'

'He told me privately.'

'Oh, he *told* you, did he?' Freya gave a pitying laugh. 'You haven't actually seen it for yourself?'

They all looked at her as if she were crazy. Perhaps

her curiosity was on the prurient side, but now she'd started she had to bluff it out. 'Well, have you?'

'Of course I haven't *seen* it. Don't be stupid.'

'Why not? And don't call me stupid.'

'He can't exactly show it to me.'

'Why can't he?'

'It's in the bank, dummy.'

'He keeps his penis in the bank?!' Freya's eyebrows soared.

Five seconds of silence. Five pairs of male eyes looking at her with pitying disgust.

Jack cleared his throat. 'Al didn't say penis, Freya, he said bonus.'

'Oh.'

The blush that she had kept at bay during her unseemly interrogation now lit her body like a flash fire. Suddenly she was back at junior school, a foot taller than every other girl, singing out a beat too early in the carol service. She saw Leo give Jack a look that said, *Where did you find this fluff-head?* and was mortified when Jack gave a responsive flicker of his fingers: *I know, but let it go.* Freya forced a jaunty chuckle. 'Just as well I'm not Freud's secretary, huh?'

She got them to laugh, but she felt an idiot. From now on she'd keep her mouth shut – except for drinking purposes. Freya reached for the Southern Comfort, but all it did was fuzz her brain. In a round of five-card draw she misread a six for a nine, and made a fuss when she lost. She found she was out of chips again, and signed another IOU. Her eyes itched from the smoke; her skin felt dry and tight.

At the end of another disastrous hand, Freya rested her head on the table and closed her eyes. She felt terrible. Why had she come? She'd lost all her money and made a fool of herself. They all thought she was stupid. Nobody loved her. Nobody would ever love her. She wanted to go to bed.

*Bed!*

'Wait a second,' she croaked, trying to straighten up and focus. Someone was dealing the cards, floating them across the table. 'I have to make a call.' She groped for her phone and started pressing buttons. Nothing happened. She banged it on the table and tried again. 'Stupid thing won't work.'

'Maybe that's because you're trying to make a telephone call from a pocket calculator.' Leo's voice was as dry as the Sahara.

Everyone found this hilarious. Freya heard their donkey laughter. She saw Jack grinning openly at her from across the table, flashing his rich boy's teeth. Aflame with alcohol and bad temper, she threw the calculator straight at him. It crashed into his glass, splashing drink all over him.

'Freya! What do you think you're doing?'

'Fuck off, Jack. It didn't even touch you.'

'She's drunk.'

'Fuck off, Al. I am *not drunk*.'

'Let's call her a cab.'

'Fuck off, Gus. I don't need a cab.'

Something weird was happening to the room. The walls were billowing in and out like sails. The floor was tilting.

Someone bent close beside her. 'Are you all right, sweetheart?'

'Fuck off, Larry. I'm fine,' she mumbled, and passed out.

# 3

The bed was hot and sweaty. Sunlight glared through thin curtains. Somewhere a fly was buzzing. Jack groaned through mummified lips. His mouth felt like a bat cave. He turned on to his stomach and buried his face in the pillow.

The buzz came again: not a fly, but the doorbell. Jack opened a gummy eye and squinted at the bedside clock. It was almost noon. He rolled over and levered his body into a sitting position. After a painful interval his brain followed. Hemingway had probably felt like this much of his life, Jack told himself, a cheering thought that enabled him to rise to his feet and pull on a pair of jeans over his undershorts. He added a cleanish white T-shirt, raked his fingernails through his hair, and stumbled to the front door. On the way, something bit into his bare foot. Hopping and cursing, Jack dislodged a metal bottle top from the soft flesh and flicked it back on to the floor. He remembered that Hemingway had shot himself in the end.

On his doorstep a pretty young woman was smiling up at him. Automatically, Jack smiled back. It took only seconds to recognize her as one of his students from the creative writing seminar he taught on

Tuesday evenings, Candace Something-or-other. They had gone out for a drink after class last week. He'd been much struck by her listening skills.

'I hope it's okay to drop by,' she began shyly. 'You said the other night that if I was in the neighbourhood . . . We were going to do some more work on my structure, remember?' She gestured at her chest, which was ample and deliciously rounded, and after a moment of confusion Jack saw that she was clasping a bundle of books and papers. 'But if this is a bad time . . . ?'

'No, no.' Jack found his voice. Dark hair fell to her shoulders in a glossy wave. Her skin was smooth and glowing. 'It's a perfect time.' He smiled down at her. 'Just perfect. Come in.' He stepped back to let her pass inside, inhaling a fresh smell of soap that took him right back to high school.

'Beautiful glass,' she said, admiring the etched panel in the door. 'I love these old places. They're so full of – '

'Shit!' Jack recoiled from a rancid blast of last night's fumes as he opened the living room door. The scene that met his eyes, bathed in a lurid, curtained half-light, reminded him of a Tarantino movie. 'I forgot.' He rubbed a stubbly cheek. 'Wait here a minute, will you?'

She stopped obediently in the doorway. Moving swiftly, Jack pulled open the curtains, then toured the room picking up bottles, glasses, ashtrays, squashed potato chip bags and other jetsam, which he piled higgledy-piggledy on to the centre of the table. With an expertise born of practice he then flipped up the corners of the tablecloth, drew them tight to create a giant makeshift sack, and carried the whole clanking mess out to the kitchen. Returning, he opened a window, flipped over the seat cushions of the couch to dislodge any remaining debris, and patted one invitingly. 'Sit down. I'll make some coffee.'

Candace was leaning against the door jamb, watching him in frank amusement, a tip of pink tongue curled against her upper lip.

'What's so funny?' he asked.

Her smile broadened, revealing straight pearly teeth. 'You are.'

Jack decided this would be a good moment to tuck his T-shirt into his jeans. 'Party last night,' he growled cryptically.

'I guessed.' Candace swayed over to the couch, sat down and crossed her bare legs. She gave a dreamy sigh. 'I love parties.'

'Not that kind of party.' Jack set her straight. 'This was a boys' night. Cards and booze and all that bad stuff. You're much too young and innocent for that kind of thing.'

'I'm twenty-two!' Candace protested.

'Exactly.'

Jack retreated to the kitchen, smiling to himself: young girls were so adorable. He tried to recall which story she was working on. Was it the monologue of the suicidal teenager, or the one about the wolf? He had to stop drinking so much.

While the coffee heated, he ducked into the bathroom, located some headache pills and washed them down with a whole glass of water. Then he squeezed out a gob of toothpaste and squelched it around his mouth with his tongue. That was better. Body cleansed, his memory followed suit, and now he remembered how Candace had approached him as he was leaving the seminar room and asked him something about *The Sound and the Fury*. Well, that was it. William Faulkner was his hero: a Southerner, a genius, a whisky drinker. The fact that this fresh-faced young woman had ventured beyond the cordon sanitaire enclosing Sylvia Plath, Toni Morrison and the usual crew of politically correct writers was stirring. He wanted to find out more about her. Three beers later, he was still holding forth about Faulkner, the South, literature and himself, prompted by her flattering attentiveness and a need to dodge her more alarming questions about 'modality' and 'semiotics'. That was the trouble with these self-educated or semi-educated students; sometimes they knew more lit. crit. jargon than he did. The next thing he knew it was midnight; somehow they never did get around to Candace herself, though he had a dim memory that she'd said she was a secretary, originally from one of those dismal industrial towns like Pittsburgh or New London. He must have given her his address and some vague invitation as he left, though it was hard to remember now. He really must stop drinking.

When he returned with the coffee he found Candace examining his shelves.

'All these books!' Her tone was admiring. 'I can hardly believe you've read them all.'

Jack could hardly believe it either. 'Publishers send me things for endorsement. And I do some reviewing.' He shrugged modestly, slopping coffee.

'Here, let me do that.' Candace took charge of the tray, pouring coffee from the pot and milk from a carton in neat, efficient movements while Jack sprawled in an armchair.

'So this is the home of Jack Madison,' she said, settling herself back on the couch. 'You can't imagine how exciting it is for me to see how a real writer lives.'

Jack glanced vaguely around the familiar room. Piles of old magazines were stacked on the floor. A lampshade hung off its metal frame, where someone had bumped into it last night. The smell of dope still hung in the air. 'It's kind of messy, I guess.'

'Creativity *is* messy. Writing is just so involving, I'm beginning to discover that. If my room-mate talks to me I'm, like, leave me alone, I'm thinking.' She paused. 'Do you find that?'

'Absolutely.' Jack felt a prickle of familiar panic. He did *not* have writer's block; he was just allowing time for his novel to ripen in his imagination.

'But maybe you don't have a room-mate to bother you?' Candace cocked her head enquiringly.

'What? Oh no. I hate sharing with other people.'

'Even . . . women?'

'Especially women. All those fights about the garbage, or who finished the milk. Who cares? I like to be able to do what I want when I want.'

Candace nodded. 'Solitude is an essential prerequisite for the artist.'

'Yeah. Right.' She was very articulate for a twenty-two-year-old.

'So tell me, Jack, what are you?'

Jack was nonplussed. 'A writer, I guess.'

'No, what star sign?' Candace laughed at his foolishness. 'Wait, let me guess.' Her brow furrowed as she considered the alternatives. 'Let's see. You're creative, sensitive, intelligent . . .'

'Keep going.'

' . . . and a little egotistical. Hmm. Aquarius?' Her head tilted. 'Am I right?'

'No idea. My birthday's February first, if that's any help.'

'I knew it!' Candace clapped her hands with excitement. Her brown eyes grew wide. 'That's so awesome. It must be the Sagittarius in me – you know, intuition and stuff. I'm on the cusp with Scorpio.'

Jack had no idea what she was talking about, but she looked so cute and perky that he smiled back.

'I have a favour to ask.' Candace took a pen out of her purse, then reached towards her pile of papers. Jack's heart sank. He didn't want to spend his

Saturday in textual analysis of someone else's dreary prose.

She held something out to him. 'I know it's corny, but would you . . . ?'

Jack was gratified to recognize his own book, the collection of short stories that had launched his career on a tide of rave reviews. In hardback, too. 'Aw, you shouldn't have wasted your money.'

'I found it on sale, reduced to half price. Wasn't that lucky?'

Jack frowned. This was not something authors liked to hear. He turned to the title page, took the pen Candace offered and thought for a moment. Then he wrote 'Candy is dandy', and signed his name with a flourish. He closed the book and handed it back.

Candace stroked the dust jacket reverently. 'If I saw my name on a real book I think I'd die.'

'You'd have an awfully short career.'

Candace laughed and hugged the book tight, so that her breasts plumped up above the stretchy top she was wearing. Jack wondered if that was what people called a 'boob tube'. Or a *bustier*? – or a *basque*? Whatever it was, he'd like to shake its inventor by the hand.

'Listen,' he said casually, 'are you doing anything tonight?'

'Me?' Candace's eyebrows rose in surprise. 'Not especially. Why?'

'I was thinking, you could leave me your script to read, and we could talk about it over dinner.'

'Just you and me?'

'Just you and me.'

'But it's Saturday night.' Her lips curved flirtatiously. 'You must have plans. Isn't there somebody – ?'

'Nobody,' Jack said firmly. 'Not a thing. No plans, no ties, no – '

A sudden commotion interrupted him. There was a yelp of pain, a vengeful thump, and a muttered tirade as a whey-faced figure limped into view, wearing nothing but a striped shirt Jack vaguely recognized. He stared. It was *his* shirt. And the woman inside was Freya. He'd forgotten all about her.

''Scuse me,' she croaked. 'Oof!' She winced as the slanting sunlight hit her face and flung up a protective hand, then shuffled blindly across the room, depositing a metal bottle top on the table as she passed. Jack watched, speechless, as she continued through to the passage beyond. There was the slam of the bathroom door, then the sound of somebody throwing up.

'I have to go now.' Candace was already on her feet. The sparkle had gone from her face.

'But you've just come!' Jack sprang out of his chair, blocking her way. He wanted to strangle Freya. 'Look, you haven't even finished your coffee. Sit down.'

Candace shook her head. 'I need to do some shopping. And you're busy.'

'No, I'm not. Oh, you mean *her*?' Jack sounded incredulous. 'That's just someone who came to play cards last night and got drunk. She'll be okay.'

'You said it was a boys' night.'

'I don't think of Freya as a *girl*.' Jack chuckled at the very notion. 'She's an old friend. An old, old friend. I mean, really old.' He swallowed. 'Practically forty.'

Candace's eyes darted to his. She looked suitably shocked.

'Personally,' Jack lowered his voice, 'I think it's kind of sad when someone of that age gets out of control and has to be put to bed *in the guest room*, don't you?'

Candace shrugged.

'Actually, my study. It's so frustrating. I haven't been able to do any work all morning. The sooner I can get her out of here, and back uptown with her boyfriend, the better.'

'That's up to you.' Candace tossed her hair. 'I mean, it's none of my business.'

'Good. So are we meeting tonight?'

'I don't know . . .'

'Come on,' Jack drawled persuasively. 'How will I ever finish my novel if you don't tell me all about semantics.'

'Semiotics.' Was that the suspicion of a smile?

'See, I can't even pronounce it right. Why don't you write down your phone number? When I've gotten rid of Freya I'll give you a call.'

'I don't know,' she repeated, twisting a lock of hair. 'I might be busy after all.'

'Write it down anyway. Just in case.'

Minutes later, Jack was standing on the sidewalk

watching Candace's tilting hips as she receded down the street. Sunlight gleamed on the curves of her smooth calves; he caught the flash of a gold ankle-chain. Everything about her signalled availability. Well, why not? he thought – so long as Freya hadn't ruined the whole thing. Jack jabbed his hands deep into his jeans pockets and scowled. *Thanks, Freya, you're a pal.*

Back inside, Jack looked around for her. She could at least help him clear up last night's mess. But it seemed she had gone back to bed with her hangover. It was somehow unsettling to think of her lying asleep in his apartment. Jack rubbed a hand across his chest, wondering what to do. He was sorry that Freya didn't feel well, naturally, but she had already caused him major embarrassment and it wasn't as if she was *his* girlfriend. Far from it. Michael could take care of her, he'd be good at that. Jack headed for the telephone. Unconsciously, his lips pursed and his steps became mincing as he pictured Michael prissily carrying a pot of tea and plumping up pillows. Then his expression sobered. What exactly was the etiquette of calling up another man to inform him that his girlfriend had just spent the night in your apartment?

Pondering this problem, Jack slumped in a chair by the telephone and flipped idly through his address book. The pages were worn and dog-eared, each one crammed with names and numbers inked in, crossed out, scribbled over, doodled around, mysteriously emphasized with stars, tantalizingly cryptic. 'Barbie (C's sister)' – who was she? 'Angelo's Bar (payphone)'

– what was that? He could remember when the pages were crisp and white and empty, the leather binding a sensuous, glossy tan stamped with his initials – a going away present from Lauren, his stepmother, 'for all the wonderful friends you'll make'. She'd already partially filled in the personal information on the first page, so that it read 'Name: John Randolph Caldwell Madison III. Address: New York City. Occupation: Writer.' Jack recalled how his younger self had swelled at the stark magnificence of this description, though he had sheepishly discarded the page after a couple of weeks of city sophistication.

Now the book was a satisfyingly fat compendium of publishers, movie theatres, girlfriends, favourite bars, magazine editors, libraries, pool clubs, restaurants, bookstores, photocopy shops – and friends, of course. Freya's name sprouted all over the F section, like thistles in a meadow. He'd never known anyone who moved as often as she did. The very first entry, now crossed through, gave the address of that leaky old boarding house in Brooklyn where he'd come looking for a cheap room his very first week in New York. An image flashed up of long blonde hair fanning out around her upside-down face as she leaned over a top floor banister to call out to him.

In those days Freya had struck him as an impossibly superior being, a sophisticated twenty-five to his raw twenty-two. She knew where you could fill up on soup and bagels for five dollars, which flea markets sold the cheapest furniture, how to sneak into openings and gorge on canapés and champagne for free, which movie theatre let you see the picture twice around to keep warm. She'd introduced him to 'the gang' – a loose group of would-be artists, actors, musicians and writers who shivered together through the winters, dragged their mattresses on to roofs and fire escapes in summer, gossiped at Ambrosio's over coffee and doughnuts, borrowed money and clothes, and assured one another they were geniuses. Freya was famed for her 'celebration spaghetti' that marked their inching achievements, invariably followed by a disgusting English dessert called 'bread and butter pudding', which Jack had learned to make almost palatable with a thick mulch of American ice-cream. From the first Jack had enjoyed her sharp wit and independence of mind – even her cool mockery, which was quite different from the flirtatious brand of teasing he was used to from the girls back home. There had even been a time, one particular night years ago, when he'd –

Jack frowned. He did not wish to revisit that humiliating occasion. He was different then, and so was Freya. Returning to the address book, he leapfrogged swiftly from one Freya entry to the next – uptown, downtown, this boyfriend, that boyfriend, this job, that job. Yes, ten years was a long time. They were still friends, would surely always be friends – but he had his own life to lead, and she had hers. He found Michael's number and dialled.

# 4

*... A wisp of silver strayed diaphonous beneath the moon, suspended in the inky well of night. Watching it, something dark and primitive stirred in Garth's loins, and he emitted a groan of longing, like the honk of a lonely goose. He felt himself spinning down, down, down, in a vortex of despair. Was there to be no love for him in this cruel world, just because his skin was black?*

Jack grabbed the pencil from behind his ear. His hand hesitated over the page. Where to begin? In the end, he contented himself with correcting the spelling of diaphanous, ringed the dangling participle, and gave his pencil a couple of vicious bites before returning it to its resting place.

It was mid-afternoon. Over the last couple of hours he had done the dishes, cleaned up the living room, left a cup of tea by the bedside of a comatose Freya, and taken out the trash. Now he was lying on the couch under the large window, sneakered feet comfortably propped on the far armrest, a sheaf of papers on his chest.

He checked to see how many pages remained, and sighed. From what he could make out, 'Forbidden', world copyright Candace Twink, was a story of doomed love set in the Civil War, featuring a feminist version of Scarlett O'Hara and a black slave apparently familiar with existentialism. Experience told him that it was not a parody.

What was he going to tell her? Not the truth, obviously. Parts of her script were very nearly not bad; but as a whole it was crap. Sometimes, Jack privately wondered whether creative writing could be taught. He loathed the word 'creative', which brought to mind women in floaty garments dancing barefoot, and pointless artefacts made from sea-shells. Good writing was a craft; great writing was an art; creative writing was all too often neither. But he needed the money. He wrote reviews and magazine pieces for the same reason. His allowance simply wasn't enough to live on any more. Jack thought resentfully of his father, with his beach house and his mountain house as well as the Madison mansion, his expensive cigars and even more expensive wives. Dad had no idea how much it cost to live in Manhattan. Jack's allowance barely covered the rental for this apartment; but when he tried to ask for more, all he got was his father's famous cock-of-the-walk smile and the suggestion that Jack got himself a 'real' job. No wonder his novel wasn't finished. A writer needed to breathe the pure Olympian air of the imagination, untrammelled by petty anxieties, not to pollute his talent with demeaning hack work.

Still, there were compensations. He skipped ahead through Candace's script to see if there were any sexy bits; he might pick up some useful tips for tonight – assuming he talked her round, of course. Disappointingly, Candace favoured metaphor, though Jack was encouraged by one reference to the 'proud swell of manhood'. He leaned his head back against the armrest of the couch and closed his eyes, trying to picture the shape of the evening. First he'd take Candace for drinks at Z Bar, where they could sip cocktails on the roof terrace and spy on any celebs; girls always liked that. It would be important to get the business part over at the beginning, so pretty soon he'd take out her script and give her his critique. He practised a few phrases in his head: original concept . . . acute observation . . . interesting – no, arresting use of simile. *Excellent* punctuation. Then, over the second cocktail, he'd suggest one ruthless cut – dropping the subplot about the amputee, for example – something to get her emotions going. They'd fight, she might cry, he'd apologize, they'd make up, and afterwards they'd move on to some dark, funky restaurant, then back to her place.

Satisfied with his plan, Jack returned 'Forbidden' to its nifty folder. After all that work he was starving; he would make himself a sandwich and refresh his intellect with the *New York Review of Books* – or perhaps a game on TV if the Yankees were playing. He got up from the couch, stretched his arms wide and yawned, sucking in his breath so vigorously that it made a curious noise in his throat. Hark! Was that, perchance, the honk of a lonely goose? He tucked his fists into his armpits and flapped his elbows experimentally.

'Taking off somewhere?' said a voice.

Jack whirled around. 'Oh, hi, Freya.' He tried to turn the flapping into a vigorous rib-massage. 'Uh, feeling better?'

'Fine.' She was fully dressed in last night's clothes, purse over her shoulder, ready to go. 'I just came to say goodbye, and thank you. I'm sorry to have been such a nuisance.'

'That's okay.' Her formal manner caught Jack off guard. He scanned her more closely. She looked very pale. 'Can I get you some coffee? Aspirin?'

She shook her head. 'I'd better get back.'

'Right.' Jack hesitated, wondering how much he dared question her. Freya always acted as if her private life was a state secret. 'Back where?' he ventured finally.

'Home, of course.'

It was the 'of course' that did it, uttered with such condescension that Jack was piqued into saying, 'Why don't you call Michael? He must be worried about you.'

Immediately he regretted his cruel impulse. Freya's face closed tight, like a fragile sea creature poked with a stick. 'Oh . . . you know . . . let him stew. I'm not a dog you can whistle home.' She gave him one of her looks. 'You know how to whistle, don't you?'

'You just put your lips together and blow.' Automatically he finished off the quote. It was an old game.

Freya was unzipping her purse. 'I'm sure I must owe everyone money from last night.'

'Afraid so. Don't worry, I paid for you since you were . . .'

'Asleep.' She pulled out her wallet.

'Whatever. The total's kind of steep – two hundred and forty-seven dollars.'

Her hand froze. 'I don't seem to have my cheque-book on me right now. Is it okay if I pay you back next week?'

'Well, of course it is!' What was the matter with her? 'Take as long as you like.'

'Thanks, Jack.' Her face softened, but only for a moment. 'I'm sorry about this morning, by the way. I hope I didn't interrupt anything.'

It seemed to Jack that her eyebrows arched in a knowing way. He did not care for the insinuation. 'That was one of my students,' he said reprovingly.

'Really? Are you teaching her the A, B, C?'

Jack glowered. 'I'll come and help you get a cab.'

'No! I mean, thanks, but I think I'll hop on a bus.' She half turned away, hesitated, then stepped towards him in that decisive, long-legged way she had. They kissed cheeks. 'Thanks for the game, and thanks for the bed. See you soon.'

'See you,' Jack echoed, following her into the hall. He opened the door for her and watched her walk out to the street. He wondered where she was going. Some friend? Another man? She obviously didn't want to tell him, and he knew better than to ask. Fine. He shut the door.

Cheese and peanut butter, he thought, with a smidge of piccalilli, corn chips on the side and an ice-cold beer. Yum. His mouth was already watering. He headed for the kitchen, yanked open the fridge door and started assembling ingredients. What a mystery women were. He'd known Freya for over ten years, yet she wouldn't tell him she'd split up with her boyfriend; whereas Michael, whom he'd met about twice and didn't even like, had told him right away. Men were so straightforward. Jack still didn't know the exact reasons for the break-up, but it was pretty clear that Michael wasn't expecting Freya back. When Jack had protested that Freya was sick and needed somewhere to go, Michael had responded, 'You're her friend, you take care of her.'

Of course that was impossible. He had a novel to write. Jack ran a forefinger round the inside rim of the peanut butter jar and put it in his mouth: sensational. Anyway, you might as well try to take care of a sabre-toothed tiger: Freya did exactly as she pleased, and always had. It was her own fault that she'd never settled into an apartment of her own, claiming that she liked to be 'free'. Jack flicked a splodge of piccalilli on top of the cheese, pressed a piece of only slightly stale bread on top to complete his sandwich, and took a large bite. The real conundrum was how Freya and Michael ever got together in the first place. What could she see in a nine-to-five lawyer from one of those tight-assed Midwest states? And the guy had no style. He had actually complained to Jack that the bill at Phood had come to three hundred and sixty-five dollars, 'not including tip'. Jack chuckled, spraying out a few crumbs. He loved that – Michael's entire character summed up in three words. In fact, it was so good that he wanted to write it down. Taking his sandwich with him, he walked through to his study so he could scribble a note for his 'Ideas' file, a cornucopia of observations, bons mots and scraps of overheard dialogue that was now actually longer than his novel.

When he opened the door, the first thing that caught his eye was the narrow divan bed. Normally a repository for papers, dirty laundry, broken electrical equipment and other random articles, it was now a vision of tidiness. The bedspread lay flat and scrupulously symmetrical; in the exact centre was a neat pile of folded sheets, with his striped shirt and a ten-dollar bill on top. Next to the money was a note: 'For laundry – F'. Jack picked up the note, smiling at the familiar, cryptic signature. What a funny person she was, for all her hoity-toity ways. He remembered all the crazy, caffeine-fuelled discussions she'd presided over at Ambrosio's; the surprise party she'd organized for Larry when he got his first job in TV; the scores of old movies the two of them had seen together, legs hooked over the seats in front, sharing popcorn with double butter. The nagging guilt he'd been trying to ignore all morning exploded into some much larger emotion – concern? affection? shame? When he asked her where she was going, she'd said 'Home, of course.' Except Freya didn't have a home. Her family lived thousands of miles away in England. Michael had thrown her out. She was alone in the loneliest city in the world. And he was supposed to be her friend.

Jack tossed the remains of his sandwich on to his desk. Stupid woman! Why did she have to be so proud? He hurried to grab his keys and ran to the front door. Wait a minute – what about his bicycle? Jack manhandled it outside, cursing as his sticky hands made him clumsy. He half scooted, half hopped down the path and across the sidewalk, bumped down into the street and, swinging his leg over the bike, raced in the direction she had taken. Cars beeped at him. A voice yelled, 'Hey, bozo, one-way street!' *Yeah, yeah.* Jack sped on regardless. There was no sign of her.

At the intersection he came to a slithering halt. An uptown bus lumbered into view, gathering speed from the corner bus stop. Jack peered inside as it passed, but the windows were smeared with grime and he didn't have his glasses on. Anyway, if she wasn't going back to Michael she wouldn't be going uptown, would she? *Excellent, Watson.* So where had she gone?

He wove his way perilously across the stream of traffic, without waiting for the green light, and pedalled head-down towards Seventh Avenue and the down-town bus stop. This is crazy, he told himself, as his ancient bike juddered and squeaked. She could be walking on any of a dozen different streets. She could be in a coffee bar. She could have caught a cab after all – except she probably didn't have any money. *You're a bastard*, Jack told himself, clicking the rusty gear into first.

When he was four years old his parents had divorced, and his mother had taken him and Lane, his baby brother, to live with her in Atlanta. The house on Benning Street was the first place that he remembered – his bed made of hickory, a maid called Abigail shelling pecan nuts on the back porch, and a school with girls in dresses, whose sashes he liked to pull. He didn't remember his mother much – she was out a lot – but Jack remembered being happy. Then one day everything changed. He learned that his mother was to marry again and was going to live somewhere far away. She wanted to take Jack with her, of course she did, but his father wouldn't allow that; it was time for 'the boy' to claim his heritage and learn to be a Madison. Jack remembered the rumble of arguments and late-night conferences and the arrival of letters that made his mother's voice harsh and scary. And then, shortly after his seventh birthday, the arrival outside the house of a big shiny car, his suitcases on the stoop, Abigail sobbing into her apron, and his father, a stranger tall and golden as a god, laying a heavy, claiming hand on his shoulder, saying, 'Son, I've come to take you home.'

Was that her? Jack squinted at a tall figure in black, walking purposefully. 'Freya!' he shouted. But when he got near, it turned out to be a young Indian boy with made-up eyes and lips – a gay cruiser looking for some action.

At the next block he swooped left, joining the stream of traffic. Shit, he could see a bus ahead of him, letting out a pair of gym-bunnies with their sports bags. There was a line of people waiting to get on. Jack bounced his bike on to the sidewalk and rode down it, swerving around pedestrians. 'Excuse me, sir . . . excuse me, ma'am.' He thought he could make out a dark figure with pale hair. Was that her? He started ringing his bicycle bell.

By the time he reached the bus, she had one foot on the first step of the bus, one hand on the rail.

'Freya! Wait!' he called.

She looked around, blinking, as if roused from a dream. Her eyes focused on him. He'd have said she'd been crying if he didn't know that Freya never cried.

'Jack . . .? What's the matter?' she said.

There was no time for tact. 'I know about Michael,' he bawled across the other passengers. 'I called him this morning. You haven't anywhere to go, have you?'

Freya's mouth opened and closed. 'Yes, I have.'

'Oh yeah? Where?' Jesus, she was stubborn. He rolled the bike forward, balancing on his toes.

She stood there, half on, half off the bus. Other passengers pushed past – a couple of old men in skull caps, some *hausfraus* with bulging shopping bags, a fat black lady carrying a bunch of wilted flowers.

'Come and stay with me. Just until you get yourself fixed up.'

'No, Jack. You've got your writing and all your . . . students. I'd cramp your style.'

'No, you wouldn't.' Of course she'd cramp his style!

'I'll come if she don't,' chuckled the black lady, her mountainous body aquiver.

'Hey, Romeo, get lost!' barked a voice. It was the driver, mirrored sunglasses flashing, forearms the colour of lard bulging from short sleeves. He bared his teeth at Freya in a sinister leer. 'Come on, lady. Make my day.'

Freya leapt back on to the sidewalk. The doors closed behind her with a swoosh of compressed air, and the bus took off.

'It's okay, Jack. Really.' Freya's eyes flicked up from the sidewalk and back.

'Have you got a place to stay?' he demanded.

'Not yet. But . . .'

'Then come home with me.'

No answer. Her eyes were lowered, her lips pinched tight.

He wanted to put his arm around her, but he didn't dare.

'There's grease on your jeans,' she said at last.

Jack smiled at this typical evasion. He turned his bike around, making a big production of it, giving them both time. Suddenly he had an idea.

'Frankly, Freya, I need the rent.'

That got her attention. 'You? Don't make me laugh . . . Oh God, you're not serious, are you?'

'Perfectly serious.' Moving slowly, as if she were a jittery horse, Jack took her purse off her shoulder and put it in his bicycle basket. She didn't seem to notice. 'Twenty dollars a day, two weeks absolute max.' He held out his hand, palm upward. 'Deal?'

She wavered for about five seconds, then gave his palm a decisive slap. 'I warn you, I'm hell to live with.'

Jack nodded. He could well believe it.

## 5

'Men are such pigs.' Cat's dark eyes glowed with sympathetic indignation. 'So then what happened?'

'Well, after he'd fished out his stupid ring and made the waiter bring him a bowl of water so he could clean it up, he told me I wasn't committed to him. Can you believe it? The creep dumps me, then twists the whole thing around so that it's *my* fault!'

'Typical male rationalization. I remember when I was going out with Perfidious Peter – '

'He said I didn't "relate" to him, that I didn't listen enough, that I was always criticizing him. He complained that I corrected his stories in public.'

'Did you?'

'Only when he was wrong.'

'Men are never wrong.'

'Oh yeah. I forgot.'

Freya and Cat exchanged a smile of female solidarity. They were sitting opposite each other at a Formica-topped table in a cramped restaurant in Chinatown. A teapot and two cups, pale blue with pink dragons, steamed between them. It was Monday lunchtime. The courthouse district was just around the corner, and the place was bursting with journalists, lawyers, policemen and paunchy City Hall apparatchiks talking at top volume, as well as local Chinese workers and a group of docile-looking shaven-heads from the Buddhist temple nearby. Cat spent a lot of time down here in the course of her work as a family lawyer, and this was one of her favourite eateries. Freya had met her here before and couldn't honestly share Cat's enthusiasm, but she wasn't about to complain. Officially, Cat was supposed to be working, but like a true friend she had cancelled an appointment to hear Freya's tale of woe.

'When I think of all the hoops I jumped through for him!' Freya continued. 'Drinking skimmed milk because of his cholesterol count, not seeing my friends so we could "*beee* together", pretending I liked those dreary concerts he took me to.' Her brow cleared momentarily. 'One good thing: at least I won't have to sit through that bloody *Ring Cycle*.'

'At the Met? Freya, those tickets are like gold dust. And you're practically German: how can you not like Wagner?'

'All that yearning and churning.' Freya shuddered. 'And my mother was Swedish: quite different. I'm a totally Kraut-free zone.'

'Well, I'm Italian, and I adore Wagner. He's so romantic.'

'Not the R-word. Please.' Freya pressed a hand to her forehead.

'Of course. I'm sorry.'

A Chinese woman in worn slippers halted by their

table and gave a surly jerk of her head to show that she was ready to take their order.

'I'll have a number five,' said Cat. 'What about you, Freya?'

'I couldn't eat.'

'Of course you can eat. Now hurry up and decide.'

Freya stared at the inscrutable menu. A Bloody Mary with extra Tabasco was what she wanted, but they didn't serve alcohol here. The restaurant specialized in *tong shui*, a type of Chinese health food that tasted good, but had an eye-of-newt and toe-of-frog quality that always made her scrutinize each mouthful for alien substances.

'You choose,' she said. 'Nothing with more than four legs.'

When the waitress had gone Freya finished her story, then sank her chin in her hands and fixed Cat with a mournful look. 'Be honest, Cat. Why didn't Michael want to marry me? What's wrong with me?'

'Nothing!' Cat was gloriously emphatic. 'You're gorgeous, smart, funny. What's wrong with *him* is the question. If I could get my hands on that Michael I'd feed him through my mincing attachment. Hmmm . . . Minced Michael – I could add him to my collection.'

Cat always invented epithets for her men. There'd been Simian Simon, Rod the Bod, Dandruff Dylan. It was her form of self-defence when relationships ended. But they weren't talking about Cat's men. Freya wrenched the subject back to herself.

63

'I find the only man in New York who actually wants to commit – but he doesn't want to commit to me. Why not?'

Cat considered. 'You don't think – ?'

'What?'

'You don't think he could have found another woman?'

'Michael? Don't be ridiculous.'

'In that case, he probably got cold feet. Personally, I blame the media. Every time you open a magazine, there's another article about how desperate women are to get married. No wonder men are scared. If you ask them to pass the butter they flinch. Ten years ago it was HIV; now it's single women: the new plague. Run for your lives!'

Freya giggled, forgetting for a moment how miserable she was. Cat always made her laugh. They had met years ago, at a tap-dancing class of all places, where Cat had broken her ankle while attempting a double pick-up. Freya, temporarily homeless, had ended up taking care of her and sleeping on her pull-out bed. The two of them had bonded over chilled vermouth, fiery *penne a l'arabiata*, old Bruce Springsteen tapes and killer games of backgammon. Freya had discovered that Cat's Latin temper, Columbia-educated mind, and I-want-it-and-I-want-it-*now* attitude of the native New Yorker concealed the most generous heart she knew. Cat adored her family, a huge Italian–American tribe based in Staten Island. She knew all her neighbours in her apartment block by name. She had a passionate social conscience and contributed hours of free legal work to those who couldn't afford the fees. Despite her feminist principles, you could make her cry by telling her that Rhett and Scarlett never did get back together again. Their relationship might have started out by Freya looking after Cat, but both knew that the reverse was now true. It was Cat who cooked Freya meals when she was down, listened to her moans about Lola, bought her a pot plant every time she moved apartments (it always died), and picked up the pieces when some man let her down. Freya had many close acquaintances in this town – friends in the art world, a few of the old Brooklyn gang, people who invited her to parties and dinners and did the kissy-kissy bit when they met – but Cat was a real friend. Freya trusted her absolutely.

The food came with indecent speed, confounding any pretence that it had been freshly made. Picturing an array of witches' cauldrons in a health inspector's nightmare kitchen, Freya took a tentative bite.

'Maybe it was a mistake to walk out on Michael.' Cat was thinking aloud. 'I mean, what if he was testing you, to see if you'd come up with a more positive response? If you'd stayed at the restaurant and talked through the situation, he might have changed his mind.' She shot Freya a speculative look. 'Even now, he could be reconsidering.'

'What?' Freya choked on a noodle.

'Just think. It could still all be yours: house, children, Connecticut.'

'But – '

'Station wagon. PTA. Country club.'

'Don't!'

'A nice big Lassie dog to play with the kids.'

'Stop trying to torture me.'

'Ah-hah! I thought so. Admit: you liked the *idea* of getting married, like those sad women who fantasize over *Brides* magazine.'

Freya glowered at her health-slop. She didn't want to admit anything of the kind. Michael had *rejected* her. It *hurt*.

'I'd like to have seen you in pink, though.' Cat gave her rippling chuckle. '*Pink!*'

'Oh, shut up.'

'I'm sorry, sweetie.' Cat reached out impulsively for her hand. 'I'm sorry it didn't work out with Michael. But you could be awfully disparaging about him. You never even let me meet him.'

'I know.' Freya was embarrassed. For some reason she was always secretive about her emotional life. Or maybe she felt Cat knew her too well and would judge her too severely on her choice? Anyway, Cat would have scared the pants off Michael. She shrugged. 'You'd hate Michael. He's so straight.'

'But you wanted to marry him?'

Freya squirmed under Cat's challenging gaze. She probably did want to marry someone, sometime. The fact that she might have rejected Michael in the end was beside the point; he hadn't even given her the option. 'Well, I thought I did,' she mumbled, absently twiddling the bottle of chilli sauce. 'Mind you, he was never exactly King Kong in the bedroom.'

'Really?' Cat was agog. 'You mean . . . technical problems?'

'No, the equipment worked. Let's just say that I think he must have read about the importance of foreplay in some magazine.'

'But foreplay's my second favourite part!'

'Depends how it's done.' Freya pulled her chair close and leaned across the table. 'Say you decide to have a really nice dinner, at the dining table, at home – but naked. And the rule is, you're not allowed to touch until dessert. Now that's fun.'

'I'll say.'

'But with Michael it was a bit like going to the dentist. You know, first you make an appointment, then you sit in the waiting room reading a magazine, then the hygienist cleans your teeth and tells you all about her vacation in Florida, and then you rinse and spit, and spit and rinse, until you think "For Chrissakes, get out the bloody drill!"'

Cat yelped with laughter, making heads turn. 'That's so cruel.'

'What are these crunchy bits, by the way?' Freya poked moodily at her food. 'Toad's testicles?'

'Probably ginkgo nuts, or lotus seeds. Every dish has a perfect balance of yin and yang. I haven't had a single cold since I started coming here.'

'Maybe that's what's wrong with Michael – too much yin, or too little. He's always blowing his nose, or asking me if I have a Kleenex. It drives me mad. *Drove*,' she amended.

There was a thoughtful pause. 'You know, Freya, sometimes a person really needs a Kleenex and doesn't have one. It doesn't mean they're a wimp.'

Freya slapped the table. 'For me, it's simply not sexy. End of story.' She glowered at her friend. 'You're too nice. Promise me, you'll never marry someone just because you feel sorry for him.'

Cat straightened her spine and fixed Freya with a portentous stare. 'I'm not going to marry anyone,' she announced. 'It's official.'

'What do you mean?'

Cat wiped her mouth carefully with a paper napkin. 'I've made a policy decision. I'm not dating any more. I'm not "putting out". I'm going to stop searching, even subconsciously, for Mister Right. I've had enough of getting dressed up, and wondering if I smell nice, and taking an interest in his work, and waiting for that phone call. The fact is, *I don't need a man*.'

She looked so fierce that Freya nodded dumbly.

'I have a good job, enough money, my own apart-ment. A husband would only mess things up. Frankly, I'm not at all sure that the ideologies of marriage and feminism mesh. No. I have seen the future as a single woman – and it works.'

Freya couldn't help feeling sceptical. Anyone could see that Cat was made to have a husband, a home and a tribe of children to manage.

'What about love?' she asked.

'Pure make-believe. I see husbands and wives every day in my work, and the truth is they hate each other. The men beat up their wives, steal from them, cheat on them. I've got a case right now of a woman in her *seventies* who's suing for divorce on the grounds of unfaithfulness.' Cat sighed.

'But sometimes you need a man, as an accessory. Say there's a business dinner and you're invited to bring your partner. What happens then?'

'You hire one.'

'What?'

'Sure. From an escort agency. My friend Rosa does it all the time. She says you can tell them exactly what to wear and how to behave. They don't get drunk, or tell embarrassing stories about you. Afterwards, instead of listening to them complain how bored they were, you pay them off and go home.' Cat looked at her triumphantly.

'What about kids? You love children.'

'There's always the turkey baster.'

'Cat!'

'I'm serious. There's an AI clinic right in the building where I work. All I have to do one day is get out of the elevator at the fifth floor instead of the ninth, and I could walk out pregnant.'

'Hmmm.' Freya tried to picture herself proud and free and single, an Amazon towering above the petty squabbles of the sex war. 'What about sex?' she said.

'You don't need a husband for that,' Cat scoffed. 'No. The fact is that women want romance, affection, fidelity, children, and an adult mind to engage with. Men want sex, unquestioning admiration, absolutely no responsibility and a regular turnover. There's no synergy.' She lifted her chin defiantly. 'I can't tell you how relieved I am since I made this decision. Frankly, I'm amazed you haven't commented on my new aura of serenity. Now let's have some lychees. Then I must run.'

While Cat tried to attract the waitress's attention, Freya stared thoughtfully at her friend – at her vibrant, expressive face, her creamy skin and mass of curly black hair, her voluptuous figure that scorned the cult of the body skeletal – and felt suddenly furious at the doltish male population of New York. Men should be falling over themselves to get hold of Cat.

'If you've given up dating,' Freya asked, 'where were you on Friday when I needed you?'

'At my sister's, babysitting. I gave Tonito his bottle and sang him a song, then I had two vodka martinis and reheated *spaghetti alla matriciana*, watched *When Harry Met Sally* for the umpteenth time, and fell asleep on the couch.'

'The perfect evening.'

'I rest my case.' Cat looked smug. 'Now listen, sweetie, I'm sorry I wasn't home Friday, but you're welcome to come and sleep on my couch for as long as you want. I'd adore it.'

'Thanks, Cat, but I might as well stay at Jack's, now I'm there.'

'Is that the big blond guy who was at the beach party last year?'

'If he was carrying a six-pack of nymphets, probably.'

'Mmm-mmm.' Cat smacked her lips in a vulgar Italian manner. 'Maybe you should introduce me properly one day.'

Freya frowned. 'You just said you were off men.'

'I said marriage was an untenable position for a feminist. I can always research my theory.' Cat's eyes sparkled.

'Well . . . just so long as you understand that Jack is not marriage material.' Freya felt it was her duty to warn her friend. 'If you wanted to go dancing, say, or see an old film, or do something dotty like ice-skating in Rockefeller Center, Jack would be the perfect partner. In all other respects his knuckles are still scraping along the ground.'

'But *you* like him,' Cat pointed out.

'I'm different. I'm immune.'

'I see. Well, stay with him if you want to, but be careful.'

'Of what, for heaven's sake? We're just friends.'

'Men are funny. They see you wandering around in a bath towel, or hanging out your underwear, and suddenly they want to *pounce*. It's an instinct thing.'

'Pounce?' spluttered Freya. 'Jack?' She pictured a

blond gorilla in cut-off jeans and glasses, leering at her from the jungly undergrowth.

'You may laugh, but proximity is the first law of sexual attraction. Men are lazy: they grab what's under their noses. That's why they all run off with their secretaries. People think it's because the secretaries are young and beautiful and subservient, but really it's just because they're *there*. If men could send out from their desks, they would.' Cat held an imaginary phone to her ear, and lowered her voice an octave. '"One woman, medium rare, sex on the side, hold the nagging."'

'Stop!' Freya clutched her throat. 'I nearly swallowed my lychee stone.'

Cat was checking her watch. 'Sweetheart, I hate to say this but I really must go.'

'I'll walk you back. And I'm paying. No arguments.'

Outside, Freya hooked her arm into Cat's and gave it a squeeze as they set off down the street. Maybe Cat was right. Here they were, two single women together, perfectly happy. No husbands to irritate them. No children to rush home to. Just friends. Suddenly Freya felt optimistic again. She had taken this afternoon off work so that she could sneak into Michael's apartment and grab the clothes she needed while he was safely at the office. Then she would start looking for somewhere to live, and figure out what to do about England now that Michael had let her down. Somehow the future would sort itself out.

Freya lifted her head and looked about her. The

morning's rain had cleared, leaving the air summery and fresh, a good ten degrees cooler than yesterday. Sunlight filtered through a silvery sky, bouncing rainbow reflections off the World Trade Center in the distance. People forgot that New York was a seaside city, with its own special quality of light. You sometimes got fantastic effects at dawn or sunset, when the sky turned lime green or shocking pink. It was good to appreciate such things, instead of always rushing, head down, like that boring herd of office workers in their boring suits and –

Freya gasped. 'Quick!' She yanked Cat backwards and turned to duck into the shelter of the nearest building entrance. There was a door in front of them – some kind of shop. Freya pushed it open and drew her friend inside.

'What's going on?' Cat shook her off.

Freya whipped round, and peered out through the shopfront window. 'It's him!' she whispered.

'Who?' Cat whispered back.

'Michael! You don't think he followed me here, do you?'

'Which one?'

'Tan briefcase, blue shirt, crossing the road. Oh my God, he's looking this way!'

'Hmmm. Nice suit.'

'Bugger his suit. What's he doing here?'

'He's a lawyer. That's the courthouse. And I'm Einstein.' Cat smirked.

Freya watched the dark figure retreating, one

businessman in a shoal of lookalikes. Her hand was still pressed to her heart, but she was shocked to realize that, beyond a desire to remain invisible, she felt absolutely nothing. This was surreal. She'd lived with that man for months. Three days ago she'd been thinking of marrying him. A rejected lover had once told her that she had no heart, only a block of ice. Maybe he was right.

'Anything I can do for you?'

A husky voice behind them made Freya jump. She turned around to see a very tall, well-built peroxide blonde smiling at her through sugar-pink lips.

'We're just looking, thanks.'

'Two little ladies on their lonesome ownsome. Now what could you be missing? Maybe one of these?'

The woman whipped out a drawer from under the counter and plonked it down under their noses. Freya stared. Why would anyone think she needed a torch, especially a pink one with bristly bits on top?

'Or you may prefer one of our celebrity models,' the woman continued. 'The Rock Hudson, the Errol Flynn . . .'

Thoroughly bemused, Freya glanced around for enlightenment, and suddenly grasped the significance of what she was seeing – leather harnesses, handcuffs, a life-sized doll saying 'Oh'. They were in a sex shop! She looked round to warn Cat.

'What does this big black one do?' Cat was asking, taking something out of its box.

'I'll get a battery and show you.'

Freya marched over to Cat, gripped her arm so tightly that she cried out, and propelled her towards the door. 'We have an appointment,' she explained to the blonde with insane politeness.

'Too bad. Have a nice day, now.'

They exited in dignified silence. As soon as the door banged shut behind them, they erupted into hysterical giggles, clutching each other and stumbling down the street like two drunks.

'Well,' said Cat finally, wiping her eyes, 'there's the answer to our man problem.'

'We're not that desperate,' Freya protested.

'Fits in your purse,' Cat pointed out. 'Hits the spot every time. No weird positions. No "How was it for you?" And the size!'

They walked on in pensive silence, arm in arm, past the Chinese grocery stores. Freya averted her gaze from the mounds of strangely shaped vegetables laid out on the street stalls. She wished Cat could find herself a real man for keeps. But not too soon: it was comforting to have Cat always available, the fold-out bed if she was desperate, the undivided force of her affection and loyalty. If Cat fell in love, where would that leave *her*?

'Tell you one thing.' Cat's uninhibited voice cut across her thoughts. 'Those gadgets knock Dangly Dave into a cocked hat.'

# 6

'The important question,' said Leo, 'is how you're going to position yourself.'

'Right here on this barstool seems pretty good to me.' Jack grinned, and tipped a bottle of beer to his lips.

The truth was, he was hellishly uncomfortable on the moulded plastic seat, raised on its slim chromium stalk to an awkward height that left him pawing alternately for the footrest and the floor. These things might look cool, but they were made for Italians, not a six-foot four American who liked to slouch. But he wasn't about to complain. When it came to a free lunch he could take the rough with the smooth.

They were sitting at a shiny horseshoe-shaped bar that projected deep into the room, imprisoning two ludicrously handsome barmen, one black, one white, who co-ordinated beautifully with the decor – couches and chairs in charcoal and beige leather, casually grouped around a scattering of zebra rugs. Colour came in brash primaries from paintings on the wall, and piles of oranges and lemons in steel baskets on the bar. Something by U2 was playing on the sound system. There was a buzz of chatter from the lunchtime crowd, a mixture of sharp suits, leather jackets, ponytails and arrestingly short dresses.

This was Club SoHo, a new members-only media hang-out, sited in a handsome old cast-iron building embellished with Italianate pillars and curlicues, like a New World palazzo. Jack had read about its glitzy membership – screenwriters, actors, agents, producers – but this was the first time he'd been inside. He liked it. The atmosphere was casual, classless, anti-puritan and about as far as you could get from the old-fashioned college clubs with their scary acoustics, moribund attendants and preppy clones. Although he had not actually noticed a sign outside saying 'No admittance for the over forty-fives', the message hung in the ether: no corporate geeks, no has-beens from the seventies, no old money. If you were here you were hip. You could write your own rules. The fact that Leo was smoking and hadn't been lynched spoke for itself.

'I'm serious,' Leo persisted. 'People don't have time to figure things out for themselves any more. You have to tell them what to think. Get the juices flowing. Connect.'

'"Only connect",' Jack muttered vaguely. 'Who wrote that?'

Leo plucked at his tie, a bold snakeskin pattern aggressively teamed with a crimson shirt. 'No idea. I never went to college.'

This was a daring admission from someone in the literary world. Jack was curious. 'How come?'

'No time. No money.'

'Didn't your parents – ?'

'My Dad was a failed boxer, my mother an Irish Catholic who left school at fourteen. Both boozers. Both dead. I came to books late. But I'm making up for it now.' Leo gave a sly grin and stubbed out his cigarette. 'Let's go eat.'

Jack followed him up the stairs, trying to fit this interesting piece of information into the Leo jigsaw. The two men had been aware of each other for some years, as they both circled the literary pond, waiting for an opportunity to jump in and make a splash, but they'd been acquaintances rather than friends. Leo used to be almost a figure of fun, a shameless net-worker and publishing wonk who could cite every major author's advance and sales figures, and name the winner of each literary prize for the last twenty years. The joke was that he took facts and figures to bed with him every night, instead of women. Until the other week, when they'd got talking at some book party and Jack invited him on impulse to the poker game, they hadn't met in a long while. But Jack was well aware of Leo's rocketing reputation. However weird his approach, the fact was that in the last couple of years Leo had emerged as a hugely successful literary agent. He was still only thirty-one. Not everyone approved of his methods of acquiring writers – often 'rustling' them from the quieter pastures of other agents – but there was no denying that when he zeroed in on talent he knew how to make it pay.

Jack wondered if he was about to be wooed, and felt a kick of excitement.

The dining room was on the first floor, plain but stylish, lit by three high, arched windows overlooking the street. You could see partway into the kitchen, where a wood-burning oven shaped like a giant beehive took up most of one wall. Its iron door was open, offering a glimpse of glowing embers and the seductive, smoky smell of roasting food. On the way to their table, Leo stopped to say hello to a man who turned out to be Carson McGuire, though he didn't look anything like his author photograph. McGuire's first novel, *Vanderbilt's Thumb*, had been on the best-seller list for weeks. Everyone said it was a masterpiece. Jack hadn't read it yet, in case it was.

In the flesh McGuire was unprepossessing: squat, fortyish, Bruce Willis haircut. Yet the sheen of success was upon him. His cheeks were plump and smooth, his jacket uncreased, his body language subtly assertive. With him was a tempestuous-looking young woman with slanting cats' eyes and a thrilling acreage of bare flesh. Jack hovered at Leo's shoulder, a half-smile on his face, while the other three chatted about a party they'd all been to, laughing and bandying names. He was beginning to feel painfully conspicuous in his jeans and shabby jacket when Leo at last turned to include him in the group.

'Carson, do you know Jack Madison? He wrote that terrific collection, *Big Sky*, a couple of years back.'

'For sure.' McGuire did the professional handshake/eye contact number. 'Great book. Nice to meet you, Jake.'

'Yes. Thank you. Uh, great.'

What wit! What suavity! Carson McGuire would certainly remember *him* next time. Jack lumbered after Leo to their table, feeling as ridiculous as a dancing bear. It was obvious that McGuire had never read *Big Sky*, probably not even heard of it.

'Great guy, Carson,' said Leo, once they had taken their seats. 'Absolutely one of my favourite clients. I think I'm just about to clinch a Hollywood deal for him – enough zeroes to make his eyes spin – but don't tell him, huh?' Leo winked.

'How would I? We don't move in the same circles.'

'You will, Jack, you will.'

Leo spoke with such confidence that Jack felt ashamed of his sulkiness. He made an effort to rise above it. 'A movie deal, Leo: that's wonderful. Carson's a lucky man to have you for an agent. Good taste in women, too.' He cocked an eyebrow at the dark temptress.

'That's Mercedes. She's a model, from Venezuela or somewhere. Carson's married, of course, and he's planning to move his family to New York, but there's a glitch. The house sale fell through, or his wife's mother is dying – I forget what. Still, while the cat's away . . .' He shot Jack a man-to-man smile.

'Yeah.' Jack chuckled. 'Cute mouse.'

'By the way, what happened to that poor woman the other night?'

'What poor woman?' Jack's smile faded.

'Your fancy English friend who threw the calculator at you. She was hilarious!'

'She's fine.'

'Got rid of her okay, did you? Some ditzy woman once passed out like that at my place, and I caught her crawling into my bed at five in the morning. I told her, "If you're sober enough to get here from the couch, you're sober enough to go home." I put her in a cab, quick, before she started getting ideas.'

'Freya's not like that.'

'Come on, Jack, once they pass thirty they're all like that. Hormones in overdrive, bodies in free-fall, careers a little shaky. They put those soft pussycat paws on you and suddenly – ouch! – in go the claws.'

Jack gave a weak laugh. Freya was probably moving her things into his apartment at this very moment.

'Older women are so demanding! *Talk to me. Listen to me. Not like that, like this.* They feel they have some goddamn right to criticize how you look, your tastes, even what you do in bed.'

'Freya's just a friend.'

'They're the worst. They think they "understand" you.' Leo grimaced. 'They squirm their way in by making you dinner, or doing little favours like stocking your fridge or taking your stuff to the repair shop. One minute they're telling you that they'll always "be there" for you; the next, they're always *there*, period.'

'Ha ha.' Jack wished Leo would order some more booze.

'Secretly, of course, older women *hate* men. They know we can wait for ever to get married and have children, whereas they have to do it by the time they're forty – and they *can't stand it*. It blows their equality theory to hell. I like to stick with the under twenty-fives, myself. All they want is fun.'

'And they think we're God, right?' Jack grinned, remembering Candace. 'I'm seeing an adorable twenty-two-year-old at the moment.'

'Way to go.' Leo reached across to give him an approving punch on the arm. 'Now, what are you drinking?'

A pretty waitress took their order and brought a bottle of wine. To Jack's relief, Leo began talking about the publishing industry. Jack watched his sharp, clever face and emphatic hand gestures, half listening to an energetic commentary on takeovers, book fairs, trips to LA, six-figure deals, seven-figure deals. From time to time he gave an intelligent grunt. *Relax*, he told himself. Leo didn't know that he was stuck on his novel. Leo didn't know how he woke suddenly in the night, breathless with the fear that he might never write another word – that he was no good, had never been any good. Leo liked *Big Sky*; he'd said it was 'terrific'.

'She's got her nerve, coming in here.' Leo broke off from his lecture on internet selling. 'See that woman over there, the desperate-looking blonde? She's been banned from Barnes and Noble because she went into her local store every morning and put piles of her book *Susan's Secret* on top of *Vanderbilt's Thumb*, hoping people would buy it instead.' He gave a malicious chuckle. 'Last time I looked she was number ninety-five on the list.'

'The book's no good, then?'

Leo found this question so amusing he choked on his focaccia. 'It's totally irrelevant whether the book is good.' He wiped the crumbs from his face. 'The point is that it was never *positioned*. Nobody knew whether it was a girly romp or a feminist rant or a plate of cupcakes. Nobody had been *told* that it was good.'

Jack was puzzled. 'But surely it would sell if – '

'Jack, Jack, Jack, Jack.' Leo shook his head sorrowfully. 'People think that if you write a brilliant book the world will recognize it. Ain't so. Nobody has time to read the actual book, so you sell the idea instead, preferably in under ten words. Let's see . . . "Abused woman finds love – and a psycho in the attic!" Recognize that?'

'*Jane Eyre*?'

'You got it. "Wealthy adulteress commits suicide on Moscow train track."'

'*Anna Karenina*.'

'"Student's dilemma: marry his girlfriend or avenge his father's murder."'

'*Hamlet*.'

'See, it's easy. You can do it with authors, too. "Man in a white suit."'

'Tom Wolfe.' Jack was enjoying this. He felt like the smart alec on a TV quiz programme.

'"Out-of-town lawyer defends the little man."'

'John Grisham.'

'"Manhattan cokehead beds blondes." Shit! don't answer that. He's over there.'

Jack busied himself with a mouthful of guinea fowl before turning his head surreptitiously to catch a glimpse of literature's latest *enfant terrible*. This was a cool place.

'You see, in the old days publishers relied on good reviews to sell a book – but who gives a shit about reviews these days? In the eighties and nineties, they advertised a book into the charts – but that got too expensive. Nowadays you have to be smarter. It's like the movies: the pitch is everything. You have to make a book sound hot, irresistible, must-have.' Leo pushed away his plate, his food half-finished. 'So, Jack. Tell me about your new book.'

'Oh. Well it's, you know, okay. Going well, in fact. Slow, but – '

'What's it called?'

'*The Long Summer*.' Saying it aloud was painful. 'At the moment.'

'Good title. Don't change it. Is it long?'

'Longish. Probably.'

'Contemporary setting?'

'Yes, but it sort of weaves back, you know, into some family, uh, history.'

'Sounds fascinating.'

'Not *history* history, dates and stuff, but the – you know, the – '

'The past?'

'Right. The past,' Jack accepted the word gratefully. 'And there's a kind of love story except it doesn't – well, anyway, a love story. Kind of. I'm not too good at describing my plots.' Understatement of the year! Why hadn't he rehearsed? Jack grabbed his wine glass and drained it.

'A Southern setting?'

'Yes.'

'Anything about slaves?'

'No.'

'Wonderful. I can't wait to read it.'

Mercifully, Leo changed the subject. 'How do you like the club?'

'Great spot. Is it easy to get membership?'

'Almost impossible. But I know the owner. I could probably swing it for you. You want to get in soon, though, before they increase the fee again.'

'How much is it now?'

'Four thousand dollars.'

'Whoooh! I think I'll have to wait for my inheritance.'

'With your talent? I could get you an advance tomorrow, so big you wouldn't have to worry about such things.'

Jack stared at Leo. Could he really do that?

'Of course I know you already have an agent,' Leo said.

'Well . . .'

'Ella Fogarty, isn't it?'

'She's . . . I . . . We go way back.'

'A really nice woman, no question. I admire your loyalty, Jack. Now what about dessert? I recommend the *tarte tatin*.'

Jack nodded his acceptance, and fell silent. He felt crushed. It seemed that Leo was not interested in him after all.

After lunch Leo suggested they go downstairs again to 'The Den' and shoot some pool. In the corridor Jack paused to admire an Annie Leibowitz portrait of Truman Capote. Hurrying to catch up, he bumped into someone, a man wearing a peacock-coloured shirt that marked out the club staff.

'Excuse me.'

'That's okay.'

For a moment the two men looked at each other. Jack felt a jolt of recognition, and on its heels something else – a backlash of embarrassment that made him hesitate. Before he could say hello, the other man turned abruptly and walked away.

'Someone you know?' Leo was holding the door open for Jack, one eyebrow raised.

'Not really.'

But as they busied themselves putting the balls out on the table and gathering them into the wooden triangle, Jack reflected uneasily on his small lie. The man was Howard Gurnard – Howie – someone he'd known years ago when he first came to New York, an aspiring writer like himself. But Howie had never got anything published. When Jack sold his first story,

Howie had been flatteringly in awe of Jack's success, and Jack had been willing, even gratified, to be quizzed about editors and agents and writing methods. Then Howie became a pest. He learned about 'the gang' and Ambrosio's, and turned up there so often that Freya had nicknamed him Howdy Doody. He'd bring his rejection letters, and harangue them all about the death of literature, until they felt obliged to pay for his coffee and food. They began to dread his appearance – hang-dog, needy, sour with desperation. Jack started to avoid him, and had gradually, guiltily, dropped him. And now here he was, a *waiter* or minion of some kind at Club SoHo, probably the nearest he would ever get to fame and success.

Leo tossed a dime to see who would break first. Jack won. Still upset, he put far too much power behind his cue and scattered the balls in all directions without pocketing a single one.

'Hmmm,' murmured Leo. He chalked his cue and blew off the dust, then prowled around the table, planning his attack. He lined up his cue on the chosen ball, then checked the angle from the pocket side before returning to his original position. He sighted along the cue again. There was a sharp *crack!*, and a red ball spotted with white shot into a corner pocket.

'See, positioning is all.' Leo grinned. 'Stripes for you, spots for me.'

Jack was still thinking about Howie. 'Tell me, Leo, what do you think makes a successful author?' he asked.

'Four things.' Leo potted a second ball. 'First, youth. Young is good; young is fabulous. If you can get a book out before an author turns twenty-five, you're home. And if they're that young, they're probably single, which means you can get pictures of them into the magazines, posing with models or movie actors or media movers, with no husbands or wives to make trouble. Shit!' His next ball had spun around the edge of a pocket and bounced out again. 'Though trouble can be good copy, too, of course.'

Now it was Jack's turn. He potted an easy ball, while Leo leaned on his cue like a warrior on his spear, and continued his lecture.

'Second is looks. Natural good looks are best, but you can do a lot with accessories and camera angles. Oh, too bad! . . . If they're women and you can get them to pose naked, great. Tasteful pictures, obviously.'

He positioned himself at the table again, and despatched another ball. 'Third, contacts. That's basically anyone you know who's rich, famous or influential. It's generally better if you aren't any of these things yourself. No one likes a smart-ass.'

Leo attempted a fancy ricochet shot off the side, but he mishit and almost potted the white. Jack circled the table looking for something he could hit; he was distracted, and playing badly.

'Finally, there's the gimmick,' said Leo. 'This can be anything, though it's usually something sad or bad. Former drug addiction, kooky religions, sexual abuse –

though that's a little passé now. Lesbianism sometimes works; male homosexuality is okay, but limited. Diseases can be great, so long as they're not contagious or – what's the word?' He snapped his fingers.

'Terminal?'

'Disfiguring. Funnily enough, terminal can be quite successful if death coincides with publication. No backlist, of course.'

Leo watched critically as Jack leaned so far across the table that he was practically lying down. 'If you're going for the blue, you need the rest.' He unhooked it from the wall and handed it to Jack, then continued. 'For a woman, confessing to gross overweight is a surefire winner, providing she's now whip thin and comes across with the fatso pictures for the promo. Yup. Those are the crucial things, my golden four: youth, looks, contacts, gimmick. I made up an acronym to remind me. You Love Counting Greenbacks.' Leo chuckled. 'Uh-oh, I think you're snookered.'

*But what about talent? What about style? What about passion and wit and humanity?* Jack kept the words to himself. He didn't want to appear foolish. Instead he asked, 'What if the author's sort of boring – over twenty-five, ordinary looking, no contacts, no scandal?'

'There's always a way.' Leo spun a ball out of trouble. 'I'll give you an example. "Simple Kentucky rancher writes novel of love and betrayal, and is tipped for the Pulitzer."'

89

'That's McGuire, isn't it?'

'Yes and no. In fact, Carson is rather well-educated, and he's a horse-owner, not a hired hand. He's sent himself on scads of creative writing courses; that's how I found him. I could see the fiction market was tiring of urban sophistication – drugs, models, mutilation – so I was hunting for some down-home macho realism. Carson was perfect, but it took me a while to figure out how to sell him. There were downsides. He's not exactly young, and he's no Adonis, and his real name's Carson Blossom.'

'Blossom?' Jack couldn't help smirking.

'I know, a real killer. With a name like that the poor guy was never going to win anything besides a dairy cow competition. But then I discovered that his middle name was McGuire, and bingo! Look at all the writers who've been successful recently – Cormac McCarthy, Tom McGuane, Jay McInerney, Frank McCourt. So we dropped the Blossom, dug out Carson's old grandmammy – a crazy Kentucky character, great copy – sent down a top photographer, and the press ran with it. We never claimed that Carson was a ranch hand; people deduced it from the cowboy hat, though we only used the hat to hide his baldness. Serendipity!'

'I guess.' Jack was reeling from these revelations. 'But isn't that kind of crass?'

'It totally sucks. But that's the way the world is. You have to use dirty means to achieve a pure end.'

'Even lying?'

'Lying is just a different way of telling the truth.' Leo gave his leprechaun grin. 'My game, by the way.'

It was true: Leo had won.

'Of course you have to have the right product. And you' — Leo pointed his cue at Jack — 'are terrific product.'

'I am?' Jack couldn't stop a gratified smile tugging at his mouth.

'Yup. Because you are the real thing. In fact, you're *better* than Carson.'

'I don't know . . .'

'But I do.' Leo laid down his cue along the edge of the table, and looked across at Jack, controlled and confident. 'Listen to me, Jack. You have talent. You are going to be a star. All you need is a little help. If you want it, I'm here. Understand?'

Jack met Leo's intense gaze and nodded solemnly. 'Thanks. I — I'll think about it.'

'You do that. Now, what do you say to another game?'

It was past three by the time Jack stumbled out into the daylight. He walked down the street with a vague, foolish smile on his face, oblivious of passers-by. His chest swelled. He was going to be a star! — not a loser like Howie. He was going to be rich! — in his own right, not dependent on his Dad. There would be book signings and a coast-to-coast publicity tour. Television interviews. Fan letters. (*Dear Mr Madison, I cannot tell you how much* . . .) People would no longer ask him what he 'did', they would know. Jack pictured himself dropping by Club SoHo – *his* club. The bartenders would get to know him. 'Hey, Jack!' they'd shout in welcome (he wouldn't object to the familiarity), setting up his favoured tipple as he pushed his way through a back-slapping crowd. While he waited for his dazzling lunch partner to show up, he would bitch with other writers about the hell of creative struggle. Or would he be too grand to mingle? *Better than Carson* . . . Carson Blossom! Jack guffawed loudly. A woman approaching him gave him a suspicious look and veered around him as if he were a nutcase.

Little did she know. He was an artist; artists were allowed to behave in weird and lordly ways. Jack smiled gleefully up into the sky, and walked slap into a small tree. His thoughts returned to earth. He'd never leave Ella, of course he wouldn't. He'd finish his novel and let Ella sell it for what it was worth. But what was it worth? What was *he* worth, without a Leo to spin him to success. *The pitch is everything*: could that be right? Jack frowned: of course not.

But as he wandered through the streets, inhaling the smell of summer, woozy with drink and flattery, he couldn't help trying out something in his head. 'And the winner of this year's Pulitzer Prize is . . . Jack McMadison.'

## 7

Freya twisted her key in the familiar lock and pushed open the door of apartment 12B. She took a tentative step inside. There was the stale smell of trapped air, a faint purr from the fridge, nothing else.

'Hello?' she called out.

But of course there was no answer. Michael was safely at work. She had the place to herself.

Letting the heavy door snick shut, she walked quietly into the apartment and looked around her, feeling like an interloper. In the galley-kitchen Michael's breakfast cup and cereal bowl (muesli with extra bran) sat upturned on the drainer. The cushions on the living room couch were rumpled and squashed where he had last sat on them. A copy of *The Harvard Law Review* lay folded open on the low table alongside. She noticed with a shock that all her art magazines were gone. Could he have already packed up her things, perhaps even thrown them away?

Swiftly she crossed the living room and opened the bedroom door, but no, everything in here was the same – the clutter of bottles and make-up tubes on her chest of drawers, her kimono hooked on the back of the door, a single black stocking (where had that come from?) draped over a chair. The bed was unmade.

Freya was strangely touched to see that Michael still slept on 'his' side. She walked over to the window and leant her forehead across the glass, staring out. This was what she had always liked best about the apartment: its wide, calming view over Riverside Park and across the Hudson to the smokestacks of New Jersey. It was exhilarating to float here above the swarming streets, to escape the maze of dwarfing, cliff-faced buildings that blocked out the sky. Sometimes Michael used to find her like this at night, standing silent and alone in the dark, and he would exclaim in alarm and switch on lights, as if he found her behaviour weird.

Michael. She sighed. Another era over. She wasn't exactly heart-broken, but she felt . . . tired. Why was it that her life no longer seemed to progress? When she looked back over the last few years, there seemed to be no development, just one damned thing after another: another man, another job, another apartment. Something must be the matter with her.

Michael was one of the few single men in New York actively seeking a long-term partner – okay, *wife* – yet he had discounted her as a possibility. Why? Was she too tall? Too thin? Were her breasts too small? Her knees too bony? Had she teased him too much about his funny little habits? Or was she simply too old – not only to win someone else's heart, but to give her own? In the restaurant, Michael had turned sad, brown eyes to hers and said simply, devastatingly: 'You don't love me.' It was true.

Other people said confidently that they were 'in love'. How could they tell? Mere companionship was not enough; she knew that now. Yet there must be more to love than the skittishness that attended every new affair, the coiled-up excitement that could be triggered into passion by a single glance or the touch of a finger. Passion burned very prettily, but sooner or later the flames went out – or left a scar.

Freya's love life had taken her down some strange back alleys. A couple of years ago, in the darkest, nastiest alley of all she had found Todd. Tall, beautiful and charming, almost the only art dealer who was unarguably heterosexual, he had literally bewitched her. Within minutes of their meeting – a casual intro-duction at a dull party – he had caught her hungry, speculative look and warned, 'Don't even think of it. I'm much too dangerous for you.' But she hadn't listened. His eyes were hot and dark, and looked at her in a certain way; even before he took her to bed that night, she was enslaved. This was love at last, the real thing.

All her usual rules of conduct flew out the window. She left in the middle of dinner parties if he wanted her, cancelled engagements in case he called, forgave him instantly when he didn't turn up. She told him that she loved him and asked him repeatedly, shamelessly, twenty times a day, if he loved her too. ('Of course I do.') She worshipped his bevelled cheekbones, as smoothly sculpted as stones on a beach, the long muscular legs that twined with hers, the smell of his sweat. She was so aroused herself that for a while she didn't think it strange that he never had an orgasm; he told her it was her fault for being too eager. She began trying new tricks, even things she didn't like doing. Always, he held himself aloof. He made her reveal her fantasies and fears, but never told her about himself. Sometimes, during sex, he pressed his forearm against her throat until she struggled for breath, but she didn't complain. He was looking for the perfect woman, he said. For six long months Freya really thought it might be her. Each mark on her body was a battle scar, a token of their passion for each other. They were Antony and Cleopatra, Troilus and Cressida, Heathcliff and Cathy.

The more abject she was, the more critical he became. She began to worry that she was too fat, not sexy enough, that she smelled wrong. She went on diets, changed her hair, topped up her confidence with booze. She missed meetings, ignored invitations. Friends and colleagues began asking her if she was okay; she answered that she'd never been happier. One night Todd went too far and she blacked out, waking in bright sunlight the next day, alone, in a pool of cold vomit with her throat in agony. Somehow she got herself home, pulled the plug on her phone and went to bed with the whisky bottle and a handful of aspirin – no, not enough to kill herself, she wasn't that stupid, though when Cat found her she had been frightened enough to call a doctor. Eventually Freya had understood that Todd had not been looking for the perfect woman to love, but to hate. They were never Antony and Cleopatra; they weren't even a couple, just one another's dirty little secret. For months afterwards she'd felt bruised and shaken and disgusted with herself. Then she had met Michael. What had he seen in her, she wondered? Whatever it was, it seemed he hadn't cared for it on closer inspection.

Freya blinked her eyes and hauled herself back into the present. Her breath had steamed a cloudy circle on the window. She wiped it clear with the sleeve of her sweatshirt. Twice in a row she had been the victim of her own fantasies – Todd's passionate lover, Michael's domestic companion. Next time she was going to be more careful – if there was a next time.

She turned away from the window. Stop wittering; get packing. She dragged a chair over to the closet and reached for her two suitcases, old friends, stacked on a high shelf. When she yanked them down, dust and debris showered on to her head and drifted to the floor. Damn. She fetched a dustpan and brush to sweep up the mess, and a long apron to protect her clothes, then dusted off her hair and found an old cotton scarf to tie washerwoman-style around her head. It was funny to think this had been a quasi-feminist fashion some time back in the eighties. She wondered if she looked like Simone de Beauvoir.

She made the bed roughly and put her suitcases on top, lids flipped open. The good thing about having no fixed address was that you never accumulated too much stuff. Not for her the rubble of old letters and photographs and theatre programmes, the personal collection of books with one's own signature written with increasing fluency on the fly-leaf, the balding childhood bunny-rabbit, the gewgaws and love gifts, vases, bowls, framed reproductions and other sentimental nonsense that most people seemed unable to live without. A truly independent woman, Freya told herself, ought to be able to pack up her life in an hour, max. Besides, when you were five foot ten no one offered to carry your luggage.

First, the essentials: passport, underwear, shoes. The passport was easily stowed in her handbag; her extensive collection of fancy lingerie and footwear, however, required an entire case to themselves. Freya sat on the lid and bounced out the air until it shut. She filled the other suitcase, staggered to the elevator with both of them, and stowed them downstairs in the doorman's cubbyhole until she was ready to take a cab to Jack's. On the next trip she fetched a bulging dress-bag. By this time she was feeling dishevelled, and grumpy with hunger. Her yin and yang might be marvellously balanced, but she was starving. She stood in the kitchen and chomped eight Ritz crackers in a row; she had bought them herself, so it wasn't stealing. Her eyes roved around the neat, familiar room. She pictured Michael in his striped apron, sleeves rolled up, meticulously chopping and measuring, frowning over his recipe book like a small boy doing his homework. He was a good cook, and at the beginning this had pleased and impressed her. She was useless in the kitchen; there'd been nobody to teach her. Recently it had sometimes seemed a burden to be presented with a complicated meal over which she was meant to rhapsodize, when all she'd wanted in the first place was cheese on toast and a good book in bed. Yet she couldn't help feeling a stab of regret for what might have been.

Swallowing hastily, she grabbed a couple of plastic shopping bags and did a final sweep of the apartment, dropping in small items – bottles of goop from the bathroom, the new Matisse biography she was reading, some favourite sounds from the rack by the stereo: Billie Holiday, Elgar, Blondie, Verdi's Requiem, César Franck, Bruce Springsteen, the Commitments, Cole Porter – hey, a perfect Desert Island eight!

Last of all she located her handbag and the two items that she had laid ready on top of the chest of drawers, now empty and otherwise bare. One was a small framed photograph of her mother, glamorous in boots and a Russian hat, laughing in a blur of pigeons: Paris, Place Vendôme, 1972 – the last week, possibly the last day, Freya had seen her. For a moment Freya held the photo in her palm, staring down at it: *Why aren't you here?* The carefree eyes smiled back. Her mother had been only thirty-one, four years younger than Freya was now, when she died. Freya stroked the cold glass with a fingertip, then carefully slotted the picture into an inner pocket of her bag.

The other item was an airline wallet containing two

tickets for England, one for her and one for . . . well, who? The wedding was less than three weeks away. Freya felt a burst of anger that Michael couldn't have waited a bit longer to ditch her. She couldn't go alone; she *couldn't*. Her imagination raced ahead, conjuring up scenes of embarrassment and humiliation – and that's when she remembered the hat. She had bought it specially. Where was it? Climbing on to the chair once again, she foraged in the clutter of overnight bags, tennis-ball cans, rolled-up posters and exercise weights until she spied a smartly striped box. She quailed at adding yet another item to her heap of luggage, but without a hat it was unthinkable to –

*What was that?* Freya froze, arm arrested in mid-air. She could hear a distinct metallic scuffling, horribly like the sound of a key in a lock. Instinctively, she crouched low and slid off the chair. It couldn't be!

But it was. Freya felt a faint draught of air as the apartment door opened. She heard footsteps, the rustle of clothing or shopping bags, then a slam loud enough to make her jump. She checked her watch: barely five o'clock, much too early for Michael. Besides, she could smell perfume. She remembered Cat's theory that Michael might have found another woman, and her own scoffing denial. Or what if it was a robber? No law said that all robbers were men. She grabbed the dustpan and brush, and holding them before her like shield and dagger, edged cautiously into the corridor.

An elderly woman was hanging something up in

the hall closet. She wore a neat, old-fashioned suit of celery green, its pleated skirt falling modestly to her plump calves, and had a nimbus of fluffy white hair sculpted like a meringue. Freya must have made some small sound, for the woman suddenly turned, saw her, and clutched the pussycat bow at her neck. 'My goodness! You practically scared me to death!'

Freya stared. Who was this person?

Whoever she was, she seemed quite unabashed. 'I thought you came on Tuesdays,' she said, closing the closet door with a firm hand. She advanced on Freya, head high, a tsarina approaching a serf. 'Do you speak English?'

Freya opened her mouth, but no words emerged.

The woman aimed an index finger at her own heart. 'I,' she said, slowly and distinctly, 'am Mrs Petersen, Mr Petersen's mother.' She thought for a moment. '*La madre de Signor Petersen. Comprendo?*'

Freya's brain raced. What was Michael's mother doing here? And why was she speaking in mangled Spanish? Freya knew nothing about Mrs Petersen except that she was divorced, worshipped her son, worked as an administrator at some fancy girls' school in Minnesota, and had consistently refused to acknowledge Freya's existence. On the few occasions when Freya had happened to answer the phone, Mrs Petersen had deflected any attempts at small talk with a curt, 'May I please speak to my son?' – always in a tone of aggrieved suspicion, as if Freya had broken into the apartment and was holding Michael at gunpoint.

'Oh, never mind. Come with me.' Mrs Petersen beckoned commandingly and bustled towards the kitchen.

Freya hesitated. Did she really look like a maid? A *Mexican* maid? She caught a glimpse of herself in a far mirror, complete with dustpan, apron and knotted headscarf: not so much Simone de Beauvoir as Mrs Mop. She allowed herself to be led zombie-like into the kitchen where Mrs Petersen demonstrated exactly how she was to defrost the fridge, empty and wipe clean the food cabinets, and polish the kettle. She tut-tutted over a circular burn mark on one of the wooden counters, where Michael had once placed a sizzling wok during his stir-fry craze: Freya could tell that Mrs Petersen had already convicted her of the crime. Next stop was the bathroom, where Freya was instructed to disinfect the tiles and scrub the toilet.

'*Si, si.*' She nodded meekly.

When they reached the bedroom, Mrs Petersen eyed the open closet, and its line of bare hangers, with satisfaction. She checked that Freya's chest of drawers was empty, ran one dustometer finger across the top, and grimaced. Freya noticed with dismay that her handbag was sitting on a chair next to the chest, conspicuous as an elephant. Giving a theatrical gasp, she ran across the room to screen the bag, and pointed open-mouthed at the empty closet. 'Pliss, hhhhwhere ees Mees Freya?'

'Gone.' Mrs Petersen gestured like someone shooing geese. '*Vamoose.*'

Freya crossed herself.

'No, no, Juanita, or whatever your name is, it's all for the best. *No bueno muchacha. Artista.*' Mrs Petersen frowned. '*Inglesi.*'

'Ah.' Freya sighed in condolence.

Mrs Petersen was now rifling through her son's clothes, pulling out his suits and laying them on the bed. 'I want all these to go to the cleaners, understand? *Launderio.*'

'*Si.*' Did the woman think Freya carried the Black Death?

'You get started, then. I have some calls to make. *Telephonio.*'

Freya listened to the retreating tattoo of Mrs Petersen's heels. Then she took off the apron, folded it, and placed it in the middle of Michael's bed, with the apartment key on top. She considered leaving a note, but there seemed nothing to say. Quickly she assembled her belongings – purse, plastic bags, hat box – wondering how she was going to sneak out of here. From the living room Mrs Petersen's voice rose in a girlish gush. Evidently she and an old friend had been telephonically reunited. Freya lurked just out of sight in the bedroom doorway, ears cocked, waiting for an opportunity to escape.

' . . . not too bad. I have the maid here, getting everything back into shape. I think I'll rearrange the furniture, too. It's so important for Mikey to have a fresh start, with no reminders.'

*Mikey?* Freya rolled her eyes.

' . . . of course it was his decision, Myra. You know I never interfere.'

*Ha!*

'He knew in his heart that she wasn't the woman for him. She was always so off-hand when I called. You know what these city girls are like nowadays. Well, I say "girl", but from what Mikey told me she sounded quite "experienced", if you know what I mean.'

*Bastard!*

' . . . Yes, I do know times have changed. I may not be an Eastern liberal, but that doesn't mean I'm unworldly. I see those magazines at the hairdressers with all the articles about ess ee ex. There are pernicious forces abroad in these United States of ours. We have to fight to protect those we love. My Michael has always been such a sweet, innocent boy. Did I ever tell you that darling thing he said once at Sunday School?'

*Only nine billion times, I bet.*

' . . . Oh. Well, anyway, I know what's right for my son: a nice American girl, somebody young and fresh who can make him a lovely home, not some Mata Hari.'

Freya ground her teeth.

' . . . not actually Dutch, no. I understand she's British. But these foreign women are all the same. He told me she never cooked him a real breakfast, not once. She wouldn't even sew on a button for him, though she's been living off him for months.'

By now Freya was burning with indignation. How

could Michael have been so disloyal? It was intolerable to think that all the time she had been trying to fit in with his lifestyle, he had been giving his mother weekly bulletins on her behaviour. She glared malevolently round the bedroom, centre of their supposed togetherness. Her eye fell upon the pile of clothes that Mrs Petersen had instructed her to take to the cleaners. It gave her an idea.

' . . . I imagine it was one of those, you know, *physical* things. But that always wears off doesn't it? Which reminds me, how's Harold? Still enjoying his ham radio? *And where do you think you're going?*'

These last words were addressed to Freya, who was walking boldly across the living room to the front door. Wedged between her arms and chin was a great heap of Michael's suits, under which she had contrived to conceal her own possessions. Mrs Petersen stiffened in her chair. Her eyes bulged with outrage.

For explanation, Freya nodded at her overflowing armful. '*Si si por favor y viva espana hasta la vista,*' she gabbled frantically, trying to open the apartment door with her little finger. It was maddeningly resistant. '*Enchillada Lope de Vega agua minerale la cucuracha.*'

The door yielded explosively, nearly toppling her backwards. She headed for the elevator at a rapid waddle and stabbed the down button. *Quick!* she prayed, glancing back at the door of 12B, which had slammed behind her and so far remained shut. As soon as the elevator arrived Freya leapt inside, threw everything on the floor, and pressed L for Lobby. She checked once more to see that she was safe, and nearly froze with horror to see Mrs Petersen's white little-old-lady head playing peekaboo round the apartment door.

'The rain in Spain stays mainly in the plain,' Freya told her, in her haughtiest English accent, and stepped back smartly. The elevator doors lumbered shut an inch from her nose.

Five minutes later she tumbled into Joe's Dri-Kleen and dumped Michael's suits in a slithery pile on the counter. Her arms ached. She felt sweaty and untidy and unattractive and extremely angry.

'Name?'

'Petersen.' Freya spelt it out for him, impatience rising.

'Regular or rush?'

'Whatever's most expensive.'

While Joe filled out the tickets, Freya rested her elbows on the counter, scowling at a sign that read, 'Repairs on the premises. Just ask!' What was she doing here? What kind of a person took her ex-lover's clothes to the dry cleaners, at the behest of her ex-lover's mother, who thought she was the cleaning lady? An idiot, that's who. How dared Michael complain about her to his mother?

'I forgot to say,' she called out. 'All the trousers need shortening.'

'Okey dokey.' Joe picked up his pen again.

He copied down her instructions obediently, and handed her the tickets. She stuffed them into her pocket. Michael had a brain, didn't he? He'd track down his suits eventually. It was a pity she couldn't be present when he put one on. She pulled open the rickety door to the street.

'Hey, just a minute! These trousers: did you say *six inches*?'

Freya paused, hand on the doorknob. Then she turned and fixed Joe with a dazzling smile.

'Haven't you heard? Short is the new long.'

# 8

Jack opened the door of his bedroom. He was wearing a sleep-creased T-shirt, and faded undershorts with a lipstick kiss imprinted on the right buttock. After steadying himself on the door jamb, he launched himself on a trajectory that should, with luck, lead him across the north side of the living room and around the corner to the bathroom. Walking on auto-pilot, eyes squinched with sleep, he successfully nego-tiated the corner and biffed the bathroom door with the heel of his hand, as he always did. Normally it flew open with a satisfying *pop!* Today it nearly broke his wrist. It was locked! He recoiled sharply and cradled his arm, panting with the pain.

'Out in a sec,' chirruped a voice, a female voice: Freya. He kept forgetting she was here.

Next there came the hiss of water, which meant that she was only just beginning her shower. Women always took for ever. Muttering to himself, Jack stomped through the kitchen and unlocked the door to the back yard, a wasteland of weeds and rotting cardboard boxes. He took a couple of paces across the cracked concrete and peed vigorously on to a patch of dandelions. As his senses juddered into focus, he became aware of an annoying whistling noise.

Eventually Jack made out a little brown thing on the back wall. Hop hop. Tweet tweet. Dumb bird. He hated cheerfulness in the morning.

Something was fluttering at the edge of his vision. Jack turned his head and gaped. A makeshift washing line had been strung out across one corner of the yard. From it dangled various pieces of unmistakably female apparel, including flimsy wisps of underwear. This was awful. What would the neighbours think? – especially Henpecked Harry from upstairs, who was practically Velcroed to his wife and depended on Jack to live a life of brutal, undomesticated masculinity. Jack winced his way across the prickly terrain, snatched the clothes off the line, and took them inside.

His plan had been to position himself in an armchair bang in the middle of Freya's path back to her room, so that he could rustle a newspaper impatiently when she finally emerged. But to his surprise he found the bathroom already vacated and exuding warm, scented steam. Jack wrinkled his nose. What if that stuff got into the water system? He didn't want to wind up smelling like a girl.

He shut himself in the bathroom, only realizing once he was inside that he still had Freya's clothes. He dumped them in a pile on the toilet seat, then ran water into the basin and lathered his face with shaving foam. He dipped his razor into the warm water, and cut a long swathe through the foam. Ouch! Whimpering softly, Jack bathed his stinging cheek in cold water, then peered in the mirror to examine the damage. One side of his face was covered with tiny red pinpricks beginning to exude blood. What had happened to his razor? But he already knew the answer. He flung open the bathroom door.

'Freya!' he bellowed.

'Morning, Jack,' said a voice about three feet away from him. 'I was about to make some coffee. Want some?' She was standing at the entrance to the kitchen, immaculate and aloof, already dressed in her zippy career-woman suit.

Jack brandished his razor in the air, as if he was about to lasso a steer. 'Have you been using this to shave your legs?'

'I might have. Oh, all right, I did. Sorry. I left mine at Michael's.'

'Then buy yourself a new one. Look at my face! I'm going to have to go around all day with Kleenex polkadots, like a nerdy teenager.'

'Sorry,' she said again, but she didn't sound properly penitent.

'And you locked the bathroom door. I practically broke my wrist on it.'

'Bollocks.'

'You could have stopped me working for weeks. I need my hands. A writer is like a concert pianist.'

She folded her arms and gave him a smile he didn't altogether like. 'Which one, oh Toscanini?'

'Huh?'

'Which wrist sustained the near-fatal injury? The

one you're waving your razor around with, or the one you're using to prop up the wall?'

Jack glowered. 'Kiss my ass,' he said nastily, and turned to go back into the bathroom.

'Looks like somebody already did,' she called after him. 'Love the shorts.'

Jack slammed the door, readjusted the shower head to its harshest setting and stood under the drumming water. It was only a temporary arrangement, he reminded himself, trying to calm his heartbeat. 'Two weeks,' he'd said, 'two weeks *max*.' If today was Tuesday, that meant only nine more days of cohabit-ation. *Only* nine days? Only *nine* (9) days? Only nine *days*? He closed his eyes and tipped back his head, as if in supplication to a compassionate deity. Water ran down his face like tears.

The best policy was simply to avoid one another. So far, he'd managed this rather successfully. Jack's mood brightened as he recalled how he had charmed Candace off her high horse and persuaded her to come out with him Saturday night, as he'd known she would, though he'd delayed calling until six-thirty to keep her guessing. When she answered at the first ring, he knew he was in. Girls! The evening had gone pretty much according to plan, though their discussion of Candace's writing was bumpier than expected: who would have guessed that she'd set such store by her adverbs? Candace herself, in a skimpy black dress, was even prettier than he had realized. Out of the black dress, she was sensational. At the end of the evening he had escorted her home, like the Southern gentleman he was, learned that her room-mate was fortuitously absent (another giveaway) and decided to stay.

Jack stepped out of the shower and grabbed a towel to frisk himself dry. Candace was a sweet girl, too. When they finally got out of bed, she'd insisted on making him waffles and maple syrup for breakfast. He didn't especially like waffles, but he'd enjoyed watching her make the effort for him. After that, frankly, he'd become restless. Candace's apartment was tiny, its windows looking straight into other windows or at blank, dirty walls – probably the best she could afford, but it made Jack feel claustrophobic. She'd suggested going to the park (what for?), but he got away by claiming to have a squash date, which was true once he had called Gus to arrange it.

Jack's thoughts reverted to Freya. So far, they'd got through three days without difficulty; there was no reason why the remaining time shouldn't pass smoothly, as long as they were both polite and respected each other's space. They were mature adults, after all. One tiny niggle remained, which was that he still hadn't got around to telling Candace about Freya moving in. But he'd been busy. A man couldn't do everything.

Wrapping the towel around his waist, Jack returned to his bedroom to dress. As he pulled on his usual jeans and comfortable shirt he sniffed appreciatively at the smell of coffee and toast. There were some good things about having a woman about the place. He arrived in the kitchen, determined to be good-humoured, and looked around for his cup of coffee and his plate of toast. Neither was to be seen.

'Didn't you make me any toast?'

'Hmm?' Freya was sitting on the only stool – his stool – and appeared to be totally absorbed in reading the newspaper – his newspaper.

Jack cleared his throat testily, making his point. When she didn't react, he began to fix his own break-fast, rustling the plastic bread bag and banging the toaster loudly enough to shame her into an apology.

Sure enough, her head suddenly lifted. 'Listen to this: Bliss and Ricky have split up!'

Jack waited a few withering seconds. 'And who, may one enquire, are "Bliss" and "Ricky"?'

'Bliss Bogardo the supermodel, you cretin. Ricky Radical, the rock star. She caught him with a female drummer and set fire to his maracas. What a hoot!' She returned eagerly to the paper, shedding buttery crumbs.

'Stupid names,' said Jack. 'They can't be real.'

'Of course they're not real. Have you been living in a cave?'

'I prefer not to clutter my mind with trivia. Now, might I trouble you for the sports section?'

She gave him a look, then disengaged the relevant pages. As she handed them over, Jack caught sight of the headline: 'Strained Pinky Threatens Yankee Chances.' His heart contracted. This was cataclysmically bad news.

'Dear me, a strained pinky,' murmured Freya. 'Just as well it's nothing *trivial*.'

Silence followed while Jack poured himself some coffee, put his plate of toast on the table and set the paper next to it. He opened the refrigerator door and closed it again.

'Where did you put the milk?'

'All gone, I'm afraid. There was only a teensy bit left anyway.'

Black coffee. Jack hated black coffee. He would have thrown it down the sink if he weren't above childish gestures. Instead he heaved a chair from the living room, grunting loudly with effort, and seated himself at the rickety table. He reached for the butter – at least she hadn't finished that too – and spread a generous amount across his cooling toast, aware of Freya's critical gaze.

'You certainly like butter.'

'Yes. I do,' he said evenly.

'Frightfully fattening.'

'Are you trying to tell me something?'

'No.' She crunched into her second – third? – piece of toast. 'Though you have put on weight since I first met you.'

Automatically Jack sucked in his stomach. 'That's muscle. I've been playing a lot of squash.'

'Muscle!' Freya cackled with merry laughter.

Jack picked up the paper and held it in front of his face. The news wasn't as bad as he'd feared. The star pitcher was fine, but –

'I've been thinking,' said a voice behind his paper. 'If I'm going to be staying here for a bit, we need to establish some ground rules.'

Jack flapped the paper and read on.

'I mean, people who share a place usually have house rules . . . Hello? Are you there?'

'*What?*'

'Don't you want to give me instructions about garbage and laundry, and who does the dishes or cooks dinner?'

'No.'

'What about cleaning? That bathroom's a health hazard.'

'Cleaning is not one of my interests.'

'What about bringing people home?'

'I usually go to their place.' Then the full implications of her question struck him. He lowered his paper. 'You mean – *you?*'

'No. Rudolph the red-nosed reindeer.'

'Well . . .' Jack was flummoxed. Was Freya really intending to bring another man *here*, to his apartment, to his study, to his inner sanctum, and – and – *fool around*? She'd only just broken up with Michael. Where were her standards? 'I guess we could let each other know beforehand if we wanted to . . .' He coughed gruffly. 'The other one can stay out of the way, so we'll have some . . .'

'Privacy?' She pronounced the word the English way – 'priv' to rhyme with 'give'.

'*Pry*-vacy,' he corrected.

'Righty-ho. One more thing: I'd like to make some contribution to the household. I thought I'd try to get to the market today – stock up the fridge. Is there anything you'd particularly like?'

'Peanut bu – '

Jack bit back his words. *Stock the fridge*. Wasn't this what Leo had warned him about? The older woman, the supposed 'friend' who wormed her way into your life and NEVER LEFT.

'No! Do *not* go to the market.'

She gave him a mystified look, then shrugged. 'Okay. You go. I hate buying food anyway.'

Jack also hated buying food. How had he got himself into this mess? He watched grumpily as Freya got up and put her cup and plate into the sink – unwashed, he noticed. But at least she was going. Jack returned to his paper. Peace at last.

But instead of leaving, she opened the back door, looked into the yard and shrieked.

'Someone's stolen my underwear!'

'I brought it in.'

'*You* took my underwear? Why?'

'Because – because it was dry!'

'So where is it?'

'I don't know.' How could anyone think about

underwear when the Yankees were in trouble? He forced himself to concentrate. 'I – uh, I think I left it in the bathroom.'

'And why exactly did you need to take my underwear into the bathroom with you?' Freya's voice was suddenly steely.

Jack slammed down his paper. 'I didn't *need* to. I forgot I had the damn stuff. Jesus, Freya, stop looking at me as if I'm a pervert.'

'I'm not!'

'You are!'

'I'm not.'

'You are.'

'Not.'

'Are.'

'Not.'

'Are.'

'Not.'

'Are.'

'Not.'

'For Chrissakes, are you ever going to work?'

'Right now. Don't be so touchy.'

'I'm not.'

'Are.'

'Not.'

'Are, are, are.'

Freya seemed to think this was an amusing game. Jack clamped his lips together, refusing to be caught again. Now Freya was leaving the kitchen. In a minute or two she would be gone.

But she wasn't. First she brushed her teeth, then she disappeared to her room for what seemed hours, then she came out, went back in, came out, uttered a feminine little *tut!* of surprise as if she'd forgotten something, went back in, came out. Her footsteps clacked across the floor and she reappeared in the doorway, armed with her briefcase, standing as stiff and straight as if she had been frogmarched to this precise spot.

'I just want you to know how much I appreciate your having me here.' She spoke with the cheery spontaneity of a Greek messenger announcing a massacre in Sparta.

Jack grunted.

'Perhaps, as a gesture, I could make you dinner tonight?'

Ohhh no. She wasn't going to catch him that easily. 'I'm going out.'

'Alternatively, I've noticed a number of broken electrical items in my room. If I could assist you by taking them to the repair shop – '

'No.' These women were as cunning as fiends. 'I like them that way.'

'You like broken irons?'

'Definitely.'

'And broken alarm clocks?'

'Passionately.'

'And broken – ?'

'I like everything except broken records. Stop

nagging, Freya. If I wanted a wife, I'd be married by now.'

'*A* wife, singular? You're slipping, Jack.'

'Don't you have somewhere to go – like a public flogging?'

Hah! That got her. She tossed her hair, what there was of it, and turned on her heel. She was leaving! Click-clack, click-clack went her shoes – one of the five thousand pairs she had felt it necessary to stash in his study. He heard the front door open, the sound of traffic from the street, then . . . nothing. Time ticked by as he awaited the blessed slam of the door. It didn't come. The pressure in his head became so great he feared his ears might fly off. What was she waiting for? Unable to stand the suspense, he lurched up from the table and strode out to see what was going on.

There she was on the threshold, head down, leg crooked to support a big, lumpy purse in which she was rummaging like a squirrel digging for winter nuts. Why did women buy bags that size if they could never find anything?

'Oh Jack,' she said in a vague, maddening way, 'do you have any quarters for the bus?'

'*No. I do not have any fucking quarters for the fucking bus!*'

She raised her head. There was an odd, shocked look on her face. He almost wondered if he had hurt her feelings. But then she shouldered her bag, stepped outside, and turned to present him with a phoney smile.

'Goodbye, darling,' she cooed. 'Have a wonderful day at the office. Aren't you going to kiss me goodbye?'

Jack slammed the door in her face.

# 9

When Freya returned from work that evening, she was relieved to find the apartment empty. After Jack's deplorable bout of bad temper this morning she realized that Cat was right: men and women were simply not designed to live together in harmony. Besides, his absence gave her a chance to make some essential domestic improvements. She carried a large brown-paper bag through to the kitchen and banged it down on the counter. From it she took a can of scouring powder, a bottle of toilet bleach, a scrubbing brush, cleaning cloths, rubber gloves. Mess was one thing; a shower cubicle where you could scratch your name in grime was another.

She hurried to change her clothes, not wishing to be caught by Jack in the middle of this demeaning job in case it gave him false notions about the roles of the sexes. The sight of her room was depressing. Small to begin with – a single bed at one end, Jack's desk under the window at the other – it was now absurdly cramped. Stacks of shoeboxes took up most of the floor space, along with the suitcase she used as a chest of drawers. Her clothes hung high above the bed from a heating pipe. She might as well be nineteen again. Still, this was only a temporary arrangement.

Tomorrow she'd get up early so she could buy *The Village Voice* hot off the press, and check out the apartment rentals. With luck, she might find a cheap summer sub-let.

Within a few minutes she had tidied away her work clothes, pulled on a T-shirt, ancient jogging pants and sneakers, and was standing in the shower in a snowstorm of scouring powder. She hefted the big scrubbing brush and set to work. It was surprisingly satisfying. Nothing could be duller than routine cleaning, but visible dirt was a challenge. After half an hour of steamy labour the light and dark grey tiles were revealed to be white and black, the toilet foamed with a sinister froth of chemical blue, and she could read the manufacturer's name on the whisker-free basin. Since she was now so dirty and the bathroom so clean, it seemed a good idea to market-test her handiwork immediately by taking a shower. She had just finished rinsing shampoo out of her hair when the doorbell rang. It was almost certainly Jack, too lazy to face the effort of getting his own key out of his own pocket. Freya took no notice. She was not his butler, after all. Stepping out of the shower, she dried herself and slipped on her kimono, and was twisting a towel around her hair when the bell sounded again. Freya growled with exasperation. The idiot must have forgotten his key.

She slapped her way to the front door, leaving a trail of damp footprints. 'Yes, suh, Massa Madison,' she croaked, in what she imagined to be a Southern accent. 'I's a-comin'.'

But it wasn't Jack. It was a young woman, whose expertly mascara'd eyes mirrored Freya's own surprise.

Freya put up a hand to steady her towel turban. 'Yes?' she enquired.

'Is – is Jack at home?'

'No.'

'Oh . . . He said to meet him here.'

'What for?'

'It's Creative Writing night. We're going together.'

'How sweet. You'd better come in.'

Freya stepped back and opened the door wide. She recognized the girl now. It was Little Miss ABC, Jack's 'student' from the other morning. With her cute, plump cheeks and flirty skirt, she looked about seventeen. As she jiggled past on high-heeled sandals, Freya was easily tall enough to see straight down her cleavage. That would explain Jack's reference to her fine mind. Freya re-tied her kimono tightly around herself and followed the girl into the living room, watching her scan the apartment with a proprietary air, as if to check that Jack was indeed out. At length she turned back to Freya and gave her a pert, lip-gloss smile.

'I'm Candace,' she announced.

'The perfect name. I bet Jack calls you "Candy", am I right?'

Candace flushed. 'Sometimes.' Her little bunny nose twitched. 'What's that smell?'

'Cleanliness. Marvellous, isn't it? And before you ask, no, I am not the maid.'

'Who said you were?' Candace looked ruffled. 'I saw you here Saturday. Jack said you were an old friend.'

'What a flatterer he is!' Freya gave a brittle laugh.

'He didn't tell me you were *living* here.'

'Men.' Freya rolled her eyes. 'They're so forgetful. Now, if you'll excuse me, I must hobble back to my knitting. Help yourself to anything you want from the kitchen – Diet Coke, lemonade, milk and cookies . . .'

And with that Freya escaped to her room, cheeks flushed, lips set in annoyance. She disliked being caught at a disadvantage. Why hadn't Jack warned her? A glance in the mirror showed her unattractively naked face, her turban askew, the fraying silk at the neck of her kimono. A contrasting vision of Candace's coiffed and perfumed perfection rose in her mind. Candace was short and small-boned, with ripe flesh that swelled and bounced in all the right places. Freya scowled at her reflection. She must look like an alleycat next to a fluffy Persian kitten.

She threw off the kimono and rapidly started to dress in her favourite jeans and a skinny black top. Why did Jack always go for these brainless bimbos? She could barely remember the last girlfriend of his that she'd liked. Freya's face was stern as she slicked her damp hair behind her ears and began to apply make-up. Didn't he realize how inconsiderate this was – how difficult it was for the rest of them, Larry and Gus and the gang, to have to deal with someone whose earliest cultural references were *Star Wars* and Wham? More than one reunion of old friends had been spoiled by some Candy or Mandy or Bonnie or Connie canoodling with Jack, when the rest of them wanted to relax and reminisce. It was time he grew up.

When she returned she found Candace charmingly posed on the couch, head bent over Jack's copy of Aristotle's *Poetics*.

'Only me,' said Freya. At least the girl had the book the right way up. Freya fixed herself a bourbon on the rocks, and perched on the arm of a squashy chair, swinging one long leg. Candace stared at her warily.

'You're Frieda, aren't you?' she said.

'Almost. Eight out of ten. Actually, it's Freya.'

'Jack said you lived uptown with your boyfriend.'

'I did.' Freya's smile hardened.

'So what happened?'

Freya hesitated. She did not need to explain herself to this pinhead. 'If you must know, he wanted to get married and I didn't.'

'Really?'

'Yes, really. Is that so difficult to believe?'

'No. I admire you,' Candace paused, 'for making such a brave decision.'

Freya frowned suspiciously. 'What's so brave about it?'

'Just . . . I mean, at your age . . .' Candace lowered

her eyes and shrugged. Her entire upper body seemed to sway and re-form with the movement, like a water-balloon. Freya wondered how it would feel to be as massively endowed as that; it must be like having two giant guinea pigs stuffed down your front. Candace probably couldn't see her own feet when she was standing up.

Freya folded her arms across her own, less seismic frontage. 'Are you implying that's the last proposal I'll ever get?'

'I didn't say that. My Aunt Rochelle didn't get married until she was forty-two. She never had children, of course. And she's divorced now.'

'What an inspiring story. Thank you, Candace.'

They sat in silence. Candace looked at her watch. 'He's late,' she said.

'Jack's always late.'

'How long have you known him?'

'Ten years. And you?'

A holy expression came over Candace's face. 'You can't measure a relationship in time. Not chronological time, anyway.'

'Oh well, if it's *chronological* time you're talking about . . .'

'I mean, with Jack and I it's a – a coop de food.'

'I beg your pardon?'

'Coop de food. It means, like, love at first sight. That's French.'

'I see. How wise of you not to attempt the accent.'

Candace wasn't listening. Her full lips parted in a

secret smile, revealing sparkling, tombstone teeth. 'When he walked into my first class I almost died,' she confided.

'Almost? That's a relief.'

'Isn't he just the handsomest man in the whole world? Those blue eyes . . .' Candace gave an ecstatic shiver. 'Plus, I felt so in awe of his talent.'

Freya crunched an ice cube.

'At the beginning I wasn't sure he even noticed me – as a woman, I mean. But then I sort of bumped into him after class, and I felt this incredible *connection* . . .'

'Oh dear. Not painful, I hope?'

' . . . even though he's above me in so many ways, so much smarter and deeper and . . .'

'Older?'

Candace looked stern. 'Age is about the number of years you've been on the planet, not how human beings interact emotion-wise.'

'How true.'

There was the sound of a key in the lock. Both women's eyes swivelled to the living room door. They waited in silence, listening to Jack manoeuvring his bike into the hall. Candace moistened her lips and shook back her hair in preparation for his entrance.

The door opened and Jack ambled in, sliding his wire-rimmed glasses into place with a forefinger. For a split-second Freya saw him through Candace's eyes – hunky, masculine, appealingly dishevelled, the sort of man you kidded yourself you could 'save'. Then she almost laughed out loud as Jack caught sight of them both and halted abruptly, as astounded as if he'd found Hitler *and* Stalin in his living room.

'Well, well, *well!*' He was suddenly as jovial as Santa Claus. 'My two favourite women. Together! How – how wonderful!'

'I know. Isn't it marvellous?' Freya mimicked his rapturous tone.

Jack shot her a dirty look, and rubbed his hands with hectic bonhomie. 'So!' he enthused. 'I guess you two girls have met!'

'We two girls certainly have.'

Candace could resist him no longer. With a tremulous cry, she launched herself from the couch and almost ran to throw her arms around Jack's waist. Freya watched deadpan as Candace gazed up at him adoringly, a darling little daisy turning its face to the sun. If she had called out 'Daddy!' Freya wouldn't have been in the least surprised.

Jack mussed Candace's hair with a casual hand, and disengaged himself. 'Okay, everyone!' he cried, his jollity control still on maximum. 'I'll just, uh, get my papers, and we'll go!'

'W – we?' faltered Candace, staring at Freya in panic.

'No, no.' She waved a hand. 'You young people run along and enjoy yourselves. I want to stay home and give my dentures a good soak.'

The two of them quickly made their escape. Freya could hear them going down the path – the slow rumble of Jack's voice, Candace's happy, answering giggle. The sounds died away; then there was silence, and the long evening ahead.

Freya topped up her drink, slotted a tape into the stereo, and flopped on to the couch. On the floor beside it was the inevitable teetering pile of Jack's magazines, mostly copies of *The New York Review of Books*. She hoisted a handful on to her stomach, and shuffled through them idly, while Billie Holiday poured her tender melancholy into the room. '*I don't know why, but I'm feeling so sad . . .*' Names leapt out at Freya from the magazine covers – Updike, Roth, Isaiah Berlin, Nijinsky, William James, Velázquez. How could a man who revelled in the intellectual fireworks of these articles spend his leisure time with the Candaces of this world?

Freya suspected it was sheer laziness. There was something about Jack that made women drop into his hand like ripe fruit from a tree; he didn't have to bother to pick them. She remembered when she had first seen him, fresh off the plane from North Carolina. It was August: steam-room heat, eyes prickling with heat and grime, the maggoty smell of sun-baked garbage. Those were the days when she was mixing with a bohemian crowd and living uncomfortably close to the breadline. You had to watch out for the druggies and weirdos on the street. The men she knew, however friendly, even loveable, tended to be hairy and not very clean. Jack had strolled on to the drab set of their existence, with his beautiful leather luggage and that old beat-up typewriter he was so proud of, looking like Robert Redford in *Barefoot in the Park*. He'd been so young, so eager. So *clean*. So polite! One of the girls in the rooming-house swore he smelled of fresh grass. He said he was going to be a writer.

It hadn't taken long to scuff him up. They'd all teased him like crazy – for his beautiful shirts, his rich Daddy, the slow rise and fall of his accent, his fancy hardback edition of Proust's *Remembrance of Things Past* (unread). Jack took it all in good humour. His family was rich but he wasn't, he said; he'd had a big bust-up with his father and for the time being, anyway, he was one of them. Freya took him under her wing. Jack was funny; he was generous with what he had; he wasn't ashamed to be enthusiastic; and he was serious about his work. She liked him.

And he liked her. But that was all. He was too young for her. And there was already a queue for him. It was tacitly agreed that they would be friends.

And they still were friends. Freya turned back to her magazines and flicked idly through the pages. She was glad she'd never got involved with Jack. He was good fun and good company, but his relationships with intelligent women – the few she could remember – never seemed to last long, probably because he couldn't stand the competition. He used to talk about Fayette, the girl at the University of North Carolina who had been perfect in every way and who had supposedly broken his heart, but Freya suspected that he used her as an excuse not to commit himself. It was easier to drift along with only a fraction of his brain engaged. Men liked intellectual challenges, and they liked attractive women: they just didn't like the two in combination.

Or did they? Freya's attention sharpened as she reached the back pages of the *Review* and discovered the 'Personal' advertisements.

> Yale grad DWF seeks attractive,
> cultured companion for excursions
> to theatre, exhibitions, country
> and – who knows? – more
> private places.

Well, well.

> Bogart (JNRD) in search of
> Bergman. Let's play it again.

Freya sat up excitedly and looked around for a pen. This could be the answer to her problem.

'*Lover man, oh where can you be?*' wailed Billie. Freya didn't exactly need a lover man, but she did desperately need a man, and she needed him within the next two weeks. Anyone presentable would do. Readers of the *New York Review of Books* were bound to be a cut above the usual lonely hearts; these men would be respectable, educated, sophisticated . . .

> I am a recent widower,
> but almost ageless, often
> mistaken for Einstein.

Wise Owl, nest, feathered,
seeks dove for occasional
migrations.

Or bonkers.

Still, it was worth a try. Freya found the three most recent issues and started to compile a shortlist. The abbreviations were troubling. Could DWF really mean a dwarf? And what about MWM – marvellous, wonderful me? Murderer with mange? Magnificent white mouse? She tapped her pen thoughtfully against pursed lips.

First she eliminated those who didn't give an e-mail address; there wasn't enough time to contact box numbers, and telephoning seemed dangerously direct. Then she cut out anyone who admitted to being bearded, fit, over forty-five, married, or had used the words 'intimate', 'fun', or 'threesome'. She was left with a meagre choice, but all she needed was one lucky strike. A faint smile curved her mouth as she began to draft a reply in her head. This was fun, sort of like mail-order shopping.

Suddenly brisk, Freya gathered together her bundle of magazines, got up from the couch and walked purposefully across the living room. Jack's computer was in her room, the room that she *rented*. If she used it to send out one or two teensy messages he could hardly object. Could he?

# 10

*The ship came into the harbour.*

Hmm.

*The ship entered the harbour.*

Better, but –

*Entering the harbour, the ship . . .*

Jack drummed nervy fingertips across his computer keyboard, and frowned at these clunking efforts.

*The ship chugged? – glided? – sailed? – sped? – cruised?*

No. *Think*. The ship he had in mind was a big old tub, forcing its way through rough waves. What about this?

*The ship ploughed into the harbour.*

Oh yeah, brilliant. He'd made it sound as though the ship was demolishing the harbour. Jack put his finger on the Delete key, and pressed hard.

Now there was only the white cursor flashing at him, a frenzied lighthouse beam in the flat, empty blue of his screen. He shut his eyes, trying to dream himself into the moment.

*The ship lumbered into harbour on a foggy February night, its rusty metal creaking with cold.*

That was better. He had told the reader that it was a cold night, that the ship was old and big. He liked the alliteration of 'foggy February' and 'creaking with cold'. He read the sentence aloud to himself, to check how its rhythm struck the ear. Not bad. But there was nothing individual about his phrasing, no way of telling whether the writer was Jack Madison or Somerset Maugham or Irving P. Nobody. Would the sentence be more exciting backwards?

*On a foggy February night the ship lumbered into harbour . . .*

Or broken up, like bad poetry?

*Foggy February. Cold creak of rusty metal.*

*. . . Rusting? rusted?*

Jack scratched his nose. Did metal creak when it was cold? Was it a ship exactly, or a boat? He decided to look up 'Shipping' in his encyclopaedia. A description, or a picture, might inspire him. Half an hour later he was a great deal better informed about Saskatchewan (cold), Seventh Day Adventists (weird) and the Seleucid Dynasty (Syria *c.* 312–64BC). He had also, after extensive nautical research, ascertained that the word 'ship' meant 'a vessel with a bowsprit and three, four or five square rigging masts' or 'any large sea-going vessel'; whereas a 'boat' was 'a small, open, oared or sailing vessel, fishing-vessel, mail packet or small steamer'. Ship it was, then. Okay: so the ship was in the harbour. What next? He checked his watch. Hey, time for coffee!

The kitchen was a mess. So much for having a woman around the place. While the coffee heated, Jack decided it really was time that someone cleaned up. He filled the sink with hot soapy water, and dabbed one or two plates with a cloth before realizing that the best policy would be to let everything soak itself clean. Instead, he checked through the newspaper to see if there was anything important he'd missed. It was 105 degrees Fahrenheit in Riyadh, yet only 35 in Anchorage; New York, at 70 degrees, was exactly in between the two – amazing. He poured out his coffee and was about to carry it back to his desk when he remembered the loose hinge on one of the cabinets that he'd been meaning to fix for weeks. He sighed with exasperation: another delay. Still, no time like the present. Now, where had he put his screwdrivers?

Twenty minutes later he was back where he started that morning, staring at a blank screen – except he now had a pink bandage around one thumbnail. He picked at it absently, waiting for inspiration to strike. His head felt as if it was clogged with porridge. He lowered it into his hands and groaned. Why couldn't he write like he used to? What had happened? Words used to gush out of him; once he had written a story in a single day. In his eagerness to get something – anything – published, he hadn't stopped to agonize over every word, or to fret about his position in the literary pantheon. Yet he had scored a bull's-eye with his very first shot. At the time he had accepted his success as simple, wonderful luck. Everything was new to him – proofs to correct (his words looked so wonderful in print that he missed all the typos); alternative jacket designs to consider (they were all fabulous); blurbs to write (pompous as hell, he later realized). And then the reviews, falling at his feet thick and beautiful as peach blossom in springtime.

Jack opened the deep bottom drawer of his desk. Furtive as someone reaching for his porn stash, he pulled something out from the very back. It was his clippings file. Balancing the fat folder on his knees, he swung his chair away from the screen and began to leaf through the pages. As he read, a self-satisfied smile crept across his mouth. Here was a good one: 'Madison springs his narrative traps with the ruthless expertise of a professional, whilst never losing his compassion for their victims' (*New York Times*). And another old favourite: 'furiously intelligent . . . written with the kind of grace many older writers can only daydream about' (*Washington Post*). 'Brilliant' – what about that? Okay, so it was only the *Little Rock Post*, but not everyone from Arkansas was stupid. Apart from a certain H. Hirschberg – who complained that Jack had 'not fully embraced post-modernism' (whatever that meant), and whose own first novel Jack prayed might one day fall into his hands for review – every commentator made the same point: he was good.

Was. Had been. Jack caught sight of the date of one of the reviews, and snapped the folder shut. He had long ago passed his publisher's deadline for delivery of his new novel. He must hurry up! Jack stared at his empty screen, his brain a jumble of fragmented thoughts. All he wanted was to combine the virtues of *Great Expectations*, *The Great Gatsby*, *Catcher in the Rye*, and *The Sound and the Fury*. The story was in his head, somewhere, a perfect artefact. But the words wouldn't come.

Jack looked at his watch. He'd give anything for the phone to ring and someone to invite him out for a long oblivious lunch. He ground out two more sentences, spell-checked what he had written so far, printed it out in several different typefaces to see which looked more impressive, and allowed his computer to tell him how many words he had produced (163). Maybe he'd feel more sparkling when he'd had some-thing to eat.

In the kitchen he began to compile a sandwich – ham, cheese, dill pickle, mustard, a couple of shots of Tabasco – while his mind tussled with a complex calculation. Suppose he wrote two hundred words a day: that was a thousand a week, which meant that, allowing for vacations and other interruptions, it would take him another – Jesus! – two *years* to finish. He'd be thirty-four, almost halfway through his whole life! And would he do it? If he was honest, his productivity in the last two years had been unimpressive: one story, a flurry of showy but forgettable magazine articles and a couple of dozen reviews. ('But who gives a shit about reviews these days?' Leo's sardonic voice echoed in his ear.)

Jack carried his sandwich into the living room, popped a tube of lemony fizz and turned on the TV. It was important to keep abreast of popular culture. He could hardly work while he was eating, could he? For five fascinated minutes he watched an overweight young woman in cowboy boots confess to sex addiction. A man in a toupee, dressed as if for the golf course, coaxed detail after salacious detail from her until she broke down in sobs, provoking the bovine studio audience into applause. Public executions must have been like this, Jack reflected as he surfed the channels – the same mixture of titillation, boredom, and careless cruelty. He began to formulate a theory about cultural maturity, whereby contemporary America could be said to have roughly the same mental age as medieval Europe, before being distracted by a quiz programme in which blindfolded newlyweds were cross-examined about their partners' domestic and sexual preferences. Jack shook his head sorrowfully, and flicked onward. Sometimes he wondered why he bothered with literature. If this was what the masses wanted, he'd be better off in Hollywood, prostituting his talent as a sleazy screenwriter. Oh look! – *Buffy the Vampire Slayer*. Jack slumped back contentedly.

He was halfway through the show, and had just stuffed the rest of his sandwich into his mouth, when the phone rang. With a rhinoceros snort at this interruption, Jack levered himself out of his chair, zapped off the sound, and sidled across the room, keeping his eyes on the screen. He picked up the receiver.

'Yeah?' Uh-oh. It looked like Buffy was in trouble with some creepy guy with red eyes.

'Hi! Is Freya there?' It was a man's voice. He pronounced her name 'Fryer'.

'No,' mumbled Jack, still chewing.

'Will she be home tonight?'

'Guess so.'

'Okay, I'll try later. Tell her Max called, willya?' He hung up.

Five minutes later, exactly the same thing happened, except the man was called Norman. Jack felt a flicker of irritation. He was not Freya's secretary, after all; he had work to do. As soon as he found out what happened to Buffy he'd –

Damn it! The phone again. Didn't these people have the courtesy to wait for the commercial break? A man named Lucas claimed to be calling from his 'limo'. Freya certainly had some tacky friends.

'Who are you, by the way?' asked Lucas. 'Not her husband, ha ha?'

'I'm – I *live* here.' Jack was indignant.

'Oh . . .' The voice was full of innuendo. 'You the gay one?'

'*No!*'

Jack slammed down the phone. How could a man work with such interruptions? He turned back to the television screen, where the shot of an overjoyed woman in pristine tennis whites was swiftly eclipsed by a close-up of a tampon package. Terrific. On top of everything else, he'd missed the climax of the show.

He switched off the television and returned to his office in a sour mood. Freya's things cluttered his space – dresses hanging hither and yon, bottles of face stuff clogging the edge of a bookshelf, her perfume in the air. She'd even put some damned flowers on the windowsill – irises, were they? Gladioli? Tall purply things anyway, the kind you'd see in a wishy-washy watercolour. A man needed order if he was to work efficiently, with everything plain and shipshape; this wasn't a hair salon. Suddenly Jack caught sight of a sprawl of magazines under the bed, and let out a hiss of outrage: she'd stolen his *New York Reviews*! How did she know he wouldn't need to refer to one of the articles? He could have wasted hours of valuable time searching for them. She'd even left half of them folded inside-out. Jack snatched them up angrily, noticing that some of the pages had been defaced by scribbles and circles. A loose piece of paper fluttered to the floor, probably one of those tedious promotional inserts. He stooped to pick it up and carried it over to his desk.

It was the draft of a letter. As he began to read, a smile of glee spread across his face. It seemed that Freya was on the hunt for a new boyfriend to torment.

To: . . . . . . . . . . . . . .
From: Freya c/o jackmad@aol.com
Subject: Dating

I saw your ad in the New York Review of Books. If you are interested in having dinner this weekend with a tall [attractive *crossed out*, slim *crossed out*], blonde, professional woman [35 *crossed out*, 33 *crossed out*, 29 *crossed out*] in her thirties, then contact me and convince me why we should meet. Telephone evenings only, email <u>midnight to 7a.m. only</u>.

PS. If a man answers the phone, that's my room-mate. [He's just a friend *crossed out*. He's my brother *crossed out*] He's gay.

Jack smashed his fist on the desk. He seized her stupid flowers and wrung their necks like so many chickens, then tossed the corpses into his wastepaper basket. How dare she give out his e-mail address to a bunch of lonely-heart losers? How could she contaminate his computer, sacred repository of his most precious thoughts and ambitions, with her tawdry billets-doux? Who was she calling gay? He paced the small room, kicking shoeboxes out of his way. She'd even given out his telephone number, which was not only insanely dangerous but meant that he'd be the one fielding the crazy calls long after she'd moved out. How selfish could you get?

When the phone rang again, he let out a roar of fury and charged into the living room like a bull into the ring. He snatched up the receiver and shouted into it, '*She's not here!*'

'Jack? Is that you?' A man's voice. 'It's Michael Petersen here. You feeling okay?'

'Fine, fine.' Jack forced out a genial chuckle. 'In another world, I guess. Writing is so absorbing.'

'Pardon me for interrupting the great work, but I wanted to get your address. There's some mail I need to send over to Freya.'

Jack dictated his address in a laboured, grudging tone. Just because you were at home in the daytime, people assumed you weren't really working and could be interrupted by any manner of trivial queries. Why couldn't the guy call Freya, and interrupt *her* work? 'Freya's here most evenings,' he said pointedly, 'if you require further information.'

'Thank you.' Michael was equally formal. Then he continued, sounding rather aggrieved, Jack thought, 'I guess you two must be enjoying each other's company.'

'*Enjoying?*' Jack practically spat the word. He was

about to launch into a savage diatribe about Freya, when he had a brainwave. The sheer beauty of it made his scalp tingle. He would persuade Michael to *take her back!* With Freya out of the apartment, he could take showers whenever he wanted, read the sports pages in peace, fill the place with beautiful girls whom he could ravish in rotation. Jack could barely restrain a shout of hysterical joy. With difficulty, he modulated his voice to a persuasive molasses drawl.

'How could anybody not enjoy being with Freya? She's such a good companion, so much fun, so . . . helpful. But you know what?' His tone became solemn. 'I'm worried about her.'

'Oh?'

'She's not herself. She looks sad and lonely. I think she's missing you.'

'Really.' Michael's voice was unaccountably cold.

'Oh, she pretends. She smiles. But underneath' – Jack paused for pathos – 'underneath, her heart is breaking.'

'Good,' said Michael.

*Good?* Whoa, there. Who was writing this script?

'Allow me to tell you what happened in my apartment on Monday.' Michael clipped his words with vicious precision, a prosecuting attorney in action.

Jack listened in awed silence. It seemed that Michael's mother had suffered some kind of nervous breakdown following a bizarre encounter with Freya in Michael's apartment. Mrs Petersen had since checked into the Plaza and was consoling herself with shopping and room service, at Michael's expense. There was worse to come.

'Six *inches*?' Jack repeated, when Michael reached the final catastrophe of his story. 'That's – that's terrible.' Unfortunately, a guffaw escaped him as he pictured a finicky, besuited Michael revealing an expanse of executive hosiery and hairy calf.

'Obviously you find Freya more amusing than I do,' said Michael. 'Some of those suits cost a thousand dollars apiece. I'm thinking of suing her.'

'Good idea.' Jack's tone was robust. 'Not that I don't adore Freya, but I admit she can be pretty headstrong. It's always the same with women: they're wonderful creatures, until you try to live with them.'

'I don't know what happened to Freya,' Michael said plaintively. 'She was so sweet at the beginning.'

*Sweet?*

'Then suddenly everything about me was stupid or wrong. If Freya doesn't have the whip hand in every situation, she breaks out in anti-social behaviour. That's what the couple therapist said, anyway.'

*Couple therapist!* Jack couldn't wait to tease Freya about that one.

'So you think that the, uh, trouser-shortening was a symbolic act of emasculation?' Jack could barely keep a straight face. 'Or could it be a cry for help?'

But it seemed that Michael was not as dull-witted as Jack imagined. 'Don't think you can patronize me, Jack Madison, just because you have a private income and call yourself a writer. I'm telling you, Freya's a disturbed person. She has severe relationship problems. You want to watch out.' With that, he hung up.

Jack returned to his desk, chafing at Michael's remarks. How come these office clones always thought they were God's gift? Jack turned on his computer and pulled up the file he'd been working on. The reason he called himself a writer, *actually*, was because he wrote. If it hadn't been for these ceaseless interruptions – all Freya's fault – he could have written an entire chapter by now. Or two. Now let's see: the ship was in the harbour . . .

Jack's eyes strayed to Freya's letter. 'Convince me why we should meet' – how typical of her lofty manner. He pitied the poor sap who fell for that line. A thought struck him. At least three men had ignored Freya's instructions to telephone in the evening: what if the e-mailers had done the same? What if there were some replies she hadn't seen yet? Jack scented revenge. Eagerly, he began tapping keys, then clicked the mouse.

Eureka!

*To: Freya c/o jackmad@aol.com*
*From: Tomcat*
*Subject: Dating*
*Hi, babe! Couldn't wait til midnight. How did you know*
*blonde is my favourite colour!!! I am six feet tall, rugged,*
*around forty, with my own funeral parlor business. I adore*
*fur, long legs, oysters, and dead bodies (just joking!!!). I can*

*meet you any time, any place, anywhere this weekend.*

*Let's make music!*

*Tom*

Jack flipped in fascination to the next e-mail.

*Dear Ms Penrose, Your message saved me from the brink of suicide. My wife left me last Christmas. She took the apartment and all my money, and turned my children against me (Lois 7, Elijah 6, Tiffany 5, Clinton 4). I lost my job due to severe depression and alcohol dependency, though I'm hardly ever violent. I need the love of a good woman. Please meet me. Lenny*

*PS. Maybe we could meet in the park and go for a walk with my dog Burton, as I cannot afford to go out to dinner.*

Poor guy. Jack clicked again.

*Dear Freya, I'm afraid my ad misled you. The truth is, I am a gay man who needs a female companion for business events three or four times a year. I am civilized, educated, good-looking, and this is a straightforward, no-strings offer. You sound perfect for my purposes. I would pay all your expenses. If you needed a special dress for a particular occasion, I would buy it for you – or you could borrow one of mine! Christopher.*

The final e-mail he found was personalized with a little icon at the top, which Jack recognized as the famous portrait of Shakespeare, in his ruff, peeking out over two crossed quills. Immediately below was the heading, *Bernard S. Parkenrider Associate Professor, BA, MA, PhD.* Jack gave a snort. The text ran:

> *Dear Freya,*
> <u>*La table est reservé!*</u> *I look forward to meeting you tomorrow (and tomorrow and tomorrow, as the Bard would say!). Yours in great expectation, Bernard*

Well, well. So Freya thought she'd found Mr Right. Jack doubted it. He ran through the messages again, trying to marry them up with the advertisements Freya had circled. If Bernard was the 'university professor', Jack thought she had some surprises in store. What a silly girl she was. Still, she deserved to be taught a lesson. She had abused his hospitality, and intimidated his adorable little Candace. Thanks to Freya, Mrs Petersen had suffered a nervous breakdown, and Michael was walking around with his ankles showing.

Jack sat for a moment in silent concentration. His mind moved with a speed and infernal ingenuity he hadn't achieved in months. Within ten minutes he had registered a new hot-mail address, laid out a rough imitation of Prof. Parkenrider's absurd Shakespearean letterhead, and composed a poem to Freya, which he sent purportedly from Bernard.

> *My Sweet: 'Tis meet that we should meet*
> *Not like strangers in the street*

*But somewhere private, somewhere cosy*
*Far from friends and neighbours nosy.*
*I'm so glad we've made a date*
*This Friday night arou-hound eight.*
*If you don't like me (or my poem)*
*You can always just go ho-em!*

Then he invented a message to Bernard from Freya.

*Dear Bernard,*
*I am so thrilled to be meeting a genuine scholar! I want to*
*hear EVERYTHING about your work. You may like*
*to know a little more about me before we meet. Besides my*
*'artistic' inclinations, I like to think of myself as an*
*intellectual – though of course I enjoy fun. Among my interests*
*are couple therapy, men's fashions and German opera. I*
*also have a keen interest in footwear. My friends joke that*
*I am rather bossy and always like to have the whip hand (!),*
*but I'm sure you can deal with that.*

*PS I adore hairy legs!*

Jack rubbed his hands. That should spice up their romantic little tryst. He reached for the mouse and pressed 'Send'.

Freya turned off Fifth Avenue and walked briskly towards Madison on high, spiked heels. It was a warm evening, and she felt good to be out in the Friday night bustle, with somewhere to go and someone to meet. Apart from one evening at Cat's, helping to make lemon polenta cake for yet another da Fillipo family feast, she'd been stuck in the apartment all week, prey to Jack's grouchy temper and oafish humour, until she was screaming to escape. Jack wanted her out tonight anyway: Candace was coming over to 'cook dinner' for him, ho, ho. It had given Freya considerable satisfaction to inform him that, as it happened, she had a date already.

'Oh yeah?' Jack's incredulous smirk had been intensely irritating.

'Yes. As a matter of fact, I'm meeting a most interesting professor of English literature. It will be nice to have some intellectual stimulation, for a change.'

This, apparently, was so hilarious that Jack could only raise sceptical eyebrows, as if Freya's experience could hardly match the kind of 'stimulation' he was anticipating with Candace. Men were so crude. Distracted by their own sweaty animal grapplings, they did not understand the importance, to women, of the life of the mind.

Thankfully, there were exceptions. Freya repeated to herself the words of the advertisement that had initially sparked her attention. *DWM, university professor, 39, cultured, humorous, battered but unbowed, seeks superior female for invigorating encounters.* DWM, she had discovered, stood for divorced white male, and she had at once pictured an attractively rumpled figure in corduroy, with amused eyes and a wry smile. They had since spoken on the phone, and she had been struck by his polite, almost courtly manner and his flattering eagerness to meet her. He had even tossed in a quotation from Shakespeare, the subject of his latest 'magnum opus', as he called it. (Freya hoped there wouldn't be too much Latin.)

His name was Bernard, pronounced the American way with the emphasis on the second syllable — so much more classy than the plodding English *Ber*nard. Unconsciously Freya raised her chin, congratulating herself on her choice. Ber*nard* was an educated man, mature but not old, tempered in life's fiery furnace yet not jaded. His taste was for 'superior' women, not teenyboppers from the Planet Bubblegum. A blind date was nothing to be ashamed of. If Bernard turned out to be unsuitable for her purposes, she would at least have enjoyed an evening of intelligent conversation.

Here was the restaurant. Freya pushed the door open and stepped inside its chic, minimalist gloom.

While the manager consulted his book to check whether Professor Parkenrider had arrived, she paused by the fish tank, trying not to catch the protuberant eyes of the clawed and whiskered creatures inside. Japanese food was not her favourite, but so long as she was not required to eat anything actually alive she should be fine.

'This way, please. The gentleman is waiting.'

They passed the sushi bar, where a man in white was slashing vegetables to ribbons one-handed, and headed for the sleek ebony tables beyond. From one of them, a lone figure rose to greet her – tall, slightly stooped, and grinning as if he could hardly believe his eyes.

'Bernard?' Freya put out her hand.

Instead of shaking it, he clasped her hand in his and raised it to his lips with a galumphing gallantry that Freya told herself was charming. 'Ah, Freya. We meet at last.'

'Yes . . . Hello.' Freya reclaimed her hand. 'Shall we sit down?'

As she settled herself at the table, a quick glance confirmed her first impression. Bernard's looks were not immediately prepossessing. He had pale, pouched eyes and straggly hair, brown with a reddish cast, that curled behind his ears. Over a white nylon shirt stretched across his sloping chest, he wore a vivid tie and – yes – a chocolate-brown corduroy jacket lightly sprinkled with dandruff. If he was thirty-nine, then she was Pollyanna: fifty was more like it. Still, she must not be judgemental. Looks weren't everything. Wit and brains were equally important. Think of Cyrano de Bergerac. Or Quasimodo.

Bernard picked up a jug and poured sake into the small cup in front of Freya. 'Come, let the festivities begin!'

Freya took a sip, resisting his efforts to clink cups. She remembered all those magazine articles about dating that she'd read at the hairdressers: be interested, be interesting, go to *give* a good time, not just *get* a good time.

'So tell me, Bernard.' She kept her voice light and brisk. 'Where exactly do you teach?'

Bernard cleared his throat with some thoroughness while he formulated his answer. 'At this present time,' he began, 'I am attached to a small but elite junior college in southern New Jersey. In point of fact, my duties are more of a bibliographic nature, involving the cataloguing, purchasing, issuing and recalling of diverse printed materials.'

'You mean, you work in a library?'

'To be sure.' Bernard nodded ponderously. 'At all events, that is my *job*. My *work* involves lucubrations of a quite different order.'

'Lucu-what?' Freya gave a perky laugh, trying to lighten the atmosphere. Bernard seemed very serious.

'From the Latin *lucubro, lucubrare, lucubravi, lucubratum*, meaning to labour by lamplight. I refer, in short, to the work of Shakespearean scholarship on which I am embarked. A small thing, but mine own.'

'Shakespeare! How fascinating. You must tell me all about it.'

After half an hour, Freya had to admit that she had condemned herself to dine with a Grade One, twenty-four carat, bona fide bore. The seaweed and shrimps had come and gone with agonizing slowness: when Bernard opened his mouth it was not to eat but to pontificate. Now a platter of raw fish dotted with rice mounds sat between them. (Bernard had chosen a Japanese place, he told her, because he knew that 'you girls' had to watch their weight in case they turned into fat pigs.) As Freya listened to his interminable catalogue of Shakespeare's use of phallic imagery, she feared that by the time the platter was empty she would have died of boredom. She glanced enviously at the lively groups around her. Even the flashy exec at the next table, accompanied only by his briefcase and mobile phone, looked a more interesting companion.

' . . . And here's another example. "When *icicles* hang by the wall, and *Dick* the shepherd *blows* his *nail*, and Tom bears *logs* into the hall . . ."' At each key word Bernard paused to shoot Freya a glance loaded with innuendo. ' "Tu-whit, tu-who – a merry note, While *greasy* Joan doth *keel the pot*." That's *Love's Labour's Lost*, of course.'

Freya suppressed a yawn.

'I'm considering entitling my book *The Merchant of Venus: Freudian Analogues and Dialectics in the Works of William Shakespeare*.'

'Very impressive.'

'Alternatively, though I fear this might go over the heads of the groundlings' – Bernard's smug chuckle signalled another witticism on its way – 'I am sorely tempted to call it *In the Canon's Mouth*. You see, that's – '

'A pun. Yes. How clever.' Freya stabbed her chopsticks into the rice.

'As I was saying, that's a play on two words in the English language which are phonetically similar but orthographically and, to be sure, connotatively different. Firstly, "canon" with one "n", signifying an author's complete works; second and subsequently, "cannon" with two "n"s, meaning – '

'Bang! Bang! You're dead!' Freya burst out, with a trill of hysterical laughter. The exec looked up, startled, from his conversation about plane arrival times. Freya tried to compose herself. Every nerve in her body twitched with suppressed energy. She wanted to whirl her arms in the air and run around the room screaming.

'Furthermore, and not inappropriately, as you will no doubt perceive, "in the cannon's mouth" is a direct quotation from the Swan of Avon himself: *As You Like It*, Act Two, Scene Six . . . Or is it Seven?' Bernard dabbed reflectively at a mole on his cheek. Freya saw that the nail of his little finger was almost an inch long, carefully shaped and filed for a purpose she dared not imagine.

She stood up abruptly. 'Excuse me a moment.'

In the ladies' loo, fortunately empty, she pulled

faces at herself in the mirror until she felt almost normal, then she crept out and hovered in the passageway until one of the waiters passed by.

'Psssst!'

He came over, polite but dubious. 'I need a taxi,' Freya told him, pressing a ten-dollar bill into his hand. 'Urgently. In fact, *now*.'

Then she fluffed out her hair, assumed an innocent smile, and returned to the table under Bernard's unnerving, gloating gaze.

'Wonderful shoes,' he commented, as she sat down. 'Are they as painful as they look?'

'Not really.' Freya shrugged. 'I like wearing heels.'

'I mean, painful for anyone you stepped on.'

Freya stared at him. His mouth hung open in a slack, suggestive smile. She hoped he didn't mean what his words seemed to imply. 'Why would I want to step on people?'

Bernard gave her a sly wink.

'And stop winking at me!' she hissed.

'Okay, okay. Mercy, mistress.' Bernard threw up his hands in mock surrender. 'I like this game.' He licked his lips.

Freya drummed her fingers on the table. How could she have picked such a sicko? No wonder his wife had left him. 'You're divorced, aren't you?' she said, filling the silence.

Bernard sighed. ''Tis true, 'tis pity; and pity 'tis, 'tis true.'

'So what happened? In plain language.'

'In plain language, Lucretia was a bitch. I was glad to get rid of her. She was my research assistant, you know. I taught her everything – let her do all my typing and library work. Then she started saying she was too busy to help me. I discovered she was working on a PhD behind my back – on Shakespeare, mark you, *my* subject. The betrayal was shattering.'

'Mmm,' said Freya. Where was that taxi?

'It's taken me a long time to learn to trust again.' Bernard's eyes were bleary with self-pity. 'But with you, I feel there could be hope.' He reached across to place one moist hand on top of hers.

'I don't think so.' Freya removed her hand. 'I'm not looking for a long-term relationship at the moment.'

'Oh?' Bernard did not look as disheartened as she had anticipated. 'Short term is fine, too,' he leered. Then, with a portentous cough, he pushed out one leg from beneath the table, and twitched up his trousers to reveal an expanse of naked calf. 'I apologize if my trousers are rather *short* – or my socks insufficiently *long*.' He waggled his eyebrows suggestively.

'What?' Freya stared in disgust at the scurfy skin brindled with gingery hairs.

'I must say, I feel not unlike Malvolio in his "crossed garters". Ha, ha.'

'I'm sorry. I don't know what you're talking about,' Freya said crossly. 'Do put that horrible leg away. People are staring.'

Bernard gave her a waggish look. 'The lady doth protest too much, methinks.'

At that moment, Freya heard the words she had been waiting for. 'Miss, your cab is here.' Unfortunately, so did Bernard.

'Are we going back to your dungeon?' He rubbed his hands. ' "Now might I do it pat." '

'*We* are not going anywhere.' Freya threw some dollar bills on the table. 'I am going home. Alone. You seem to have got some kinky idea about me. I don't know why or how, but – '

'From you, of course!' Bernard was loudly indignant. 'From your e-mail.'

'Keep your voice down. All I said was that I was tall and – '

'No, the second one. The hairy legs . . . the whip hand . . . artistic . . .'

At the next table Mr Mobile Phone stared into space with an eavesdropper's frozen concentration.

'You've confused me with someone else,' Freya snapped. So *that* was what he had meant by 'invigorating encounters'. She rose to her feet and glowered down at Bernard. 'I did *not* send you a second e-mail, and I am most definitely *not* interested in kinky sex. Or in William bloody Shakespeare, for that matter.'

'Zounds! You're beautiful when you're angry! Is this part of the punishment? I promise to be a good boy.'

'You're sick, you know that? Goodbye!' Freya turned on her heel and strode towards the door, her cheeks hot with embarrassment. Heads turned curiously as she passed.

She heard the scrape of a chair behind her. 'Wait!' Bernard shuffled after her, bleating pitifully, 'I am a man more sinned against than sinning.'

As he spoke, there was a terrific clap of thunder outside. When Freya opened the door to the street she was confronted by a wall of water falling from the sky, as if a giant had upended a colossal bucket. Her cab glowed like a beacon of hope. She raced across the slick sidewalk before some bastard New Yorker could steal it.

'Drive!' she shouted, as she plunged inside. Her back was already drenched.

'You tell me where we're going, and I'll drive.' The cab driver folded the newspaper he'd been reading with maddening nonchalance.

'Anywhere! Just drive!'

There was a *rat-tat-tat* on her window. A sodden Bernard loomed at her through the misty glass.

'Move it!' she shrieked.

'When shall we two meet again?' he called, running alongside the cab as it began to accelerate.

'In thunder, lightning or in – ?'

The cab shot into a gap in the traffic, drowning his words in the whine of the engine. Freya sank back damply against the seat and closed her eyes, thanking God for her deliverance. From now on she would be a better person, she vowed – kind, tolerant, forgiving, sweet-tempered.

'Quarrel with your boyfriend?' asked the cab driver. She caught his snide smile in the rear-view mirror.

'Just drive around the block, and shut up!' she told him.

*Click-clack* went the windscreen wipers as Freya huddled in the back seat, watching the city lights come and go in a watery blur. She was cold and damp, and itched to hit something, hard. It was far too early to go home. Even if she didn't care about interrupting Jack and Candace, the thought that they might pity her, or laugh behind her back, was unbearable. After Bernard, she didn't want to go to a bar and submit herself to more male gropings. A cinema would at least be dry, but she hated watching films by herself, and she was too consumed by rage to sit still. Cat might be home, but Freya wasn't in the mood for another lecture about the joys of the single life. Meanwhile, the meter crept steadily upward.

'Take me downtown,' she called out to the driver.

Half an hour later, dressed in a singlet and shorts retrieved from her locker, Freya had bicycled four gruelling miles while remaining in exactly the same place. Sweat gathered at her temples as she vented the frustrations of the evening on the chrome and rubber machine. There were two other women in the gym, either glued to MTV or staring fiercely at their own toned reflections. What are we all *doing* here, Freya wondered, with our fat-free bodies and our lonely lives, our expensive haircuts and our mobile phones that nobody calls? God, another hill. Freya strained at the pedals until her sinews ached.

Now for the treadmill. She adjusted the setting and

started walking at a fast, steady pace, pumping her arms, trying to obliterate the vision of Bernard's moist mouth and yearning eyes. She should have stabbed him with one of her spiked heels – except he would have enjoyed that. Freya increased the speed and began to run. Fuelled by oxygen, her brain moved up a gear. What could have made Bernard suppose that she was into punishment? What was all that about a second e-mail?

Freya's pace faltered, and she almost toppled backwards off the running machine. *Bloody Jack!* So that's why her messages didn't immediately show up on the screen; she'd blamed her own unfamiliarity with his computer, but the real reason was that he'd read them first: read them, doctored them, and invented his own replies. It wasn't Bernard who'd sent the silly poem that had made her smile; it was Jack, making a fool of her. Freya upped the speed again, pounding the smooth, sliding rubber under her feet. Sweat poured down her body. *Just you wait, Mr Jack Madison III.*

'We're closing now, miss. Time to go home.' A man in overalls, holding the hose of his vacuum cleaner, smiled kindly at Freya from the doorway of the exercise room.

After showering and changing, Freya found that her legs were trembling from exhaustion. She trudged to a coffee bar, ordered a cappuccino, mineral water and three cinnamon doughnuts, and sat on a high stool at the window, watching the spatter and trickle of raindrops. Tonight had been a mistake. She'd been a fool to think she could find the perfect man, even a short-term partner, just like that. Even Jack, it seemed, had correctly decoded Bernard's advertisement; though it was hard to understand why he should have wanted to play such a cruel joke on her. Anyway, who cared?

Freya leaned her head on her hand and stared into her coffee, eavesdropping on a conversation between two women behind her, evidently a mother and daughter. Their talk was desultory and mundane – gossip about family and friends, a delicious non-fattening recipe for chicken salad, whether the daughter should repaint her living room peach or yellow – but listening to them, Freya felt a pang of longing. For most of her life she had fantasized about having a real mother, someone who would love her unconditionally and listen to whatever nonsense she cared to pour out, who would tell her that she was beautiful and clever and give her refuge when she needed it. Sometimes she talked to her mother in her head. *What do you think?* she'd ask about some new boyfriend. *Is this how it was with you and Daddy?* But there was never any answer. She didn't have a Mummy; she had a stepmother.

Freya had been thirteen years old when her father told her that he and his new friend Annabelle were getting married, and that they were all going to live in a big house in Cornwall. Her first reaction was simple astonishment. How could he want to change the unique perfection of their life together? For the last seven years, there had been just the two of them. In term-time she went to school while he researched and wrote his books in the large, untidy London flat, rescued from domestic chaos by a wiry Portuguese woman of unconquerable energy and good humour called Mrs Silva. In the holidays they travelled together in Europe, visiting museums, churches, libraries and the homes of her father's art historian friends. 'You can come too,' her father had told her, when she begged not to be left behind, 'so long as you never complain of being bored.' And she hadn't. Her father talked to her, took her to dinner with him, asked her opinion of buildings, food, people. He taught her to play chess and poker and solo whist, how to tell if an oyster was fresh, the meanings of spinnaker and pantheon. Sometimes he let her watch him shave, drawing clownish patterns in the foam with his razor to make her laugh. Freya learnt how to pack her own suitcase, wash out her underwear in a hand basin, and to ask for the bill: *l'addition, il conto, la cuenta*. She learned not to disturb him when he was reading the newspaper, in the lavatory, writing in his notebook or 'thinking' – and *never* to ask if he was lost or had run out of money. They stayed in cheap *pensions* with peculiar bathroom arrangements and scratchy toilet paper, in borrowed flats smelling of unfamiliar food, and occasionally in a grand hotel, where they would dress up and pretend to be royalty in disguise. 'May I say, Princess Freyskanini, how exceptionally lovely you are looking tonight? Your shoe buckles quite dazzle the eye.'

There were women, of course. Her father was a handsome man. Freya had taken a certain pride in his conquests, knowing they could not last. For an unseen third accompanied them wherever they went, the memory of a loving, laughing woman who had risen early one morning to buy croissants for breakfast, failed to look the right way crossing the rue du Bac and died instantly under the wheels of a delivery truck. Years later, overhearing gossip, Freya understood that her mother had been in the early stages of pregnancy.

Annabelle, too, was a mother – of Natasha, aged three. Freya's father explained that Tash had no Daddy, just as she had no Mummy, so they were joining up to make a new family. Freya, who loved her father more than anyone in the world, accepted it. At the Register Office in London she stood behind him clutching the stiff, wired handle of her bridesmaid's bouquet and watched his blunt-tipped fingers, familiar as her own, slide the ring on to the hand of another woman. *So this is marriage.* Annabelle was very nice to her, but she was a brisk, definite person; Freya had the uneasy suspicion that she was about to be knocked into shape.

At first it was almost okay. There was the excitement of a new bedroom and a new house – an extraordinary house near the tip of Cornwall, big enough to get lost in, with a maze of a garden that fell in a green tumble to the shingly edge of the sea. There was a forest of plants with leaves the size of tablecloths, prickled underneath, and windows with glass that made the view waver intriguingly. There were barns and a crumbling dovecote and a small chapel, cold as winter. To begin with, there had been nothing to object to about Tash, a portly three-year-old with a direct stare and a snotty nose. It was easy enough to outrun her, or hide from her tiny despotic presence. *Tash up! Tash banana! Mine!*

Freya's first shock had been Annabelle's request, polite but firm, that she should knock before entering her father's bedroom, now also Annabelle's bedroom. Next was the decision to send Freya to boarding school, as no local school was deemed ' appropriate'. Freya hadn't complained; she hadn't wanted to upset her father. For the same reason she endured Annabelle's painful intrusiveness: how often was Freya washing her hair? Should she be watching so much television? Didn't she need a bigger bra? It was Annabelle who now accompanied her father on his trips.

In Freya's absence at school, Tash dominated the household. As the only child of a woman who had already suffered one tragic loss, and the stepchild of a man trying hard to pull his new family together, Tash was cosseted and indulged. She resented sharing the spotlight. At first Freya couldn't believe that a small child could be so manipulative and malevolent. Tash crayoned all over her books, borrowed things from her room and hid them, and once broke an ornament of Swedish glass, a precious present from Freya's mother – deliberately dropped it in front of her eyes. When Freya got angry, Tash would run to her mother and scream that Freya had hit her. Annabelle had words with Freya's father, who took Freya aside, embarrassed, and suggested she should be nicer to her 'sister'. Just at the time when Freya hit the gawky, self-conscious stage, here was an adorable toddler claiming everyone's indulgence while Freya was expected to act like a grown-up. One holiday she returned to find that Tash had started to call her father 'Daddy' – and he did not correct her. His betrayal was like a knife in her heart; the hidden wound festered and spread. Freya understood that the life she and her father had lived together – the easy companionship with no rules, no *need* for rules – was over for good. Instinctively she began to turn her gaze elsewhere. She studied hard, developed her own interests, retreated into secrecy. The summer she left school, she took a job as an au pair in New Jersey. The plan was that she would return in the autumn to start at university; instead, she had discovered New York, and stayed.

Freya's thoughts drifted off, conjuring up images of how her life should be, or could have been, or might be, until the rattle of cups alerted her to the fact that it was almost midnight. She paid her bill, popped a mint in her mouth to keep herself going, and caught the uptown bus home.

The lights were out in the apartment. To be on the safe side, Freya inserted her key with silent stealth and, once the front door was open, took off her shoes and tucked them under her arm. All was quiet. She tiptoed into the hall, and waited for her eyes to adjust. The living room door was open. She could make out humps of furniture in the half-dark; a green pinprick light indicated that the stereo had been left on. She was moving forward to turn it off when she was halted by a tiny sound, the merest breath of a sigh. Someone was in the room.

Freya stood still, nerves tingling. Just then a car entered the street. Its approaching headlights cast a fuzzy, sulphurous glow through the curtains. As in a slow-motion dream, Freya made out the erect shapes of wine bottles and guttered candles on the central table, then the dark pools of discarded clothing that formed a trail across the floor, finally the saggy couch where it appeared that some strange, shadowy beast lay sprawled in sleep. There was an orange flash as the car passed, and all became clear. Jack lay with his back to her, naked. She caught a blond spark of tousled hair, the gleam of one smooth shoulder flexed to hold an almost invisible Candace, the tangle of four legs crooked into the sofa's embrace. Candace's small, ringed hand rested intimately on the muscled curve of his buttocks.

The light disappeared, eclipsing the coupled figures and leaving Freya blind. But the image remained vivid in her mind. She was aware of her heart urgently beating. It was the surprise, she told herself. Moving as quickly as she dared, almost hurrying, she entered her own room and closed the door.

# I 2

'Sshhh!' hissed a voice.

Freya, who was standing at the kitchen sink, elbow-deep in dishwater, twisted her head to find Candace glaring at her from the doorway. In the full force of daylight, without make-up and enveloped in Jack's dressing gown, she looked very young. Her toenails were painted dark plum.

'He's trying to sleep!' she protested.

Freya hoisted a handful of cutlery out of the water, held it in the air for a few pointed seconds, then dropped the lot on to the steel drainer.

'Who?' she asked, when the jangle had subsided.

'Jack, of course! His head hurts, poor baby. I think he's sick.'

'Huh! Hangover, more like. I cleared away about ten million bottles. Not to mention all this other rubbish. Anyway, it's practically afternoon.' Freya added a lid to a pile of pans, which collapsed with a crash.

'You don't have to do that, you know,' said Candace. 'I like cleaning up.'

Freya gave a martyred shrug. 'It's done now.'

There was a moan from Jack's bedroom, and at

once, with a cheep of distress, Candace fled from the room.

Within a minute she was back. 'Do you have any orange juice?' she asked.

Freya dried her hands on the dishcloth, considering this question. '*I* have orange juice, yes. Jack does not. He likes us to shop separately. That means I shop and he doesn't. Where's my coffee, by the way?'

'Oh. Was that *your* . . . ?' Candace's voice trailed into silence under Freya's glowering gaze.

'Great! Fantastic!' Freya snapped her wet dishcloth angrily. 'How marvellously bohemian of Jack to rise above the banality of the grocery store.'

Candace stepped back a pace. Her eyes were wide and eloquent. Crazy, they said. Cracking up. Menopausal.

With difficulty, Freya pulled herself together. She stalked to the fridge and threw it open. In one swift movement, she grabbed the juice and plonked it on the counter.

'There! To you, Candace, I grant the freedom of the orange-juice carton, to do with as you will.'

Candace's brow wrinkled. 'Does that mean I can take some to Jack?'

'Yes, yes, yes, yes, *yes*! God! It's not as though he can't afford the stuff. Bloody Jack Madison the bloody Third.'

'The Third?' Candace paused in her search for a glass.

'Ridiculous, isn't it? You'd think he was royalty. He

probably is, down on the ol' plantation, with the magnolia a-blossomin' and the bullfrogs a-croakin' and the Cadillacs a-revvin'.'

'Every man likes to be king in his own home. I think that's nice.'

Freya made a gagging noise.

Candace eyed her suspiciously. 'Are you a feminist?'

'If that means being equal to men, of course. Aren't you?'

Candace thought about this while she poured out the juice. 'I have respect for myself as a woman. But men and women are different. I mean, look at our bodies.'

What drivel she talked. Freya folded her arms. 'Tell me, Candace, what exactly do you do? I mean, what's your job?'

'I'm in marketing?' Candace's questioning cadence suggested that Freya might be unfamiliar with the concept. 'Right now I'm a telemarketing operative, but my boss says he wants to promote me.'

'So what do you market?'

'A whole bunch of stuff. It's really interesting. Though I don't want to do it for ever. A career is so restricting.'

Not nearly as restricting as not having a career, thought Freya. Aloud she asked, 'What would you like to do?'

'Be rich and famous.' Candace gave a confident smile. 'Shop, travel, develop myself as a person.'

Freya arched an eyebrow. 'Ambitious stuff.'

'I think so. What about you?'

Freya had a standard answer to this commonplace enquiry: set up her own gallery, develop artists she had chosen – at *their* pace, not according to the whims of the market, blah blah. But explaining it to this lamebrain was a waste of breath. She cocked her head. 'Uh-oh. Was that the Master's voice?'

Candace scurried away with her precious juice, boobs bouncing, leaving Freya to flick her hair in irritation. The idea of playing piggy-in-the-middle with Jack and Candace all weekend made the blood thrum in her ears. She couldn't imagine why no one had invited her to Connecticut or the Island. Since no one had, she would make her own escape, but not before she'd had a little word with Jack – if he ever got out of bed. *His head hurts, poor baby.* Perhaps it was a brain tumour. Freya decided that now would be a good moment to reorganize the saucepan cupboard. As she did so, she sang softly under her breath to the tune of 'Chitty Bang Bang': *Bounce bounce, titty-titty bounce bounce titty-titty bounce bounce, we love you . . .* Eventually, sounds indicated that the lovebirds were finally leaving their downy nest.

Earlier, from her vantage point at the sink, Freya had noticed that someone had set out some tatty deckchairs in the back yard. It was a sparkling day, the sky washed to a clear cerulean blue by last night's rain. Fetching the newspaper and a pile of envelopes from the hall floor, she carried them outside and settled herself in the hot sunshine. She leafed through the post, mostly dull-looking brown jobs apart from a thick, cream envelope addressed to Jack. She turned it over, and idly rubbed a thumb across the embossed flap, which proclaimed the sender to be Jack's father. With any luck he had decided to disinherit his useless son.

There was one item for her, a large padded envelope re-directed from Michael's address, franked by a London PR firm whose name she recognized. Freya's face tightened. Tash had never written to her once in all the years she'd lived in New York. If she was doing so now, it would hardly be out of sisterly affection. Freya ripped the envelope open and pulled out a glossy magazine. Good grief! – *Country Life.* She flipped through the pages depicting clipped yew hedges, prize bulls and luscious English country houses until she found a compliment slip covered in huge scrawly writing: *Daddy said I should send this to you. See p. 51. – T.*

Freya pursed her lips and turned to the relevant spot, where she found a full-page colour photograph of Tash on the girls-in-pearls page. *Country Life* had always featured a portrait like this – the English middle-class equivalent of a *Playboy* centrefold – which advertised the charms of a well-born or aspirant young lovely, usually on the occasion of her engagement or marriage. No wonder Tash was thrilled. But surely the girls used to wear high-necked frilly blouses and Alice bands, and were snapped in mid-embrace of a labrador or a cherry tree in blossom, not sprawled half naked across a red velvet chaise longue. *Country Life* had certainly changed. Freya smoothed the page flat and stared stonily at Tash's flawless young skin, her greeny-hazel eyes innocently wide, the showy ring oh-so-casually prominent on one perfectly manicured hand. Underneath the portrait was the usual formulaic caption:

Miss Natasha Penrose, 25, only daughter of the late Mr John Huffington and Mrs Guy Penrose of Trewennack, Cornwall, is to be married to Roland Swindon-Smythe, only son of Mr and Mrs Barry Swindon-Smythe of The Shrubberies, Totteridge Common, Essex.

Reading the announcement in black and white made Freya catch her breath in panic. The wedding was exactly two weeks away, and she had nobody to go with. *What was she going to do?* She slammed the magazine to the ground upside-down and picked up today's newspaper instead, hoping to distract her thoughts.

She was trying to concentrate on a lament for the demise of the formal dining room when Jack stumbled out from the kitchen. God! that's all she needed. He was wearing shorts and a giant T-shirt with the words 'Think Sausage' printed on it. Freya had once owned its exact twin, both party-bag freebies from some restaurant launch they had crashed together years ago – only she had possessed the good taste to throw hers out.

Jack slumped in a chair and put his head in his hands. 'Urghh,' he said.

Freya read her paper in icy silence.

'I think I might be dead. No flowers, please.'

Freya ignored him – the cheap, slobbish, cruel, selfish bastard.

He stretched noisily and let out an uninhibited yawn. The silence ticked by. Freya waited. Finally he asked, in a carefully casual voice, 'How was your evening?'

'Sensational, thank you.'

'Really?' Jack's eyes widened in surprise.

'Pure poetry. There's nothing like a man who worships the ground you walk on – particularly if it's his own body. Excuse me, his own *hairy* body. Though those handcuffs need some new padding, that I will say.'

Jack was looking at her in alarm. 'You're kidding.'

'Of course I'm kidding!' Freya jumped to her feet and began thwacking him about the head with her newspaper. 'How dare you set me up with a pervert?'

'I didn't – ow! – set you up. You answered the ad yourself. It was your choice. Stop that!' With mortifying ease, Jack relieved her of the paper and held her at arm's length. 'I don't get it, Freya. Can't you even last a week without a man?'

'Look who's talking!' Freya twisted out of his grasp. 'You can't let even a *day* pass without picking up some woman – however feeble-minded.'

Jack bared his teeth in a taunting smile. 'Maybe it's not their minds that interest me.'

'Where's the "maybe" in that? No wonder you can't write any more, Jack. You're about as intellectually challenged as a piece of plankton.'

His eyes flickered. 'At least I don't need to scour the lonely hearts ads.'

They glared at each other.

'I almost forgot.' Freya reached into her shorts pocket. 'Last week's rent. Thank you so much for the privilege.' She tossed a wad of dollar bills in his general direction. The notes separated and fluttered on to the rough grass.

After a pointed pause, Jack bent to pick them up and folded them with exaggerated care. He sagged back in his chair and considered her through eyes narrowed against the sun. 'You're really not going to like yourself when you read my novel,' he told her.

'You can't put me in your novel. That's libel.'

'A woman like you.'

'What happens to her in the end? After she's raped by the pervert, that is.'

Jack's face clouded over. 'I don't know. Speaking of libel, I had a talk with Michael yesterday. Someone mutilated his wardrobe. He's thinking of suing.'

'He wouldn't dare.'

'Gives the word "lawsuit" a whole new meaning, doesn't it?'

'Hi, everybody,' chirruped a voice. 'I've made us all some lemonade.'

Candace tripped out to them with a tray, fully dressed and restored to bandbox perfection – lips glossed, hair smoothed, and no doubt manicured, waxed, depilated and hygienically sprayed in all problem areas. Freya looked down at her bare legs and scuffed trainers. Time to leave.

'Thank you, Candace.' She took a glass and drained it. 'You don't mind if I borrow Rosinante, do you, Jack?'

'Yes, I do.'

'Rosie who?' Candace frowned suspiciously.

'Rosinante is Jack's pet bicycle,' said Freya, 'and after you, Candace, the thing he loves most in the world. It's named after Don Quixote's horse.'

'Oh, right. Don. He was in *The Waltons*, wasn't he?'

'Come on, Jack.' Freya kicked him, none too gently, on the leg. 'It's in your interest: I'm going to check out some apartments.'

He looked up sharply. 'You're moving out?'

'Are you begging me to stay?'

'Let me know when I can crack open the champagne.'

'Is this your sister?' interrupted Candace. She had picked up the magazine which Freya had stupidly left lying open on the grass.

'Stepsister,' Freya agreed shortly.

'Let's see.' Jack held out his hand. Obediently, Candace gave him the magazine and draped herself over the back of his chair, her cheek next to his, so that they could read it together.

Jack examined the photograph, and whistled. 'I thought you said she was a schoolgirl, Freya.'

'She was. She grew up.'

'I'll say.'

'Look, Jack!' Candace pointed excitedly. 'It says she's getting married! Isn't that amazing?'

'An event of truly world-shattering significance.' Freya snatched the magazine out of Jack's grasp and slapped it shut. 'You do have your own post, Jack.' She bent down and scooped up the small pile. 'Or is this some new kind of group therapy where we all get to paw through each other's letters? There's one here from your father. Shall I read it aloud?'

Jack looked at her with dislike. 'Take the bike,' he said.

'What?'

'I said, take the goddamned bike!'

Freya hesitated for a moment, then tossed the letters at his feet. 'Fine,' she said.

Bicycling forty-odd blocks from Chelsea to Central Park on a hot Saturday was madness; to do so on Jack's clanking, three-speed antique, amid crazy traffic and death-jets of pollution, was the kind of suicide mission Freya was determined to enjoy. *I can do this*, she told herself, pedalling across intersections just as the lights turned red, banging on the roofs of cars that crowded her space. Back in the old days she had bicycled everywhere – but that was because she was penniless, not because she was some *poseur* 'artist' like

Jack, who thought a battered bike enhanced his boyish, bookish charm, and who could always grab a cab if it looked like rain. When she thought of all the cruddy jobs she had taken just to stay alive in this city – sandwich deliverer, telephone sex-line receptionist, rollerskating waitress (in obligatory pigtails), human guinea pig in hospital drug trials, the kind of maid employed to clean up other people's vomit after parties, tour guide in 'colonial' costume (complete with a stupid bonnet she called her 'Dutch cap') – Jack's fecklessness enraged her. He thought he was a hero because he'd survived in New York one whole year before his Daddy relented and put him back on an allowance. He'd never missed a meal to pay tuition fees, as she had, or spent a winter sleeping on a strip of foam with a charity-shop fur coat as a blanket. Even now, her bank balance regularly tipped into minus; since the pink dress and poker disaster she hadn't dared open a statement. And if Michael seriously intended to sue her . . . Freya groaned. She'd call Cat this afternoon and unleash her on the case.

Freya rose in the saddle as she pumped steadily northwards on an incline invisible to the eye but palpable to the calves. Block by block the character of the urban landscape changed – from flowers to fur, synagogues to churches, diamonds to books, theatres to office blocks, from rich to poor and back again, while the buildings rose and the wedges of sky narrowed. She caught the smells of hot-dog stands and melting tar and suntan lotion, and the occasional tang of the Hudson — part oil, part brine — wafted eastwards by cross-town winds. Heat pulsed from granite and bounced off glass. Tourists and Saturday shoppers dawdled at crossings. Young men in trucks shouted at her as they roared past, hoping to scare her into a tailspin. Freya put her head down and pushed on grimly, counting off the landmarks: the National Debt Clock, Macy's, the Town Hall, the RCA building with its enchanting slim spire, the sinister black glass cube of the CBS building plonked down on the corner of 53rd like a gigantic blank television screen. She passed Jim Dine's sculptures parked on the back lot of the Museum of Modern Art, a trio of bronze Venuses that were unquestionably female in form, but headless, armless and enormous. Was that secretly how men saw women? She thought of Candace's ample curves and Bernard's yellow-toothed leer; and heard again the tremor of amusement in Jack's voice when he enquired about her date. She had lied when she told him she was going to look at apartments. She was going to the park for some privacy, so she could plot her revenge.

Sweaty and breathless — but alive — Freya at last crossed into the park. The whole place seethed with bikers, joggers, lovers, rollerbladers, ball-players, sunbathers, men with babies, women with dogs, children licking ice-cream cones. Slowing her pace, Freya slipped gratefully on to the tree-shaded cycle track and rode one-handed towards the lake. At a streetcart along the way she waited in line to buy mineral water, popped the dewy bottle in her bicycle basket, and continued to the Ramble in search of an unoccupied spot amid its supposedly 'wild' tangle of streams, woodland and artfully placed boulders. Dismounting faithful Rosinante, Freya wheeled her through the bushes and laid her against a tree. She sat down on a shaded patch of worn grass and took a deep, cooling swig of water from her bottle, then reached for the rucksack she had carried in the bicycle basket. From it she drew a pen and notepaper. For a long while she chewed her pen thoughtfully, frowning down at the noisy chaos of rowing boats on the lake below. Then she began to write.

After several efforts, she had the letter as she wanted it. Next, she transferred the pen to her left hand and practised her psychotic blackmailer's handwriting. Finally, she took a fresh sheet of paper and wrote, in erratically capitalized lettering:

> You think your such a big shot, but be warNed –
> the FORCES OF DARKNESS are gathering. I
> know what's going on with you and Her. If she gets
> an A and I don't, you will be Punished for GROSS
> moral turpatude and SEXUAL favors. Nobody can
> be aloud to stand in the way of my GENIUS. So
> watch your step. Or else.
> 'A Friend'

Freya re-read the letter and smiled with satisfaction. Everybody knew that people attracted to creative writing courses were by definition paranoid and deluded; Freya liked to think of Jack torturing himself by trying to identify the perpetrator out of so many suspects. She folded the letter in two, slid it into an envelope and wrote out Jack's name and address in the same misshapen print. Then she took a stamp from her wallet, licked it, and stuck it on at a deranged angle. That should fix him. Suddenly exhausted, Freya lay back against the tree trunk and closed her eyes. The park was extraordinarily unpeaceful. Dogs barked, children whooped, music blared, men with jumpy eyes came over to ask her the time, lovers giggled in the dusty bushes. From time to time a park ranger issued warnings concerning boat safety from a loud-hailer. Freya endured it until a mountain-biker burst sweatily from the undergrowth and ran over her foot. Serenity was what she wanted; she knew the perfect place.

The room was cool and silent. High above her head was an elegantly corniced ceiling; a faint smell of polish rose from the wooden floor with its square of green carpet. The paintings that surrounded her – by Gainsborough, Romney, Reynolds, Hogarth – exuded English eighteenth-century confidence and calm. Freya was standing in the dining room of an elegant Beaux Arts mansion, now a museum, that provided a lush cultural oasis in the desert of gentility known as the Upper East Side. It had been an easy ride across the park; on the way she had passed a mailbox and deposited the letter to Jack. There was something about museums that made her feel safe, perhaps because she had spent so many hours in them as a child, her hand snug in her father's. The Frick Collection never changed, though occasionally items were moved around; the paintings were old friends. Wandering alone, and at her own pace, through these graceful rooms in the company of El Greco, Vermeer, Holbein, Titian, she felt simultaneously soothed and refreshed.

Normally she bypassed the Fragonard Room, with its rococo furnishings and chocolate-boxy depictions of young lovers, all rosebuds and flouncy dresses. But for some reason, today she stepped inside and found her attention caught by the series of four large paintings known as the Progress of Love. It told a familiar story. First, The Pursuit: a young man proffering a rose to an alarmed young girl, caught unawares in a flowery garden. Two cupids observe the encounter from their position on a phallus-shaped fountainhead, gushing water. Next, The Meeting, in which the young man, dressed in the red of passion, scales a wall to encounter his still-hesitant quarry. By the third painting, she has yielded; complacently she allows him to nuzzle her neck, while a small dog, symbol of fidelity, lies at her feet. Finally, in The Lover Crowned, he is in full, triumphant possession under a limitless sky; the happy couple smile out of a canvas awash with symbols of fertility and happiness.

And that was it: 'The End' – just like old movies,

where the two words actually came up on screen after the final kiss. Freya folded her arms and pursed her lips consideringly. It didn't seem that simple nowadays. Fragonard depicted love as a game for the young and innocent, in which both parties knew the rules. But there were no rules any more. No one was innocent; they were guarded and cynical, anxious to keep their options open, wary of being trapped yet terrified of missing out.

What was the secret of true love between a man and a woman, she wondered? Sex, certainly; romance, ideally; domestic stability, probably. Anything else? She shrugged: whatever it was, she hadn't found it yet. Freya rubbed her upper arms, suddenly cold in the air-conditioning. Could it be that the fault lay with her, that she was *unworthy* of love? Everyone abandoned her, in the end. Her heart welled with self-pity.

A German couple entered the room, arguing about which of them had forgotten the camera, and interrupted her thoughts. Freya shook off her melancholy mood, and moved towards the door. Her eyes swept over the paintings again as she passed, taking in the girl's blushing cheeks and plump bosom. Though scorning Fragonard's prettification of love, she couldn't help feeling a wistful pang for the sheer optimism and energy of youth. She moved on dreamily through the house, then sat for a while in the courtyard, with its small pond and plants and classical columns, and gave herself a lecture about being a nicer person – more open-hearted, more receptive, less critical. On the way out she noticed, for the first time, the size of the codpiece on a portrait by Bronzino: probably padding, or the sixteenth-century equivalent of photographic retouching, but massively impressive nevertheless. There was a smile on her face as she stepped out on to 70th Street, only to discover that Rosinante's rear tyre was flat.

This was not a likely area for a repair shop. After stopping to ask several passers-by, Freya learned that there was some kind of a bike place several blocks north, and made her way there, hoping it really existed and had not closed yet. She was in luck. In a junky street off Second Avenue she found a big old garage smelling of rubber, with a row of bicycles parked on the sidewalk and a throng of muscled youths inside, clinking spanners, hefting saddlebags, conferring over spinning wheels. As she took her place in the queue for the counter, her fingers slipped on the handlebars and Rosinante lurched sideways, ramming the person in front.

'I'm so sorry,' said Freya.

''S okay.' It was a young man, with a friendly smile. 'I was just trying to persuade myself I needed a Tour de France water bottle, but I'm already way deep in accessory overload. What's the problem with your bike?'

'Puncture.' Freya sighed with self-pity.

He looked at her in puzzlement.

'Flat tyre,' she translated.

'Is that all? Why don't you fix it?'

'Well. I . . . er . . . don't have the equipment. It's not my bike.'

'Sure you do.' He showed her a pouch thing strapped behind the bicycle seat.

'I thought that was a first aid kit,' Freya admitted.

He laughed as if she'd cracked a terrific joke, revealing perfectly straight, dazzling white teeth. Freya realized that he was extremely good-looking.

'Listen,' he said. 'Let's go back outside, and I'll fix it for you. They'll charge you crazy money to do it here. Come on.'

Freya followed him outside and watched him lean his own machine tenderly against the wall. Then he came over and took the bike from her hands. He was exactly the same height as her. Straight dark hair sprang from his forehead. He was wearing a tight black T-shirt and stone-coloured shorts cut high on his thighs.

'Let's get her on her back first,' he said commandingly. 'No, out of the way. I'll do this.'

Freya watched him flip the bike upside-down. He certainly seemed very fit.

'Shit, that's heavy! You shouldn't have to drag around a thing like that. I can lift my bike with one hand. Watch!'

He walked over and proudly hoisted his own sleek, slim, gunmetal super-bike into the air. His T-shirt rose with the action, revealing a rippled band of caramel skin.

'Amazing,' said Freya.

'That's the titanium, you see,' he explained seriously.

'I see.' Freya raised her eyes to his and smiled. He blushed! She wondered how old he was.

'Yeah, a real museum piece,' he muttered, fiddling with some kind of metal tool. 'Wonder how old she is.'

For a ghastly moment Freya thought he might be referring to herself.

'Got to be before 1973,' he continued. 'That's when they put casings on the off-side wing-nuts and brought in the bifurcated flange.' Anyway, something like that. Freya was busy marvelling at the musculature in the young man's legs as he bobbed up and down in attendance on her bike.

'1973!' He shot her a dazzling grin. 'That's even older than me!'

Freya made a rapid mental calculation. He must be eight years younger than her, at least. There was a time when she'd dismissed boys his age as cocky little twerps. Now she wondered why she hadn't helped herself to boat-loads when she'd had the chance.

A group of bikers swooped out of the garage. Someone called, 'Coming to the park, Brett?'

The young man glanced at Freya. 'Maybe later.'

'Please don't stay because of me,' she said quickly. 'I can easily get the bike fixed inside.' It would be awful if he felt stuck with her, like some old lady he had helped across the road and was too polite to abandon.

'Nah, it's okay. I want to. We can talk.'

So Freya perched on a fire hydrant and listened to him talk, watching his lean fingers move skilfully around her bike. Brett was an actor – well, mainly a waiter and bar person, if he was honest, though as a matter of fact he was opening next week in a really challenging production – a non-speaking role, unfortunately, and unpaid, but still, it was a start, wasn't it? He'd only been in the city ten months, sharing a loft space in the West Village with three others – strangers to begin with, but a great bunch. He'd be getting his own place as soon as he'd landed a good part – ideally something by Mamet or Stoppard: he had some good contacts.

Listening to him, Freya felt an ache of nostalgia. Had they all been this eager and hopeful in the Brooklyn days? Had they been this attractive and energetic and firm-fleshed? Back then, 'real' life lay in the future, somewhere over the rainbow, waiting for when they were ready; now they were drowning in it. Brett's enthusiasm about the details of her own life was infectious. It was 'cool' that she was English; 'really cool' that she ran a gallery. When she told him she was temporarily living in Chelsea, he thought that was cool too. Meanwhile, the glances he gave her, which had at first made her wonder whether she had bicycle oil on her face or had suddenly sprouted a varicose vein, confirmed the flattering truth that he found her attractive. Freya began fiddling with her hair and rearranging her legs. Quite suddenly she developed amnesia about the exact chronology of her life to date. Her heart was as light as a bubble.

At length Brett righted the bicycle and squared his shoulders in triumph.

'Marvellous.' Freya stood up and dusted off her shorts. 'Thank you so much.'

'No sweat.'

His hand rested in a proprietary way on her bicycle seat. Freya was mesmerized by the twin bones of his wrist and the golden hairs that dusted his smooth arm. When he squeezed the seat gently, she felt such a fierce leap of lust that she had to dig her fingernails into her palms.

'Well . . .' she said.

Brett grinned at her, looked off into space, glanced back, bounced on his toes, ducked his head.

'I was going to take a loop round the park,' he said. 'Maybe get a drink. Hang out. Want to come?'

Freya thought of the crowds, the noise, the heat, and her aching legs. She reminded herself that she was thirty-five years old, and hadn't combed her hair since this morning. She thought of Jack and Candace on the couch, and Fragonard's young lover with the rose, and Tash's cat-with-the-cream smile. She saw the invitation in Brett's eyes, and read the eager vitality of his tapping foot. She remembered the Bronzino codpiece.

'Why not?' she said.

# 13

Michael hurried out of the elevator and down the hall, the trousers of his ill-fitting new suit flapping around his ankles. He was late, and he couldn't find the right office.

'Excuse me!' He flagged down a young woman carrying an armful of legal folders. 'Can you tell me how to find Suite 719 – the Birnbaum case?'

Her eyes gave him a quick up-and-down scrutiny and returned to his face unimpressed. 'Do you mean Blumberg?' she enquired.

'Atshoo!' Michael sneezed heavily. 'That's it: Blumberg.'

The woman gave him directions, keeping her distance from his germy presence. Michael hurried on, wiping his sore nose with a handkerchief. He hated this kind of situation, where he had to take over a case with no notice and no background knowledge of the participants. But Fred Reinertson, his boss, had been rushed to hospital with suspected colitis; he could be out of action for weeks, and had specifically requested that Michael handle the case. Michael was unsure whether this was an honour or a test. Either way, his partnership could depend upon his performance.

The case was Blumberg v. Blumberg. He was representing Mr Lawrence Blumberg, aged seventy-six, of Queens, New York, against his wife, Mrs Jessica Blumberg, aged seventy-four. It was not the kind of high-profile divorce case normally handled by a senior partner like Fred, but apparently there was some family connection with Mr Blumberg which Fred had chosen to honour with his personal services. The case seemed straightforward enough, though there had been no time to meet his client in person, nor to review the paperwork as thoroughly as he would have liked. Michael had never felt so stressed: Freya, his mother, the game of hide-and-seek with his dry cleaning, emergency shopping. His routine had gone haywire. As a result he had caught this crippling cold, which showed ominous signs of turning to flu. Michael put a hand to his chest, and listened uneasily to its hoarse wheeze. It could even be pneumonia.

Here was Suite 719 at last. Michael straightened the knot of his tie, gave his nose a last-minute blow, and opened the door. An elderly man with sparse grey hair and a doleful expression was sitting in the small reception area. He looked doubtfully up at Michael over half-moon glasses.

'You the young fellow from Reinertsons?'

'Yes, that's right, Mr Birnberg – uh, Blumbaum – that is . . .'

'*Blumberg.* You're late.'

'Well, I'm here now.' Idiotically, Michael held his briefcase aloft, as if to prove he really was a lawyer.

'Jessie's already in there.' Mr Blumberg nodded his head towards another door. 'With her lawyer – a woman. Seems a very commanding young lady. Everything at her fingertips, if you know what I mean.' His expression implied that he did not necessarily feel the same way about Michael.

Michael hid his irritation with a professional smile. 'I'm sure you and I will be more than a match for them.' He sat down next to Mr Blumberg, and took a folder from his briefcase. 'Now, if we could just run through a few points before we go in . . .'

Mr Blumberg was extremely definite in his instructions, but so long-winded that it was a good ten minutes before Michael was able to lead the way to the inner office. He knocked once, and opened the door. It was the usual square, unadorned room, furnished with chairs and a small conference table, where two people sat facing him, each provided with a paper cup. Mrs Blumberg was handsome and stern-looking, with snowy hair pinned in a bun. Next to her was a much younger woman, presumably Mrs Blumberg's attorney; though Michael noted, with fleeting disapproval, the distinctly unlawyerly flamboyance of her brilliant turquoise shirt and riot of jet-black hair.

Michael adopted his best smile. 'Good afternoon, everybody. I'm so sorry – '

'What do you think you're doing here?'

To Michael's astonishment, the young woman with the hair had leapt to her feet and fixed him with an accusing glare.

'I'm Michael Petersen, from – '

'I know who you are,' she said in tones of loathing. 'What I asked was why you're here.' She kneed her chair out of the way and stepped towards him. 'Let me tell you, I will not have you interrupting this meeting so that you can slap some ridiculous lawsuit on one of my clients.'

Michael stood frozen in the doorway, opening and closing his mouth like a fish. What lawsuit? Which client? She must have mistaken him for someone else.

'Michael Petersen,' he repeated stubbornly, 'from Reinertson & Klang. I'm here to represent Mr Blumberg.' Belatedly, he stepped forward, allowing Mr Blumberg to enter the room. 'Mr Reinertson's been taken sick,' he added.

'Oh.' Far from offering him an apology, the mad woman folded her arms and glowered.

'And you,' Michael scoured his sluggish memory, 'must be Ms da Fillipo.' He tried to inject a cheery note into his voice.

She tossed her head as if this was obvious. 'You say you're here as Mr Blumberg's attorney – instead of Fred Reinertson?' She seemed unwilling to accept this fact. 'Why wasn't I informed of this substitution?'

'Didn't our office – ?'

'No, they did not.'

'Well, I apologize for that, naturally, but . . . *atshoo*!' The sneeze shook him from head to toe. Droplets sprayed into the air. 'Excuse me. I'm so sorry.' Once again, he dragged his long-suffering handkerchief from his pocket. He felt wretched.

Ms da Fillipo's smouldering brown eyes rested on his face for a moment. Then she dropped her eyelids, turned on her heel and returned to her place next to Mrs Blumberg. She gave the old woman's hand a reassuring squeeze. 'There's nothing to worry about, Jessie,' she told her – prematurely, in Michael's opinion.

He had hardly sat down with his client before she rapped a pencil on the table. 'Okay, let's get started, now that Mr Petersen has condescended to join us. The purpose of this meeting, as you know, is to talk through your reasons for wanting a divorce and, if you are resolved on such a course, to reach a settlement without having to resort to the expense and stress of a courtroom procedure.'

'But I don't want a divorce,' Mr Blumberg said mulishly.

'Well, I do,' said his wife.

'She doesn't.' Mr Blumberg nudged Michael. 'She's being stubborn. Can't you make her come home? I'm lonely, and I can't find anything.'

Ms da Fillipo bristled. 'I hardly think those are convincing reasons for maintaining a relationship. My client has a very serious grievance. Perhaps, Jessie, you would like to tell us about that.'

But now that her moment had come, Mrs Blumberg was strangely reluctant. The proximity of her husband of fifty years, sitting right opposite her, seemed to unsettle her.

'Well, he snores,' she offered.

Michael couldn't help smiling. Ms da Fillipo shot him a look of contempt.

'And what else?' she prompted.

Mrs Blumberg stared at her clasped hands. In a low, tight voice she claimed that her husband also left his slippers under the bed instead of putting them in the closet, and that they sometimes fought about what to watch on TV. Finally, at the end of a stumbling catalogue, she suddenly burst out:

'And he's having an affair with Mrs Lemke from upstairs!'

Mr Blumberg groaned and smacked his forehead, as if this ground had been gone over many times. 'All I did was ask her if she remembered how to foxtrot. Before I could stop her, she'd grabbed hold of me and – '

'What kind of a woman dances with strange men in her kitchen in the middle of the day?' Mrs Blumberg demanded darkly.

'Now, Jessie: Doris is sixty-five years old,' protested Mr Blumberg.

'Doris, is it now? Well, pardon me.'

'She just moved into our building. She's a widow. I was being neighbourly.'

'Neighbourly! Is that why you snuck out to have lunch with her when I was visiting my sister?'

'I did not sneak.'

Back and forth they went. Michael was amazed at their passion. Privately, Mr Blumberg had conceded to him that for two brief weeks he'd had 'a crazy thing' with sixty-five-year-old Doris, though the craziness had consisted of little more than a kiss on the cheek and the odd bunch of flowers. Mr Blumberg now regarded the episode as closed; he couldn't see why his wife was making such a fuss, or why he had to apologize. Mrs Blumberg, on the other hand, felt betrayed; she wanted her pound of flesh.

'I just want to get divorced,' she said, terminating the argument. 'It's the end of the road.'

Ms da Fillipo looked at Michael triumphantly. She must really hate men, he thought.

The discussion moved on to an examination of the Blumberg assets and the settlement to which Mrs Blumberg might be entitled. Michael protested that Ms da Fillipo's demands were absurdly high, but every time he attempted to object, Mr Blumberg, looking more depressed by the minute, cut the ground from under his feet by saying he didn't care. Until, that is, Ms da Fillipo uttered the words, 'And what about Pookie?'

'Ha! I thought we'd get to that,' said Mr Blumberg, showing more animation than he had all afternoon.

'Pookie's *my* baby,' said Mrs Blumberg stubbornly.

'That's right,' nodded Ms da Fillipo.

'Well, I've got her, and I'm keeping her.' Mr Blumberg stuck out his chin.

'No, you're not.'

'Yes, I am.'

Michael was floundering. He tried unobtrusively to

peek through his notes. 'Let's see now . . . What exact kind of, uh, baby are we talking about here?'

Three pairs of eyes regarded him with scorn.

'Creeping Jesus!' exclaimed Ms da Fillipo. 'I always knew that you macho power-freaks at Reinertson & Klang had no compassion for the *humanity* of these sad situations, but I thought you might at least have done your homework. Pookie is a five-year-old pedigree Highland terrier, purchased *in person* by my client, as the breeder will testify.'

'Paid for with *my* money,' Mr Blumberg pointed out. 'Jessie doesn't have any money of her own; she's never worked.'

'Never worked? *Never worked!*' Ms da Fillipo flung back her head and stared down her high-bridged nose at poor Mr Blumberg. 'The woman who has made your home, who cooked your dinner, who bore your children; the woman who tends to you when you're sick, who listens to the trivia of your working day and gives you the warmth of her body at night – *for fifty years:* how can you say that woman has never worked?'

There was an intimidated silence. Michael tried to remember what he knew of this da Fillipo woman: nothing, except that she worked for a family law partnership which had a radical reputation and handled a lot of legal aid cases. The word 'feminist' formed in his mind.

'Isn't that just typical of men?' she continued, in a quiet, sinister voice. Unnervingly, her laser gaze now moved to Michael. 'Does the woman not contribute to your life who shares your bed, who puts up with your musical tastes even when she doesn't like opera – ?'

'Opera?' both Blumbergs chorused in surprise.

' – who drinks skimmed milk because of *your* dietary requirements – '

'Skimmed milk?'

' – and endures your sexual inadequacies?'

'Jessie! How could you?'

Michael's head spun. It was almost as if she was talking about himself and Freya. But how could that be?

'You pursue this woman.' Ms da Fillipo thundered on like a runaway juggernaut. 'You send her flowers. You beg her to share your life. Then one day – *pfff!* – you decide you don't need her any more. So what do you do? You take her to a *public place* and cast her off.'

'But Jessie left *me*,' objected the old man.

'Of course I left you! You were having an affair with Mrs Lemke.'

'Once and for all, I was not – '

'You cast her off, I say – homeless, alone, crying her heart out, like an old – an old – '

'Like an old, homeless, lonely shoe,' Michael offered drily. 'In tears.'

Miss da Fillipo glared at him. The Blumbergs were looking bewildered and hurt.

Michael rose to his feet. 'Ms da Fillipo, I wonder if we might step next door for a moment?'

'Gladly,' she answered, her cheeks flushed.

Michael crossed to the door and held it open with elaborate politeness, then stepped after her into the outer room. Behind him he could hear Mrs Blumberg wailing, 'But I don't understand . . .' He closed the door firmly.

'Now.' He rounded on Ms da Fillipo. 'Would you please tell me what's been going on in there?'

'Don't play the innocent with me.' Her eyes flashed. '*I know everything.* And I am not embarrassed to tell you to your face that you have treated Freya abominably. If you dare to sue her over those trousers, I shall defend her personally, to the Supreme Court if necessary.'

Michael looked down on her in perplexity, mildly disconcerted by how small she was, close to. His brain struggled to figure out how she knew so much about Freya and his trousers. It was hard to believe that Freya had gone to the trouble of hiring an attorney, just *in case* he sued. And why the ferocious attitude? How come this Caterina da Fillipo was taking it all so personally? Caterina . . . The penny dropped with a clunk. 'You're Cat,' he said.

'Of course.' She eyed him defiantly, arms clasped tight beneath rounded breasts. Somehow he had never imagined Cat looking like this.

'Well, listen, Ca – that is, Ms da Fillipo. I am not, as it happens, intending to sue Freya – not that it's any business of yours. Moreover, I would like to remind you that I am not on trial here, and I consider it highly unprofessional of you to allow personal feelings to interfere with a case of law.'

'Oh, do you?' Her chin lifted; her eyebrows soared: it was one of the most expressive faces he had ever seen. 'I'm sorry, but I can't suppress my feelings the way you men can. I'm glad to hear that you've backed down over the lawsuit. That's something, at least.'

'I haven't "backed down". I never even – '

'And I cannot agree that personal emotions are irrelevant to a case of law. That's the difference between men and women: for me, divorce is about people; for you, it's all about money.'

Suddenly Michael was almost angry enough to slap her. 'How dare you presume to tell me what I feel? As a matter of fact, I think divorce is a tragic, cruel, painful business. Yes, I make money from it – and so do you. I'm proud to do my job well. I'm proud that I, for one, can keep my emotions under control.'

Michael stopped, stunned by his own outburst. His nose was running. He groped for his handkerchief, but he must have left it in the other room.

'Here.' Cat handed him a folded Kleenex from her skirt pocket.

'I'm *never* going to get divorced.' Michael blew his nose with a loud honk. 'The thing to do is to pick the right person – and stick.'

'You didn't stick with Freya,' she pointed out.

Michael jerked his head in exasperation. 'I didn't ask her to marry me either.' He added, more quietly, 'I don't think she wanted to. Do you?'

Cat didn't answer. She was looking at him as if he presented some puzzle she couldn't figure out. Now that his explosion of anger had subsided, Michael felt foolish, exposed.

'Let's get back to the case, shall we?' he said. 'So far, there aren't any real obstacles to a smooth divorce except this dog business.'

' "Dog business",' mimicked Cat. 'Pookie is her *child*. You're a man: you can't understand what that means.'

'Of course I can understand what it means! Anyway, Mr Blumberg's a man, and he loves . . . the dog.'

'See, you can't even say "Pookie" out loud. You think it's sissy.'

'No, I don't.'

'Say it, then.'

Michael rolled his eyes. This was absurd. He had never met such an unreasonable woman. 'Pookie,' he grunted.

Those fierce brown eyes stared into his, and suddenly a kind of craziness swept through him. 'Pookie, Pookie, Pookie. I love you, Pookie. Come to Mamma, Pookie. Stop crapping on the carpet, Pookie.'

Cat's mouth had gone a very peculiar shape. She was laughing!

There was the rattle of a doorknob, and a voice growled, 'Are you two people interested in our case? Or are you just going to stand out there yakking?'

'Of course we're interested, Mr Blumberg,' Michael replied smoothly. 'In fact, we were just discussing a pertinent legal technicality concerning canine apportionment.'

'Hmph.'

They had returned to the table and resumed negotiations when a sudden trill sent both Michael and Cat scrabbling in their briefcases for their mobile phones. The call was for Michael. He tossed Cat a superior look and opened his phone importantly. 'Petersen here.'

'Mikey! Thank goodness I've reached you.'

His mother: that's all he needed.

'What seems to be the problem?' he said, in what he hoped was a businesslike voice. 'I'm just wrapping up an important case here for Mr Reinertson, so I can't – '

'I want you to come over right away. It's sweltering in this room, and I can't get the air-conditioning to work. I think I'm going to have one of my attacks.'

Michael swung away from the table and hunched himself over the phone. 'Are you sure you turned it on correctly?' he asked in a low voice.

'Speak up, Mikey. You're mumbling.'

'Can't you get Room Service to fix it?' he asked, painfully aware of six eyes watching him, and six ears listening.

'They're so busy. I don't like to bother them.'

'Mother, it's a hotel. That's what they're for.'

'Can't you come over just for a minute? It's such a little favour to ask. Or do you want your poor old mother dying all alone in a strange place?'

'The Plaza Hotel is hardly – '

'Is this a professional meeting or a goddamned circus?' demanded Mr Blumberg, slamming one palm on the table.

'Now, Lawrence, don't get all riled up. It's bad for your ulcer.'

'So what? These people don't care about us, Jessie. All they want is money, money, money. Pah! Plaza Hotel. I'm going to talk to Fred about this. What kind of a rinky-dink outfit is he running anyway? Fellow didn't even know who Pookie was.'

Michael felt the sweat break out on his forehead. He put his thumb over the earpiece of his phone, and stood up. 'Excuse me, Mr Blumberg . . . Mrs Blumberg . . . Ms da Fillipo. This is an, um, emergency call. I'll be right back.' With that, he escaped into the outer room, accompanied by a faint parrot squawk. 'Mikey? Mikey? *Mikey!*'

'Mother, will you please stop shouting? I am in the middle of a business meeting. I can't come now. Call Room Service, and I'll see you at dinner, as we agreed.'

There was a long silence. Then a sulky voice said, 'Maybe I'll just take the plane home.'

'If that's what you want.'

'I might as well not be here. You've neglected me all week.'

'I have not neglected you. I've been at work.'

'If I'd known you were going to turn out like this, I wouldn't have scrimped and saved all those years to put you through college.'

Michael removed the phone from his ear and bashed it hard against his head.

'What's that noise? Did you hear what I said?'

'I heard. Now I'm going to say goodbye.'

'You're with a woman, aren't you? I can tell by your voice. Some flashy, New York – '

Suddenly Michael couldn't take any more. He cut the call, snapped his cellphone shut, and leaned his head against the cool wall. His nose was running and his eyes itched. He was tempted to walk away and leave the whole Blumberg mess behind. He'd blown this case, possibly even blown his chances of a partnership. Then he remembered Ms da Fillipo's scornful eyes: she'd think he was a wimp – as well as a male-chauvinist stuffed shirt with no feelings. Not that it mattered what she thought. Michael gave a bracing sniff, squared his shoulders and re-entered the room.

An extraordinary scene met his eyes. All three of them were sitting cosily together on the same side of the table. Cat held a handkerchief to her eyes as if she'd been crying; the Blumbergs sat solicitously on either side of her, like ministering angels.

'Well, young man.' Mrs Blumberg gave him a stern look. 'I think you owe Caterina here an apology.'

Michael frowned. 'Now what?'

'Don't be like that. You've got to learn to get over these little problems. All lovers have quarrels, even old stagers like us.'

*Lovers!* Michael looked wildly at Cat, whose eyes commanded silence.

'You have to learn to say you're sorry,' continued Mrs Blumberg. She smiled across at her chastened-looking husband. 'Imagine: we were actually thinking of getting divorced after fifty happy years.'

'Imagine . . .' Michael repeated faintly. He had no idea what was going on.

'Well,' prompted Mrs Blumberg, 'aren't you going to apologize to Caterina?'

There seemed nothing to do but go along with this pantomime. Michael looked at Caterina, and swallowed. 'I'm very sorry.'

'That's okay.' She seemed equally embarrassed by this charade.

'Well, go on, give her a nice big hug.'

After a small hesitation Michael stepped forward, and Caterina rose from her chair to meet him. He held his arms out stiffly, and she leant her head against his chest. Automatically his arms closed around her. She felt warm and womanly under his hands. Her hair smelt spicy. *Caterina* . . . The syllables sang in his head.

'All right, that's enough,' joked Mr Blumberg.

Michael relinquished his hold, and Caterina stepped back, eyes lowered.

'We'll leave you now, so you can be alone,' said Mrs Blumberg. 'Come along, Lawrence.'

'Don't forget your bag, Jessie. She always forgets her bag.'

'Look who's talking! What about your reading glasses? Lawrence can't go anywhere without losing his reading glasses.'

'Yes, I can. I've got them right here.'

'Only because I gave them to you.'

Arm in arm, bickering gently, they left the room.

Michael waited until he heard the outer door close, then turned to Caterina. 'What happened?' he demanded. 'What did you say?'

She moved to the table and started gathering up her papers. 'All I said was that you'd broken off our engagement.'

'Our *what*?'

'I told them that your mother didn't approve, and was trying to make you give me up.' She flashed him a defiant glance. 'I had to think of something.'

'But – but why?'

'For the Blumbergs' sake. Obviously.'

'But –?'

'It was quite clear they didn't want to get divorced. I thought we might as well all stop playing games.'

'But just now – you were crying!'

'That's my party trick.' She tossed her thundercloud of hair. 'I can cry on demand.'

'I see,' said Michael. He didn't, in fact, understand a single, solitary thing, except that a few minutes ago there had been an impossible tangle, which this extraordinary woman had somehow pulled into a smooth ribbon of silk. He watched the capable way she squared her papers and rapped them firmly on the table.

'Well . . . thanks,' he said at last.

She caught his eye and smiled. The transformation was astonishing.

Michael took a step forward and opened his mouth. 'At*choooo*,' he said.

'You want to take care of that sniffle,' Caterina told him calmly.

Michael was suddenly aware of how unattractive he must look, with his red nose and watery eyes, dressed in this awful suit. 'I'm trying to,' he said. 'Codex, Codeine, Flugo, Dri-noze: I've got them all.'

'Tchah! Your yin and yang are out of balance. I recognize the signs. What you need are some vitamins. Do you like nuts?'

'Uh . . . yes. In their place.'

'Well, their place is inside your stomach. You need some Vitamin E to get those antibodies going. There's a good health store not too far away where you can get the right stuff. Here: I'll write down the address for you.'

With the passionate energy that seemed to infuse everything she did, she tore a strip off her yellow notepad, scribbled something in a bold hand, then folded the paper and handed it to him. 'Now, I must rush.'

'Thank you. Uh, Ms da Fillipo . . . Caterina –' Michael broke off. He wanted to keep her here a little longer, but he couldn't think of anything to say.

'Yes?' She shot him a glance of cautious curiosity, as if he were an unfamiliar and unpredictable beast. Michael couldn't remember a woman looking at him in quite this way before. Her eyes were not brown after all, he saw, but flecked with fiery sparks of yellow.

'I, um . . .' Michael frowned. His mind was blank. Then he had an inspiration. 'I'd be very grateful if you would clear up this misunderstanding about a lawsuit – you know, talk to Freya.'

'*Freya?*' His request seemed to startle her.

'You'll be seeing her, won't you?'

'Sure. Absolutely. Of course.' Suddenly she was cramming her belongings into her briefcase and busily snapping the catches. She was leaving!

'Wait! I'll ride down in the elevator with you.' Belatedly, Michael started to clear up his own things. But he was too slow.

'Sorry. Got to go. 'Bye!'

Moving like a small, vivid blue whirlwind, she picked up her briefcase, whisked herself to the doorway, and was gone with a wave of her hand.

Michael stood alone in the dismal little room. He looked down at the piece of yellow paper he was holding, and unfolded it. There was the address of a store called Aphrodisia and the names of a couple of products: nothing else. He crushed the paper in his fist and let out a curse of frustration.

'Nuts!' he said.

# 14

' . . . and I thought the part where Mack chopped up his mother was a little clichéd.'

'That was *intentional*, Mona. It's an ironic commentary on the banality of violence in our society.'

'But he didn't have to eat her, too.'

'Of course he had to eat her. That's the "devouring passion" foreshadowed in my very first paragraph.'

'With ketchup?'

'You don't get it, do you? The ketchup is symbolic.'

'Oh yeah? Of what exactly?'

'Of blood, I imagine.' Jack cut in smoothly. 'Am I right, Lester?'

Lester gave his usual psychopath's stare, then jerked his head in a nod. As always, he was wearing a tie over an obsessively well-pressed shirt; his scalp gleamed white through a born-again-Christian haircut. Jack wondered: could Lester have written the threatening letter? Lester was always the first student to arrive for class, and always sat in the same seat. This latest story – about a son so grotesquely overfed by his mother that he became a prisoner of his own obesity, and eventually ate his mother's corpse – was typical of his work. If anyone knew about 'the Forces of Darkness', it would be Lester.

'Why do men always have to chop up their mothers? Why not their fathers? Give me a good castration scene any day.' That was Rita, fat and fifty, an enthusiastic latecomer to feminism. But Rita was all bluster; her hatred of men was purely theoretical. If she knew about Candace and him, she'd just laugh. Wouldn't she?

Jack forced himself to concentrate. His gaze travelled around the faces at the seminar table, drawing their attention. 'Let's look for a moment at character development in "Big Mack". Who wants to comment on that?'

As usual, Nathan began to shoot his mouth off. Meanwhile Mona, who clearly felt she had been snubbed over the symbolic ketchup, began to clean her nails with a hair pin. She was one of those pale, skinny women who cultivated the 'damaged' look, and told anyone who would listen how she had been abused by her high school English teacher. Jack studied her bony profile; maybe *she* had written the note, as a form of vicarious revenge.

The letter had arrived yesterday in the mail. Fortunately, Freya had gone to work by then, so there was no one to witness his shock. And Jack had been shocked. He was used to being liked; hell, he was a likeable guy ... wasn't he? To begin with, he had screwed up the letter and thrown it away. But all morning, while he tried to write, he found his thoughts dwelling uneasily on its threatening malice. Eventually, he had retrieved the crumpled paper from the waste basket and smoothed it out, scanning it for clues. It was upsetting to know that someone out there hated him this much. He wondered if a similar letter had been sent to his employers. Part of his training course to become a creative writing instructor had included a lecture on 'appropriate' behaviour. Jack hadn't paid much attention. He wasn't a dirty old man, and there were plenty of girls around without having to resort to your own students. Though that, of course, was exactly what he had done. Jack frowned; it occurred to him that he might have been rather stupid.

Whatever his private opinion of certain teachers of creative writing (undistinguished graduates whose sole achievement had been to publish a couple of stories in journals with names like *Mirage, Semiotext(e)* and *The Skunksville Review*), or of most students (unable to spell, ignorant of grammar, utterly unwilling to read), creative writing courses formed a respectable and lucrative part of America's academic institutions. Jack's own credentials were potentially impressive; he had published a whole book, by a publisher everyone had heard of, and was a regular contributor to national magazines. At the back of his mind was the notion that one day, when he had tired of the New York literary scene, he might take a professor's job in some agreeable university town. He didn't imagine the teaching would be very onerous; there'd be plenty of time for his own writing.

Now that little fantasy was under threat. American academia was going through a McCarthyite phase at the moment. Teachers didn't necessarily have to be good, but they did absolutely have to be squeaky clean. They didn't dare even shut their office doors during a private interview with a student, for fear of accusations of sexual harassment. Any hint of fraternization, favouritism or hanky-panky could be punished by dismissal and a mark on one's record as fearsome as the black spot.

Jack glanced at Candace, sitting right down the other end of the table, uncharacteristically silent and demure, and felt a twinge of exasperation at her blatant overacting. Without mentioning the note, Jack had told her that they must be more discreet; but not that she should impersonate a nun. Everyone must have noticed that she hadn't opened her mouth all evening. Feeling his eyes on her, Candace glanced up, bit her lip, and blushed deeply. Jesus!

Nathan and Lester, meanwhile, were approaching danger level in their argument about whether character was an outmoded concept in contemporary fiction. Jack wished he had never set this assignment. Write a story about love, he'd said – any kind of love. The results had been depressing. Terrified of being accused by their peers of writing mush, his students had subverted the brief in the most perverse ways they could think of: love of drugs, love of killing, love in the Holocaust, love that turned to rape, and of course incest, tiresome hallmark of the beginner. The one shining exception had been a story about the friend-ship between two misfits at school, and its betrayal –

a piece of writing so tender and subtle that Jack was half-tempted to steal it. He might as well. Carlos, the author, was an obsessional re-writer; he would never send the story to a magazine because it would never, in his view, be 'finished'.

That was the trouble with teaching. Even if you were lucky enough to find one or two students with genuine talent, they always found ways to sabotage it. Desperate to be 'original', they wrote thrillers that didn't thrill, love stories barren of love, mysteries that penetrated no further than the detective's own angst-ridden maunderings – usually in sub-Raymond Carver prose. Writers were their own worst enemies; they resented being helped. *You think you're such a bigshot* . . .

Jack smoothed back his hair. Relax. What did it matter if he lost this job? It was only money. The academic world wasn't so wonderful that he needed to join the scrabble for position of eager-beavers flashing their diplomas and publication lists, especially if that meant tailoring his personal life – and his intellect – to some moronic standard of 'correctness'. Why the hell shouldn't he form a relationship with a consenting adult of twenty-two?

Re-entering the discussion, Jack steered it deftly onwards until the class concluded that 'Big Mack', despite its imaginative strengths and some impressive turns of phrase, hadn't quite 'worked'.

'Why not?' Jack prompted.

Silence.

A hesitant voice spoke up. 'I know this is probably my fault – Lester's a better writer than I'll ever be – but I didn't really *feel* anything.'

'Feel!' scoffed Lester.

'Girls' stuff,' agreed Nathan.

The woman who had spoken, fortyish and frumpy, turned fiery red. Jack remembered that she worked in a daycare centre, and had never graduated from high school.

'That's very perceptive of you, Lisa,' he said warmly. 'You've hit on a key point.'

He leaned back and clasped his hands behind his head. 'All right. What's the most important thing you need to do as a writer?'

'Get yourself a shit-hot agent,' Nathan shot back.

The class laughed.

Jack acknowledged the joke with a smile, and waited for the class to settle. 'The most important thing a writer can do is to be truthful. I'm talking here about emotional truth. That means that you don't try to bullshit your readers. Don't *tell* me how shocked I must be, or how sad or happy: make me *feel* it.'

'Is that what you do? Sir?' Nathan's tone was offensive.

'I try to.'

'We're all real eager to see that novel you've been working on.'

Jack refused to be distracted. 'Forget my work. Choose someone you admire, anyone you like, and see how they do it.'

'You mean, like Carson McGuire?' asked Mona. 'He's brilliant, isn't he?'

'Anyone you like,' Jack repeated. 'Remember, in order to make your reader feel, you've got to feel too. So far in this course we've been concentrating on techniques – imagery, dialogue, point of view. These are all important, but it's no good hiding under a glittering surface. Come out. Show yourselves. Tonight I want to see you naked.'

'Not me.' Rita gave a raucous chuckle.

'Yes, all of you.'

'Pervert,' growled Nathan, flexing his tattooed biceps.

Jack looked at his watch. There was still an hour left of the three-hour session, and he wanted to put a lid on Nathan's aggression before it got out of hand. 'Okay. Exercise time.'

The class groaned.

'I want you to spend the next forty minutes writing a scene that moves me.'

Nathan folded his arms. 'I'm not in the mood.'

' "You can't wait for inspiration; you have to go after it with a club": Jack London. Anyone failing to attempt this assignment will be graded accordingly.' Jack looked carefully around the circle of faces. 'They certainly won't get an A.'

'I can't do it!' Carlos's voice was anguished. 'There isn't enough time.'

'Try. The difference between a would-be writer and a real writer is finishing. Now: any questions?'

Lester's hand shot into the air like a Nazi salute. 'Should we write on just one side of the paper, or both?'

'One, both, any, all. You can write upside-down or backwards. You can write a poem, or a scene of dialogue, or even a letter. You can tell me how much you love your cat. I don't care. Just be honest. Make me feel something genuine. Look into your hearts and write.'

After a certain amount of fuss the students settled to their task. A pleasing, concentrated stillness fell on the room. Through the high windows, street lights glowed in the night sky. Jack looked around the square room with its institutional blue paint and its tickle of chalk in the nose, and contemplated his class – his twelve disciples – slouching, doodling, writing, chewing their pens, occasionally gazing hopefully at him as if he might impart the trick of turning water into wine. Jack felt his heart expand. He did like teaching. He liked the combination of pure ideas and muddled humanity. He liked the arguments and the jokes, and the intense satisfaction when a student's comprehension opened like a flower. He didn't want to lose this job, or the chance of others like it. He wondered which of the twelve was Judas.

There was a rustle of paper as Rita turned over her page and raced to set down the words that spilled out of her brain. Jack was amazed by the confidence of some of his students. His own desire to be a writer had been slow and stealthy. Sometimes he felt a fraud, that he couldn't be a 'real' writer because he hadn't written obsessively from childhood. His had not been a literary household. His father read the stockmarket pages; his mother had liked fat, floppy magazines with pictures of other people's homes and other people's clothes. But Jack had observed. As stepmothers and stepfathers came and went, and he shuttled from one home to another, he had learned to read the emotional temperature, and to record it in his head. If the life he was living seemed imperfect, he fantasized a different one.

When Jack was ten, his father had remarried. Lauren had gusted into their lives, bringing with her trunkfuls of books and the fresh, tantalizing whiff of a different world. Jack discovered that reading could be a serious, even an admired pursuit. Lauren bought him books, read aloud to him, explained new words and concepts, listened to his opinions. Jack's relationship with her had survived the inevitable divorce some years later, and Lauren had encouraged him when he began, tentatively and in secret, to commit some of his imaginings to words. He had dedicated *Big Sky* to her.

For Jack, writing was a liberation, like discovering an extra limb or a new dimension. He liked the process that went on in his head: first, the open, instinctive rush of words, then the gritty, cerebral tussle of revision. He loved the notion that a good writer could create anything he liked, and make the reader believe it.

Except he was blocked. Stymied. Stuck. Grounded. Perhaps he was a fraud, a one-book wonder. He'd have to go home to Oaksboro and take some dreary job in the family business – maybe running the warehouse, or taking charge of advertising. ('Hey, Jack: you're supposed to be good with words.') He remembered with a flicker of anxiety that it was this weekend that his father was flying up to New York for a series of business meetings the following week. There had been the usual two-line letter, typed by his secretary, informing Jack of this fact and stating that he would be free to see his son some time on Sunday. It irritated the hell out of Jack the way his father always assumed that Jack himself would be free. Dad didn't rate writing as 'work'. They'd had many bitter struggles, starting way back when Jack had dropped out of the school football team to concentrate on his studies. ('Hell, son, who needs to study when they're going to inherit Madison Paper?') Then there was the time Jack announced that he wanted to stay on at college to take a Master of Fine Arts degree. ('*What* arts? Fine *what*?') At last the day had come when Jack had proudly presented his father with a copy of his book, the first fruit of his labours. His father had merely flipped through the pages and commented with a chuckle that Jack could have produced a million of these by now if he'd been working at Madison Paper. Jack was sure he'd never read it. Maybe if his next book got on to the bestseller list – or won the Pulitzer! – his father would finally stop jeering.

At the end of the session Jack collected up the students' efforts and distributed copies of a piece for next week's discussion. When Candace handed him her paper she surreptitiously showed him the palm of one hand, on which she had written 'See you Saturday!' with a smiley face underneath. As Jack rattled homewards on the subway, he realized that he was relieved not to have her chattering at his side, even though he was warmed by her girlish affection. Candace was a doll, but sometimes he needed to relax and think his own thoughts. Like why he couldn't write, for example. The question became more agonized and urgent each day, but there was no one he could talk to about it. *Be honest*, he'd told his students. *Look into your heart and write*. But he couldn't do it. Something blocked his view.

Jack remembered Carlos's wonderful story, and his own impulse to steal it, and a flash of shame seared through him. He vowed that, without telling Carlos, he would send it off to a couple of the better publications, just as it was, unrevised, 'unfinished'. A good editor – at *Antaeus*, maybe, or the *Iowa Review* – would surely spot the talent. Jack pictured it all – the editor's enthusiastic reply, Jack's revelation of his little subterfuge, Carlos's gratitude and subsequent glittering career (not too glittering, of course). Jack smiled as he emerged from the subway station, warmed by the fantasy.

He caught the eye of a woman walking towards him – stylish, self-possessed, maybe forty-five, very attractive. As she passed, she gave him a look of cool amusement, as if to say, 'Yes, I'm marvellous. Thanks for noticing. Now get lost.' Jack loved women like that. He wondered where she was going, whether she was married, what she liked to talk about. He began to compose a scene in his head: a dusky summer's evening, two people in a restaurant, both attractive and intelligent – himself, say (a little thinner), and the mystery woman (a little younger). They would be arguing – an intellectual argument, not a domestic squabble, but with an undertow of intimacy. She would be married, or unavailable for some reason, but the reader wouldn't know that yet. He could see the woman leaning towards him, her face beautiful and fierce, her expressive hands cutting the air as she –

Wait. Here was the pizza place. Jack pushed the door open and sniffed appreciatively. He was starving. He'd grab a slice and take it home to eat in the back yard, so long as the mosquitoes kept their distance. As he debated what to choose, his thoughts turned to Freya, wondering if she'd be in the apartment when he got back. Probably. She didn't seem to be having much of a social life at the moment. Poor old Freya. Her attempts to find Mr Perfect weren't working out; they never did. Look at all the losers and bores she'd hooked up with over the years. Women acted so picky; then they went and chose a dud. No wonder she was so bad-tempered; it must be frustration. She should just dip in and out of the sexual smorgasbord, as he did. Of course, that was easier for men.

Suddenly Jack had a marvellous idea: why didn't he buy Freya a pizza, too? He knew what she liked: no mushrooms, no pepperoni, double anchovies and lots of olives – black not green. It would be a peace offering. He'd played a mean trick on her, but the Bernard thing was only a joke. She was a good sport; she'd get over it. Jack pictured his arrival at the apartment. She'd be washing her hair, or watching TV; she wouldn't have bothered to eat, so she'd be hungry, and grateful. They'd sit outside and talk. He'd tell her about Candace's cloak-and-dagger act in class tonight, and make her laugh. It would be like old times.

# 15

Freya could bear it no longer. She shifted her weight off one numbed buttock, uncrossed her legs, and recrossed them the other way. The seat beneath her let out a loud creak, and the guy in front of her twisted his head to glare. The ring through his eyebrow gave him a particularly malevolent look.

'Sorry,' she mouthed.

She returned her attention to the stage, where an actor dressed as a Buddhist monk had been standing in the same spotlit position for the last twenty minutes, eyes lowered, palms pressed together. So far nothing else had happened. Freya wasn't sure whether this was very meaningful or if something had gone wrong back stage. This was off-*off* Broadway, after all.

Wait, she could hear something: a low, rhythmic hum like a fridge in the night. Very gradually, body parts began to emerge from the darkness of the wings – one hand, a bare foot, a flexed elbow, a head penitently bowed. Over the next ten minutes or so they inched onstage in a series of agonized t'ai chi movements, eventually revealing a group of very solemn young American men and women dressed in sarongs and shifts made of drab sacking. Brett was not among them. Freya curbed her impatience;

perhaps they were saving him for a special role – a naked god, for example. She had asked Brett about his part, but all he'd said, with that shy half-smile that seemed to sock her about four inches below her belly button, was, 'We're opening Tuesday night. Why don't you come?'

Freya's fingers tightened on her rolled-up programme as her mind drifted back to last Saturday and the image of Brett's back view cycling ahead of her – rather fast, frankly; it had taken some effort to summon a breezy smile when he looked back at her, and find breath in her lungs to answer his shouted remarks. But there had been ample opportunity to take in the athletic, pumping legs and the broad back, with its peekaboo strip of bare flesh, flaring out from taut, slim hips. Once they were in the park he had slowed his pace and started to do tricks for her – riding no-handed, slaloming along the track with a graceful weave of his body, turning back with a grin to check that she was watching, while the wind flipped up his hair. Freya laughed and began to copy him, and soon they were playing follow-my-leader. Overtaking him, Freya lifted her feet from the pedals and stuck her legs out sideways; she flapped her elbows like a funky chicken; and for a brief, wobbly moment let go of the handlebars and stretched her arms wide with a whoop of triumph. Then it was Brett's turn again. Passers-by paused to watch them, and smiled. It was fun, flirtatious, exhilarating. She realized what she'd been missing with Michael, whom she could not imagine on a bicycle, unless equipped with a safety helmet, military-style shorts and a rucksack. By the time they stopped, breathless with laughter, they were halfway to intimacy.

'Come on, you crazy girl. I'll buy you an orange juice.'

'No way. *I'm* buying.'

And they'd fought about it; and that was fun, too. Once they were in the juice bar, there didn't seem much to say. Freya liked it that way. Sitting opposite each other, he smiled at her and she smiled at him as they sucked frothy, fruity slush through straws. She discovered that he came from Denver and was one-eighth Iroquois, which explained the angled planes of his face and the slanted eyes set under straight, black eyebrows. Physically, he was the human equivalent of a T-bone steak; looking at him made her hungry. Of course he was ridiculously young. But did age really matter? In her heart, Freya felt no older than twenty-three. It was a relief to jettison all that baggage of career and family and failed relationships to be, well, just a 'crazy girl'.

Freya blinked, and refocused her vacant gaze on the stage. She really must concentrate. The humming had now been enlivened by a random warble from an unseen flute-like instrument, while the actors (pilgrims? peasants? nameless husks of humanity?) separated into groups to enact slow-motion panto-mimes – tilling soil, drawing water, scattering seeds. Centre stage, a couple appeared to be copulating joylessly; on one side of them, a woman was making heavy weather of childbirth; on the other, a tubby man lay on the floor, arms outflung, head back – presumably dead: the cycle of life, Freya deduced. She had been to art shows like this, except the crowd was better dressed.

Probably it was very good, if you were in the right mood. The audience seemed rapt. When the 'dead' man suddenly sneezed, they politely ignored him. Freya tried to rehearse what to say when she went back stage. She remembered that Noel Coward had solved this problem with 'Darling! Marvellous *isn't* the word!', but wasn't convinced she could deliver the line effectively.

A slow drumbeat began. *Bong. Bong. Bong.* The actors stopped what they were doing – all but the monk, who was still praying – and turned their faces wonderingly upwards. Was it going to rain? The drumbeat speeded up, the harsh lighting turned soft and golden, and grains of rice – real rice – began to shower on to the stage. Oh, right: the harvest. Released from their sluggish trance, the actors began to whirl and leap and stamp in a frenzied dance, while falling rice caught the light and sparkled like golden rain. Sarongs flew and shifts twirled as the drum built up to an ecstatic crescendo. After a good five minutes of this the actors catapulted themselves offstage and into the wings, one by one, until only the monk remained, impassive under a final trickle of rice that pinged on to his pate. Freya remembered now that the play was called *Grains of Truth*. Aha!

The drum stopped abruptly. In the stark silence that followed, Freya could hear the blood in her ears. The audience held its breath. Into this silence stepped Brett, dressed in a saffron-yellow loin-cloth and carrying a long wooden rake over one shoulder. Freya leaned forward. He walked with slow solemnity to the centre of the stage, lowered his rake to the floor in a graceful curve, and began to draw the piles of fallen rice, slowly and rhythmically, into a pattern, while the unseen flute recommenced its husky drone. Brett's head was bowed, his expression concentrated and inward. Golden light streamed across the stage at an angle, emphasizing shapes and shadows. Brett's body had been covered with gleaming make-up that accentuated every bone and muscle. Now *this* part of the show was very effective, Freya thought approvingly. Evidently others thought so too, for they watched in rapt attention while Brett circled the stage with his rake, round and round, sweeping the rice into a pleasing spiral pattern. When at length he reached the front he straightened up and lifted the rake back on to his shoulder. There was a final *bong!* from the drum, then the rest of the cast emerged from the wings in a dignified procession and lined up on either side of him. It was the end.

The small theatre erupted in generous applause, surprising the actors into smiles that instantly took ten years off their ages. Freya let go of her programme and clapped enthusiastically, sitting tall in her seat, her eyes on Brett. When he caught sight of her, he lost his composure and had to hide his face by bowing prematurely. Freya laughed aloud with delight.

The stage emptied, the lights dimmed, the theatre filled with the bustle of departure and a rising roar of chatter. The audience was mainly young, probably friends and rivals of the cast, with a smattering of older luvvies and professionals and a few overdressed couples whom Freya took to be parents in various stages of pride or bemusement. Freya joined the shuffling exodus, keeping her ears pricked for flattering titbits to feed Brett.

' . . . not surprised there was no interval. Everyone would've stayed in the bar . . .'

'Now *that's* what I call theatre. I feel spiritually *purged* . . .'

'Poor darling Basil never will realize that less is not always more . . .'

'I am not angry with you, Deborah. I'm simply asking why you booked the restaurant for ten-thirty if you knew the show ended at nine-thirty . . .'

Oh well, she'd have to make something up.

When she reached the foyer, Freya ducked into the Ladies to check herself out in the mirror: ripped, faded jeans teamed with an immaculate white T-shirt and minimal make-up. She had opted for the dressed-down look, one of the kids rather than the glamorous older woman. Was this right? She caught her reflection grinning at her, goofy as a teenager, and turned away, embarrassed by her own excitement. He was only a man, for God's sake.

At the stage door she joined a small scrum of hangers-on, and gave her name to the guy on the door. A few moments later Brett burst out of the exit, still in his costume, glowing and gorgeous, adrenalin pumping from every pore. Before she could formulate her congratulations, he threw his arms around her.

'Wasn't that *great*?' he demanded.

He smelt of make-up and sweat and excitement. His skin was hot and slick against hers.

'Fabulous.' It came out in a croak. She took a breath and tried again. 'Totally fabulous.'

'I wasn't sure you'd come. When I saw you there I couldn't believe it!' he gabbled. 'Listen, I'll be a few minutes. I need to help bag up the rice and get cleaned up and stuff. Will you wait?'

'Probably.' But she was smiling.

'We're all going over to Julio's to celebrate. I'll be as quick as I can.' He bounded off, then pivoted neatly in the doorway and fixed her with a slow-burn look. 'Don't go away.'

Freya shook her head. As if she could.

Julio's turned out to be a scruffy, studenty tapas bar, much frequented by the cast during rehearsals, to judge by the proprietor's ebullient welcome. In the noisy confusion of their arrival, as bags were stored and tables pushed together, Freya made her way to the bar and quietly paid for two bottles of champagne before taking her place next to Brett, now dressed in black jeans and a soft blue shirt, hair still gleaming from his shower. Everyone talked at once, drowning out the flamenco music. There was a rumour that Hal Prince had been out front. Or was it Cameron Mackintosh? No, it was Cameron Diaz. Bullshit: Cameron Diaz was shooting in Nevada; there'd been a picture in *Screen*. Well, anyway, some of the papers had sent a critic – the *Post*, *Village Voice*, *Paper*. What would the reviews say? Oh God, it was too agonizing to think about.

The champagne arrived, provoking an excited whoop and a flurry of speculation. When the waiter indicated who had bought it, eyes swivelled curiously to Freya, then to Brett.

'This is Freya, everyone,' he announced. 'She came to see the show tonight.'

There was a tiny, awkward pause. Freya saw that her extravagant gesture had been misjudged. It set her apart: not one of the kids but someone richer, superior, different – a sugar Mommy. She grabbed her glass and raised it. 'You were all fantastic,' she told the blur of young faces. 'Here's to' – her memory stumbled sickeningly, then righted itself – 'here's to *Grains of Truth*.'

The toast was taken up enthusiastically, everyone clinked glasses, and to Freya's relief the hubbub continued.

'Hey, that was really nice of you.' Brett's voice was low and warm in her ear. She turned her head to find his eyes inches from her own. The open collar of his shirt had slid sideways, revealing the smooth skin of his shoulder. She wanted to go to bed with him. *Now.*

'I got you something, too,' she said, reaching into her bag. She had spent hours trawling through the shelves of the Gotham Book Mart looking for the perfect present, toying with second-hand editions of famous plays or Broadway memoirs, before settling on a paperback copy of Anthony Hopkins's autobiography. After a great deal of thought and several false starts she had inscribed it, 'For Brett, on his opening night – one of many', signing herself simply 'Freya'.

Brett unwrapped the package. His handsome face lit up. 'Cool!' He leaned over and gave her a brief kiss on the cheek. 'Thanks,' he said. He smelt of clean, male skin.

'You're welcome,' she said lightly, and turned blindly to the person on her other side, a heavy-set young man slumped on one elbow.

'Aren't you drinking?' she asked, focusing on his empty glass.

'I couldn't.' He shuddered. 'Not after that performance.'

'Why? What was wrong with it?'

'Don't pretend you didn't notice. I corpsed.'

'You what?'

'I corpsed. I died. I might as well leave town – or shoot myself.' His expression trembled on the brink of tragedy. 'Every single rehearsal I've lain as still as a stone. Then, on opening night, I have to sneeze. I'm supposed to be dead, for Chrissakes! It was totally out of character.'

Freya reached for a bottle. 'Well, I didn't notice, and I was sitting in the fifth row,' she lied, pouring champagne into his glass. 'The way you positioned your arms,' she improvised, 'I thought that was very realistic.'

'Wes is a perfectionist. Aren't you, babe?' A woman across the table reached over and poked him in the arm. She wore her hennaed hair in pigtails that stuck out from the sides of her head, like Dorothy in *The Wizard of Oz*. Her gaze moved on to Freya and hardened. 'So how long have you known Brett?'

'About three days.'

Both women glanced automatically at Brett, who was trying not to laugh while one of the actresses dangled a spear of asparagus vinaigrette over his open mouth.

'Cute, isn't he?' said the woman.

Freya shrugged, as if she hadn't really noticed.

'You know, it's fascinating what you said about my arms.' Wes's beefy shoulder nudged hers. 'Arms are so important. I studied a lot of pictures of dead bodies to feel my way into the part. I don't know whether you're familiar with Stanislavsky's theory of Method Acting, but . . .'

On he droned. Freya noticed that he had found the courage to empty his glass after all. Meanwhile, the table filled up with small plates of olives and shrimps and smoked ham and things on sticks, and the champagne was succeeded by a rough red wine that rasped her throat. Conversation about people she didn't know, and things she didn't want to know, dinned in her ears: auditions, impro classes, throat pills, summer stock, bastard directors, what A said to B about C. Even while she spoke and listened and acted normally, more or less, she was aware of Brett's proximity, caught within his magnetic field. Every time he accidentally brushed her arm or her leg, a current of desire jolted through her. She drank steadily.

Wes was still in full flow when she felt a gentle squeeze on her leg. 'How're you doing?' asked Brett. He had a trick of looking up at her from under his eyebrows, that she found wildly seductive.

'Fine.' *Kiss me*, she ordered silently.

He leaned closer and ran the back of one finger down her bare arm, erasing her brain cells with one swipe. 'I've hardly talked to you.'

'There are a lot of people,' she said stupidly.

'We could go if you want.'

Freya bit her lip. 'Could we?'

Five minutes later they were standing outside in the hot night. The air smelled of hamburger and dirt; headlights bounced through the darkness. Good old New York.

'So . . .' Brett scuffed his sneaker back and forth on the sidewalk. 'Don't you live somewhere around here?'

'A few blocks away,' Freya agreed. She stuck her thumbs in the front pockets of her jeans and examined her toecaps, suddenly as awkward as a farm boy. 'You want to walk me home?'

Brett's smile widened. 'Sure.'

They walked a few yards in silence. *Do you have a girlfriend?* Freya wanted to ask. *What about that actress person with the pigtails? Do you think I'm attractive? How about coming to England with me?*

'I was wondering . . .' Brett began.

Freya swallowed. 'Yes?'

'What did you *really* think of my performance?'

So they talked about Brett: his talents and ambitions, and the stresses of this particular show, which was so demanding – 'mind-fuck' was Brett's expression – that they could perform it only on alternate days. As well as maintaining a peak of physical fitness, the cast was required to meditate for an hour before each performance to clear their mental space. Brett had given up red meat, doubled the frequency of his yoga classes and was seriously thinking of turning Buddhist. 'Except I'm too vain to shave my head,' he admitted, with a boyish grin that made him seem more charming than ever.

'Of course I'd like to do more commercial stuff. There's an audition coming up for *Cats*.'

'Do you know, I saw that in London on opening night.'

'But . . . wasn't that way back in the *eighties*?'

Whoops. Freya's brain whirled with mental calculations. Brett must have been – yikes! – seven or eight years old, a kid on a bike.

'School trip,' she explained blithely. 'I can't have been more than thirteen. Or twelve, even. Eleven or twelve. Though I might as well confess I probably am a little older than you . . . Almost thirty.' She sneaked a glance at his face, waiting for his reaction.

'Who cares?' Brett turned to her, looking genuinely surprised that she should think it mattered.

That was what was so great about younger men, Freya told herself: they didn't have any macho hang-ups. Plus they were younger.

Brett smiled into her eyes and dropped an arm around her shoulders. 'I like you,' he said. 'That's all that matters.'

'Good.' After the tiniest beat Freya slid her hand around his back, as she had ached to do for hours, and curled her fingers around his hip bone. They walked on together, body to body, striking sparks. The silence sizzled between them. Freya's skin tingled where his arm grazed the back of her neck. Every sense was on red-alert, yet she felt exquisitely languid at the same time. It seemed to her that they floated down the dusky streets like two sleepwalkers in the same dream.

*I like you: that's all that matters.* How true! How simple, how unpretentious. What a change from the usual jockeying for status with older men.

She stole a glance at his profile – at the sweet curve of his lips and smudge of dark eyelashes. His body felt warm and solid under her hand. She remembered the sight of his slatted ribs and flat stomach disappearing into the saffron loin-cloth. Yes, this was the answer: a younger man, eager and unspoiled.

Outside Jack's house she stopped and turned into the curve of Brett's arm. 'We're here,' she told him.

'Are we?' He smiled shyly.

Freya registered a flicker of irritation that he wasn't a little more assertive. Her own instinct was to drag him inside and eat him alive. 'You could come in for a drink, if you like,' she suggested.

His eyes met hers. 'I like.'

Flustered, she couldn't at first find her key; then she kept trying to put it in upside-down. On the way to the basement door, she had noticed with relief that the windows were dark – not that it took a genius to guess that Jack would be staying out with Candace after his class. Even if he came back late, and caught her canoodling in the darkness with a young whipper-snapper – on the couch, for example – so what?

At length, Freya got the door open and led the way inside. Before you could say 'cradle-snatcher' she had turned on a table lamp – nothing too bright – slotted Billie into the stereo, kicked off her shoes, and was in the kitchen hacking ice from the ice-tray with trembling hands. Music, lights, action!

'Great place!' called Brett from the living room.

Freya raised her eyebrows. As usual, Jack's apartment was a tip; and she'd never thought of Chelsea as particularly upmarket. But to someone sharing a room with three others it probably looked like a palace.

'It belongs to a friend,' she called back. 'I'm between apartments at the moment, so I'm using his guest room for a couple of weeks.' She paused. 'He's out tonight.'

When Freya carried in the drinks, Brett was sitting on the couch. She caught him smoothing back his hair with a nervous gesture. Weren't young men adorable? She walked across to him in her bare feet, letting her hips sway, invitation in her eyes.

'Here you go.' She leaned down to hand him his glass. At the same time he made a clumsy lunge at her arm, to pull her down next to him. Freya half-sat, half-fell on to the couch. Drink splashed down her front.

'Whoa! What are you doing?' she giggled, putting down the glasses. 'I'm soaked.' She flicked at the moisture on her T-shirt, and saw how her nipples swelled visibly through the wet material.

Brett saw too. His face grew intent. Suddenly his musky weight was on top of her, pressing her back against the couch. His lips found hers, warm and insistent. Freya closed her eyes and surrendered with a sigh, opening her mouth beneath his. Her hand slid up over his shoulder to cup the back of his neck. His tongue leapt and darted in her mouth; she felt him plucking at her T-shirt, and almost smiled at his eagerness. But the touch of his fingers on her bare skin made her catch her breath. Her back arched as his hand travelled upward; she gave a sigh of pleasure. She reached down to yank Brett's shirt free, hungry for the feel of his body against hers. She wanted more. Everything. *Now.*

Suddenly Brett pulled away. 'What was that?' he asked.

'Nothing!' She grabbed him back.

But even as she spoke, she heard it too – a scuffle in the lock, then the sound of the front door slamming.

'He-e-e-re's Jackie,' swooped a horribly familiar voice.

Freya barely had time to straighten up and pull down her T-shirt before the living room door swung open and Jack entered, stage left, carrying two pizza cartons balanced high on one palm. 'Larks' tongues for her ladyship!' he announced. Then he spotted Brett, and his face changed. He lowered the pizzas to a more conventional position. There was a charged silence.

'What are you doing here?' snapped Freya.

Jack did a comic double-take. 'I, uh, live here . . . don't I?' Now he did his Stan Laurel head-scratch. Very funny.

'This is Brett,' she told him coldly.

'And I'm Jack,' said Jack. 'Freya's room-mate. I'm gay.'

'Oh, right. Hi, Jack.' Brett sketched a nervous wave. He was now crouched on the very edge of the couch.

'Kind of dark in here.' Jack flicked on an overhead light and dumped the pizzas casually on the central table. 'Anybody hungry?'

'No!' Freya scowled.

236

'You don't mind if I go ahead?'

'Yes, we do. Can't you eat in the kitchen?'

Brett jumped up from the couch. 'It's time I was leaving anyway.'

Freya wanted to scream with frustration. 'Don't be silly. You only just got here.'

'The night is young,' agreed Jack, dropping a hunk of *quattro staggione* into his mouth. Even sitting down, he dominated the room. 'I could show you the video of me fishing.'

'No, really,' Brett stammered. 'I'm on the early shift at Bagels R Us. I should get some sleep.'

Jack cocked an eyebrow. 'You a cook, Brad?'

'*Brett!*' Freya almost stamped her foot.

'No, a waiter – well, an actor, really – at least, trying to be.'

'An actor!' Jack greeted this news with enthusiasm. 'You really should stay. Freya's probably too modest to tell you this, but she's quite an expert on the plays of Shakespeare.'

'Shut up, Jack!'

What had put him in such a vile mood? It was unbearable to watch him turn Brett into a shrinking schoolboy.

'He's joking. Take no notice.' Freya smiled at Brett and took his hand. 'Come on, I'll walk you to the door.'

She closed the living room door firmly behind them, shutting Jack out, then opened the front door for Brett.

'Jack is an oaf,' she explained, stepping outside with

him. 'Needless to say, he's not gay, nor does he possess a fishing video – just a weird sense of humour. Now where were we?'

She leaned back against the brick wall, half-hoping to continue where they left off. But it was no good. Brett was twitchy and self-conscious. 'I'll call you,' he said. 'Thanks for a wonderful evening,' she replied, and they kissed cheeks. But it was an empty ritual. The romance had gone.

She watched him walk out to the street, then stormed back into the living room, slamming both doors behind her, and plonked her hands on her hips. 'How *dare* you?' she shouted.

Jack looked up innocently from his pizza. 'What did I do?'

'You know perfectly well what you did. You scared him away. How could you do that?'

'I'm sorry. I didn't know it was such a big deal.'

'I didn't say it was a big deal. I just like him. I'd like to see him again. I'd like him to have stayed longer.'

'Oh.'

'What do you mean, "oh"?'

'Nothing.'

'Come on, Jack, you always mean something. You said "oh" as if you were surprised.'

Jack chomped carelessly. 'It simply struck me that he seemed somewhat on the youthful side. To tell the truth, I wondered at first if he'd got lost on the way home from school and was waiting to be picked up by his Mommy.'

'I knew it!' Freya spun round in a fury, slapping herself on the thigh. '*You* go out with someone ten years younger, who can barely string two woofs together, but that's just hunky-dory because you're a man. But if a woman does it – how tacky, how embarrassing, what could he possibly see in her?' Freya grabbed the back of a chair to steady herself. 'The truth is, Jack, you're selfish. You do whatever you like, but you don't want anyone else to have fun.'

'Well, if you really want to fool around with some – '

'His name's Brett. Not Brad or Brat or Skipper or Chippy or Junior or any of the hilarious alternatives I know you can dream up when you're pretending to write your so-called novel. Brett. B-R-E-T-T. Aged twenty-six, if you want to know.' She blew out a furious breath. 'At least I'm not screwing one of my own students. You can get fired for that, you know. Sexual harassment, gross moral turpitude . . . Where is the little munchkin, by the way?'

The words froze on her lips as Jack's head snapped round. 'It was you!' he exclaimed, his face dark with accusation.

'What was me?'

Jack rose from the table with a crash. 'Don't give me that "what was me" crap. Who else would use a phrase like "gross moral turpitude"? Jesus, Freya, I've been having nightmares about that letter. How could you *do* that?' He flung one of the pizza boxes at her, spattering her with tomato sauce.

'How could *I* do that?' She flung the box back. 'Who set me up with that Bernard creep?'

'You know what your problem is?' Jack jabbed a finger. 'You're jealous.'

'Jealous!'

'Yes, jealous. Because I can get any woman I want, and you can never hold on to your men.'

'You don't "get" any women, Jack. They get *you* — if they're stupid enough to want you.'

His face tightened. They were both breathing like prize-fighters.

'Isn't it time you moved out?' he asked. 'I said two weeks, tops.'

'I'll call Cat. She'll have me.'

'You do that. Meanwhile, let's stay out of each other's way.' Jack strode towards his bedroom. 'If I need to tell you anything, I'll write you a note.'

'If I'm *very* bored, I might read it.'

Jack turned, and shook his head in disgust. 'I can't believe I ever liked you.'

'You used to be different.'

'I used to be a lot of things.' He banged the door behind him.

# 16

'Ms da Fillipo, is it all right if I go now?'

Cat looked up from her desk to see her new assistant, Becky, hovering in the doorway, her bag already hooked over her shoulder.

'It's just that it's my boyfriend's birthday,' Becky explained. 'There's going to be this big dinner, and I need to get dressed up.'

Cat checked her watch, amazed to find that it was getting on for six o'clock. 'My God, what happened to today?' she demanded.

Becky stared at her dumbly with anxious eyes. Cat noted the gleam of her freshly washed hair and the flush on her smooth young cheeks.

'So . . . can I go?' she repeated.

'Of course you can go.' Cat beamed her warmest smile, trying to dispel an unwelcome image of herself as a terrifying old dragon standing guard over a beautiful princess. 'Have a great evening.'

'Thanks.' Becky's voice was breathy with relief. Just before she made her escape, she turned back and added politely, 'You, too.'

Cat nodded. She could tell that Becky found it inconceivable that someone as boring as herself – an unmarried woman heading for forty, living alone, wedded to her career – could possibly have a great evening. Which just showed how wrong you could be. As it happened, Cat was meeting her brother for a movie and dim sum – and looking forward to it. She glanced out at the sky, sallow with heat and humidity, and decided to go home first to freshen up. Besides, she needed to feed her neighbour's cat, which she had volunteered to take care of in her own apartment so that the neighbour could visit her daughter in Florida. Stanley was a fat neutered tabby who was already beginning to wear a hollow in the seat cushion of her best chair, but he was an affectionate old thing. He was company.

Cat sorted through her papers and stacked them in order of priority: an injunction to keep a violent man away from his wife; that custody dispute that had suddenly turned nasty; evidence to sift in a case of sexual abuse of a two-year-old child. However much City Hall boasted of zero tolerance and the 'new', cleaned-up New York, the city's social problems were as severe as ever. The new measures simply swept them under the carpet; it made her mad as fire. Cat shut down her computer, packed up her briefcase, and checked her desk for anything she might have forgotten. Her eyes rested for a moment on the bunch of flowers that had arrived yesterday from the florist's, accompanied by a card that read: 'With so much gratitude – and good luck with your young man! – Jessica Blumberg.' She turned and marched towards the elevator.

It was, of course, out of the question that Michael Petersen could ever be *her* 'young man'. That would be unforgivably disloyal. Michael Petersen had dumped her best friend – just tossed her out on to the street without warning. Cat stabbed the 'Down' button. The bastard! The brute! She couldn't imagine what crazy impulse had made her invent that silly story of a broken engagement. Maybe she had felt sorry for him because of his cold. She'd fallen for that old sympathy trick before. Think of Whiny Wayne. And Deathbed Doug.

The elevator doors slid open. Cat wedged herself into the crowded car and stared blankly at the jacket of the man in front of her. To be scrupulously fair – and Cat prided herself on her fairness – Michael wasn't quite as obnoxious as she'd imagined. She hadn't expected him to have a sense of humour ('canine apportionment'!); and he'd been very nice to his mother. She approved of that, even if the mother sounded a nightmare. He wasn't bad looking, either. Those nice brown eyes were deceptively warm and honest, and she'd always liked that kind of hair – thick and springy, with a kind of kink to it. In actual fact, when Mr Blumberg had made them hug each other she had felt a spark of attraction – well, more of a thunderbolt. Cat lowered her eyes. That showed how untrustworthy one's baser instincts could be. It was just as well she had given up men for good. Imagine being engaged to a guy like that! Yes, imagine . . .

She gave a start when the elevator bumped to a

halt, and walked briskly through the lobby. *Get real, Caterina*. Apart from anything else, Michael would never go for her. If he hadn't thought Freya good enough, with her gorgeous legs and classy accent, he was hardly going to fall for a dumpy Italian from Staten Island. Cat smoothed her canary-yellow dress over her hips. She would put Mr Michael Petersen right out of her head. Fortunately, she was unlikely to see him ever again.

But as she pushed through the revolving door to the street, the very first person she saw was Michael. He was standing a little way down the sidewalk, gazing distractedly into the sky as if he was trying to memorize something. Cat's heart tapped a Fred Astaire number in her chest, and in a very un-Catlike manner she bolted back inside and hid behind a large pot plant. Fumbling frantically for her sunglasses, she slid them on to her nose and peeked out cautiously. She was not hallucinating. It was definitely him. What was he doing here?

She watched him smooth his hair. He looked nervous, and rather forlorn. Was he waiting for someone – for her? Explanations darted through Cat's brain. Maybe there was a loose end on the Blumberg case; or he wanted to consult her on some general legal point; or he'd decided he wanted Freya back, and needed her help. The brute. There was only one way to find out.

Cat came out of the door like a bullet and marched

right up to him. 'What are you hanging around here for?'

Michael gaped at her. A slow smile of amazement lit his face. 'I – I was waiting for you.'

'Why?' snapped Cat. He wasn't good-looking, he was gorgeous.

'Caterina . . . could we go somewhere for a cup of coffee?' Michael gestured vaguely at a coffee shop across the street, but his eyes were fixed on hers with mesmerizing intensity.

'Okay,' Cat heard herself say. Quickly she tried to regain control of the situation. 'But not that place. Their coffee tastes like goat piss. Let's go around the corner.'

They walked in nervy silence. Holy Mary! What had made her say 'piss' out loud? He already had her down as a loud-mouthed, bossy feminist – not that his opinion mattered in the slightest.

Café Ole was the usual affair of white walls, blond wood, hissing steel machines and classical music on the sound system. Michael insisted that she sat down at a small table, while he lined up for their order. The chair beneath her was utterly ordinary, but Cat felt as dizzy and disorientated as if she was perched on the edge of a precipice. Something terrible was about to happen – or something wonderful; she couldn't tell which. For someone who had always boasted of having a brain in her head and two feet planted firmly on the ground, this was unnerving.

Michael brought two cups over on a tray. His movements were neat and careful. He had nice hands, with clean, blunt nails. When he sat down opposite her, barely two feet away, his physical presence seemed overwhelming. Her painfully sharpened perception registered the weave of his shirt, the spirals of his ears, a shallow cleft in his square chin.

'So what did you want to talk to me about?' she demanded.

'Well . . .' Michael put a sugar lump in his coffee and stirred it about fifteen times. 'I wanted to thank you for helping me out with the Blumbergs the other day.' He looked up and smiled at her admiringly. 'You were fantastic.'

'I was insane!' Cat tossed her head, but she couldn't help feeling a glow of pleasure. 'Jessica Blumberg sent me some flowers.'

'I got a bottle of wine.'

Cat wondered if he had also got a card wishing him good luck with his 'young woman', and felt a blush flood upwards. 'Well, you've thanked me now.' She gave a businesslike nod.

'And I also wanted to talk to you about Freya.'

*Freya.* Of course. 'What's to talk about? You dumped her, and she's very upset. Those are the plain facts. As her best friend, I feel very uncomfortable even sitting here drinking coffee with you.'

'I didn't "dump" Freya!' Michael protested.

'What else do you call it when you invite the woman you're living with to a special dinner, and instead of – ' Cat bit back the words. It would be disloyal to reveal Freya's expectations of a proposal of marriage.

'I can see I did it all wrong.' Michael frowned unhappily.

'And now you've changed your mind.'

'No!' He looked astounded. 'Absolutely not.' He plucked rather wildly at the knot of his tie.

'You can take that thing off if you want,' Cat said.

He looked at her as if she'd made a daring suggestion, then slid the tie from around his neck and undid the top button of his shirt. Suddenly he looked much younger.

'I wanted to tell you about Freya because of what you said the other day. You seemed very angry, and I – well, I don't want you to think badly of me.'

'I see.' Cat's heart began to thump. She couldn't take her eyes off him.

Slowly and hesitantly he began to explain why he had ended the relationship as he had. The plan had been that he and Freya would go together to this wedding in England – Cat must know about that. She nodded. But as the date approached he had felt increasingly uncomfortable. He knew in his heart that the relationship had no future; and he had genuinely thought that Freya sensed it too. Much as he admired her and cared for her, they were simply wrong for each other. It was nobody's fault, just one of those things. To accompany Freya to England, and be presented to her family as her 'partner', would raise certain expectations that he realized he couldn't honourably meet. Rather than place them both in a false position, he had decided to take the initiative and discuss the situation openly with Freya. Of course, he had messed it up; he'd never been very good with words.

An extraordinary sensation came over Cat as she watched Michael's face and listened to his halting account. She *knew* this man. How and why was a mystery, but she could read the contours of his mind and heart as if she possessed a map. She saw his insecurities and kindness, his hopes and doubts, his principles and longings. She ached to reach out and touch him. Instead, she smiled into his eyes and said again, 'I see.'

Michael leaned forward. 'Is she *very* upset?'

'Who? Oh – Freya.' Cat gave a guilty start. She struggled to recapture her sense of righteous indignation on Freya's behalf, but there had been such a radical shift in her perception that she couldn't. Freya was all wrong for Michael, and vice versa: any fool could see that. Anyway, hadn't there been a breathy phone call about some hunky young guy on a bicycle? Freya wasn't exactly in mourning; it would be unfair to mislead Michael when he had been so transparently honest with her. 'She'll get over it,' Cat said briskly.

'It was my own mistake,' Michael admitted. 'That first time I saw her, she looked so beautiful and lost. I had this . . . fantasy, I guess, of making her happy.'

'You're a romantic,' Cat told him. Suddenly, she felt indescribably happy herself.

'Am I? No one's ever called me that before.' But he looked rather thrilled. 'Actually, I think I bored her sometimes. She's so quick-witted and reckless. Do you know she once lost *fifty dollars* in a poker game?'

'No!' Cat widened her eyes, teasing him.

Michael acknowledged his own stuffiness with an abashed chuckle. 'I guess lawyers *are* kind of boring.'

'Well, thanks!'

'Not you, of course. You could never be boring, Caterina.' He smiled with such warmth that Cat's defences melted further. It wasn't disloyal just to *talk* to Michael. She decided that she'd tell Freya that the two of them had met – but that's all. There could be no virtue in troubling her with a more detailed confession that might, quite unnecessarily, throw a spanner into their long friendship.

Michael and Cat began to talk about law – where they had each studied, how they liked their jobs, that pig of a judge who always made their female clients cry. The conversation caught fire, and before they knew it they were vigorously debating the relative merits of the botanical gardens in Staten Island and Minneapolis, by way of New York politics, Cat's relatives in Calabria and the appropriate use of truffle oil. Michael didn't seem to be having any problem whatsoever with words. He leant across the table to her, eager and bright-eyed, completely transformed from the man she'd encountered with the Blumbergs two days ago.

'What happened to your cold?' Cat asked suddenly.

'Gone! I went to that place you recommended, and they gave me some amazing stuff.'

'Really? You went there?'

'Of course.'

Cat felt ridiculously flattered.

'You know, it's so funny we never met before,' Michael said. 'I used to hear about you all the time: Cat this, Cat that.'

'And I used to hear about you. Michael, Michael, Michael. But Freya's always been sort of secretive.'

'Maybe she didn't think we'd get along,' Michael suggested.

They looked at each other. Neither said a word, but the truth rose warm and palpable between them. They got along just fine. Cat felt she could sit here with him for ever.

'Oh my God!' she exclaimed, looking at her watch. 'I have to go.'

Michael's face fell. 'Already?'

'I'm meeting someone.'

'Oh.' He looked completely crushed. 'Of course. I see.'

No, he didn't see, the great lummox. 'I'm meeting my kid brother,' she told him. 'Well, he's almost thirty but you wouldn't believe the messes he gets himself into.'

'Brother,' Michael echoed, cheering up.

'Youngest of five and spoilt rotten. I'm going to

read him the riot act tonight. Now, where did I put my briefcase?'

'It's here.' Michael reached down for it. 'I wish I'd had a big family,' he said. 'They sound such fun. I'm the only one.'

Another door opened in Cat's perception. She had the sense that Michael had been on his best behaviour all his life – devoted son, good grades, solid job, decent citizen. Yet there were other, more passionate impulses straining to break free. His wooing of Freya, fervent if wildly misguided, had been one example. Cat thought – in fact, she very much hoped – that lying in wait outside her office today was another. But what if she was mistaken? Michael hadn't suggested another meeting, and any minute she'd be gone. She stood up reluctantly. 'Time to catch that subway.'

Michael jumped to his feet and asked politely if he could walk her to her stop. He opened the door for her, and insisted on carrying her briefcase. Oh, this was so regressive! Cat loved it. And she loved the way he used her real name. 'Cat' was the pugnacious lawyer, the dependable friend, the upfront city girl; 'Caterina' was someone much more feminine and mysterious. She could see this other self reflected in Michael's ardent face every time he glanced at her, though still he said nothing aloud. Unconsciously she began humming a tune that had been playing in the coffee shop – the duet from *La Bohème*.

Michael stopped dead in the street and turned to her. Speculation leapt in his eyes. 'You like opera?'

'Of course I like opera. I'm Italian.'

'Even . . . Wagner?'

'Especially Wagner.'

He gave a great sigh, as if a weight had slid from his shoulders. 'That's good. Because it just so happens that I have an extra ticket for the *Ring Cycle*.'

# 17

Jack:

Called Cat today, but she was in a meeting and couldn't talk. Says she'll ring me back. Please explain the situation if she calls when I'm out.

Messages:
1. Ella wants you to call her a.s.a.p.

2. <u>Voilà</u> says you're late with your review of <u>Dumb Beasts</u>.

3. The newspaper guy wants you to pay your bill.

For the second time this week I've come home to find a plate of melted butter on the kitchen table. After breakfast PLEASE remember to put it back in the fridge. (That's the big white thing in the kitchen.) – F


Freya:

So <u>that's</u> the refrigerator. No wonder my laundry never comes out clean.
Trust you're using 'home' in the purely temporary sense of the word.
No word from Cat. The meter's running . . . J

Jack:

Spoke to Cat at last. She's dying to have me stay with her, but there's a problem. Her neighbour's cat puked on her fold-down bed and she's having the mattress cleaned. So I can either stay here until Wednesday, when I'd be leaving anyway, or move into a hotel. Let me know which.

Ella called again. She wants to set up a meeting. PLEASE ring her back.

Message on the machine from that creep Leo Brannigan, too. What's going on?

By the way, Michael is NOT suing me about his trousers. Cat ran into him at some law thing and asked him straight out. So screw you. F

PS Did anyone call?


Freya:

So Cat's cat opened the bed all by himself! Smart pussy – or the least convincing excuse I've ever heard.

Since you ask so prettily, okay: next Wednesday LATEST. And you can pay the newspaper bill.

No, anyone did not call. Actors are busy fellows: all those yodelling classes and hair workshops.

Is it you who bought that indigestible white stuff in the cellophane wrapper? Found it in the refrigerator and tried some in my sandwich today. Not a success, even with Hellmann's and dill pickle. Must be some English delicacy – tripe??? J

Jack:

Ha ha. Lots of women chill their underwear when the weather's hot. Leave it ALONE.

Your father rang – what a charmer! I understand genes often skip a generation. He wants you to go over to his hotel for cocktails at 6.00 on Sunday – call his 'usual suite' to confirm. He invited me too – said I sounded 'a delightful young lady'. Can't wait to meet him. F

PS. See giant cockroach (trapped under glass). I knew this would happen.

Freya:

Don't get excited: Dad will flirt with a baked potato if there's nothing better around. Besides, you're way too old for him. But thanks for passing on the invitation, which Candace and I will be delighted to accept.

Garbled message on machine from Tash – about

bridesmaids, I think. Laughed so hard trying to picture you in pink satin I missed most of it. Is there something you feel you should tell me?

Took the cockroach back to JBJ Discount. The assistant confirmed it was a Madagascan Hissing Roach, <u>not</u> indigenous to Manhattan, bought yesterday by a 'tall blonde lady'. I explained that my wife had mental trouble and we'd decided on a dachshund instead. Good joke, though!

Oh – almost forgot. Your young gentleman caller called. B-R-E-T-T (though I understand the final 't' is silent). He wonders what you're doing Saturday night. I said you'd probably be washing your hair, but I'd put in a good word for him. Here are a few favourites: discobolus, crapulent, prestidigitation, sesquipedalian, hippogryph, polyanthus.

Or was it Bernard?

No, Brett, I'm almost sure.

Anyway, it began with B. – J

Jack:

Here's my rent money. Thanks for another wonderful week. F

PS. Steven Spielberg called – wants to buy movie rights in <u>Big Sky</u>. He left a number, but I didn't have any paper so I wrote it on my hand. Then I washed your dirty dishes . . . Silly me!

PPS. It was Brett.

# 18

Strawberries . . .? Or raspberries?

Freya barely hesitated before adding both to the mounting pile in her shopping cart. She gave a happy sigh. It was Saturday morning. Seven hours from now Brett would be picking her up at the apartment for a night out – their first real date. *Hubba hubba!* as they said in America.

She had woken early, wound tight with anticipation. By eleven she had worked out at the gym, eaten breakfast, spied a fabulous dress in the window of a Village boutique and bought it, and returned to find the apartment silent and Jack apparently asleep. Still brimming with energy, she had decided on a trip to the food stores, to stock the apartment with goodies. It was not, after all, impossible that Brett could still be around tomorrow, or for some days (and nights) to come. A healthy young man like that needed feeding. Jack could have the leftovers for his sandwiches.

Freya pushed her cart over to the pastry section, wondering if Brett liked croissants for breakfast. Or would he prefer muffins? Or pancakes? Or eggs? Maybe he ate that super-healthy cereal stuff that looked like gravel chippings. Freya decided to buy the lot, and threw in some organic goat's yoghurt for good measure. She was tasting salamis at the deli counter when she felt a tap on her shoulder.

'Hello, Candace,' she said, surprised. 'How are you?'

Candace stuck out her tongue.

Freya flinched. 'Yeuch! What's that?'

'A tongue stud.' Candace looked smug. 'It's a surprise for Jack.'

'Yes . . . I imagine it might be.'

'He wouldn't let me see him all week because of the teacher/student thing. So I thought, why not seize the opportunity? It takes a few days for the swelling to go down.'

'Wasn't it horribly painful?' The silvery chip was embedded like a gob of fat in Candace's purplish tongue. Freya decided to forgo the salami.

'Jack's worth it. Actually, I came in here to buy him coffee and stuff for breakfast. You guys never have anything to eat in your apartment.'

'We do now.' Freya gestured at the cart. 'In fact, I'm very glad you turned up, Candace. After I've bought some cheese, you can help me carry everything home.'

Candace responded to this request with surprising enthusiasm. She was a good-natured girl, Freya realized, even if her elevator did not quite reach the top floor.

'How's Jack?' asked Candace, while Freya fretted over the ripeness of the *Torta di San Gardenzio*. 'I didn't want to call him because my tongue made me talk funny.'

Freya frowned. 'We're not on speaking terms.'

'That's too bad. I thought you were such good friends. Jack's told me all about you – how you came to New York without any money and put yourself through art school, and did all those awful jobs, and how you discovered that famous artist, and how you two lived in the same rooming-house and always went to the movies together.'

'My goodness, Candace, are you planning to write my biography?' Freya didn't know whether to be annoyed or flattered by the extent of Jack's revelations.

'I was jealous,' Candace confessed. 'Crazy, isn't it? But I kept pestering him, until he explained why he could never feel that way about you.'

'Ditto,' agreed Freya crisply.

'You two should make up. Everyone needs friends in this world.'

'Fine with me.'

'Let me talk to him. He could at least be grateful that you're buying all this stuff for the apartment.'

'Well, it's not exactly – '

But Candace had spied the magazine rack and darted away. She rejoined Freya at the check-out, and even tossed in twenty dollars towards the bill. They walked back together, arms wrapped around big brown bags, sunglasses slipping in the heat.

'They say it could get up to ninety today,' said Candace. 'I'm like totally smothered in sunblock.'

'Gorgeous, isn't it?' said Freya, daydreaming about Brett and tonight. Her new dress was short and strappy, in a shade of aquamarine she knew suited her, made of a strange, stretchy fabric that glistened like fish scales. She wondered if she should buy some of that fake-tanning stuff to warm up her pale skin. Should she put it on all over, or only on the bits that showed? What if she turned orange? She sneaked a glance at Candace's skin for comparison, lavishly exposed by a scarlet mini-dress with bows tied at the shoulders, and a generous impulse slipped past her guard.

'I think I should warn you: Jack's father is in town, and he's invited you and Jack for drinks tomorrow evening. At the St Regis.'

'The St Regis!' squeaked Candace. 'The one with all the marble, and a little brass house for the doorman?'

'Jack's father has a special suite.'

Freya watched the implications sink in. After a pause Candace asked, 'Are the Madisons – I mean, are they an *old* family?'

'God, no! *Arrivistes* of the 1930s, I should think, but stinking rich. You're an American, you know how these things work: Madison Street, the Madison Foundation, Madison Civic Center, the Madison playground for disadvantaged children – all that crap. Mind you, Jack's Dad must be slashing his way through the family fortune with all his alimony payments; he gets divorced on a regular basis. With luck, Jack won't inherit a penny.'

Candace was silent – probably nervous, poor thing.

'Don't worry.' Freya gave Candace an encouraging smile. 'I've spoken to Mr Madison on the phone, and he sounds delightful.'

'I think I'll wear my black.'

'Perfect. I'm sure he'll love you.'

Back in the apartment they deposited their groceries on the kitchen floor with grunts of relief. There was no sign of Jack; his bedroom door was still shut.

'I told him I'd be here by noon.' There was an edge of exasperation in Candace's voice.

'No doubt you can find a way to wake him up,' said Freya, thinking of the tongue stud.

But Candace had other ideas. She went into the living room and reappeared shortly with a music tape in her hand, which she held up for Freya's inspection.

'How about this?'

Freya grinned. 'Yep, that should do it.'

Within five minutes Jack appeared in the doorway, sketchily dressed in jeans and T-shirt, aghast to find the apartment rocking with music, the kitchen floor strewn with bulging shopping bags, and Candace and Freya reading aloud to each other from a women's magazine.

'What's going on?' he growled.

'Hello, Jack.' Candace flashed him a smile, then turned back to Freya. 'Okay, next question. "You're at a club with your date, when a gorgeous hunk cuts in and asks you to accompany him to Paris for a weekend of passion. Do you (a) tell him to get lost;

(b) collect your passport and go; or (c) say, 'Great! Let's make it a threesome'?"'

'Definitely c,' answered Freya, in high spirits. 'It's a quiz,' she told Jack. ' "How sexy are you?" I think I'm winning.'

'Dumb-belles of the world, unite! You have nothing to lose but your brains.' Jack exuded masculine scorn. 'How can anyone be expected to write the Great American Novel when they're swamped by trivia?'

'Were you writing? We thought you were asleep.' Candace caught Freya's eye and giggled at her own boldness. 'Still, now that you're here, you can help us put away all these wonderful groceries Freya's bought for you.'

'What?'

Candace stood up from the table, pulled something at random from one of the bags – a package of rice – and dumped it into Jack's arms. 'Food,' she explained. 'For you. All you have to do is put it away.'

'But I don't even know where – '

'In here,' said Freya, who had stationed herself by a cupboard on the far side of the kitchen. 'Come on, chuck it over.'

'And I'll stash the cold things,' Candace volunteered. She pulled open the fridge door and stood beside it, hand on hip, smiling expectantly at Jack.

'This is ridiculous,' he said, still holding the rice as gingerly as if it was a new-born baby.

But at that moment 'Saturday Night Fever' pounded out of the stereo, and a sudden madness overtook them all. Candace started it by waggling her hips to the music and beckoning to Jack like a siren. Infected by the beat, Freya copied her. She'd scored forty-six out of fifty in the quiz, which put her in the 'red-hot' category. Thinking of Brett and tonight and how she'd look in the aquamarine dress, she laughed into Jack's outraged eyes and undulated her long body.

With a sudden God-help-me grin, Jack capitulated. In a flash he had tossed Freya the rice, bent to one of the grocery bags, armed himself with a banana and a cucumber, and was stabbing the air, north-east and south-west, John Travolta-style. Candace whooped with delight. Encouraged, he spun around and treated them to the sight of his thrusting backside as he stabbed again, this time north-west and south-east. After that, there was no holding him. He did a kind of limbo dance with a strawberry before snapping it in two with his teeth. He shook packets of dry pasta like maracas. He clashed tins, juggled grapefruit, spun frozen pizza on one finger, and tangoed with Aunt Jemima's Pancake Mix. Candace laughed so hard she dropped the eggs. Jack stubbed his bare toe on a table-leg. Freya lobbed things higgledy-piggledy into the cupboard with a huge grin on her face. She'd almost forgotten that Jack could be like this. And he did have a great bum.

When the track had finished they collapsed at the table, laughing and out of breath. Two eggs were cracked, several apples bruised, and the pitta bread that Jack had frisbeed across the kitchen had failed to survive the trip, but everyone was in a good mood. Candace put coffee on the stove, Jack squeezed fresh orange juice, Freya sacrificed Brett's putative muffins to the general good, and the three of them breakfasted together, talking companionably of nothing in particular.

'So what are we doing tonight?' Candace asked Jack.

'Whatever you want. See a movie. Grab something to eat. Why, do you have something special in mind?'

'Yes, I do.' Candace straightened in her chair, important as a pouter pigeon. 'I think it would be a lovely idea if we invited Freya to join us.'

'*What?*' Jack and Freya pounced as one.

'Look how friendly you two can be if you only make an effort. Socializing improves relationships: it's a known fact.'

'Thanks, but I have plans,' Freya said coolly.

'Why, what are you doing?'

Freya gritted her teeth. 'I am going out, Candace. With a man.'

'Oh yes, so you are!' said Jack, with that hearty bonhomie Freya had learned to distrust. 'Freya has a new boyfriend,' he stage-whispered to Candace.

Freya felt herself start to blush, and gabbled on to hide her embarrassment. 'We're taking the train out to Coney Island, as a matter of fact. Very tacky, Candace. Not your scene at all.'

'But I adore Coney Island!' Jack protested. 'I haven't been there for – well, probably not since I went with you, Freya. Was that the time Larry lost his hot dog on the Wonder Wheel?'

'I've always wanted to go to Coney Island,' Candace announced, clasping her little hamster hands. 'It sounds so much fun.'

'No,' said Freya, feeling trapped.

'A double date!' Jack enthused. 'Very retro. Very Travolta. Heck, where'd I put my white suit?'

'No,' she repeated.

'I think it could be a really, like, bonding experience.'

'I said no! And that's final.'

# 19

' . . . He was a left-hander, of course – tall guy, graceful as an acrobat – and he hit that ball clear over the lights in right field. You should have seen it, Brett.'

'Sounds a cool game, Jack. There's something about left-handers that gives them that extra edge. Do you remember when the Tigers . . .?'

The two men moseyed on down the boardwalk, beer cans in hand, shirtsleeves flapping in the off-shore breeze – oblivious of the last shreds of purple twilight and brightening stars, blind to the gaudy funfair delights around them, and totally ignoring the two women who trailed at their heels – like a couple of housewives from the burbs, Freya thought savagely. She had told Jack to 'be nice' to Brett, not to turn the evening into a symposium on bloody baseball.

'The cuticle's the really important part,' Candace twittered at her shoulder. 'My manicurist swears that – '

'How can you call it the *World* Series when no other nation even plays baseball?' Freya yelled at the men's backs.

At the sound of her voice, Brett and Jack turned politely, finished what they were saying, and gave her identical, preoccupied smiles.

'Hmm . . .?'

'What's that, Freya?'

She toned down her glare. 'I was just wondering: are we going to do something, or what?'

A split-second glance of understanding passed between the two men. Brett came over and took her hand. 'Of course.' He smiled at her. 'What do you want to do?'

'I dunno,' she murmured, swinging his hand.

She wanted him to tell her she looked beautiful. She wanted to put her lips to that boyish groove at the back of his neck, where a soft ducktail of black hair met tanned skin. She wanted to laugh and be silly. She wanted to fall in love. Or something.

So they went to a shooting gallery. Candace let Jack show her how to line up the gun, wriggling and giggling in the circle of his arms so that she missed every time. Freya meanwhile armed herself with her own rifle and hit three targets with three shots.

'Ten in a row, and you get a prize. Come on Brett: your turn.'

Cheered on by Freya, he got another three points; then passed the gun on to Jack, who won three more. That was nine: one to go.

'Here, Brett, you take the last shot,' Jack offered courteously.

'It's okay.'

'No, go ahead.'

'No, really – '

'What about me?' Freya demanded.

'It's Brett's job,' Jack insisted.

Poor Brett, nervous under the intent stare of three pairs of eyes, missed.

'Too bad.' Jack gave him a hearty clap on the shoulder, smiling genially down from his superior height.

Freya linked her arm protectively with Brett's. 'Never mind,' she told him. 'What shall we do next?'

Brett gazed about him vaguely. 'Whatever you want.'

'We don't have to stay with the others, you know.'

'That's okay. They seem really nice.'

'Do they? Well, all right. But no more talking about sport.'

'Yes, boss.'

The four of them strolled on through the amusement park, washed this way and that by the mainly black crowd – harassed Dads chasing after runaway toddlers, large women ladled into shorts, children glued to their cotton candy, teenage girls wearing almost nothing, tenuously paired with teenage boys apparently dressed in the clothes of their much bigger brothers. Coloured lights flashed as the fairground machines swooped and spun. Music thumped. Loudspeakers touted prizes and trinkets in nasal Brooklyn accents. Salt hung in the humid air and clung to the skin. Freya had suggested Coney Island to Brett because it was cheap and different, and because that's where she'd often gone to have fun when she was twenty-six. Its glory days as the 'World's Largest

Playground' for New York's huddled masses were long gone: by day it was a junkyard of clapped-out equipment and hot-dog stands, with grim tenement blocks on one side and a strip of trampled beach on the other, packed with oiled bodies and beach umbrellas. But at night, when darkness hid the litter and peeling paint, the combination of bright lights and the slow lap of the ocean gave it a kind of magic. Freya showed Brett her favourite landmarks – the sea-serpent humps of the old wooden roller-coaster; the famous stall that had sold frankfurters and fabulously greasy crinkle-cut chips for almost a century; the lights of Rockaway Point across the inlet, with the black ocean beyond, rolling its way to Europe.

'I can't believe you've never been to England,' she told him, as they leaned elbow to elbow on a railing, staring out to sea. 'It's absolutely brilliant for theatre. You'd love it.'

'My aunt went last summer. She said it rained every day.'

'We do have roofs, you know. And umbrellas. If you, er, won a free air ticket, for example – you'd go, wouldn't you?'

'Of course – depending on my work.'

'What? You'd pass up a free trip to England just to slog your guts out at Bagels R Us?'

Brett frowned. 'My acting work, I mean.'

'Oh. Yes. Of course.' Freya flushed at her *faux pas*. 'But *Grains of Truth* is closing on Wednesday, isn't it?'

'Thanks for reminding me.'

For despite the audience's enthusiasm on opening night, the reviews had been so-so. There was talk of a Boston venue, but nothing had been settled.

'I'm sure you'll land another part soon,' Freya said.

*But not too soon*, she added silently. The spare plane ticket to England, bought originally for Michael, still lay snugly next to her own in the airline wallet in her suitcase. She could just see herself at Tash's wedding with Brett on her arm, indisputably desirable – a trophy escort. *Twenty-six, actually*, she'd say, if anyone asked. There would be no need to explain her single state; its attractions would be obvious. Freya stole a glance at Brett's sculpted profile. He was handsome, fun, sexy – and he liked her. He would jump at the chance.

She now set herself to the task of being the life and soul of the party, with particular reference to Brett. She dragged them all into the Hall of Mirrors and persuaded a grotesquely short, fat Brett to declaim one of his audition pieces. Then they rode on the Dodgems, swirling giddily around the black-rubber floor to ear-splitting technobeat. Freya let Brett drive, while she muffled her ear against his shoulder and urged him to crash into Jack and Candace. Somewhere along the line Jack won a goldfish, which he gave to a little girl who was crying because she'd dropped her ice-cream out of its cone. Brett won a Coney Island baseball cap, and insisted on wearing it backwards, even though Freya told him he looked stupid with a tuft of hair poking out like that. Eventually their meanderings brought them into the criss-cross shadows beneath the huge wooden piers that supported the roller-coaster. Above them, they could hear the escalating rattle of cars speeding overhead, then a chorus of screams as they plummeted downwards.

'The Cyclone.' Jack rubbed his hands in anticipation. 'Hold on to your stomachs, folks.'

'Is that thing safe?' asked Brett, peering up dubiously.

'Course it's safe,' swaggered Freya. 'I've been on it loads of times. Four tickets, please,' she told the attendant.

But at this point Candace put down her tiny, sandalled foot, scarlet nails and all. Nothing would induce her to step inside one of those death machines.

'Well, I'm going,' Jack declared.

'So are we,' said Freya firmly, looking at Brett.

He ducked his head. 'It's okay. You go. I'll stay and keep Candace company.'

'She'll be all right.' Freya flapped her hand, as if swatting a fly.

'Thank you, Brett.' Candace gave him a dazzling smile. 'How very gallant.'

Before Freya could protest further, Jack had bought two tickets and was leading the way up to the waiting cars. Freya followed grumpily. This was not at all what she had planned. She took her place beside Jack, then glanced back to where Candace and Brett seemed already absorbed in conversation.

Jack followed her gaze. 'How could Candace even

think of another man when she has *me*?' he teased.

Freya twitched a shoulder.

'Not that young Brett isn't a delightful piece of arm candy.'

'What a revolting phrase! Brett is a nice, intelligent, charming person – not a fashion accessory.'

'If you say so. Doesn't have much of a head for heights, though.'

'He's being gentlemanly – something you wouldn't understand.'

They strapped themselves in and sat in silence, waiting for the cars to fill up. The air was warm and humid, almost tactile, like velvet against her skin. Every time she moved, her dress gleamed with a silvery light. It was funny that no one had been moved to compliment her on it. Was it too short, too tight, too teenage? She fiddled self-consciously with the skirt, trying to stretch it down over her thighs.

'You know, the first time I ever came to Coney Island was with you,' said Jack.

'Was it? I don't remember.'

'We came with Larry, and that Spanish girl from downstairs who drove us wild with her guitar, and some weird vegetarian person in a headband.'

'Ash.' Freya smiled at the memory. 'Ashley Franks, sculptor and bean freak. He thought all the world's geo-political problems could be solved if only we ate more beans. And I thought he was marvellous. Briefly.'

'You all seemed so exotic. I felt like Gulliver.'

Freya nodded dreamily, staring at her knees.

'You had long hair then. When we went on the Cyclone, I remember it streamed across my face, blinding me. I didn't know if I was up or down.'

'No danger of that tonight.' Freya ran a hand over her boyish crop, wondering if his words were an implied criticism. 'Did you ever call Ella, by the way?'

'We're meeting Monday. Don't nag.'

The car began to move, ratcheting its way up the first steep incline, hoisting them into a sky now truly dark, with a sliver of moon hanging high over the ocean. At the top it wobbled perilously for a few gathering seconds.

'We're going to die,' said Jack, stating a fact.

Freya felt her body tense with a mixture of terror and exultation. She filled her lungs with air as the car tilted sickeningly into a nose-dive. '*Eeeeeeee . . .*' she screamed.

'*Aaaaaah . . .*' roared Jack.

Eyes squeezed tight-shut, Freya gripped the safety bar and abandoned herself to the plunging, lurching, oaring movement. There was thunder in her ears; wind rushed into her open mouth. Up and down and up and around they went; then again, that thrilling leap into the sky. Any second they were going to hurtle straight off the track into space, but she didn't care. She felt as if she could fly all the way to the stars.

The roller-coaster slowed at last, and trundled back to its starting point. Freya let out a shaky sigh and blinked her eyes open.

'I've just thought of a scene for a novel.' Jack's

breath tickled her ear. 'A proposal of marriage on the Cyclone. Wouldn't that be great?'

'Hmmm. Sort of *Strangers on a Train* meets *North by Northwest*?'

'Exactly. How well I've educated you. When I first met you, the only Hitchcock movie you'd seen was *Psycho*.'

'But the Cyclone's so noisy. She'd never hear the question; and if she did, he'd never hear the answer.'

'That would be part of the plot: the psychological complication.'

Freya turned to look at him. His hair stood up on end, as if he'd been electrocuted. 'You know your problem, don't you?'

'Too perfect? Too brilliant?'

'You're a fantasist.'

'I'm a writer.'

*Writers write*, Freya almost said. But she was in too good a mood to start a quarrel with Jack. 'And I'm starving,' she announced, climbing out of the car.

'Me too. What about heading over to Brighton Beach for some vodka and seafood?'

Freya groaned aloud at the temptation. 'We can't,' she said. 'Brett couldn't afford it, and I don't want to embarrass him by paying myself. We'll have to make do with a hot dog or some clams.'

'The last time I ate clams off the street I spent the next day hugging the toilet bowl. What if I pick up the tab?'

'Great!' she said, accepting this magnanimous offer.

'You can pay me back afterwards.'

When they emerged into the crowds, Candace and Brett were nowhere to be seen.

'Maybe they've eloped,' said Jack.

'There they are.' Freya pointed up some steps to the boardwalk, where a group of black teenagers was dancing in a tight, jittery circle to some unseen source of music that pounded out a hiccuping rhythm. The two white faces bobbing at the edge of the circle were easy to pick out.

'Where?' Jack peered, fumbling in his shirt pocket for his glasses.

'Come on, let's join them,' she said, hurrying ahead.

But when she reached the group, she didn't have the nerve. The sheer intensity of the dancers, absorbed and unsmiling, excluded her. She watched Brett twirl his limber body, arms high in the air, while Candace jiggled and swayed. When the track ended, Brett threaded his way over to her. His eyes were shining; heat rose off his body like steam. 'That was fun,' he said breathlessly.

'Time for dinner,' Jack announced, taking command. 'My treat.'

He set off down the boardwalk with Candace, casually holding the back of her neck between thumb and forefinger in a gesture Freya had seen in countless American high school films. For the first time in years, she longed to be cute and kittenish, so that Brett would drape a proprietary arm around her, too, instead of bouncing along beside her, hands in his pockets,

276

talking about clubs and bands she'd never heard of.

The lights and noise of the funfair receded, until all they could see, when they looked back, was the glow of the big wheel, pink and purple against the black sky, its tiny cable cars glinting like charms on a bracelet. Suddenly everyone around them was white and speaking Russian: elderly couples walking their dogs; young girls in tight, chattering groups; middle-aged women in halter tops and miniskirts, black roots showing through their bleached hair, looking for Saturday night excitement.

'This is incredible!' exclaimed Brett.

Freya smiled back. 'Russian émigrés started settling here back in the fifties. They call it Little Odessa. I thought you'd like it.'

They came to a strip of beach restaurants, with tables outside, crowded with families and festive parties. Pretty waitresses in short aprons carried trays back and forth from the steamy back kitchens, under the watchful eyes of the proprietors, sinister in dark glasses and soft white shoes. Lively band music wafted out across the sand. The atmosphere was wholly European: no hamburgers, no musak, no Manhattan execs, no Fifth Avenue divas starved to perfection – just the clink and roar of ordinary people having a good time. Freya always imagined that this was how it must be in summer on the Black Sea.

Eventually Freya spotted an empty table, and they sat down. Jack took charge of the ordering: vodka, of course; eggplant caviar, potato salad, smoked eel –

'And herrings,' Freya reminded him. 'Those fat, pickled ones.'

'Good thinking.'

'And beetroot with sour cream.'

'Yeah, yeah. Who's ordering this anyway?'

Freya left him to it, and went to the loo, accompanied by Candace.

'I love Brett,' Candace confided from the next cubicle. 'He's a riot.'

'Good.' Freya frowned at the back of the door. She hadn't seen as much as she would like of Brett's riotous side. He didn't seem to have grasped that this was supposed to be a heavy date, not a jolly outing.

While washing her hands she stared at herself critically in the mirror. 'Tell me, Candace, what do you think of this dress? Truthfully. Do I look stupid?'

Candace turned from her own reflection to scrutinize Freya, giving the question serious consideration. 'You can get away with it,' she concluded kindly. 'You're very well-preserved.'

When they returned to the table, Jack was telling Brett his old joke about the Pole and the eye chart.

' . . . and the Polish guy says to the optician, "Can I read it? He's my cousin!"'

'That's not how it goes,' Freya objected, taking her seat opposite him. 'He's supposed to say, "That's my *uncle*."'

'What's the difference?'

'I'm just telling you how it's supposed to go.'

'It doesn't matter how it goes, so long as it's funny. Brett laughed. Didn't you, Brett?'

'Absolutely. Very funny, Jack.'

Jack jutted his chin at Freya. 'QED.'

'The QED,' Candace breathed rapturously. 'I've always wanted to travel on an ocean liner.'

'Me, too,' agreed Brett.

Freya's eyes met Jack's. She couldn't help it: she laid her head on her arms and howled.

'What's so funny?' demanded Candace.

But all Freya could hear were Jack's deep, infectious guffaws; she laughed until her eyes streamed.

Finally Brett – nice, sweet Brett – said, 'Private joke, I guess. Let me pour you some more vodka.'

The food arrived in a succession of small dishes. Freya explained each one to Brett, and popped delicacies into his mouth. Conversation flowed back and forth: body-piercing, apartment rentals, the horrors of open auditions, the artificiality of bestseller lists.

Brett was impressed to discover that Jack had published a book. 'What name do you write under?' he asked.

'His own, of course,' Freya chipped in quickly. She knew that this was number one in Jack's chart of crass things to say to an author.

'Oh, right.' Brett nodded. 'I'll look out for it in the library.' That was number two.

Freya moved the conversation on to the subject of Russia and Russians, though this led to another sticky moment when Jack and Brett locked horns over the Second World War.

'But the Russians were our enemies,' Brett insisted.

'They weren't, you know,' Jack said mildly. 'Think of Yalta.'

Brett looked ruffled. 'Well, in all the movies I've ever seen, the Russians were the baddies.'

'Absolutely right, Brett.' Freya kicked Jack under the table. 'The Cold War and all that.'

Jack looked at Freya open-mouthed. She gave him a quelling look. Brett might not be Einstein, but she would not have him squashed by Jack. She had not chosen Brett for his academic qualifications. Fortunately, at this moment Candace started to tell them all about a TV show she'd seen, featuring an unspeakably evil character with a Russian accent. Brett had seen it, too, and the two of them launched into an animated discussion. Freya hadn't a clue what they were talking about. In the end she gave up and chatted amiably enough to Jack. The uneasy thought occurred to her that a stranger observing their table might pair off the four of them in a different way from the reality.

Meanwhile, the noise level rose implacably. Around midnight the singing started – jolly, rhythmic songs involving repetitive choruses and clapping. Then dancing broke out, as twirling girls in nylon disco-dresses spilled outside, eventually sweeping all four of them into a ragged line that hopped, bopped, kicked and sang its way around the tables. Freya held on to Brett's waist. His shirt hung loose; her thumbs grazed his warm, smooth skin. She closed her eyes and pressed her cheek against his bouncing back. Her head spun. It was time to go home.

Not for nothing was the train back into the city known as the Trans-Siberian Express. The view was monotonous, the journey interminable, and the other passengers as cheerful as transported prisoners – apart from Candace, still firing on all cylinders, who swung herself round and round one of the metal poles, singing 'I'm as horny as Kansas in August' and waggling her tongue-stud at Jack. Thank goodness we're not so blatant, thought Freya, sitting with her arm linked in Brett's, his baseball cap on her head. She had started calling him 'Brettski'.

'You don't mind if Brett stays over?' she had asked Jack in a private moment during dinner.

'Does he want to?'

Freya glared. Well, of course he'd want to! Jack acted as if he was the only person in the universe entitled to sex. 'His bicycle's at the apartment,' she'd answered evasively. 'With all this vodka, I'm not sure he could make it back to his place anyway.'

'Bet you wouldn't care if *I* had to cycle across town.'

'You? Don't be ridiculous.'

'Candace is coming home, too, you know. There won't be much privacy.'

'Honestly, Jack, don't be a prude.'

But when they finally tumbled into the apartment, Freya felt the awkwardness of their situation, as the four of them stood blinking at each other in the over-bright living room. It was two in the morning. Too much alcohol and the long journey home had taken the gloss off the evening. As Jack had hinted, the geography of the apartment was not conducive to privacy. Both bedrooms gave on to the living room, and shared one wall that was only partially sound-proofed by closets. To reach the bathroom from either, one had to traverse the open arena of the living room.

'Who needs a drink?' demanded Freya, wanting the party mood to continue – to carry her into romantic oblivion.

But Candace had already grasped Jack by the waist-band of his trousers, and was pulling him backwards towards his bedroom. 'You're coming with me, loverboy.'

Jack spread his hands helplessly. 'When you gotta go, you gotta go.' His smug expression seemed to linger, Cheshire cat-like, even after the bedroom door had closed behind the pair of them. Freya took it as a challenge.

She fixed a couple of drinks in the kitchen and carried them back over to Brett, who was sitting on the squashy arm of a chair, jiggling one leg. She'd forgotten that about young men; it must be all the testosterone. From Jack's room came a high-pitched giggle and the squeak of bedsprings.

'So, Brettskowich.' She ruffled his hair. 'Alone at last.'

The door of Jack's bedroom opened, and he

emerged, loosely wrapped in a towelling robe, long belt trailing. 'Still here, Brett?' he said, and headed for the bathroom.

Brett stood up. 'I think – '

'So do I.' Freya seized Brett's hand and led the way to her bedroom. 'Let's go in here. Then we won't be bothered.'

She flicked the door shut behind them, and leaned her weight against it. Light slanted in from the street, throwing Brett's face into shadow. His eyes glittered as he turned to look at her.

'Did you have a good time tonight?' she asked.

'Sure. It was great.'

He stepped towards her with a smile. His hand reached towards her face. At last! 'You've got my baseball cap,' he said, removing it.

It seemed to Freya that her heart was audibly knocking against her spine; then she realized that someone was tapping on the door at her back. She opened it a couple of inches. Candace pushed her way into the room, rosy and voluptuous, half-wound in a sheet.

'Oh, good, you're still dressed. I know this is really embarrassing, but does either of you have any . . . protection? Jack and I have gone lickety-split through our entire supply.' She looked from one to the other, smiling her pert smile, as unembarrassed as anyone Freya had ever seen. 'This is, like, a major emergency.'

Freya waited in vain for Brett to say something. Why did men always assume that this kind of thing was a woman's responsibility? Abruptly she crossed to the suitcase that doubled as her bedside table and pulled out a packet of condoms. She tried to hide it in her hand, furious to be forced to reveal that it was a brand-new packet, as if she had bought it especially for tonight. Which she had.

'Here.' She thrust the condoms into Candace's hands.

'Thanks,' gasped Candace. 'You saved my life. Literally.' She waggled her fingers at Brett and Freya – 'Have fun, you two!' – and hurried away, the sheet trailing behind her.

'Wait, Candace!' Freya sprinted out of the room and managed to catch her outside Jack's door. 'I need some too, you know,' she whispered furiously.

'Oh, sorry.' Candace began picking at the cellophane wrapper with her scarlet nails. 'How many do you need?'

'For God's sake! How many do *you* need?'

There was the sound of a toilet flushing, and Jack loomed out of the half-dark. 'What's going on?'

'Nothing,' snapped Freya.

A smug expression crept over his face as he noticed that Freya was still fully dressed. 'Brett gone home?'

'One, two, three, four, five, *six* condoms.' Freya counted them into her hand. 'That ought to last us till tomorrow morning. Thanks, Candace. Sweet dreams, Jack.'

'Oof! . . . aah . . . mmm . . .' Jack lay back on the bed, not altogether comfortably, while Candace snuffled and bounced around on top of him. Ouch – that was his stomach! He shouldn't have eaten so much.

Six condoms. *Six!* Was she showing off, or was he getting old? Or had he never been that good? For the record, he'd never received any complaints in that particular department – at least, not of the 'not enough' variety. The more usual female accusation was 'too much sex' – though what a contradiction in terms that was! – like a trustworthy politician, or a cute Dobermann.

Jesus, what was happening? Women shouldn't be allowed to whip their hair around like that. They could blind someone. Jack rearranged his head on the pillow and closed his eyes again.

*That should last us until tomorrow morning.* Assuming 'tomorrow morning' counted as, say, ten o'clock, that meant six times in under eight hours, which was once every hour and twenty minutes. Or, if you assumed four hours' sleep, once every forty minutes – six times in a row.

Shit.

Jack held his breath for a few seconds, straining to hear any sounds coming from next door, but Candace was making too much noise. Normally he rather enjoyed her running commentaries, but tonight he didn't seem able to focus properly. He wondered if Brett and Freya could hear her – or were they too busy? Busy doing what? Not talking about Plato, he bet. Freya was usually so dismissive of people who weren't as intelligent and quick-witted as herself, as

Jack knew to his cost. She'd never behaved with him in the girlish, simpering way she had tonight; or flaunted herself in a skimpy dress like that. He scowled. What exactly did she see in this six-times-a-night Brett character?

Maybe he'd sneak out in a minute and see what was going on. It was his apartment, after all. And he was getting awfully hot for some reason. He could do with a glass of water.

But just then Candace did something really rather amazing. Instantly Jack's conscious mind short-circuited into oblivion, as his brain prioritized a quite different part of his anatomy.

'I mean, Arthur Miller's a good playwright, but so is Andrew Lloyd Webber. My agent says I'm perfect for the juvenile lead in musicals, but I don't want to get typecast. What do you think?'

'I think you'd be wonderful in both.' Freya wriggled downwards on the bed, and stretched out one long leg to touch Brett's thigh encouragingly with her bare foot. Hmm. Solid muscle. Pity he still had his trousers on. 'Someone with your looks – and your talent – is bound to be successful.'

'You're just saying that.' He gave her foot a playful caress, sending desire shooting up her body. But almost at once he pulled his hand away again, looking nervous.

A throaty cooing was coming from Jack's bedroom, which Freya took to be Candace in the throes of passion. Initially, Freya had found this irritating; now she was beginning to hope that Brett would take the hint, but so far the noises from next door had had the opposite effect. Brett seemed to prefer to perch cross-legged at the end of her bed while she leaned against a pillow at the top end – for all the world like two fifth-formers in the dorm. She'd heard of foreplay, but this was ridiculous. Still, he was only twenty-six, poor boy. Naturally he would be in awe of her greater experience and, let's face it, her superior intellect. All this talk was a cover for perfectly understandable shyness. Somehow she must signal her availability.

She stretched her arms languorously above her head and gave a deep, sensuous sigh. Brett looked up. She smiled.

'Ready for bed?' he enquired.

Eureka!

'Aren't you?' Her body was turning to soup in anticipation. 'Why don't you come up here so I can examine you properly.'

Brett laughed uncertainly, as if she had cracked an obscure joke.

If the mountain would not come to Mahomet . . . Freya curled herself slowly on to all fours and crept panther-like down the bed. When she reached Brett she gave a soft growl, sat back on her haunches and slid one hand between the buttons of his shirt and on to the flat, hard plain of his stomach. Brett tensed.

'Relax . . .' she told him.

Her fingertips traced the silky arrow of hair leading

downwards. She found the dip of his belly-button and stroked it gently. Next door, the coos were turning into deeper moans, interspersed with excited yelps. She thought she caught the word 'stallion'.

Brett gave a nervous laugh and sat up. 'I'm not sure – '

'Forget about them.' Freya's voice was soothing. 'They don't matter.'

'I don't think – '

'Don't worry. You'll be fine.' Freya reached for him again. He was so warm, so smooth, so firm, so –

With a suddenness that shocked her, Brett broke away and stood up. 'Guess I'll go home now.'

'What?' Freya blinked at him from the bed.

'It's late. I should get back.' Brett started to tuck in his shirt.

'But – why?'

'I feel . . . uncomfortable.'

Freya knelt on the bed, her arms wrapped tight around her stomach, pressing against the pain of her desire and her disappointment. 'Why?' she asked again.

Brett ducked his head in a way that was now sweetly familiar. 'I don't fit in here. Weird vibes and stuff. I don't want to get into anything heavy, you know?'

Freya struggled to decode this. Had she somehow offended him? Did he feel snubbed by Jack? Was she put off by the activities next door? Didn't he *like* sex?

'You're not gay, are you?'

'No!' His chin came up. 'And I'm not a toy-boy either.'

'*What?*'

'I mean, you were the one who decided where to go tonight, like you're in charge or something. You talk about stuff I don't know about and pat me on the head like I'm six years old, and then you expect – ' He broke off, shifting his shoulders in embarrassment.

Freya stared at him, aghast. She could decode this all right. He was telling her she was too *old*. She became aware of a rhythmic banging from Jack's room, as if someone were hammering a nail into the wall.

'Right.' She stood up in one swift, smooth gesture and looked Brett in the eye. 'That's pretty clear.'

'Wait.' He put a hand on her arm. 'What I mean to say is, I like you. I like talking to you. And you're very attractive. But maybe we can be, you know, just friends.'

'Sure.' Freya managed a shrug. 'I'm going on holiday next week anyway. I might give you a call when I get back.'

'Great.'

She opened the door of her room and led the way across the living room to the hall, where Brett had left his bike. She could read his hurry and his relief in the way he unslung his helmet from the handlebar and laid his hands on his beloved machine. She prickled and stung and smarted with humiliation. Unlocking the front door, she held it open for him.

'Well, goodbye,' he said awkwardly, as he pushed the bike past her. She could see him wondering if he should give her a peck on the cheek. This was excruciating.

'Wait. Don't forget your baseball cap.' She fetched it from the bedroom, plonked it on his head – the right way – and gave the peak a playful downward tug, like she was someone's really fun aunt. Then she folded her arms across her chest and stood back.

'See you, Brettski.'

'Bye.' He scooted down the path and disappeared into the night.

For several moments Freya stood on the threshold, breathing hard through her nose. She wanted to shout after him, 'It's only sex, you know. I wasn't planning on *marrying* you.'

But she burned with shame and self-disgust. How could she have put herself through such indignities? She stomped around the front yard, torturing herself with the scenes of her humiliation. Even sprawled across the bed in the semi-darkness with her skirt rucked up, she had not been desirable. Even though Brett was drunk and tired, he had preferred to go home. Then there was that tell-tale 'but'. *You're terrific BUT . . . I really like you BUT . . . You're very attractive BUT . . .* It had been exactly the same with Michael. Why did men always want to be 'just friends' with her? She gave the rubbish bin a kick. Even her friends didn't want to be friends with her any more! Look at Cat, who had fobbed her off with the feeblest excuse in history and wasn't returning her phone calls. As for Jack . . .

A drunk was cursing his way down the street towards her. It was time to go back inside. Freya closed the front door quietly and stood in the living room, listening. All was quiet. She pictured Jack and Candace drifting off into satisfied sleep, and stamped her foot. She felt scorned, rejected, crushed, and – *dammit!* – frustrated. But worse than everything would be Jack's triumphalism when he discovered that Brett had fled. How he would swagger. How he would chortle with Candace, sexpot of the universe.

Unless . . .

Freya prowled around the living room, trying to psyche herself up. 'Mmm,' she began tentatively. 'Aah . . . ooh . . .' She leapt on to the couch and padded squashily up and down. 'Oh, Brett,' she projected throatily in the direction of Jack's bedroom. 'That's so *gooood*.'

Freya located a broken spring in the couch, which twanged in a deeply satisfying manner. She began to bounce up and down on it, flinging her arms about for good measure. 'Ah . . . ah . . . aaah!' She teetered across the couch's fat arms and along its back, occasionally hurling herself on to the seat with an uninhibited cry. 'Oh *yes*! . . . oh, Brett . . . oh – '

A shadow moved at the periphery of her vision. She froze. It was a person, carrying a glass in one hand.

'Having a good time?' enquired Jack.

# 20

Jack's father had always been a stickler for the outward forms of social behaviour. A true Southern gentleman, he liked to claim, was invariably punctual, courteous to the ladies, and mindful of 'dressing nice' – by which he meant a jacket, tie and real leather shoes with laces. (Slip-ons were for women, foreigners and Yankees.) It was therefore a well-judged twenty minutes late, wearing an open-necked shirt and sneakers, with Candace scurrying disregarded behind him, that Jack timed his appearance in the King Cole Bar of the St Regis Hotel.

Because it was a Sunday, and still early in the evening, the panelled room was sparsely populated. Even if it had been packed to bursting, Jack could have located his father simply by searching for the figure of a waiter deferentially bowed over one of the tables. At every establishment he patronized, Jack's father quickly appropriated a crony from among the staff, whom he would introduce as 'my old friend Alphonse' or 'Eddie, best barman this side of the Mason-Dixon line', before despatching them to perform some extra-curricular service. Sure enough, there in the far corner his father was comfortably ensconced at the best table in the place, shooting the breeze with some butler-type in white gloves. Jack could guess with near-certainty the topic of their one-sided conversation: either 'Bourbons I have known' or 'New York: hell-hole of the universe'.

Candace grabbed his arm. 'Is that him?' she whispered.

'Yep.' All day she'd been pestering him for details, until he'd finally snapped, 'He's just my Dad. You'll see.'

Now she gave an approving murmur. 'Isn't he handsome? He looks just like you.'

'Well, he's not.'

As he approached the table Jack experienced a confusion of filial emotions – defiance, resentment, guilt, and a kind of familiarity that approximated to affection, though he told himself it was probably no more than a crude genetic tug. Right now defiance was uppermost. He was *not* returning home to work in the family business, even if his father begged. He *was* going to ask for an increase in his paltry allowance – nothing excessive, just a reasonable increase in line with his age and lifestyle.

His father rose from his chair, as tall and as broad as Jack, looking pleased to see them. His moustache had been newly clipped; his thick white hair was scrupulously parted and combed: a handsome man, indeed, though he had turned sixty-five.

'Jack, my boy. Good to see you.' He clasped Jack's hand warmly, raising his other arm to clap Jack on the shoulder in a gesture that was part biff, part manly hug.

'And you.' Just in time, Jack bit back the 'sir' that had been drummed into him from an early age. 'This is Candace,' he said, presenting her like a trophy – or a shield.

His father's face intensified with interest. He liked women, and they liked him. Jack had protested that there was no need for Candace to get all dressed up just to meet his father, for godsakes, but he couldn't help feeling gratified by her glossy appearance in a subtly sexy black dress.

There was the bustle of seating themselves and deciding what to drink. Jack's father suggested a glass of pink champagne to Candace; both became positively rapturous about the fact that she'd never tasted it before – how thrilled she would be to try it, how honoured he was to give her the opportunity, blah blah. Just to be annoying Jack ordered a beer. In the course of this farcical rigmarole he and Candace were introduced to 'my good friend, George', the still-hovering waiter.

'Any time you'all want to drop by here, George will take real good care of you. Won't you, George?'

'It would be my pleasure, Mr Madison.'

'Why, thank you, George.' Suddenly Candace was acting like the Queen of England. 'Isn't that nice, Jack?'

Jack shrugged. 'I don't get uptown much.'

He knew that he sounded graceless, but couldn't

help it. There had been a time, in his teens, when he'd revelled in his position as 'the Madison boy'. Everywhere he went there had been a special golf caddy, a favoured barber, even a friendly police officer to smooth his path or turn a blind eye. His father had taken pleasure in initiating him into the rites of manhood – more specifically, into being a Madison. Ever since Jack had been returned by his mother to his father, like a reclaimed parcel, there had been ritual visits to the paper mills that were the foundation of the family fortune. Jack remembered feeling excited yet overwhelmed by the towering skips full of old rags, the great rolling machinery leaking oil in factory rooms as cavernous as cathedrals, the heat and the noise and the foul stench, like a dead beast rotting, that flowed out across the countryside and made Minnie the housekeeper insist, when he got home, that he took off his clothes 'right this minute' so they could be laundered. If his father had never uttered the exact words, 'One day, son, all this will be yours', they were implicit in the pride he expressed when Jack made the football team or dated the prom queen or caught his first fish – even when he got drunk on hooch and threw up all over the front porch. He was 'Little Jack', who would one day grow up to be 'Big Jack', just as his father had stepped into the shoes of 'Big Daddy Jack'. Except that he wasn't, and he didn't, and he wouldn't.

His father was telling Candace about the hotel, how it had been built for John Jacob Astor at the turn of the century, with crystal from Waterford and marble from France, in response to his demand for the finest hotel in the world. 'And in my opinion, it still is,' he said, 'even with all the new gadgets they put in during the renovation. I'll get George to show you around in a little bit, while Jack and I have a private talk. Would you like that?'

Candace wriggled her shoulders and said that she would love it. 'And is Mrs Madison here with you?' she enquired.

Jack's father looked surprised; then his eyes crinkled into laughter, and he went through an absurd panto-mime of patting his pockets. 'Nope. Don't believe I've got one with me today.' He winked at Candace and smoothed his moustache. 'Already got four wives scattered across the country – and that's four too many. Cost more 'n a decent fishing-boat these days.'

Candace gave him a look Jack could only describe as saucy. 'You're not telling me you prefer fish to women, are you, Mr Madison?'

He patted her knee delightedly. 'Well, now. That depends on how much of a fight they put up.'

Jack twisted his glass round and round, his face stony. He was long used to his father's high-flown gallantries, but that Candace should flirt back seemed a betrayal. He wondered exactly why he persisted with Candace – apart from the obvious. In the South there was a clear distinction between 'nice' girls and 'trashy' girls, though nice girls could be very trashy indeed, and trashy girls nice – but you never married them. Which was Candace, he wondered?

He listened to her prattle on about her life, glowing under the attention.

'I don't know how you all survive up here,' marvelled his father, 'with the noise and the dirt, living in those little bitty cells you call apartments.'

'I know what you mean.' Candace sighed wistfully, as if her true spiritual home were a country mansion patrolled by servants.

'Everybody looks so tired and frazzled – except you, my dear. Work, work, work, that's all these Yankees seem to think about, even on a Sunday.' He gestured across the room at a huddle of men in suits poring over conference folders.

'Dad, those are Japanese businessmen.'

'So you say. Seems to me anyone can be a Yankee these days. You don't even have to speak English.'

'I'd love to visit the South one day.' Candace leaned forward confidingly. 'You have so much history – and all those beautiful trees!'

'You'll have to get Jack to bring you down for a visit.'

'Oh, would you, Jack?' Candace turned to him in a swirl of perfume. 'It sounds such a beautiful state.'

Jack took another sip of beer. 'We'll see.'

North Carolina *was* a beautiful state, bounded by the Atlantic on one side and the Blue Ridge Mountains on the other, with rolling hills in between. The place was in his blood, and he loved it, but he couldn't live there. Even now, when he visited, he chafed at the seductive pull of history, the oppressive weight of family. To live in a town where everyone knew you, where your last name was a passport to privilege or a brand against you, where you were never free of the danger of running into someone who had dandled you on their knee, or danced with your mother at a cotillion, or who knew your crazy Aunt Milly who heard voices, or whose great-great-granddaddy had fought with your great-great-granddaddy at the Battle of Wherever-it-was: for Jack, once he grew up, it was like living in a very luxurious padded cell, with a straitjacket on his imagination. He didn't feel *real*.

They made small talk while Candace sipped her champagne. When her glass was empty, Jack's father summoned the obliging George to take her on a private tour of the hotel.

'Man's talk,' he explained to Candace with a wink. 'You understand?'

'Of course.'

'Good girl. Now take good care of her, George, y'hear?'

He withdrew his eyes with difficulty from her sashaying back view.

'Pretty girl.'

Jack nodded his agreement.

'Not one of those ball-breaking career women you get up here.'

'No.'

'Seems to me she's not the same woman I talked

to when I called your apartment last week – someone with a British accent?' He shot Jack a sly look.

'That was Freya. She's staying in my apartment.'

'Oh ho.'

'She's just a friend, Dad.'

'Hmm.' His father winked, and rattled the ice in his drink. 'So tell me, son, how is everything?'

'Pretty good.'

'Finished that book yet?'

'Almost. I've been side-tracked by a lot of journalism recently. That's the only stuff that pays.'

'Miss Holly still looks out for your articles, you know.' Miss Holly was Jack's fourth-grade teacher, now semi-retired, who helped out in the archives of the Oaksboro Public Library. 'I hear she's got quite a collection. 'Course she's pretty well senile now.'

Jack grunted, and waved a hand as if it was of no importance to him what Miss Holly did. He was well aware of local reaction to the news that he had 'gone North' to be – wait for it – a writer! New York was a den of iniquity where people went 'hog wild'. Writing was eccentric at best, sissy at worst. A state that had suffered a painful defeat in war – and for Southerners the Civil War was still a raw wound – could not afford to breed sissies. Jack felt that they were all waiting for him to come home with his tail between his legs, admit that he'd finally got that funny ol' literary bug out of his system, and settle down like a normal person. Not one of them had *any idea* of how difficult it was to write a novel.

His father waved over one of the under-waiters to bring more drinks. This time Jack ordered bourbon. Mentally he rehearsed his speech: the cost of living in New York, the incompatibility of writing fiction and journalism, his certainty that he was on the brink of a major success, if only he could buy himself a little more time. But before he could find an opening, his father leaned easily back in his seat, spread his manicured hands on the table, and began to speak.

'I'm glad we have this chance to talk, son. There've been some changes at Madison Paper, and I think it's only right to let you know what's going on in the business, even if you've never shown much interest.'

'It's not that I'm not interested, Dad. It's only – '

'I know. You've chosen to do things differently. That's why I want to talk to you, bring you up to date.'

His father began to drone on about foreign competition and new markets; labour laws and tax breaks; new technologies expensively implemented and take-over threats successfully routed. One member of the Board had died, and another was retiring . . . Jack stopped listening to the words. He thought he knew where this was leading. Sure enough, his father began a long ramble about their search for a new Board member – someone with a connection with the business, someone he could trust –

'Dad, stop right there.' Jack raised his palm. He smiled at his father, to show that what he was about to say was not meant to offend. 'I know I'm the eldest son, and I know you're thinking of my own good, but

I have to tell you that I can't come home to help run the business.'

His father looked so shocked that he added, 'I'm sorry, Dad.'

His father burst into a loud guffaw. 'You!' he exclaimed. 'Run the business!'

Now it was Jack's turn to be shocked. 'Well . . . isn't that what you're asking?'

His father brought his laughter under control. 'Jack, you've been up here in New York *ten years*. What could you possibly know about running a paper business?'

Jack stared at him, feeling utterly stupid. He was aware of the fuddled look on his face, and the dead weight of his hands in his lap.

'Of course, if you wanted to come home, I'd try to find you a position of some kind.' His father frowned dubiously. 'But it wouldn't be very well paid. You don't have any of the appropriate skills.'

'Well, maybe not. But – ' Jack broke off, confused. 'Why are you telling me all this stuff about the business, then?' he asked belligerently.

'Because I wanted you to know that, as of next month, we'll be inviting your brother Lane to join the Board.'

'Lane?' For some reason, Jack pictured his brother in his high-school football outfit, with massive padded shoulders and a helmet masking his features.

'I know he never got the grades you did, but he understands paper.'

*Lane?* As far as Jack remembered, Lane never understood anything.

'There was a time when I hoped and prayed you'd come home to Madison Paper, but you haven't, and it's too late now. Business is business. I have responsibilities – to my employees and to the community. I need someone who is committed.'

Jack nodded, his mind in a whirl. Lane had a stuffed boar's head on his wall. He subscribed to car magazines. Lane had gotten one of the Danforth girls pregnant when he was eighteen, and she'd been sent away for a hush-hush abortion.

'Up to now, I've given both you boys allowances to help you get on your feet. Lane's been learning the paper business, and you – well, I guess you've been learning your "business" too.' His father chuckled at this quaint notion. 'Of course, Lane is younger than you, but he'll be getting his Board stipend now, so it all balances out.'

'What do you mean?' Jack was floundering again. 'What balances out?'

'I mean that I'll be terminating his allowance at the same time I terminate yours.'

*Terminating!* Jack stared at him, speechless.

'You'll always be my eldest son, and of course there will be an inheritance for you when I'm gone, but the time has come for you to stand on your own two feet. Hell, by the time I was your age, I had a wife and a down payment on my own house!'

Jack tried to get a grip. 'When were you thinking . . .?'

'Next month is the last payment.'

'*Next month?*'

His father gave a shark-toothed smile that Jack knew and disliked. 'Why wait? You tell me you're doing well with the writing, and I'm sure you are. Madison Paper is a business, not a gravy train. We can't carry passengers.'

Jack took a deep slug of bourbon. *Terminate*: the word crashed and echoed around his head. Resentment burned in his throat. His father spent more on quail-shooting than he did on Jack. Why should Lane get this so-called 'stipend', just because he'd been too unadventurous to forge his own career? His eyes skittered over his father's immaculate cream suit and dandyish tie, taking in the powerful shoulders and commanding tilt of his chin. Jack swallowed his panic, and clamped his own jaw tight. He wasn't going to beg.

But his turmoil must have shown in his face. His father frowned. 'You're not in any kind of trouble, are you, son?'

Jack looked him in the eye. 'No.'

His father's expression relaxed into a bantering grin. 'You mean you always dress like a bum? I guess that's what's called "a fashion statement" nowadays. Beats me. New Yorkers used to have such *style* . . . Like her,' he added, his eyes lighting up.

Jack turned around to see Candace approaching them at her new, queenly gait. He stood up at once, rocking the table. 'We have to go now.'

'Aw, so soon?' His father rose courteously and took Candace's hand, smiling down at her. 'Maybe you'll both join me for dinner tomorrow night?'

'I don't think . . .' Jack began.

'That would be lovely,' Candace said simultaneously.

Jack seized her elbow and propelled her forward, out of the claustrophobic gloom of the bar. They skirted the Astor Lounge, with its palms and marble and cocktail couples, past glass cases displaying handmade shirts and designer ties. Jack wanted to smash one with his bare fist. He made himself focus straight ahead, on a gilt-framed painting hanging at the end of the corridor. It was the portrait of a man not much older than himself – elegant, moustachioed, confident, surrounded by the symbols of his success. Jack made out the name as he approached: *John Jacob Astor III (1822–90)*. And here he was, Jack Madison III – penniless, ousted, disenfranchised.

Candace was rhapsodizing about electronically operated drapes and giant bathtubs. Jack met John Jacob's aloof, brown gaze. *Help! I'm drowning . . .*

## 21

Freya trudged towards the bus stop, her footsteps leaving alternate red smears on the tacky sidewalk. She'd stepped on a tube of Cadmium Red while paying a morale-boosting visit to one of her artists at his studio in Alphabet City. Normally, this was the part of her job she liked best. She loved the smell of turps and linseed oil, the stacked canvases, the clutter of spraycans and stapleguns and old rags dabbed with pigment that gave off a heady sense of work in progress. She enjoyed the peculiar intimacy of her relationships with the artists themselves – coaxing them out of the doldrums, sympathizing with their struggles, steering them down new paths, getting them to trust her. Creativity was a mystery. It was like lighting a fire without matches. Sometimes, just sometimes, she was able to fan a glowing spark into flame. There was nothing to beat that moment when they yanked a sheet off an easel or turned a canvas face-out from the wall and revealed, to her privileged eyes, the fresh, raw product of their labours.

But today she had been distracted. Matt Rivera was one of her young hopefuls, whose first solo exhibition was scheduled for the autumn. He had called her this morning in a funk, telling her that he was stuck, blocked, washed up. He would never be ready; she must cancel the show. Freya had gone straight round, and had spent half the day there talking through his problems and trying to offer solutions. But nothing she had said seemed to lift his gloom. She felt she had let him down, and she was angry and disappointed with herself.

She blinked away a trickle of sweat as she watched the bus crawl towards her through the rush-hour traffic. On days like this it seemed impossible to remember why anyone found New York glamorous. It was another day of suffocating humidity. Dirt settled on her skin. She could feel her lungs silting up with every breath. Everyone looked hassled and bad-tempered. The city was the colour of a dried scab, under a putrid bandage of smog.

The bus was packed. Stray elbows jabbed her ribs. She could smell hot rubber and other people's sweat. Her chic little work dress stuck to her back. Manoeuvring her way to a square foot of standing-room, Freya grabbed an overhead handle and stared at the ads that urged her to consider health insurance and cosmetic dentistry. She felt weary of the relentless demands of this city. Wear this. Don't eat that. Sparkle. Bargain. Push. Win. Go, go, go! Sometimes she wanted to put her hands over her ears and yell, *Wait! Slow down! I want to think*. But there was never time.

A sense of hopelessness and failure washed over her. She had built up her life in New York from scratch – dollar by dollar, job by job, friend by friend – and now it was crumbling to dust at her feet. Ever since the Michael episode she had experienced one humiliation after another – and she had a horrible feeling they were all her fault. Nothing was going right in her life. She had made a fool of herself with Bernard, and a worse one with Brett. Just when she needed a friend, Cat was too 'busy' to see her – doing what, Freya couldn't imagine. She was sick of camping in the corner of someone else's study in someone else's apartment. Living with Jack, whom she'd always got on with – *always* – had turned out to be a nightmare. But the real nightmare, her overriding obsession, the thought that made her prickle and snap with panic, squeezing out every other emotion, was the knowledge that in two days she was going home for Tash's wedding. Alone.

The apartment was silent, and almost as stifling as outdoors. Jack had done nothing about the ominous clanking of the air-conditioning; now, apparently, it had conked out. If only he were here, she could cheer herself up with a thundering good row. With a sigh, Freya pulled off her shoes, dumped her briefcase and made straight for the kitchen, where she took a beer from the fridge, flipped off the cap and drank from the bottle. She undid the top two buttons of her dress and rolled the bottle across her skin. It would almost be worth going to England for the pleasure of being positively cold in midsummer. Almost . . .

Abruptly, Freya set down her beer bottle on the table, and headed for the bathroom, unbuttoning her dress as she went. She stood under the cold, cascading water, forcing herself to concentrate on the things she had to do before she left town: bubblewrap Tash's wedding present, buy her a card, decide what clothes to take, try to cash in the spare air ticket. For there was now no use pretending that she wasn't going alone. Today was Monday; her flight left on Wednesday night – she had run out of time. *Alone*: the word lodged in her heart like a splinter.

She'd told them all – boasted, if she was honest – about bringing a 'friend' with her. Everyone knew what that meant: a lover certainly, possibly a long-term partner. She'd pictured herself swanning in from the States, cool and mysterious, with Michael in tow, protected by his mere presence from speculation or the need to explain herself. But Michael had let her down, and her efforts to find a replacement had ended in disaster. She was pathetic, ridiculous, a desperate old maid. And now she was going alone.

She knew how it would be: the house in turmoil, full of strangers; her father preoccupied; her step-mother in organizational overdrive, treating her as a useful extra pair of hands; and Tash – spoilt little princess Tash – patronizing her at every turn. Poor old Freya, who couldn't keep a man – a lonely career girl whose time was running out. When Freya explained to colleagues about her forthcoming 'vacation', they gushed with vapid enthusiasm, 'Going home? For your sister's wedding? You must be so *excited*!' They didn't understand that it wasn't *her* home and it wasn't *her* sister.

Freya stepped out of the shower and towelled herself briskly. She was a tough New York cookie now. Of course she could cope with Tash's wedding alone. She heard Cat's bracing voice saying, 'I don't *need* a man.' Quite right. Wrapping herself in the towel, Freya picked up her clothes and was walking past Jack's bedroom to her own when she was startled by a sound so familiar that she could have recognized it blindfold in the middle of a party. *A-hem.* The sound of Jack clearing his throat.

She paused by his closed door and called out, 'That you, Jack?'

'Yep.'

'What are you doing?'

'Nothing.'

'That sounds fun.'

Silence.

Freya cocked one arm on her hip. 'Great job you did on the air-conditioning.'

No answer. Had he slipped into the apartment while she was in the shower, or had he been there all along? She shrugged, and continued to her room. By the time she had changed into shorts and a faded blue cotton top she was hot again. She went to retrieve her beer and found Jack in the kitchen, a chair pulled up to the open fridge and his bare feet propped on the bottom shelf. He didn't even look up.

'Mind if I join you?' she asked.

'It's a free country.'

Freya put a chair alongside his. He moved his feet over to make room for hers on the shelf, and they sat for a while in silence, staring at the random jars of mayonnaise and pickles and grape jelly.

'It's hot,' Freya offered.

'Yeah.' Jack passed a hand over his face. He looked exhausted.

'Weren't you and Candace supposed to be having dinner with your dad tonight.'

'Yep.'

'So what happened?'

'I didn't go.'

'Why not?'

'Couldn't face it.'

'Ah.'

Freya stole a look at Jack. What was the matter with him? She'd have said he was sulking, except Jack wasn't a sulker.

'So where's Candace?' she fished.

'I let her go by herself. Dad's going to show her some of his old haunts.'

'Lucky Candace.'

Jack shrugged, as if he didn't care what Candace did.

Freya tried another tack. 'How did your lunch with Ella go?'

'I don't want to talk about it.'

'Ah.'

So they sat, not speaking, in the stifling kitchen,

until the fridge began to whine with strain. Jack's black mood seeped out of him like poison gas. Freya was tempted to leave him to choke in it alone. But what if something really was wrong? She didn't like to see him down.

'Hey.' She nudged his foot. 'I'm not doing anything tonight. You're obviously not doing anything. Why don't we go to the movies. At least we'll get some decent air-conditioning.'

'I don't feel like it. You go.'

'Don't be so boring.'

'I like being boring.'

'Oh, come on.' She stood up. 'It's no fun going alone.'

He raised his head and gave her a baleful stare. 'You just want to see some goofy chick-flick.'

'I do not.' She cocked her head. 'What's the male equivalent of chick-flick, do you suppose? Dick-flick? "Hey, Buzz, throw me the alien-zapper while I practise my ape-walk and remove my brain cells."' She did a little mime.

'Dick-flick . . .' muttered Jack, but there was a twist of a smile.

'I'll buy the popcorn,' she offered.

'Bet the butter's rancid.'

'Then we won't eat it!' Freya gave his chair a shove. 'Get up, you great lump. Let's go and see what's on. You can cheer me up with your lively personality and sparkling repartee.'

'Uh,' said Jack. He wriggled his bare toes. 'I'd have

to put some shoes on.' He made this sound on a par with climbing Everest.

'So get them! Chop chop.'

Jack kicked the fridge door shut and lumbered to his feet. 'No one would call you bossy.'

'Decisive, is the word.'

'If I was your husband, I'd go crazy.'

'If I was your wife, I'd be crazy already.'

Freya went to get her own shoes and her purse, and waited outside for Jack to lock the front door. They walked down the street together, keeping to the shade of the spreading trees that were just coming into blossom. Halfway down the block, the old Italian man was sitting out on his stoop as usual, wearing a saggy grey undershirt and drinking beer; he gave a friendly nod as they passed. Freya was beginning to like Chelsea, with its quiet streets of elegant town-houses, red brick with green trim, many of them still un-yuppified and housing large, extended families or rent-controlled tenants. She liked the small secret playgrounds and hidden gardens trailing ivy, the rusty wrought-iron railings and balustrading adorned with pineapples and acanthus leaves, and the fact that everyone seemed to own a large, hairy and beloved dog. In five minutes you could be at Filene's Basement rummaging for discounted designer shoes, or sitting at the end of a pier looking down the Hudson, all the way to the Statue of Liberty. A new riverside sports area was nearing completion; people of all ages and colours flocked here to play golf or rollerblade hockey.

One day she had been astounded to peek through a construction fence and see a horse being put through its paces by a young woman in immaculate jodhpurs and mahogany boots. That was New York for you – a place where people grabbed their pleasures by the scruff of the neck and wrung the life out of them.

Their first stop was a big bookstore on Seventh that was blissfully air-conditioned. Jack went in search of the *Voice*, so they could check the listings, while Freya took her time picking out a suitable card for Tash. There might not be much sisterly affection between them, but Freya was determined that no one should find fault with her behaviour. She made her purchase and went looking for Jack. Eventually she spotted him at one of the big tables near the front of the bookstore, apparently rearranging the display. It struck her that there was something furtive about his behaviour, and she paused to watch him work his way through a tall stack of identical books. What on earth was he doing? First he picked up a book. Holding it by the spine in one hand, he flipped quickly through the pages with the other – far too quickly to read anything, more as if to check whether something was hidden inside. Then he put the book down, not back on the pile but *underneath* one of the adjacent piles of other titles. She watched him for a full minute as he repeated this procedure without variation, then manoeuvred her way quietly to his side.

'What are you doing, Jack?'

'Nothing.' Jack snapped the book shut. She saw

that it was *Vanderbilt's Thumb* by Carson McGuire. Looking along the table, she noticed that each of the neat stacks of other titles contained a rogue copy of McGuire's novel, usually near the bottom. The original McGuire pile had completely disappeared.

'Let's go,' he said, hustling her away.

Freya followed him out, thinking of all the times she'd gone into a bookshop to put *Big Sky* on top of the 'Bestseller' piles. 'That's a bit mean, isn't it?' she said, when they were back out on the street. 'What's Carson McGuire ever done to you that you want to hide his books?'

Jack flipped back his hair. 'I'm simply checking to see if his book is really selling, or if it's all some big publicity stunt. See, whenever I find a big pile like that, I take the top copy and turn down a teeny corner of one of the pages – page 313, in fact. Then the next time I go into that bookstore I can see if the copy has sold, or if it's the same old pile.'

'And was page 313 turned down?'

'No,' Jack conceded.

'But you hid all of the books anyway.'

'People can always ask for a copy if they really want one.'

Freya snorted with laughter at this pathetic behaviour. 'You're jealous!'

Jack swivelled his big shoulders. 'Stop telling me what I am!' he snapped. 'You don't know me. Nobody does.'

Freya drew away in shock. She opened her mouth

to shout back at him, but she could see he was really upset. Instead, after a moment, she gently touched the folded newspaper under his arm, and asked in a neutral voice, 'So what shall we see?'

They stopped under a store awning and huddled close, scanning the listings. Suddenly Freya exclaimed and stabbed the page. 'Look! *High Society*.'

'Fluffy,' objected Jack. 'Fluffy fluff-fluff.'

'Romantic,' Freya corrected.

'*Bing Crosby?*' Jack's eyebrows rose incredulously.

'Frank Sinatra,' she reminded him. 'Cole Porter. Grace Kelly . . . in a swim suit.'

'Okay, you win.'

It was the perfect choice. They sat in the back row of the half-empty cinema, legs propped up on the seats in front, fingers absently picking popcorn out of a carton wedged between them in a special elbow-lock they had perfected over the years. Their crabbi-ness melted as the film spun its magic out of the darkness, enveloping them in the sunny, madcap dotti-ness of a 1950s society wedding. Crosby sang about what a swell party it was. Sinatra told Grace Kelly that he didn't care if she was called 'the fair Miss Frigidaire', because she was *sensational*. Kelly herself drifted across the screen, ravishing and impossible, trying to decide whether to marry the stuffed shirt to whom she was engaged, or the tabloid journalist who gave her the facts of life straight-up, or the man she had loved all along, only she couldn't admit it. It was pure, irresist-ible hokum. When the credits rolled, they stumbled to their feet with foolish, faraway grins and wandered outside to stand on the pavement, taking time to readjust to the heat and rush of the city.

Jack took off his glasses and folded them away. He smiled down at her. 'Hungry?'

Freya gave a languorous, Grace Kelly shrug. 'Maybe an ice-cream at that Italian place on Broome Street?'

'Café Pisa? That's on Mulberry, not Broome.'

'No, it isn't.'

'Yes it is.'

Eventually they found the narrow entrance, marked by a browning evergreen in a tub. There was a plastic replica of the Leaning Tower of Pisa in the window.

'Ha! Broome Street,' said Jack.

Freya waved airily. 'It must have moved.'

They pushed past the narrow bar where old men sat on stools drinking grappa, through the noisy, crowded dining room, and out into a courtyard festooned with coloured lights. Two concrete pillars of vaguely Ionic design stood in the far corners to add authenticity. A medley of soulful songs about *l'amore* crackled out of a perilously rigged loudspeaker. They ordered ice-cream and coffee and sat in companionable silence under a Martini umbrella. Jack twiddled the ashtray round and round. Freya leaned her head in one hand and drew patterns in the dusty table top, waiting for him to tell her what was bothering him.

Finally he turned to her. 'My publishers want to cancel my book contract,' he said.

'What?' She straightened with a jerk.

'That's why Ella wanted to see me. There's some new broom in the company whose mission is to sweep away the old inefficiencies – of which I am apparently one.'

'God, Jack. Can they do that?'

It seemed that they most certainly could, despite the pleas and protestations of his loyal editor. Jack had missed his deadline. The new regime was not only cancelling his contract for 'non-performance'; they were also demanding the return of the money Jack had already received – and spent.

'The real bummer,' said Jack, 'is that my dad has chosen this moment to cut off my allowance.'

'He hasn't!'

'So I can't pay back the money. Nor can I afford to live while I finish my book. I'm completely fucked.'

'That's awful, Jack. I'm sorry.' Privately Freya reflected that if he hadn't wasted so much time going to book parties and fooling around with dimbo girl-friends, he could have finished long ago, but Jack looked so stricken that she hadn't the heart to tell him so. 'What are you going to do?' she asked.

'I don't know.'

'What does Candace think?'

'Uh, I haven't told her yet.'

'I see.'

'I'll have to give up the apartment, maybe leave New York for good. Get a job.' He raked his fingernails through his hair, pushing back the thick, unkempt swathes. For the first time Freya noticed two faint lines scored across his forehead. 'I don't know,' he repeated.

'At least you don't have to worry about me,' said Freya. 'I've found a sub-let.'

'You're moving out?' He sounded surprised.

'Yep. I'll take all my stuff away on Wednesday and dump it in the new place, ready for when I get back from England.'

'Oh yeah ... England.' Jack frowned. 'I forgot about that.' He scraped up the last of his ice-cream and dropped his spoon in the bowl with a clang. 'Well, that's my life down the drain. What's your excuse?'

'My excuse for what?'

'For your peculiar behaviour over the past couple of weeks. You're worried about something. I can tell.'

'No, I'm not.' Freya stuck her chin in the air. 'And there's been nothing "peculiar" about my behaviour.' Apart, she admitted privately, from answering lonely hearts ads, picking up young men, writing anonymous letters, simulating sex, and pretending to be a Mexican maid.

Jack gave her a look. 'You can't fool me,' he said.

In the end she found herself trying to explain the problem of a single woman of a certain age attending the wedding of her much younger sister – worse, stepsister – without an escort. It was uphill work.

'What's the problem?' Jack was mystified. 'Pick someone up when you get there. I've always found weddings a rather fertile hunting ground.'

'That's because you're a man.'

'What's the difference?'

Freya goggled at him. 'Who exactly do you think is going to pick me up?'

'I would.' He grinned.

'No you wouldn't – not when the place is crawling with scrumptious twenty-five-year-olds.'

'Ah. I take your point. But I'd still pick you up.' He smiled winningly. 'Speaking of scrumptious twenty-five-year-olds, why don't you take Little Lord Fauntleroy with you?'

'If you mean Brett, that's over.' Freya folded her arms primly. 'No, I shall go alone. At least that means I won't be encumbered when I meet Mr Perfect. Correction: *Lord* Perfect.'

Jack frowned. 'You can't do that.'

'Why not? You just said weddings provided fertile hunting grounds.'

'But then you might stay in England, and start wearing headscarves. I'd never see you again.'

'So? You're the one who's talking about leaving New York.'

'Yeah, but – '

'In a few months' time maybe neither of us will be here.'

Jack looked momentarily shocked by this thought, then gave a hopeless shrug. 'You're right.'

'Mind you, I'm still holding you to my birthday dinner, wherever we are. A bet's a bet.'

'The eighth at eight.' Jack nodded. 'I'll be there.'

'Unless I've already become Lady Perfect.'

'And I'm giving my acceptance speech for the Pulitzer.' He gave a cynical grunt. 'Seen any flying pigs recently?'

Freya suddenly felt utterly defeated. She stretched her arms wide and sank her head back to stare into the rusty-black sky, its pale stars almost eclipsed by the city's electric glow. Once, she had had long blonde hair, fizzing energy, a thrilling succession of jobs and men, friends, parties, a beckoning mystery future. Once, Jack had been the handsomest, luckiest man in New York, bursting with talent. And now look at them. Jack was broke, with his career on the skids; and she was a pathetic thirtysomething too scared to go home to a wedding without a man in tow. They had reached the end of the track, last stop on the line.

Eventually she straightened up and gave a deep sigh. Her eyes met Jack's.

'Who wants to be a millionaire?' he sang softly.

'I do,' answered Freya.

They smiled.

A waitress was passing with a tray. Jack put out an arm to call her over.

'Two grappa, please.'

'I don't need a drink,' said Freya.

'Yes, you do.'

'No, I don't.'

The waitress looked from one to the other in perplexity. Jack gave her a conspiratorial smile. '*Due grappa, per favore.*' To Freya's disgust, the waitress, who must have been fifty if she was a day, melted into flirtatiousness and tripped off to fetch the drinks with a sway of her hips. She returned within a minute, bending low as she put down the glasses to give Jack a bold smile. What pushovers some women were! Freya sank her chin on her hand and stared gloomily into space.

Suddenly Jack was jabbing her arm, repeatedly and painfully, with one finger. 'I've had a brilliant idea,' he announced.

'Stop that!' She swatted his hand.

'Listen.' He pulled his chair close. 'You want someone to come to this wedding with you, right?'

She rolled her eyes. 'Ten out of ten.'

'Someone respectable?'

'Yes.'

'Good-looking?'

'Definitely.'

'Whom you like?'

'Preferably.'

'And male.'

'Ha ha.'

'Well, then.' He sat back in his chair and folded his arms.

'Well, then what?'

Jack raised his eyebrows as if the answer was obvious. She raised hers, to show him it was not.

He spread his hands. '*Me.*'

Freya stared at him for a moment, then burst out laughing. 'Don't be ridiculous.'

His face fell. 'I hate the way you always say that. What's so ridiculous?'

She gave an exasperated sigh. 'You don't understand. I'm supposed to be going with a *boyfriend*.'

'So? Why couldn't I pretend to be your boyfriend? It's only for a couple of days.'

'Four days. Thursday through Sunday. We'd be sharing a room. You'd have to hold my hand, and gaze into my eyes, and pretend you thought I was wonderful.'

'But that's my best thing!'

'You wouldn't be able to chase after the bridesmaids, or get drunk, or contradict me all the time.'

'Who would dare to contradict you?'

'And you'd have to be charming.'

'I *am* charming! "Excuse me, Lady Basset-Hound, I believe this is your lorgnette."'

'Oh, Jack . . .' Freya couldn't help giggling.

'Well, why not?' he demanded. 'It would be fun.'

'Look at your clothes.'

'I have real clothes – I just don't wear them.'

'And your hair.'

'But my hair's always been like this!'

'Exactly.'

'What if I cut it . . . just for you? Snip, snip . . .'

He had switched that Southern charm up to maximum. Freya tried not to smile. 'You just want an excuse to escape your problems,' she said severely.

'I want to help you.'

'Do you?'

He reached out and caught her hand in his, startling her. 'We could help each other,' he amended.

His mouth curved in a familiar, teasing smile. But his blue eyes were serious. She felt his palm against hers, warm and dry, and the firm grip of his fingers. *Jack*, she thought. *Jack?* . . .

Freya disengaged her hand and picked up her grappa, staring into its swirling depths. An irresistible impulse gathered inside her, as if she was balanced on the very top of the Cyclone, waiting for that terrifying, thrilling swoop into the abyss. She set the small glass to her lips, drained it in one fiery gulp and slammed it back on the table. Her eyes, smarting with alcohol, met Jack's.

'You're on.'

'Nice bed.'

Jack bounced up and down on the four-poster, dislodging a shower of small particles from the tattered hangings. He peered upwards into the dusty gloom. It wouldn't surprise him if an entire family of mice lived up there – had lived there for generations, since the days of Queen Elizabeth I. Sir Mouse and Lady Mouse, and their aristocratic little mouselets. He pictured their coat of arms: rat rampant on a wedge of Cheddar cheese, with a Latin motto – '*In bedum non catum*'. He lay back, chuckling softly. That pink drink Freya's father had given him was powerful stuff.

'Glad you like it.' Freya unsnapped the catches of her suitcase. 'You'll be able to admire its finer points from over there' – she pointed – 'on the chaise longue.'

Jack raised himself on one elbow to squint at an angular piece of furniture that looked like a cross between a prison bunk and an old-fashioned dentist's chair.

'Aw, come on. I'm way too tall. Do you want to show up at this wedding with the Hunchback of Notre-Dame?'

'Not "noder daim". You're in Europe now.

"Notrrre dahm" is the favoured pronunciation. And stop making that horrible face.'

'*Oui, madame*. But I'm not sleeping on that thing.'

'One of us has to. We're only *pretending* to be a couple.'

'That's a relief. I don't know how much more of this warm togetherness I can take. Hah! Missed!'

Jack reached down over the edge of the bed to retrieve the missile Freya had thrown at him: one of her shoes. (Eight pairs she'd brought with her – *eight!* – as he'd discovered when he'd offered to carry her suitcase at the airport and almost got his arm yanked off.) He turned the shoe over in his hands, wondering at the fragility of the high tapering heel and the slender straps that presumably, somehow, kept the whole contraption attached to her foot. He tossed it over to her. 'Here you go, Cinderella.'

Without comment she put it in the massive carved wardrobe that leaned forward at an alarming angle on the bedroom's uneven floor, and continued unpacking. Jack decided to do the same.

She'd been like this, wound tight as a spring, ever since they landed. For the first hour or so of the long drive to Cornwall, he'd barely glanced at the passing landscape; his eyes kept straying to the speedometer of the hired car, which scarcely dropped below ninety. Freya drove the way she did everything – fast, defiantly, with an edge of danger. 'Wiltshire,' she'd announce, as they flashed down the three-lane highway, 'Somerset . . . Devon.' She hadn't seemed tired. When he had grumbled mildly about his sleepless night in the cramped, economy-class seat, she told him firmly that she didn't believe in jet-lag. He hadn't dared to mention the word 'lunch', and finally took refuge in sleep.

He'd woken in mid-afternoon to the astonishing sight of a line of high-tech windmills cresting the hill before them, arms flailing, like iron monsters sprung from the pages of H. G. Wells. Freya announced that they were now in Cornwall. Jack put on his glasses and looked about him with interest. He had visited England a couple of times, but had not strayed far beyond London and the usual tourist circuit; he had never visited real English people in a real English home. At first sight, Cornwall seemed slightly spooky, a mixture of forbidding moorland and grim, granite towns. Signposts pointed the way to places called Ventongimps, Zelah and Goonhaven. Once he spotted a tall smokestack poking eerily out of a scrubby field, which Freya told him was the relic of an old tin mine. Up and down they swooped, on a smooth, grey ribbon of road. Gradually the landscape softened into a patchwork of spreading meadows grazed by piebald cows. They passed small, quiet villages, each with its pub and square church tower. Hand-painted signs at the roadside advertised trekking, campsites, pick-your-own strawberries, Village Day celebrations, fresh mackerel and, in one intriguing instance, 'Bitches – free to good home'. Trees became scarcer and more stunted, buffeted into cockeyed shapes like umbrellas blown inside-out. Spiky, palm-like plants sprouted unexpectedly in front gardens – more Florida than England. Mile by mile, the horizon seemed to flatten itself and recede into a silvery haze. Jack felt expectancy bubble within him; they were approaching the sea.

'Next hill,' said Freya, reading his mind, and sure enough, at the next rise in the road, there was the heart-lifting sight of a sweep of sparkling water, darkening to slaty blue. She glanced over at him and smiled, as if she had magicked it forth herself.

Soon afterwards they turned off the main road and entered a maze of lanes that plunged into woody ravines and skirted narrow, secret creeks. Tangled hedgerows and white lacy flowers lined their path. New York seemed unimaginably far away. Jack rolled down his window and sniffed the sweet English air. A high midsummer sun shone out of a blue sky. He took it as a good omen.

At a dip in the road, Freya turned into an entrance flanked by battered stone posts. 'This is it,' she said, and gunned the car up a narrow lane. Trees grew thickly on either side, gnarled and bulbous with age, or rising smooth and grey as elephant hide, their leaves forming a canopy that filtered greeny-coppery light on to the potholed track. They followed this for at least half a mile, during which Jack began to revise his mental image of 'the big, old house' Freya had sometimes mentioned. She had never said much about her folks, though on the plane she had briefed him sketchily about her 'ghastly' stepfamily. At length they shot out of the woods and rattled over a cattle-grid. Open pastureland dotted with sheep sloped away on either side and tucked itself into dark folds of wood. The sea wasn't visible from here, though Jack could sense its presence in the luminous sky. Dead ahead, shaded by elegantly clustered trees, lay a large manor house of grey stone. It looked very old – four hundred years? Six hundred? Jack's eyes widened. There were decorative gables romantically covered in creepers, and a huge central window, two storeys high, studded with small panes of glass like a panel of diamonds. A forest of brick chimneys sprouted from an undulating roof of weathered slate. He could see a scatter of outbuildings – a clock tower – the cupola of something that looked like a small church.

'You never told me you lived in a place like this.'

'I don't. I live in New York. This is my stepmother's house.'

It looked like the sort of place where faithful retainers lined up at the front entrance to greet Her Ladyship as she descended from her carriage – but obviously he'd been watching too many costume dramas. In real life, Freya whizzed around the back, through a stone archway, and into a courtyard with dusty cars randomly parked, a washing line strung with dishcloths, miscellaneous piles of old bricks, a lop-sided tub of geraniums, and a few scurrying chickens. The slam of car doors summoned no grander personage than a waddling black labrador, whom Freya introduced as Bedivere.

She led Jack down a dark passage lined with muddy boots and empty wine bottles, and brass hooks laden with coats and hats, fishing nets, coiled rope, plastic supermarket bags and dog leads. They entered a large room with a beamed ceiling, bare stone floor and windows on two sides. Jack blinked in the dusty sunlight. It seemed to be a kitchen, though not of a kind he recognized: no fitted cabinets, no gleaming implements, not even a refrigerator, unless you counted that tiny thing covered in flying pig magnets. A big wooden dresser stood against one wall, crammed with jugs and plates. Its flat surface was stacked higgledy-piggledy with newspapers, letters, plastic flower pots, clothes pegs, seed packets and a hairbrush. There was a deep, square stone sink with tarnished brass taps and a yellow stain where water had dripped. In the centre of the room a long oak table was laid for five. Something was simmering on a funny looking, old-fashioned stove, its burners protected by round metal lids, like airlocks on a submarine. A delicious smell of cooking filled the room, spiced with a waft of sweet-peas from an earthenware jug and just a soupçon of dog-blanket.

'Outside, probably,' Freya said cryptically. She strode across to the open window, and – as if this was perfectly normal – climbed on to the sill by means of a sturdy block of wood, evidently placed there for this purpose, and jumped down the other side. Jack clambered after her, with the sensation of stepping through a looking-glass into an enticing wonderland.

He found himself in a small garden, enclosed by high green hedges and quartered by stone paths. Aromatic smells and a murmur of bees rose from a grey-green haze of plants, topped with yellow and purple flowers.

Freya strode towards a shadowed archway in the hedge, then turned and stopped to wait for him. He could hear voices now, female voices, raised in argument.

'But, Mummy, it's *my* wedding,' one protested petulantly.

'I know, darling, but you simply can't ask poor Reverend Thwacker to read out "The Song of Solomon" in church. Can she, Guy?'

There was a resonant smack of wood on wood, then a softer click, and a triumphant male voice shouted, 'Got you!'

Jack felt his forearm gripped in a hand of steel. 'Remember,' Freya commanded. 'Boyfriend. Madly in love. I am marvellous.'

Jack felt a flicker of irritation. He would play this game his own way. He was perfectly confident of charming the entire family – Freya included. He took her hand and pulled it through his arm, feeling the tension in her. 'Just call me "darling",' he said, and they walked through the archway together.

It was an archetypally English scene. Ahead of them stretched a long, level lawn freckled with daisies and bounded by a high hedge, with the interlocking curves of green hills beyond. There was one of those elegant, spreading conifers – cypress? cedar? – casting its shade on to a huddle of striped deckchairs and a wrought-iron table bearing a tray of drinks. No one noticed them at first. Two women stood with their backs to him, each leaning on their croquet mallets as they watched a man in a panama hat bending to position his ball by one of the white hoops. He straightened, shaded his eyes and gave a joyous shout. 'Freya!'

She tugged Jack forward a few paces, then stopped uncertainly.

The man hurried towards them. He was tall and lean, and so like his daughter that Jack almost laughed aloud: same oval face, same long nose and oblique smile, even the same set to the shoulders and tilt of the head. Only the colouring was different; Freya's eyes and hair must come from her mother.

'Here at last.' Freya's father wrapped his arms around her in an eager, uninhibited hug. 'How marvellous!' He stroked her hair in a tender gesture, and beamed.

'Hello, Freya. Lovely to see you.' This must be Annabelle, a handsome, matronly woman in a flowery, calf-length skirt and white blouse. Her dark hair was striped with grey, and held off her broad brow with a hair band. Her face was worn, but pleasant. She didn't look like a wicked stepmother. Freya allowed herself to be kissed on both cheeks.

The younger woman hung back, swinging her mallet. She was a pretty brunette with high colour, full lips, and slanted eyes that met Jack's knowingly.

She wore white trousers cut off below the knee and some kind of sleeveless top that displayed smooth, rounded arms.

'Hi, Freya.'

'Hi, Tash.'

They kept their distance, looking at each other with appraising eyes and tight smiles. *Ouch!* thought Jack.

There was an uncomfortable pause. Then Annabelle stepped towards Jack with a welcoming smile, her hand extended. 'And you must be Michael,' she said.

Jack felt his arm grabbed again. 'This is Jack,' Freya told them all, with an air of defiance. 'My – friend, Jack Madison.'

'I'm so sorry – ' Annabelle flushed.

'I did tell you,' Freya muttered irritably.

'Golly, Freya, you do have a high turnover.' Tash shot Jack a mischievous grin.

'Delighted to have you with us, Jack.' Freya's father stepped forward smoothly. 'I'm Guy Penrose, and this is my wife Annabelle. Now: let me introduce you to the mystery of Pimm's. A strange English drink, but I think you'll like it.'

With some relief Jack strolled with him to the drinks table, out of the emotional force field of the three women. Men were so much more straightforward. Mr Penrose had a small cigar tucked into the frayed hatband of his panama. Jack liked him already. They stood, talking easily, while the shadows lengthened and birds arrowed through the sky. The drink was like a punch, chock-a-block with fruit and sprigs of mint. Jack drank thirstily. The tiredness of the journey dropped away. He began to enjoy himself.

'You're not a lawyer, are you?' It was Tash, peering up into his face with her long-lashed eyes.

'No, that was Michael.' His tone was dry. If he really was Freya's lover, he'd be getting pretty annoyed by now.

'Didn't think so. Lawyers are *soooh* boring.'

'Well, thanks.' Jack laughed.

'What's the joke?' Suddenly Freya was at his side.

'Oh, Freya, I meant to say . . .' Tash's face hardened. 'You didn't mind not being a bridesmaid, did you?'

'Of course not,' Freya said stiffly.

'Goody. Only Daddy said I ought to have asked you.'

'It's okay. Jack doesn't really see me in pink satin.'

Jack now remembered the message on his phone back home. That couldn't have been much more than a week ago – kind of late, he thought, given that the wedding was taking place the day after tomorrow.

Now Tash was fluttering her fingers in Freya's face. 'Don't you want to see my ring?'

'Oh, yes.' Freya bent to study it. 'It's lovely, Tash. Really nice.' Her voice wasn't exactly warm, but Jack could tell she was making an effort.

'Rubies, you know. Cost a fortune. Luckily, Rolls is absolutely coining it. I won't have to work after we're married. Not like you, poor thing, slogging away.'

Freya arched an eyebrow. *Uh-oh*, thought Jack.

'Funny,' she murmured, 'I thought that the price of a virtuous woman was *above* rubies.'

'More Pimm's, anyone?' Jack seized the jug and sloshed the fizzy liquid willy-nilly into their glasses.

'Guy, darling, why don't you help with the suitcases while I see to dinner?' said Annabelle. 'I expect you two would like to change after your long journey.'

'Good idea,' Jack agreed heartily. 'A quick shower, and I'll be ready for anything.'

He was perplexed to see them all exchange a complicit grin.

'He's American,' Freya explained.

Of course, there was no shower. Even the so-called bathroom bore little resemblance to any bathroom Jack had ever seen. Although sumptuously large, with a beautiful stone-framed window that Freya called 'mullioned', its plumbing arrangements seemed almost as historic as the rest of the house. The toilet was a capacious mahogany throne raised on a dais and canopied by a black metal cistern, hung with a torture-room chain. Judging by the adjacent bookcase overflowing with jokey titles, it was a British habit to spend a great deal of time in this position, laughing heartily. There was a gigantic bath with clawed feet in the middle of the room, with a cold tap marked 'Hot' and a hot top marked 'Cold', as Jack discovered the hard way. He could only assume that this had been a cunning ruse to sap the morale of German invaders in World War Two.

The whole place was an intriguing mix of Hammer

House of Horror and Brideshead. There was a hallway as big as a barn with an intricate timber roof. There was Bessie's Room and the Red Room and the Mirror Room and something unnervingly known as The Crypt. There was the 'new' wing, dating from seventeen-something. There were bronze busts and interesting-looking clocks, Persian carpets crudely mended, hideous old couches covered in Indian bedspreads, a painted Chinese cabinet with a live cat on top, blinking sleepily. Decrepitude was everywhere: crumbling plaster, split panelling, fungal patches on the ceilings, damask wall-coverings hanging in shreds. He couldn't make out if the Penroses were very rich or very poor. Freya had led him, through a warren of corridors and back staircases, to this vast bedroom with its gloomy furniture and tattered carpeting, explaining nothing, acting as if it was all perfectly normal. Never mind. He would piece it all together. He might even get a novel out of it. Meanwhile, it was illuminating to observe Freya in her native habitat.

Jack had never seen her so nervous. He couldn't tell whether this was because of her family, or because of him. It was, admittedly, a little strange to be alone together in the bedroom they would have to share. The huge bed seemed to loom suggestively at them, making Freya retreat into icy hauteur while he cracked silly jokes. Still, she was the one who was so desperate for a 'boyfriend', and he was perfectly willing to play the part. It could be fun.

She unpacked; he unpacked. Jack placed his

pyjamas – bought specially, with propriety in mind – on one side of the bed. After a small hesitation, she placed hers – pale pink with black piping – on the other. Jack felt rather excited, until she picked up his pyjamas and placed them pointedly on the chaise longue. Then he went to the bathroom and changed his clothes there; she did the same, returning in tight white trousers and a lilac top that suited her colouring. While she fiddled with her hair, he stood at the bedroom window, marvelling at the magical view of the garden, the sheep-meadows and a distant sliver of sea. There were no roads to be seen, no electricity wires, no cars, nothing to remind him of the twentieth century. He wouldn't be at all surprised to glance out of this window tomorrow morning and see a jousting tournament or a maypole dance. In a place like this, anything could happen. The thought excited him.

At last she was ready, subtly transformed. Jack opened the door for her and made a sweeping gesture. 'After you – *sweetheart*.'

Freya's head jerked round. She looked so haughty that he had to laugh.

'Come on, Freya. We're in England. It's not raining. And we're madly in love. Let's make the most of it.' He offered his arm.

She capitulated with a sudden grin. 'Okay – *darling*.'

They swept down the grand staircase to dinner, arm in arm.

*

Freya turned over for the millionth time. She had tried every conceivable position on this wretched chaise longue, and they were all torture. If she sat up against the angled back, she got a crick in her neck. If she lay flat, her legs projected over its rigid end, which cut off the blood supply to her feet. If she curled up into a ball, her hip-bone went numb and her folded legs throbbed with cramp. Each time she moved, the eiderdown slithered off, exposing some part of her body to the damp night breeze. It was now nearly two in the morning, as she knew from hearing the bloody long-case clock on the stairs chime every bloody quarter of an hour.

Outside, a screech owl was doing what screech owls do best. Inside, a gentle, rhythmic snore emanated from Jack, fast asleep in the four-poster. Freya burned to go over and pummel him awake. How dare he just lie there, uncaring, when she was so miserable? She sat up irritably and glowered in his direction. The moon was full and the curtains worn. She could see his head blissfully cradled in a downy mound of pillows, and the great sprawling lump of his comatose body. How come he was there, and she was here?

She slumped back on to her bed of pain. It was her own fault. Jack had insisted that the bed was more than big enough for two, but she hadn't cared for the frisky manner in which he had made this suggestion. It was her idea that they should preclude further argument by tossing a coin for bed privileges, and she had lost. Now she cursed herself for being so idiotically fair-minded; and she cursed Jack for accepting his win so easily. A real gentleman would have protested; a real gentleman would rather have slept on the floor than deprive a lady of the comforts of sleep.

But Jack wasn't a real gentleman; he was only pretending. Freya brooded darkly on his pretence at dinner tonight, when he had shamelessly wormed his way into everyone's good graces. 'Let me carry that for you, Mrs Penrose . . . Terrific cigar, Mr Penrose.' Even Tash had held back her usual snide comments. There he'd sat, utterly at ease, in a dark blue shirt and pressed trousers she'd never even seen before, with his new haircut, entertaining them all with stories about his home town and his funny ol' Suthen ax-sent. Her father even fetched up a bottle of special port from the cellar, as if Jack were Mr Nice Guy instead of a mean, selfish, heartless, *sleeping* beast.

*Screech screech*, went the owl. *Ting ting*, went the clock. *Snore snore*, went Jack. *Scurry scurry*, went something she didn't even want to think about.

Freya threw off the eiderdown and stood up. She'd had enough. If this went on, she'd be haggard and grey by tomorrow. It was bad enough being Tash's older sister; she didn't want to be mistaken for her mother. She stomped over to the bed and scowled down at Jack. He was lying on his back now, right in the middle of the bed, with the stupid, noble expression of a felled ox.

'Jack,' she whispered experimentally.

Not a flicker.

Freya hesitated. She was so tired – and cold. She reminded herself that total strangers huddled together for warmth when lost on a snowy alp. Cowboys even slept with their *horses*. What would it matter if she borrowed a teeny corner of the bed, just for a few hours? Jack would never even know, so long as she woke early and returned to the chaise longue. It was a purely practical solution. She placed the heel of her hand against Jack's pyjama'd shoulder, and pushed. He rolled obediently away, leaving a nice, empty space for her. Freya climbed in.

*Ohhh . . . heaven!* Freya sank her head back on the pillow and stretched her legs luxuriously. The sheets were deliciously warm from Jack's body, and gave off a faint masculine smell, sweet and comforting as freshly baked bread. She almost groaned aloud with pleasure and relief. The knots in her muscles were already beginning to loosen when Jack made a sudden harrumphing noise, turned over and flung a heavy arm across her waist. Freya frowned. This, presumably, was his instinctive reaction to the presence of a female body in his bed, since he was obviously asleep. She picked off his arm and deposited it on top of the covers. After a few seconds, he gave a sleepy mutter and put it back. She picked it off again. He put it back again, and this time gathered her to him with a contented little moan. Freya gave up. She was comfortable and sleepy and warm. Really, she felt quite . . . marvellous. Her eyes closed. Her mind began to drift.

She remembered that it had been autumn. The streets were spangled with leaves as yellow as Jack's hair when he yelled up to her window the news that he had sold his first story. She had bounded down the stairs – clearing the last steps of each landing at a flying leap, swinging herself around the newel posts – to tell him that she too had marvellous news. She had at last wangled her green card, the precious document that allowed her to do a proper job in America, with a proper salary, instead of slave-labour for slave wages. On the strength of their old friendship, new wealth, and imminent fame, they'd decided on a joint celebration dinner at a ritzy restaurant. Jack had dug out a tuxedo, she'd tarted herself up in a dress and high heels, and they'd taken a cab, like a couple of swells, all the way to the smart uptown address. They'd ordered lavishly, clinking glasses in regular self-congratulatory toasts and tasting each other's food. Jack smoked a cigar, and she did too, just to keep up. They'd talked and argued and laughed until it was time to pay the outrageous bill and tipsily return home. Jack had accompanied her to her door, they'd said goodnight – and then he had spoiled it all by suddenly lunging at her and declaring that he wanted to go to bed with her. Just like that! There had been no romantic preamble, no attempt at courtship, just the sort of crude pass immature men make when they're drunk. He felt randy, Freya was to hand – hey, why not? She'd said no, of course. Who did he think he was? Just because he was attractive didn't mean that every female in New York had to fall like ninepins before his charm. Freya had no desire to be just another notch on his bedpost. Besides, he was absurdly young. Jack had been surprised at her rejection, then angry. The episode had never been mentioned since, though the memory of it was like a tiny thorn in their friendship. He'd probably forgotten about it. Certainly, he'd never repeated his advance, something she was very, very happy about. Probably he thought of her like a sister . . . an older sister.

Freya gave a tiny, silent giggle. Here she was, after all these years, in bed with Jack Madison. It wasn't so bad. Of course, he was asleep. Freya settled herself more deeply in the bed, curving her back into Jack's chest. It was an instinct thing, she told herself, a totally natural animal response. She gave a languid yawn. There was something she must remember: oh yes, to wake up early. Absolutely. No problem.

She could hear Jack's even breathing, quiet now. His head lay barely a foot away from hers. What was going on in there, she wondered? What dreams of women, fame, dark wanderings, pursuit? She yawned again. Her eyes closed. She was asleep.

## 23

Jack woke with a tremendous sense of well-being. Every muscle was relaxed, each limb exquisitely heavy; his very bones felt refreshed. For a while he lay utterly still in his warm cocoon, letting consciousness seep back, incapable of even the minor muscular effort of raising his eyelids.

Gradually he registered clues to his whereabouts: no traffic noises, no sirens, no subterranean rumblings or mechanical roars, just the pleasantly inane twitter of birds and the soothing drone of a distant lawn-mower. He could smell sweet, fresh grass and frying bacon. A golden light danced at the rims of his closed eyes, promising a sunny morning. He reached down and idly scratched his balls, then stretched his mouth wide in a long, ratcheting yawn. Oh to be in England, now that June is here. There was a complacent smile on his lips as he opened his eyes, rolled his head across the pillow to look woozily about him, and almost died of shock. Someone was in his bed! – a female someone, with short, tousled hair of a pale gold colour that was intensely familiar.

Jack leapt out of bed and stood on the frayed bedside rug, frantically smoothing his hair. What – ? How – ? When – ? He scanned the room for clues.

The chaise longue was bare. On the floor next to it, the comforter in which Freya had wrapped herself last night lay in a discarded heap. Both their clothes were neatly laid on separate chairs. He couldn't see any signs of . . . inappropriate behaviour. Struck by a sudden thought, Jack gazed wildly down at his own body: he was still wearing his pyjamas – both halves. He tiptoed to the other side of the bed, wincing at every creak from the ancient floorboards, and peeked at Freya's face. She was sound asleep. The sheet covered her almost to the chin; he couldn't see what she was wearing. Surely he would remember if . . .? He should never have drunk all that port.

How quietly she slept. The twin crescents of her eyelashes were motionless, her lips fractionally parted to allow a gentle ebb and flow of breath. She lay on her side, one cheek nudging her pillow, the other faintly flushed and sheened with sleep. Jack couldn't help smiling a little to see her so silent and unguarded. As if conscious of his scrutiny, she took a sudden deep breath. Jack jerked away, but all she did was wriggle into a new position. Still, she could wake up at any moment, and there he'd be, caught like a rabbit in that fierce blue gaze. Jack decided to escape to the bathroom and consider his position.

While hot water filled the bathtub at a grudging, gurgling trickle, he took off his pyjama jacket and lathered his face with his shaving brush. Worried eyes stared back at him from the mirror. This was not the first time he'd woken to find a woman unexpectedly in his bed. It was always embarrassing not to be able to remember exactly how she'd got there – or even who she was – though to be fair to himself, such a thing hadn't happened in a long while. But Freya! This was worse than embarrassing; it was unthinkable.

Jack squirmed at the unwelcome memory of a blunder he had made, years ago, when the two of them had gone out to celebrate the sale of his first story. Freya had been the first person he told; he so wanted to impress her. He'd never met anyone like Freya before, beautiful and quick and clever, with her tart English tongue and her air of sophistication. ('When I was in Venice . . .' she'd say – or Toledo or Oslo or Salzburg.) Back then, he'd been an eager twenty-three or four, thrilled to be out on a date with her. Of course he had lots of girlfriends, but they were just fluff. Suddenly here he was, in a fancy restaurant in New York City, with a Hitchcock blonde who had dressed herself up – for *him*. F. Scott Fitzgerald, eat your heart out. They'd talked and laughed, and he'd drunk perhaps one Armagnac too many (Armagnac! – he'd never even heard of the stuff before Freya suggested it). Afterwards, he'd escorted her home to the scruffy rooming-house a couple of blocks from his own, and said goodnight: a kiss on her perfumed cheek, a wave of the hand, the click of her door. He'd walked down two flights of stairs, then turned right around, walked back up, banged on her door and, as soon as she opened it, blurted out, 'I want to go to bed with you.'

*Ouch!* He had nicked the underside of his chin. Jack ran the cold tap and dabbed at the tiny cut. The water in his bath had now reached the eight-inch mark. He stepped out of his pyjama bottoms, climbed in and slid down against the curiously grainy surface. *I want to go to bed with you.* Jack closed his eyes. How crude, how abrupt, how record-breakingly un-suave. After a moment of cool silence, she had smiled her mocking smile, and arched her fabulous eyebrows at him: 'Don't be ridiculous, Jack. I'm far too old for you.'

The memory made him sit up in a swirl of water and reach for the soap, just for something to do. He examined the brown resinous lump with suspicion, then rubbed it vigorously across his skin. An icemaiden, that's what she was – or so he had told himself, though her serial love affairs suggested that she was nothing of the kind; it was just him she didn't fancy. Fortunately, she had never mentioned the incident again; he hoped she had forgotten. But it burned in his own memory. He had told himself that he would never, ever, make a mistake like that again.

So what about last night? Could he – ? Did she – ? Jack caught sight of a fat, black spider lurking malevolently in a high corner, and decided he had better go and find out. He released the brass plug, looped its chain around one of the taps, and climbed out of the bath on to a kind of World War One duckboard that appeared to serve as a bath mat. The awful truth was, he couldn't remember a thing about last night. He'd have to take his cue from Freya.

He dried himself off, checked that his cut had stopped bleeding, then wrapped the meagre towel around his waist, tossed his pyjamas over one bare shoulder and unlocked the door. Let's see: down those funny back stairs, then right – or was it left? He was thoroughly lost when a cheeky voice behind him said, 'Morning, Tarzan. Sleep well?'

Jack turned around to see Tash, semi-wrapped in some silky pink thing, giving him an appraising stare.

'Uh, yeah. Thanks.'

Her pussycat smile suggested that *she* knew what he'd been up to all night, even if he didn't. He put a hand to his towel, to check that it was secure.

'Your bedroom's that way.' She pointed. 'This is the family wing, actually.' She took a step backwards and waggled her fingers at him. 'See you later, alligator.'

Jack watched her retreating back view. Fleetingly, he wondered why Freya wasn't in the 'family wing', actually. Then he dismissed the thought and turned in the direction Tash had indicated. He puffed out his chest a little as he walked. Tarzan, eh?

When he found the door to his bedroom – their bedroom – he stood outside, listening. All was quiet. Perhaps Freya was still asleep, or already eating breakfast downstairs. This latter thought was heartening: it would be so much easier if their first encounter was in public. He placed his hand on the doorknob and turned it stealthily, until the door gave under his cautious pressure. He took a step forward and peered into the room.

Freya was lying against a high, white bank of pillows, wide awake and looking straight at him. There was a dreamy, contented smile on her face.

'Hi,' he offered tentatively.

'And hello to you, too.' Her husky voice and the way she ran her eyes over his bare torso seemed to append the words, 'big boy'.

Playing for time, Jack closed the door behind him and sauntered into neutral territory at the centre of the room, to survey her from a safe distance. She did look rather sexy, in a tousled, impish way, but the sheet was drawn right up to her neck. It was hard to tell if she had any clothes on.

'Did you, uh, sleep well?' he asked.

'Mmmm. Wonderful . . .' Her eyelids drooped rapturously, leaving slits of sparkling blue. 'Of course, I wasn't exactly *asleep* the whole time.'

Jack nodded sagely, wondering what the hell that meant. He felt stupid in his towel, yet he could hardly get dressed with her watching. To compensate, he found himself behaving like John Wayne. He hitched his pyjamas manfully over one shoulder, sucked in his gut and jerked a thumb towards the chaise longue. 'How was the . . .?'

'Hideous.' Freya gave a delicate shudder.

Jack nodded again, lower lip jutted. If he'd had a wad of baccy in his mouth, he'd have spat it plumb on the floor.

'No: you were right, Jack. The bed was a *much* better idea.'

Jack swallowed. His hands hung down, wide as a gunslinger's ready to draw.

She wriggled down in the bed and heaved a voluptuous sigh. 'Oh, Jack, wasn't last night unforgettable?'

Jack's eyes bulged. 'You bet!' he agreed heartily.

As the silence lengthened, he became painfully aware that this was an inadequate response. Freya's smile faltered.

'Don't tell me you don't remember?'

'Well . . . I feel grrreat.' Jack thumped his chest, Tarzan-style. 'But the details kinda escape me.'

'Oh Jack, how could you forget?' Her voice throbbed with reproach. 'The masterful way you stole all the blankets . . . That mighty snore, like the call of a wild stallion . . . The sexy way you turned over in bed, like a rampant hippotota – hittopopa – '

By this time Freya was laughing so hard that she had to climb to her knees, gasping for breath. She snickered and chortled and hooted and howled with hilarity, then toppled forward, clutching her stomach. The bedclothes fell away, revealing that she had been dressed in jeans and T-shirt all along.

'Very funny,' said Jack. He should have known. He *had* known. He walked with dignity to the wardrobe and took out a shirt, while his mind raced to invent a swift revenge.

Freya dabbed at her eyes. 'Honestly, Jack, you should have seen yourself, snoring away with your mouth open. It would have been like making love with a tranquillized sperm whale.' She lurched to her feet and staggered back and forth across the saggy mattress, growling 'I feel great' and beating her fists on her chest. Jack hadn't seen her look so pleased with herself in years.

Coolly, he began to do up his buttons. 'At least I don't talk in my sleep,' he said conversationally.

'What?' Freya stopped bouncing. 'Are you saying that I do?' Her brow furrowed. 'Bollocks,' she said.

He shrugged. 'If you don't want to know what you said, I won't tell you.'

'I never talk in my sleep.'

'Have it your own way.'

'What did I say, then?'

'I don't know if I should tell you.'

'Go on.'

'Say "please".'

Freya stamped her foot. 'Tell me!'

'All right.' Jack clasped his hands in a maidenly fashion, fluttered his eyelashes and assumed a ludicrous falsetto. 'Oh, Jack,' he fluted, 'how handsome you are. What a genius you are. Oh Jack, Jack – be gentle with me. *Oof!*'

A pillow hit him smack in the face. He threw it back. She threw another one. Soon a full-scale pillow fight was underway. Jack's aim was better, but Freya cheated by taking cover behind the bedposts. She had to come out to retrieve the pillows, though, and during one such foray Jack managed to score a direct hit, knocking her off balance. He pumped his arms in triumph, momentarily forgetting the insecure arrangement of his towel. He felt it loosen and slither to the floor. Meanwhile, Freya grabbed wildly at one of the bed-hangings, which suddenly shredded loose from its attachment and collapsed on top of her. She fought her way out of its dusty folds, emerging with fluff in her eyelashes and a smudge on her nose, just as Jack whipped his towel back into position. Around them a snowstorm of feathers drifted slowly to the floor.

Their eyes met in a truce.

'Breakfast?' said Jack.

# 24

They found Annabelle in the kitchen in sergeant-major mode, bi-focals on nose and clipboard in hand. While Freya made toast and scrambled eggs for herself and Jack, a succession of young men with earrings and local women in aprons flowed in and out of the room, taking orders about marquees, flowers, caterers, cars and bed-linen. A dozen extra people were staying in the house tonight, including a pair of bridesmaids and Roland's parents ('frightfully rich – we must make a good impression'); Roland and his mates had been booked into a local pub. Most of 'the young people' would be coming by train from London; they'd need to be fetched from the station and ferried back and forth. Freya's father had popped into Truro for a book he'd ordered ('Today of all days! Really, Freya, your father's impossible.'). Tash, apparently, was suffering from pre-wedding nerves and had gone back to bed, 'poor little love'. It was the pattern of Freya's relationship with her stepmother that Annabelle always felt impelled to give her some household chore – anything from picking roses for the dinner table to worming the dogs – and Freya always felt unable to say no. She munched her breakfast glumly, waiting for the axe to fall.

But it never did. Jack persuaded Annabelle to stop pacing and sat her down next to him with a cup of coffee. He took her through the list, listening patiently to her explanation of all the things that had to be done and why she would *never be ready*! Then he borrowed her pen and somehow reduced everything to five headings on a single piece of paper. He ringed one of the headings, labelled it 'F and J' and passed the list back to a dazed-looking Annabelle. 'We'll be back around six,' he told her.

The jobs for which Jack had volunteered included dropping by the pub, collecting an order of fresh fish from a village Freya had intended to show Jack anyway, and picking up Roland and a couple of his friends at the train station late in the afternoon. In other words, they had the day to themselves.

'How did you do that?' Freya asked as they were walking out to the car.

'Oaksboro's stuffed with women like that: never happier than when they're busy, but love to complain. Annabelle's okay. She's just a little scared of you.'

'*She's* scared of *me*?' Freya stopped dead in her tracks. She remembered the thousands of times she'd choked back her resentment and politely agreed to perform some task, so that Annabelle couldn't complain about her. 'Why? What's so frightening about me?'

'You're clever and metropolitan and tall and blonde, and her husband adores you. She's a middle-aged provincial housewife trying to keep this whole show on the road.' He waved an arm to encompass the chickens and the garden and the huge, crumbling house – even, perhaps, her father. 'Asking you to do things is her way of telling you that you're one of the family, and that this is your home – even if you hardly ever come here, and freeze her out when you do. It wouldn't hurt to be a bit nicer to her, you know. So who's driving?'

Freya was so stunned by this piece of off-the-cuff psychoanalysis that she hardly heard his question. Annabelle was the wicked stepmother who had gate-crashed her life and stolen her father. Annabelle was the woman who had landed him with a second daughter when he already had a perfectly good one of his own. The idea that Annabelle might also be a normal human being, with the average mix of strengths and weaknesses, was revolutionary. Freya became aware that Jack was watching her curiously, his palm outstretched for the car keys. She hid her eyes behind sunglasses. 'I'll drive.'

First they tootled down to the whitewashed pub overlooking the estuary, where Roland and co. were to be billeted, and checked that all was in order, as per Annabelle's instructions. Then Freya wound her way westward towards the sea, taking tiny back lanes hemmed in by hedgerows that cascaded with honeysuckle and dog roses. The sun was high and hot in a clear blue sky. Through the open car windows came the caterwauling of seagulls and a metallic whiff of the sea. For the first time since she'd arrived in England

Freya began to relax. Apart from the disaster of oversleeping and waking up in Jack's bed – a potential crisis she thought she had averted rather brilliantly – everything was going okay. The day stretched invitingly before her. She took Jack on a detour past her favourite church, right on a sandy beach, so close to the sea that in a bad storm sea water swept up the nave, though the building had stood firm for five centuries and would probably last another five. Then she looped inland and dropped back to the village where the fish man had a shop on the cobbled quayside. Boats bobbed low in the small harbour ringed by grey cottages; she saw that the tide was going out. Having dealt with Annabelle's order, Freya added a small one of her own: fresh crabmeat stuffed into two crusty rolls, which she packed into a knapsack already containing a bottle of water, a bag of juicy plums and swimming things. Her plan, endorsed by Jack at breakfast, was to walk from here along the coastal footpath to a beach, where they could picnic and swim.

Freya had never been to the country with Jack, and didn't know how he'd behave. He might be one of those pathetic men who never wanted to get out of the car and get their shoes dirty, and had to be congratulated on surviving any 'walk' more taxing than a brief stroll across level terrain. In fact, he strode along at a good pace, knapsack on his back, seeming to enjoy everything from the ingenious construction of the stone stiles, to the comical sheep that cropped the grassy headlands, to the fact that the magenta flowers that sprayed out of sword-shaped leaves were known locally as 'whistling jacks'. The narrow footpath snaked up and down, through waist-high bracken and brambly hedges, over windswept cliffs, past the ruined towers of abandoned copper mines, skirting shingly coves and bustling caravan parks, until they stood high above a curving stretch of smooth sand, lapped by an inviting blue sea. They scrambled and slithered down a precipitous rocky path and at last, hot and dusty, collapsed on to their chosen spot on an almost empty beach. A shallow cave in the cliff provided a sliver of shade for the picnic and enough privacy for Freya to change at once into her bikini.

'Last one in's a rotten egg,' she shouted childishly as she sprinted across the sand and splashed into the waves. 'Lovely,' she called to Jack, clamping her teeth against the icy cold. She watched him plunge in after her, and crowed with laughter when he reared out of the water again with a bellow of protest. She stayed in just long enough to prove how tough she was, then they chased each other down the sand until they were warm, and wandered slowly back, examining shells and birds' footprints, sending tiny crabs scurrying into their holes. They ate their lunch sitting on their towels, watching distant fishing boats wink their way to a hazy horizon, then lay on their stomachs, soaking up the sun and playing noughts and crosses in the sand. They talked in a desultory way about childhood holidays, friends they had in common, movies they had seen, and whether it was better to live in the country or the city, until sunshine and the slow rustle of the waves lulled them into contented silence. It was only when Freya felt Jack's cool shadow fall across her, and heard his voice reminding her of the time that she realized she had been asleep. On the walk back, she let Jack go ahead, hypnotically watching his tanned calves and battered sneakers march ahead of her. She felt drugged with sunshine. Her skin prickled pleasurably with salt and sand.

Back at the village, they stowed styrofoam boxes of fish, packed in crushed ice, into the boot of the car and headed towards the train station. Freya had never met Roland, though she had heard his name coupled with Tash's for a while now. All she knew was that he was twenty-nine years old and did something well-paid in property development. Tash had boasted of his ultra-smart flat – which she shared most nights – in a converted warehouse south of the river, with a fab view of Tower Bridge, which he had acquired for a snip thanks to some dodgy insider deal. But when the train arrived, there was no mistaking the three young men who erupted noisily on to the platform, gaudy shirts hanging out of baggy shorts. It was a five-hour train journey from London, and they looked like they'd used every one of them for drinking. Having loaded a baggage cart with cases, two of them pushed it down the platform at a swerving run, chanting 'Here comes the groom', while the third, presumably Roland, perched precariously on top. Dark-haired, white-skinned, with heavy-lidded eyes, he was good-looking in an insolent way. When Freya introduced herself, Roland eyed her bare legs and told her she could pick him up any time, *hurgh hurgh*. His friends were called Jamie ('rugger bugger', Freya said to herself) and Sponge (blond curls, public school, posh). All of them were in such a silly, schoolboy mood that without Jack she would never have got the luggage loaded and the three men squashed, protesting, into the back seat.

'So how's my gorgeous Tish Tash?' asked Roland, as Freya accelerated out of the station car park. 'Not changed her mind, has she?'

'Of course not,' said Freya.

'Bad luck, Rolls,' joked Jamie. 'You're a marked man now.' He hummed the opening bars of the 'Funeral March'.

'Leave it out,' growled Roland.

'He's right, you know,' said Sponge. '"Till death do us part" and all that.'

'Shut up!'

'Or divorce, I suppose,' Sponge added.

'Shut *up*!' Freya heard a smack and a scuffle from the back seat.

'Mind you, there's always tonight.' Jamie lowered his voice suggestively. 'Still time to get your oar in.'

'As the actress said to the – '

'Sh!'

The three of them collapsed in snorts and guffaws. A sour smell of beer and cigarettes filled the car.

Roland demanded silence while he made an important business call from his mobile phone.

'I could be on to a winner here,' he told them; 'commission on twenty mil.'

Freya pressed her foot on the accelerator. She didn't much care for Roland's swaggering air. But presumably Tash loved him, or at least wanted him. In some ways Freya could make sense of the match. Roland had the money; Tash had the country-house credentials. They were both greedy and ambitious. He would do deals; she would shop and lunch and oil the wheels of his career. They would be stylish and successful. It wasn't the sort of life that appealed to Freya, but perhaps it might make Roland and Tash happy. She glanced at Jack, and was amused to see him cock an eyebrow towards the back seat and roll his eyes at her in silent complicity.

Really, she thought, Jack was working out remarkably well. She'd wanted someone to make a good impression, and so far Jack had done a surprisingly good job. Freya congratulated herself on bringing him. It was so much more relaxing to be with a friend than with a lover. Friends were reliable and easygoing; one didn't have to worry about being attractive and delightful every second of the day. It wasn't even that bad sharing a bedroom with him. Suddenly Cat's face swam into her mind, leaning at her across the table in the Chinese restaurant and warning her that Jack might *pounce*. How ridiculous. Freya wondered idly what Cat would be up to tonight. Let's see . . .

Friday night. Probably chilling out with supper on her lap and *Friends* on the TV. Freya felt a surge of fondness. Good old Cat.

Back at the house, Freya lay on the bed and snoozed while Jack took a bath. When he returned they swapped round, though Freya was back in the bedroom within half a minute. There was a spider on the wall above the toilet – a huge, black one with a zillion legs, waiting to leap on to her bare neck and flitter down the inside of her kimono. She was going to have to wait until it disappeared.

'Oh, for heaven's sake.' Jack marched her back to the bathroom, where she hovered outside while he trapped the spider between cupped hands. His gesture reminded her of Michael, holding his ring: what a funny thing to remember. Jack chucked the spider out the window, gave her a withering look of masculine superiority, and withdrew.

By the time Freya returned to the bedroom, Jack had disappeared, tactfully giving her a chance to dress for tonight's party. She stood by the bedroom window and tilted her face to her hand-mirror, trying to catch the sunlight that still glowed strong through high shreds of flamingo-pink clouds. Her cheeks were faintly sunburnt, but none the worse for that. She decided to leave her skin as it was. Tonight she'd go for the natural look – though not too natural: she reached for her faithful mascara. Make-up and hair completed, she wriggled herself into her dress – the turquoise fish-scale number she had worn to Coney

Island – and sat down at the dressing table to check out the result in the mirror. Not bad.

There was a soft knock on the door.

Freya grabbed a comb. 'Yes?' she called casually.

'Only me,' said Jack, opening the door. 'You ready yet?' He ambled into the room, then paused as he registered what she was wearing. 'Oh . . . the mermaid outfit.'

'It's too bad if you don't like it,' Freya said defensively. 'I don't have money to splash out on new dresses left, right and centre.'

'Who said I didn't like it?'

She saw that Jack was wearing immaculate white jeans, an electric–blue linen shirt and black sneakers with white laces. His tawny-blond hair was clean and combed, swept back from his broad, tanned face. He looked like Mr America.

He came over and stooped low, shoulder to shoulder with her, surveying them both in the mirror in a way that Freya found disconcertingly intimate.

'The perfect couple,' Jack pronounced with a smile.

She thought he was mocking her, and got quickly to her feet. 'I want to give this to Tash, then we can join the party.' She picked up a large gift-wrapped package from the bed, where she'd put it ready.

'Here, let me carry that,' said Jack.

'Why?' she asked suspiciously.

'Why not?' He pulled the package gently from her hands.

They found Tash and Roland holding court in the

library downstairs, knee-deep in discarded wrapping paper and surrounded by the spoils of marriage: monogrammed bath towels, crystal marmalade jars, chrome gadgets, Japanese bowls, Italian espresso cups, Egyptian cotton sheets, and other essentials of modern living. Tash knelt on the floor, flushed with excitement, ripping off paper under the admiring gaze of her girlfriends. The scene reminded Freya of countless birthday parties she had endured with Tash as birthday girl and herself as a cripplingly self-conscious attendant. Roland sat behind his bride-to-be on the sofa, languidly smoking a cigarette while his bride-to-be *ooed* and *ahed* at each new acquisition. 'A pasta machine! How fabulous. Oh Roll-doll, do look.' She was wearing a flimsy, slithery dress that could have been a slip or a nightie – fuchsia pink with a turquoise bra underneath.

Freya reclaimed her parcel from Jack. As soon as there was a gap in the proceedings, she stepped forward and handed it to Tash with her best smile. Ignoring the card, whose message Freya had spent so much time composing, Tash tore off the wrapping.

'Golly, what is it?' She passed it over her head to Roland. 'By the way, everyone, this is Daddy's daughter by his first wife – the one who died. And that gorgeous hunk is her boyfriend, Jack. So hands off, girls!'

'It's a painting.' Freya kept her voice light. 'By a young artist I handle, who I think could be really big.'

Roland was looking at it with his head cocked on

361

one side, then on the other. Smoke trickled out of his nostrils. 'Which way up's it supposed to be?'

Tash giggled, and darted a look at Freya. Her eyes glowed like coals.

Freya tried to smile. 'Stick it in an attic, if you don't like it, but I'd advise you to hang on to it. It could be valuable one day.'

'Oh, right.' Roland perked up. He heaved himself off the sofa to give Freya an unnecessarily smoochy kiss on one cheek. 'Thanks very much, Freya. Jolly nice of you. Makes a change from all those toast racks anyway, doesn't it, darling?'

'Hmmm? Oh, look what Lulu's given us, Roll: a jug in the shape of a pig. Isn't that adorable?'

Freya stood straight and stiff, smiling vaguely at the bright blur of gift-wrapping and party dresses, feeling as freakish as a stork among cooing pigeons. As soon as the focus of attention shifted elsewhere she met Jack's eye and retreated through the French windows. Her heels clacked sharply across the stone terrace, startling a blackbird out of a shaggy column of box.

'Well, *I* liked it,' said Jack. 'It's a portrait, isn't it?'

'Of course it is! Even you can see that.' Freya folded her arms tight. 'Why does she always have to be so vicious?'

'She's just a young girl who's getting married tomorrow. This is her big moment.'

'"This is Daddy's daughter by his first wife",' mimicked Freya. 'She can't even bring herself to say my name out loud. Bloody hell, I tried so hard to give her a special present.'

'Let it go,' said Jack. 'She's probably a little jealous of you. Her daddy is really your daddy, and she knows it. You're taller than her, smarter than her and you have a gorgeous hunk of a boyfriend like me. Who wouldn't be jealous? Come on, let's check out the party.' He put his arm around her.

'What are you doing?' Freya wriggled her shoulders.

Calm blue eyes looked down into hers. 'I'm pretending,' Jack said smoothly. 'This is a party, and you're my girl. Remember? This is how normal couples behave.'

'Oh. Well. All right.' Freya allowed herself to relax fractionally into the warm crook of his shoulder. At least Jack was tall, so that she could wear proper high-heels.

For some time she had been subliminally aware of music and the whoop and roar of a party revving into life. Now she looked about her. A steady procession of cars was rolling up the long driveway, scattering sheep to the lengthening shadows of holm oaks and hawthorns. Colour was draining from the sky, leaving streamers of tangerine and damson cloud, and a diffuse, golden light that turned the grass chartreuse. From all directions, people were emerging from archways and sweeping across lawns to funnel down the broad path leading to the courtyard where the party was being held.

Help! There was someone she recognized, the daughter of the local Master of Foxhounds, who had been brought over to 'play' with her when she first came to Cornwall, and had become a casual holiday friend. Vicky: that was her name. Goodness, she'd gained a lot of weight. Freya caught her eye and Vicky's face lit up with recognition. She came over to greet Freya, arm in arm with her husband Toby (balding, middle-aged paunch, local solicitor). With a pleasurable spurt of one-upmanship Freya introduced Jack (young, American, a writer). The four of them joined the party crowd, chatting companionably. Freya's spirits rose. This was going to be all right.

At the entrance to the courtyard, a line of eager teenage girls and boys, recruited from the village, held trays of drinks. Freya helped herself to a Pimm's, letting her gaze roam while Vicky and Toby engaged Jack in small talk. The large courtyard, normally cluttered with firewood, machinery and rusting oddments, had been completely cleared. On a mown square of grass at the centre, a jazz band was playing 'Just One Of Those Things'. Along one wall a line of charcoal braziers glowed red, ready to barbecue the fish she and Jack had bought earlier. Next to them were trestle tables laden with sticks of bread, bowls of salad and wedges of cheese, punctuated by sheaves of wildflowers in ordinary garden buckets – simple but festive. Freya caught sight of Annabelle talking to one of the barbecue men, and on impulse excused herself from the group and strolled over to her.

'Congratulations, Annabelle. This all looks marvellous. You must have been slaving for weeks.'

'Oh . . . well . . .' Annabelle seemed flustered by the compliment. She smoothed her dress over her hips. 'It's very nice of you to come all this way,' she offered. 'I wish you'd come more often. Truly.'

Their eyes met. 'I'll try,' said Freya.

'And do bring Jack again. We all like him so much.'

'Really?' Freya swivelled round to locate Jack, wanting to share this joke with him, and saw that he was being bored stiff by Toby. Catching her gaze, Jack gave her a bug-eyed stare that begged for rescue.

Freya beckoned him over, miming an instruction that he should also bring a drink for Annabelle. Within a minute he had extricated himself and was handing Annabelle a glass. 'Here you go, Mrs Penrose. Drink up.'

'Oh, do call me Annabelle. I feel ancient enough as it is.' She took a long drink, and let out a grateful breath. 'I needed that. Thank you, my dears, both of you. Now, would you do me a favour and see what those men are up to in the Great Office?' She gestured at the dilapidated building that formed one side of the courtyard. 'Tash set her heart on having this *karawaki* thing, so of course I couldn't say no, but I don't like the idea of strange people mucking about with the electrics. It would be a pity if the place burned down after five centuries, don't you think?'

Somehow Freya and Jack managed to maintain straight faces until they were safely inside the building.

'British understatement: I love it!' exclaimed Jack. 'A five-hundred-year-old building burns down, and it's "a pity".'

'*Karawaki!*' giggled Freya. 'It sounds like a Japanese car.'

She looked around the high hall, with its ingeniously timbered roof, flagstone floor, long windows with cracked and broken panes, and an unmistakable smell of damp. The village pantomime used to be put on here at Christmas time, until the leaks in the roof got too bad. This was where she had practised her roller-skating, juddering over the uneven flags, and played marathon matches of table tennis with Vicky on rainy holiday afternoons. Here, too, Annabelle had achieved wonders. There were tables draped with pink paper tablecloths and decorated with flowers, already being colonized by guests carrying platefuls of food. A large area had been covered by a temporary dance floor; above it pink and silver balloons printed with 'Natasha' and 'Roland' hung down from the rafters. Beyond this, at the far end of the room, was a stage, where two men were setting up loudspeakers and a karaoke machine.

She followed Jack up on to the stage, and while he engaged the men in conversation about amps and fuses, peered curiously at the karaoke machine. She was joined by a young man in a glittery jacket, very full of himself, who introduced himself as Rocky and asked what she wanted to sing. 'Anything you like except "Stand By Your Man",' he told her. 'I've had requests up to here for that one.'

Freya set him straight about her ambitions to make a fool of herself in public. According to Rocky, the karaoke part of the evening would be beginning shortly; afterwards he would be shifting into DJ mode for the dancing. 'Only till midnight, mind. I've had my marching orders from Mrs P. She don't want no hangovers for the wedding tomorrow.'

The hall was beginning to fill up. There must be a hundred people altogether, mostly twentysomethings from London who had been billeted all over the surrounding countryside in cottages, hotels, pubs, spare rooms, mattresses on floors and even tents. Shrieks of excitement rose above the general buzz; the jazz band was superseded by funk-rock from the speakers; a tantalizing smell of grilled fish wafted in from outside. She saw Jack signalling to her that it was time to sit down and eat. Freya was assailed by an unfamiliar sensation: she was happy.

' . . . and my heart will go on.'

As the girl in the hippie-chick outfit yowled her way to the end of the song, the audience hooted and clapped their approval. Freya nudged Jack to pass her some more white wine, and washed down her last mouthful of raspberries and cream. She felt well-fed and mellow, comfortably hemmed in by the warm bodies of Jack on one side, and Sponge on the other. Opposite sat two interchangeably pretty bridesmaids called Polly and Lulu, both in black sleeveless dresses, both perfectly nice in their girly, giggly way. Sponge had sobered up, oddly enough; it turned out that he was Roland's best man, and endearingly nervous about his duties. Over dinner, they had all tried to help him with tomorrow's speech. In fact, Jack had practically written the whole thing for him on a paper napkin. Sponge had declared himself to be 'frightfully thick', and was much impressed to learn that Jack was a published writer.

The karaoke was a good idea. Rocky was not the most sophisticated of entertainers, but his have-a-go cockiness and inventive pronunciation of unfamiliar names, like Hamish and Letitia, had won the indulgence of his audience, breaking down the barriers between young and not so young, local and London, Tash's friends and Roland's friends. Even Vicky's husband, Toby, red-faced and sublimely off-key, had gamely ploughed his way through 'Tie a Yellow Ribbon Round the Old Oak Tree'.

'I love English weddings,' Jack said expansively to no one in particular. 'A party like this is much more fun than the rehearsal dinners we have in the States.'

'What's a rehearsal dinner?' asked Polly (or possibly Lulu).

'It's sort of like a Quaker meeting, only less lively.'

Jack began to describe the blood-chilling ritual of gathering close relatives of the bride and groom in some cheerless function room, on the eve of a wedding, where they were each required to stand up and spontaneously praise the soon-to-be-blissful couple. He was on good form tonight, Freya thought, leaning her head on her hand and watching him with a lazy smile. And his haircut suited him; she had done him a favour by insisting on it.

'Usually the two families have never met before and can't imagine why their beloved son or daughter or sibling has made such a disastrous choice. But they have to pretend they all love each other.' Jack's voice thickened with false sentiment: '"I just wanna to say that Earl is the best brother a guy could have, and I feel in my heart that Nancy Mae is gonna make him happy – even though I happen to know for a fact that she was called 'little Nancy no pantsy' in junior high." Of course, he doesn't say that last part out loud.'

Freya heard Sponge chortling with laughter beside her. Rather worryingly, he took his paper napkin out of a pocket to make a note.

'What's really phony, these days, are all the step-parents,' said Jack. 'You've got the father-of-the-bride, mother-of-the-bride, father-of-the-bride's second wife, mother-of-the-bride's second husband, father-of-the-bride's second wife's current husband, etcetera – all spinning a line about how wonderful marriage is. If I ever got married I could probably fill the whole front row of the church single-handed.'

'And *are* you ever going to get married?' asked Lulu (or possibly Polly) with a flirtatious sparkle. Freya raised a sardonic eyebrow. She'd love to hear his answer to that one.

But at that moment their attention was distracted by Rocky's chirpy voice: ' . . . all the way from the American South, where the nights are hot and the girls are easy – *Jack Madison*. Jack's going to sing – and I hope this isn't a comment on tomorrow's wedding – "I Say a Little Prayer for You"!'

Freya turned to Jack in surprise, and found him glaring at her.

'You set me up!' he said.

'No, I didn't.'

'I *saw* you up there, schmoozing with Rocky.'

Polly and Lulu were clapping their hands delight-edly. 'Go on, Jack.'

The well-oiled audience, sensing a drama in Jack's hesitation, began to chant. 'Jack, Jack, Jack, Jack . . .'

Jack rose to his feet, and poked Freya in the arm. 'I'll get you for this later,' he growled.

Freya watched him go, hoping he wasn't going to make a fool of himself. 'Pass the wine, will you?' she asked Sponge.

Jack was on stage now, taking the microphone. The opening bar blasted out its fast, impossible rhythm. The blip of the autocue began to bounce over the words of the song, projected on to a screen onstage. He didn't sound too bad to begin with; in fact, he got a laugh for camping up the line about putting on make-up. But almost at once something went wrong. The music continued, but Jack wasn't singing. Freya craned her neck to see what was going on. Jack was squinting at the screen in a manner that was all too familiar to her. Oh, God . . . He hadn't brought his glasses, the idiot. He couldn't read a word. The audience began to murmur. Rocky was frantically leafing through sheets of paper, looking for a typed version. Freya squirmed with embarrassment.

Oh, no. Jack had put the microphone to his mouth again. He was going to have to apologize, and leave the stage in mid-song. She couldn't bear to look. Even Toby had performed better than this. She lowered her head, closed her eyes, and put her hands over her ears.

But Jack didn't apologize. He started singing.

> *'I don't know the words, dear,*
> *'Cos I ain't got my gla-ha-sse-hes up here,*
> *So say a little prayer for meee . . .'*

There was a ripple of laughter. More singing. More laughter.

> '*Whatever, whatever, whatever you know I should sing,*
> *I've sung it,*
> *However, however awful you think I am*
> *I've thunk it . . .*'

Slowly Freya raised her head and allowed herself to look. There he was, white jeans a-dazzle in the spotlight, with a cheesy grin on his face, hamming it up like the terrible show-off he was. The audience loved him; they thought he was hilarious. Relief washed through her. He looked pretty good. In fact he looked great. Her heart softened. *My hero.*

At the end of the song, he looked over in her direction.

> '*My darling, forgive me*
> *I know you can't bel-eeeve*
> *How badly I sing . . .*'

Jack left the stage in a thunder of good-humoured applause. As he threaded his way through the tables, hands reached out to pat him approvingly on the arm or shoulder – one even on the bottom, Freya noticed with a sudden frown. Hands off! When he took his place again at the table, amid rapturous tweetings from Polly and Lulu, she thought it would be a sensible idea to remind everybody what was what. She pulled

Jack close by the shirtsleeve and kissed him on the cheek.

'Darling, "marvellous" *isn't* the word,' she murmured.

He turned his head. His smiling blue eyes, disconcertingly close, rested on hers for a moment. They held surprise, and something else she couldn't quite decipher. Then he thumped the table. 'I need a drink!'

Soon afterwards, the karaoke ended and the guests deserted their tables to unleash their high spirits on the dance-floor. Gallantly, Sponge asked Freya to dance with him and she accepted, pleased to show the watching world that thirtysomethings knew how to party, too. Complete strangers smiled at her and sometimes shouted their approval of Jack's performance. She felt the warm, anonymous press of bodies, and saw how her dress shimmered in the flashing lights. Toby bopped up, jacket off, circles of sweat under his arms, and did his impersonation of a choo-choo train opposite her. She caught sight of Jack dancing with Vicky – how thoughtful! – then with one of those bridesmaid girls. Hmmm.

When she went back to her seat for a rest, everyone else had disappeared. Freya poured herself another glass of wine and frowned at the table, empty now except for crumpled paper-napkins, glasses, bottles and a litter of crumbs. Nobody came over to talk to her. Nobody asked her to dance. She was beginning to feel painfully conspicuous when someone draped an arm around her shoulder and slumped into the chair next to her.

'Hello, sis,' slurred Roland, breathing into her face.

Freya recoiled from the fumes. He pulled his chair closer. His shirt was unbuttoned. Sweat glistened on his skin.

'So. That painting. How much would you say it's worth?'

To keep him at bay, Freya rattled on about the yo-yoing values of contemporary art, while Roland stared at her with the dopey, lop-sided smile of the very drunk. 'Maybe a thousand dollars, if you bought it in a gallery,' she concluded.

He patted her thigh. 'You're a little cracker,' he told her. 'Fantastic legs. Come on, let's dance.' He grabbed her hand and staggered to his feet. Freya gritted her teeth. If it had been anyone else she would have told him to get lost; but rejecting her stepsister's chosen partner might look like sour grapes. She allowed him to lead her into the press of bodies, and went through the motions, head high and gaze abstracted, while Roland waved his arms about and ricocheted off her. Almost at once the music slowed to a smoochy number. Roland reached out and pulled her close, pressing every sweaty inch of his body to hers. He glued his sticky hair to her cheek. His hand groped her bottom and squeezed slowly, suggestively. To him she was a single girl of a certain age, and fair game. She couldn't bear it.

Quite suddenly she was free, and Jack was standing

there with a big, bland smile on his face, and his hand resting affably on Roland's collar. His teeth gleamed in the lights as he spoke into Roland's ear. The next thing she knew Jack had set his arms on her shoulders and was steering her away from a bemused-looking Roland.

Freya smiled into his face with relief. 'What did you say to him?'

'I told him they were playing our song.'

'Yuk. That's so corny.'

'You have no romance in your soul.'

'Where have you been, anyway?'

'Looking for you.'

And with that, he drew her into his arms. Freya relaxed against him and clasped her hands around his waist. Jack felt solid and comfortable and familiar. His warm breath tickled her neck as he crooned along to the music. '*Stand by me* . . .' He probably fancied himself as a singer now, after his karaoke success. Freya rested her cheek on his shoulder and gazed through half-closed eyes at the blur of bodies and shimmer of lights. His shirt smelled good.

When the tempo changed into the pounding, irresistible beat of a familiar old song they stepped apart spontaneously and carried on dancing. It was like old times. Freya undulated her arms and writhed her body. Jack spun and stamped in his sneakers. They advanced and retreated and circled, mimicking each other's gestures, laughing at the sheer silliness of it all. When they took a break and returned to the table for refuelling, Freya felt flushed and charged with energy. She watched the muscles in Jack's hand as he tipped the wine bottle.

'This is such . . . fun!'

'That's because you're not angry.'

'Angry?'

'Tight. Wound up. Snap, snap, like a vicious little crocodile.'

'Is that how you see me?' Freya was stung.

'Not tonight I don't.' Jack drained his glass and smacked his lips. 'Tonight you are a goddess. Freya, goddess of love and beauty. Come on, let's dance.'

They plunged back into the hot pack of gyrating bodies. Freya saw Tash and Roland clasped tight in a passionate snog, and Sponge leaping about with Polly (or possibly Lulu). Jamie had removed his shirt and was jumping up and down like a Masai warrior; he looked completely off his head. Jack deserted her for a moment and reappeared with a protesting Annabelle, whom he coaxed into a kind of slow rock and roll, while Freya leaned against the wall and watched with a smile. You could see why women found Jack attractive. He was tall, athletic, masculine – all that stuff. Then there were those flashing blue eyes, that looked as if he had just thought of a marvellous idea or was about to make a joke. No one was more fun to be with than Jack, when he was in a good mood. Look at him twirling Annabelle about, his thick hair now a little rumpled. He'll never go bald, she thought irrelevantly. *However*: it was important to remember that Jack preferred young girls and she was three years older than him; that flirting was as natural to Jack as breathing; that he was here to *pretend* to be crazy about her. Nothing could be worse than making a fool of herself.

When Annabelle withdrew from the dance floor, flushed and trying vainly to push her hair back into its bun, Jack reclaimed Freya and didn't let her go for the rest of the evening. Fast numbers, slow numbers, silly songs that made them fling their arms in the air, old favourites whose words they shouted aloud: they danced and drank, and drank and danced, until suddenly the music finished, the lights stopped flashing, and Rocky's voice announced that it was midnight. The party was over.

Freya stumbled out into the courtyard with Jack, dazed by the sudden darkness and cool air. Fairylights sparkled in the trees. A double line of flares lit the path. The moon was bright and benign in a pewter sky cobwebbed with cloud. She could hear her friend the owl screeching from its hidden perch; her mind shied away from the unresolved problem of who would be sleeping on the chaise longue tonight. Jack held her hand loosely as they were swept up the path with the crowd. There was a babble of voices shouting goodbye, arguing over car keys and who was sober enough to drive. Freya saw Annabelle trying to round up Roland and his chums, and shepherd them out to a waiting minibus. Then the noises receded as she and Jack veered off towards the house. They walked up stone steps and on to the terrace. The lawn was silver, shadowed by the looming shapes of clipped bushes.

'*Ah-woooh!*' Jack was howling at the moon.

Freya gave him a shove. 'You're drunk.'

'Who cares?' Jack threw out his arms and took a deep, ecstatic breath. 'I love Cornwall.'

'You don't say corn *waal*. It's Corn*wull* – veddy clipped and veddy British.'

'Oh, is it?' With a sudden grin Jack pulled her into his arms and waltzed her up the path. 'I don't care if you are called the fair Miss Frigidaire . . .'

'Cos I'm sen-SA-tional,' she sang back, then tripped on a flagstone. 'Stop!' She stumbled against his shirt front as her ankle twisted, and one of her shoes came off. She bent to retrieve it. 'Bugger. The heel's loose.'

'Uh-oh. Looks like I'm going to have to pick you up and carry you.'

Freya laughed in his face. No one had carried her since she was about eight years old. 'Don't be ridic – '

'Stop saying that!' He made a grab for her. Freya swerved out of his reach and took off along the terrace at a lolloping, peg-legged run. He chased after her. She darted in through the French windows, across the library and into the hall. As she reached the bottom of the staircase, her stockinged foot slid on the wooden step. She grabbed the newel post, breathless and dizzy, and swung herself round defensively to face Jack.

He reached out and picked her up, just like that. 'Light as a feather,' he pronounced, staggering wildly around the hall.

Freya kicked her legs. 'Put me down!'

From upstairs an unfamiliar female voice called, 'Are you all right?'

Freya and Jack looked at each other and giggled. Freya put her arms boldly around his neck. 'Okay, carry me, you he-man. Let's see how far you get.'

He shifted her weight a little and began to climb. Moonlight streamed through the big window at the turn of the stairs. Freya stared dreamily at his profile. What nice ears he had. She blew playfully on the hair at the nape of his neck. When he reached the landing, he paused.

'Out of breath already?' she teased.

He turned his head and kissed her. The shock of it ripped through her. Her eyes closed, then flew open.

'Freya,' he whispered. His voice was full of longing.

'Jack . . .' She put her fingers to his face. It felt soft and hard, smooth and rough, familiar yet as new and exciting as a wild frontier. Suddenly she wanted to touch every part of him – his ears and his neck and the line of his eyebrows and that corner of his mouth that curled up – just a bit, not enough for anyone but her to notice – when he was secretly amused. She slid her feet to the ground, staying within the strong clasp of his arms, feeling his body against hers. Then she wound her arms around his neck and kissed him back.

It seemed that her being split in two, so that her mind floated free in a haze of wonder and anticipation, while a drumbeat of desire propelled her body upstairs. She felt the reassuring bulk of Jack's body, his thigh hard against hers, his breath on her hair. The bedroom was bathed in moonlight. Without any conscious wish or effort she was lying down, eyes shut, arms stretched wide on a bed that tilted and swayed beneath her. Then Jack's weight was on top of her. She smiled and ran her hands down his back, feeling the ripple of his ribs under her thumbs. He pulled down the straps of her dress, then raised himself off her. Her eyelids fluttered open. He was kneeling astride her. He was undoing his shirt.

Wait . . . Undoing his shirt? Was this right? No . . . *Yes!* But the warning voice grew louder. This was Jack – her old friend, her *younger* friend, lover of Candace and a thousand interchangeable others, past and future. She was heading down a blind alley: she would get hurt. Freya put her hands flat against his chest. 'I don't think this is a good idea.' Her voice was weak and unconvincing.

Jack seized her hands and was kissing her palms. 'Of course it's a good idea,' he murmured. His eyes were half-closed, his face sharp and concentrated with desire.

'No.' She pulled herself out from under him, into a sitting position. Jack reached for her – blindly, possessively. She put out a hand to ward him off. 'No,' she said again. With a supreme effort she managed to swing her legs over the edge of the bed and stand up. She was trembling. She couldn't stop. It was embarrassing. She held on to the bedpost. 'I think

I'm a little drunk, and so are you. Let's not do anything we'll regret.'

'*I* won't regret it,' Jack said fiercely. He slid from the bed and smoothed his hands over her shoulders. He was trembling too. 'Come on, Freya, let yourself go. We've been wanting to do this for years.'

'I have *not.*'

It was a lie. She wanted to. Oh, how she wanted to. Her body was ripe and ready as a juicy fig. *It's just sex,* she told herself. She didn't want to have 'just sex' – not with Jack.

But that's what it would be. On Sunday he'd go home to Candace; she'd be no more than another name on the list. With an effort as great as slamming down a steel shutter, she made herself say, 'It's been fun pretending, Jack, but I think this game has gone far enough.'

'I'm not pretending! And neither are you.' His thumbs dug into her arms.

'Let's not forget about Candace.'

Jack tossed his head at this irrelevance. 'Freya – '

'We're friends, Jack. That's all.'

'It's not all!'

'For Christsake, let me *go!*' She was almost weeping.

His fingers tightened painfully. Then he flung her away from him. They stared at each other in distrust.

Jack's eyes narrowed to glittering slits. His mouth twisted. 'Well, what a little cock-teaser you are.'

Freya's head snapped back, as if he'd hit her. Her

nose prickled with tears that she commanded herself not to shed. Vulnerability made her caustic.

'You and your cock. That's all you think about. The only reason you want me is because I'm *here*.'

'That's not true!'

'You don't really want a woman like me. Someone who talks back. Someone who doesn't think every single thing you do is a miracle. And I don't want someone who screws around. So let's not get started, okay?' She could hear her own breath, ragged and harsh, and made an effort to calm her voice. 'I'll sleep on the chaise longue,' she said.

Jack punched the air in fury. 'You don't think I'm going to stay here, do you? Just climb into bed like a good little boy, while you lie sanctimoniously on the other side of the goddamned room? Jesus, Freya! You really have got ice in your veins.'

He backed away from her. He was buttoning his shirt, his fingers fumbling, sliding, slipping. Anger flowed out of his powerful body. He jerked open the door. His mouth twisted in a parody of the smile she loved. He cut the air with a mocking sweep of his hand.

'The bed's all yours.'

# 26

He ought to have passed out by now. Why the hell hadn't he? Jack slopped more whisky into his glass and raised it to his lips. The smell made him nauseous. He slammed down the glass and paced up and down the library, kicking errant scraps of silver ribbon and crackly paper out of his way. He was so . . . *angry*!

His first impulse had been to leave – to jump in the car, drive straight to the airport and go home. To hell with Freya and her family and this stupid wedding! But the car keys were in Freya's purse upstairs; returning to the bedroom was too humiliating to contemplate. Instead, he'd tramped around the dewy gardens for the better part of an hour, irritatingly shadowed by an inquisitive Bedivere, who clearly hoped that Jack was going to reveal the whereabouts of his bone hoard. But his efforts to calm his mind and exhaust his body had proved futile. All he'd got was wet feet. All he'd seen was the sordid debris of the party – extinguished flares, gusting napkins, the litter of cigarette butts and burst balloons. All he'd heard were the sounds of a couple copulating in a hay barn; their moans only increased his frustration.

He *hated* her, yet he couldn't get her out of his mind.

Freya running down the beach in her bikini, long legs gleaming with sea water. Freya dancing in her mermaid dress. The feel of her in his arms, the look in her eye when he'd retrieved the karaoke disaster, the tender lift of her chin as she'd raised her head to kiss him. And the kiss itself. That kiss! . . .

Jack groaned aloud and circled back towards his drink. Thank the Lord for alcohol. When at length he'd returned to the house, he'd remembered the couch where Roland had sat in state, big enough to sleep on, and the tray of drinks at his elbow, and found his way here. Now he slumped on to the worn cushions and sank his head in his hands. He needed to sleep. But he couldn't. Resentment boiled inside him. How could she do that to him? Not once, but *twice*. What did the woman want? *Come here, Jack. Go away, Jack. Isn't this fun, Jack? No, don't be ridiculous.* Push, pull, push, pull, until he was dizzy, exhausted, frustrated and furious. When he thought of how he had put himself out for her, abandoning his work, flying thousands of miles to take part in this ridiculous charade, and she couldn't even – ! He tugged at his hair. And why bring Candace up at a moment like that? He hadn't even thought of Candace since he'd been here – not once!

Jack jumped up from the couch and began pacing again, looking for distraction. The room was full of books, rows and rows of them – cloth-bound, leather-bound, jacketed; stamped, scrolled, foxed and frayed. Oh for the solace of literature, to take possession of his mind and lead it into pastures new – or at least send him to sleep. He peered at the magisterial volumes – Horace, Byron, Pepys, Boswell – and was uneasily reminded of his own novel. He moved along the shelves, looking for something taxing and intricate, which required his full concentration. Ah, Henry James: *The Golden Bowl.* That should do it. He placed the book ready by the couch, then collected all the cushions he could find for his sore head. Grunting, he bent down to unlace and remove his damp shoes. The bottoms of his trousers were wet, too. Maybe if he hung them over a chair to dry, he could use those huge wedding-present bath towels as a makeshift covering. He was starting to unzip his fly when the sensation of being watched made him turn round sharply.

A woman was standing in the open doorway. For a moment he thought it was Freya, come to beg his forgiveness, and almost threw Henry James at her. Then the figure stepped out of the dimness and came into focus.

'Can't you sleep either?' said Tash.

Jack gave a noncommittal grunt. As she strolled over to him, he saw that her feet were bare and her dark hair loose and tousled. She was wrapped in the pink thing she'd worn this morning.

'Ooh, lovely, you've found the booze.' She gave him a conspirator's smile.

'Uh, yes.' Jack realized that he must present a slightly peculiar spectacle, alone here among the wedding presents, with his shoes off, his pile of cushions, and the Penroses' half-empty whisky bottle. 'I'm afraid I helped myself. Hope that's okay.'

'Course it is, Jack! You're practically one of us. What's ours is yours.'

'Thanks.' Her friendliness was cheering. At least somebody liked him. 'Here, let me get you a glass.'

He poured her a drink and sat down. Tash clambered on to the other end of the couch and relaxed with a small sigh, tucking her legs beneath her. She raised her glass in a playful toast.

'Here's to my last few hours of freedom.'

'Freedom,' echoed Jack. Yeah, he'd drink to that.

'Just think: by tomorrow night I'll be Mrs Swindon-Smythe.' Tash giggled. 'It sounds frightfully grown up.'

'You're a brave girl.'

'Don't say that! I've got butterflies in my tummy as it is. Still, I suppose Roley's got the essentials, so what the hell?' She gave a larky grin.

'And what are the essentials for marriage – so I can be sure to avoid them?'

'Loads of dosh, for a start.'

'"Dosh"?'

'Honestly, Jack. Call yourself a writer, and you don't know a simple word like that? Lolly. Dough. Bread. Holding-folding. Roley's father practically *owns* some entire railway thingy.'

'Oh, money. That old stuff. And what else?'

'Well, he adores me, of course.'

'Of course.'

'And . . . he's *very* good in bed.'

Her wide eyes gazed cheekily into his. She was a sexy little number all right. Jack was pretty sure she didn't have a stitch on underneath her robe. Lucky Roland.

'So tell me, Jack. What are you doing down here all alone? Has she chucked you out for some frightful misdemeanour?'

'Who, Freya? Nah.' Jack waved a casual hand. 'I just . . .'

'You just what?' she asked teasingly. 'Forgot your condoms?'

'No.'

'Couldn't get it up?'

'No!'

'Don't tell me: you attempted something more exotic than the missionary position, and she freaked.'

Her outspokenness embarrassed him; irritated him; excited him. His eye fell on the navy-bound volume by his side. 'Actually, I came down to get a book.'

'A book! Golly, what an exciting sex life you two must lead. Do you always take off your shoes before reading aloud to her, you kinky thing?'

'Shut up, Tash,' Jack growled.

'Oops, sor-ree.' Tash shrank herself into a kittenish ball. 'Do I detect a lovers' tiff?'

'No, you don't!' Jack banged the arm of the couch. 'We're not lovers!'

There was a long pause.

'Really?' Tash's voice sharpened with interest.

Jack passed a hand across his aching head. He didn't have the strength to pretend any more. 'I may as well tell you.' He put down his whisky glass. 'Freya and I are just friends. We've been friends for years. She wanted someone to come over here with her, and I agreed. End of story. We've never – ' he broke off.

'What, never?' Tash smiled incredulously.

Jack shook his head.

'But you tried tonight, and she slapped you down?'

Jack looked away, saying nothing. It was humiliating to realize how he'd demeaned himself: the haircut, the smart clothes, buttering up Freya's family, following her around like a lapdog, pretending to go upstairs to bed together, then sleeping separately. Revealing his humiliation to this warm-blooded, uninhibited young girl made him feel like an impotent old fool.

'Poor old Jack.' Her voice was like molasses. 'Perhaps you need some . . . cheering up.'

Jack turned his head and looked at her. She was eyeing him over her glass. She really was very pretty, with her shiny dark hair tumbling around her face, and soft skin flushed like a ripe fruit. He could see the swell of her breasts at the opening of her robe, and the nipples that pressed through the thin, shiny material.

Tash put out the pink tip of her tongue and slowly licked the rim of her glass. She circled the smooth, curved edge, back and forth, watching him with dark, dreamy eyes. Suddenly he was conscious that his trousers were still half-unzipped beneath his loose shirt. It would look foolish to zip them up now. Frankly, he wasn't sure he could.

'Don't tease,' he said.

'Why not?' Her full lips pouted. She stretched out one smooth, bare leg and inched it across the couch and on to his lap. Her robe fell away, exposing a creamy thigh.

'Because I'm tired of games.' Jack gripped her foot, halting its progress.

'I love games,' Tash said huskily. 'It was me who put your name down for the karaoke, to see how you'd . . . perform. You were good, Jack.'

He could feel her toes stroking him, pushing his zip wider and wider. His body began to hum. 'Why are you doing this, Tash? You're getting married tomorrow.'

'That's why. One last, lovely taste of freedom. With lovely, lovely Jack.' Tash put down her glass. Keeping her eyes locked on his, she loosened her robe and wriggled it free of her shoulders. Her breasts sprang towards him – warm, soft little puppydogs with pink tongues hanging out, just asking to be stroked. She arched her back and smiled. 'What do you think?'

Jack was beginning not to think anything much. 'I think . . . you're a very naughty person.'

'It takes one to know one. I should think you could be very naughty indeed.' Her voice dropped to a throaty whisper. 'Come, on Jack. No one will find out. It can be our secret.'

The tiny corner of his brain that was still functioning told Jack that this was unusual behaviour for a bride-to-be. Still, if she wanted to, who was he to argue? It was just sex. He liked sex. He loosened his grip on her foot and let it roam, up and down and around. His fingertips slid up the inside of her leg. When he reached the soft, incredibly silky skin of her thigh, she eased her legs apart, and leaned back. Jack pushed aside the last concealment of her robe. He could see everything. He could smell her. His heartbeat began to accelerate. He'd been badly treated. He was owed.

Tash put one hand out to her glass and dabbled her middle finger in the whisky. When she took it out, he could see the liquid running down and gathering in heavy, golden drops. 'I hope you like whisky,' she said.

Maddened by her teasing, Jack launched himself on top of her. He heard her give a crow of pleasure, and felt her hot little hands slip under his loosened trousers. They pushed at the last resistance of his zip and reached around to capture him – squeezing, stroking, tickling. Her head was tipped back on the edge of the couch, hair brushing the carpet.

Jack spread his fingers across the swelling flesh of her breasts. He thrashed his legs, trying to kick free of his trousers, and the two of them tumbled together off the couch. Tash fell on her back among the crumpled sheets of wrapping paper, so hard he heard her grunt with pain. But her eyes were hot slits of desire. She liked this. Her fingers reached up and tore at his shirt. Then she half sat up and pushed at his shoulder to roll him on to his back. Her hair shadowed her face as she straddled him, lips parted, plump breasts bobbing. She smoothed her hands greedily across his abdomen, over his chest, along the hard curves of his shoulders and arms. Her cat-like face creased with pleasure. 'You're much too good for my big sister,' she murmured, and lowered herself on top of him.

She knew lots of tricks. Her slick body squirmed and squeezed and arched, until Jack grabbed hold of her and pushed her on to her back. His feet knocked something over; he heard the clatter of wood and a sharp clink of china. Tash reached up for him; he pinned her arms behind her head and pulled her tight. Thought dissolved into sensation. Then he heard her ratcheting breath, fast and on a rising pitch. He opened his eyes and saw her head tilt and her mouth widen. Some instinct made him jam the edge of his hand into her mouth to muffle her cries, while her body rippled beneath him. The savagery of her sharp little teeth made him plunge faster, deeper. One, two, three, four . . .

It was over. Jack lay with his full weight on top of her, eyes closed, mind empty, heart racing, his skin hot and sparking with sensation. Gradually his muscles relaxed, his breathing slowed. He rolled away with a groan.

He heard the delicate chiming of a clock. Consciousness returned, sudden and shocking, like a train speeding out of a dark tunnel. He lifted his head. An espresso cup lay upside down by his foot, its handle chipped off. His white trousers dangled over the edge of the couch, one leg inside out. *The Golden Bowl* had fallen to the floor and lay face down, its pages splayed open, the india paper creased.

Jack raised himself clumsily on all fours. He looked at Tash's pink and white body, sprawled like a puppet's. He saw the glint of her half-closed eyes, the slack mouth he'd been too frenzied to kiss even once. A length of ribbon, silver etched with wedding bells, was caught in the tumble of her hair. From the darkness between her legs a trickle of sperm made its pale, slow snail-track across the monogrammed towels.

# 27

Freya filled the kettle with water and plonked it on the Aga. Where the hell was he?

Probably sulking somewhere. Bloody men. Brains between their legs, egos like airships. You said no, and they called you a cock-teaser and stomped off. Typical. The really hypocritical thing was the way they pretended that their *feelings* were hurt. All they meant was that they wanted sex and they wanted it NOW.

Yes, all right, perhaps she had been a bit come-hither last night. But they were supposed to be pretending: that was the whole point of bringing him here. Okay, *okay*: so she'd got a little overexcited. She'd had a lot to drink. And Jack was an attractive man; she'd never denied that. Sex was all very well in its place. She herself had indulged in plenty of erotic flings, thank you, every bit as wham-bam as a man's. But she had not come all this way to have a one-night stand with Jack Madison!

So.

Exactly.

Freya poured boiling water on her Earl Grey tea bag. Where were his priorities, for God's sake? The wedding was only hours away. She'd scream if she had to stand all by herself in that bloody marquee, nibbling a stuffed prune and listening to Vicky's mother patronize her about Vicky's husband, Vicky's children, Vicky's wallpaper, Vicky's pergola – not to mention the softness of Vicky's hands after washing up, the miracle of the school run in Vicky's Volvo, and the quite thrilling thrust of Toby's golf-drive.

Besides, she wanted to know what he thought of her hat. It was a sizzling lime green, extravagantly brimmed, and probably visible across five counties. Yes I AM the older sister, it proclaimed – the glamorous one from glamorous New York, with the glamorous man – who still finds time in her busy schedule to witness the quaintly old-fashioned ritual of marriage, involving someone who is not even a blood relative. Buggeration: she'd spilt the milk.

Freya had not slept well. For some reason the bed seemed far less comfortable than it had the previous night, lumpy and cold. That owl kept her awake. The moonlight had been so bright she could see the red stripes of Jack's pyjamas, hanging on the back of the door. Every creak of a floorboard made her wonder if that was him, creeping back to beg her forgiveness.

There were quick steps in the passage. Annabelle burst in, her hair in rollers, eyes glassy with frenzied concentration.

'Has that kettle boiled? Freya, you're a saint. Now, where did I put the Swindon-Smythes' tea tray? They won't mind brown sugar, will they? I should have picked some flowers from the garden. Never mind. Just look at the time! Oh dear, oh dear, oh dear . . .'

And out she went again.

Freya slumped against the rail of the Aga and sipped her tea. It had begun. She could look forward to an entire day of this lunacy, until the blessed moment when Tash would toss her bouquet into the crowd and drive away. She could already hear the squawkings of the county crones. *Doesn't Tash look lovely? Isn't her dress beautiful? Don't they make a handsome couple? When is it going to be your turn, Freya?* And unless Jack turned up, she would have to endure it all alone. Where was he? Freya glowered into a corner of the room that happened to contain Bedivere's basket, with Bedivere curled inside it. He caught her eye and politely scrambled to his feet, padded over to her and lifted his nose.

Freya jumped. 'Get away, you old crotch-sniffer!' God, even the dog was at it. Bloody males. They were all the same.

'Good morning, darling. Had a good sleep?'

Her father entered the kitchen at a sprightly pace, freshly shaved and smiling, hair curling damply from his bath.

Freya raised an eyebrow. 'All spruced up to give away your daughter, I see.'

His eyes rested on hers for a moment. 'Crumpet or toast?' he asked mildly.

'Neither. I'm not hungry.'

'Nonsense. Sit down and have some breakfast with your old Dad. Tell me what you've been up to.'

'What, now? You're far too busy.'

'Plenty of time yet. I've hardly seen you since you arrived.'

There was a flurry of footsteps, and a figure whirled through the kitchen and towards the scullery, as if propelled by a force-nine gale. 'Darling, have we got any soya milk? Why didn't Barry tell me he was on a special diet? Marilyn swears she saw a mouse in the bedroom. It's too ghastly. I told you we needed more traps . . .'

Her father caught Freya's eye and winked.

' . . . Will skimmed milk do, I wonder? I hope they aren't expecting a cooked breakfast. Those girls aren't even awake yet. And the hairdresser will be here any minute. For heaven's sake, Guy! Have you forgotten Tash is getting married today? You can't just stand there!'

'Why not?'

Annabelle gave a shudder of exasperation and zoomed off.

'See what I mean?' said Freya.

'Best to lie low for a bit. She'll blow herself out. Tell you what, let's take a tray into my study. No one will bother us there.' He hesitated. 'Or would you rather go back up to Jack?'

'No,' said Freya, suddenly galvanized into activity. She strode across to a cupboard. 'Marmalade or honey?'

'Let's be devils and have both.'

The study was a beautiful room, high-ceilinged yet cosy, a perfect square of panelled walls with a fireplace on one side and a mullioned window on the other, looking out over a sweep of lawn to the sheep-meadows beyond. Freya carried in the tray and her father cleared a space on his desk, a mahogany monstrosity covered with a familiar clutter of books, papers, journals, clippings, boxes of transparencies, and miscellaneous letters weighed down with the beautiful brass paperweight, in the shape of a snail, that he'd owned as long as Freya could remember.

'Glad to see you haven't got any tidier,' she remarked. 'Do you remember how Mrs Silva used to call your study "the piggy sty"?'

Her father chuckled and closed the door. He lowered himself into an armchair and watched Freya busy herself with his plate and mug.

'How nice to be waited on by my daughter! Come and sit down.'

'What are these proofs?' Freya asked, rummaging in his papers to flip open a folded bundle. 'Have you got another book coming out?'

'No, just a contribution to one of those dreary academic series. Can't think why I do it. The pay is pitiful.' He sighed. 'I'm not sure that there's going to be another book. I'm getting to be an old man, you know.'

Freya turned sharply. 'Don't be silly,' she said.

'Stop poking about, and come and tell me what you're up to in New York. How's the job? Is the art world as dotty as it seems? Are you happy?'

Freya folded herself into an old leather armchair,

balanced her mug on the arm and began to answer his questions – the first two, anyway. She was conscious that her answers were grudging, but why should she have to reveal every little detail of her life? He wasn't really interested, anyway. He had Annabelle and Tash and the house and the dog to think about. As she spoke, her gaze hovered on the cluster of framed photographs displayed on the bookshelf behind his head, the same collection he'd had for years. One showed him and Annabelle on their wedding day, flanked by Tash and herself. They were all smiling except her. How clearly she remembered her sense of dislocation, as if her father's wedding and its attendant celebrations were all a dream and she would wake up in the London flat, just herself and her father, as it had always been. She remembered puzzling over why her father needed Annabelle, too. Wasn't she enough for him? Now the question almost made her laugh aloud. On the one hand, a gawky schoolgirl peering warily from behind that awful fringe; on the other, a full-figured woman sexually in her prime, with a child to prove it. Everything came down to sex, in the end. Jack's voice floated back to her: *What a little cock-teaser you are.* She *hated* Jack.

Her father, sensing her inattention, turned to look at the photos. His face softened. He reached out a long arm and picked one up.

'Ah, look at you.' He tilted the picture to show her. 'That was taken the very day you were born.'

'I know. You've told me.' Freya glowered at her own little monkey face.

'You were so tiny, yet you had an absolutely definite personality, as powerful as a magnetic force field. Extraordinary! You have no idea how I felt when I first held you in my arms. I wanted to protect you from everything. Funnily enough, the image I had was of greasy, long-haired louts on motorbikes coming to carry you off God knows where, when you were grown up and beautiful, and how I'd have to stand by, grinding my teeth, and let you go. I already dreaded the day when I'd have to give you away to some husband who couldn't possibly deserve you.'

Freya prickled with irritation. 'Though as it happens, it's Tash you're giving away,' she pointed out.

His smile faded. His face sagged with sudden weariness. She had hurt him. He lowered the photo to his lap with a small sigh. She noticed brown spots mottling his hand. When had those appeared?

'Tash is Tash, and you are you,' he said. 'I've done my best to be a father to her, but you're *mine*. You're special. I've always loved you and I always will love you. You're not to mind about all this wedding palaver. It has nothing to do with you and me.'

Freya gave a vague smile. She felt abashed at his warmth. She didn't know how to respond.

'I know I'm a tactless old idiot,' he continued. 'It's not important who gets married and who doesn't. But – well, I suppose the time has come when I'd like you to find someone special to care about, and to care about you – not so you can have the status of marriage but so that you can experience the big things of life. Companionship. Commitment. Sharing. Children. They . . . stretch one.'

Freya pursed her lips. Did he think she had never considered these things too? Had *ached* for such experiences – enough to pretend to herself that she wanted to marry Michael, whom she didn't even love. 'I don't think I'm the domestic type,' she said flippantly. 'Anyway, I haven't found the right man.'

Her father looked at her. 'You seem to get on very well with Jack. I like him.'

'Jack's all right.' Freya shrugged. 'He's just – ' She broke off. She'd nearly said he was just a friend. This pretence business was getting complicated.

'What happened to the chap we were expecting – Michael?'

'Oh, that's all over,' Freya said breezily.

'And now you've met Jack.'

'Yes.'

'And you like him,' her father prompted.

'Yes.' Freya squirmed.

'I suppose you must do, since you're living with him. That's right, isn't it?'

'Ye-es.'

'You don't sound very certain.'

'Well . . . Jack's a bit of a playboy.'

'Hmm. Perhaps he needs somebody fierce and sensible to sort him out.'

Freya ignored this. 'Playboys are fun, in their way. At least Jack never bores me.'

'What, never? Darling, you must bag him at once!'

'For God's sake, Daddy, it's not a big thing. Not like you and Mummy. We quarrel all the time.'

Her father's eyebrows soared. 'Do you think Karina and I never quarrelled? Good Lord, we'd hardly been married a month before I stormed out, saying we'd made a dreadful mistake and might as well get divorced at once.'

Freya was shocked. 'Why? What happened?'

'Heavens, I can't remember now.' Her father laughed at the very idea. 'People have to express their frustrations, you know.'

'But – but you loved her, didn't you?' Freya faltered.

'Of course I loved her. And she loved me. Loving someone doesn't mean that they're perfect, just that you see them clearly, flaws and all, and love them anyway. Karina was fierce and impetuous and stubborn – like someone else I know. I loved her for being the way she was, and sometimes I suffered for it too.'

Freya pictured Jack's face last night, when she'd told him she was only pretending. For a moment her bravado wavered. What if she had made a mistake? What if he had spent as miserable a night as she had? She looked down at her plate and fiddled with her toast crumbs. 'And if you had a quarrel – a bad one, I mean – what did you do?'

'Apologized. Forgave each other. Made up.' He grinned suddenly. 'That was the good bit.'

Freya smiled back. With exactly that expression he'd told her he was sneaking out to a casino to try his luck, or they were taking a boat from Venice airport, straight across the lagoon, instead of that dreary old bus.

Now he leaned towards her eagerly, forearms on his bony knees. 'It's so lovely to talk to you, darling. I wish I saw you more often. I was thinking of coming to New York in the autumn. I think I could wangle the fare out of one of those marvellous American endowment funds. I'd love it if we could spend some time together.'

Freya frowned. 'It'll be the auction season.'

'Not the whole autumn, surely.'

'I suppose Annabelle wants to do her Christmas shopping.'

'Actually, I rather thought I'd come alone. It's you I want to see – if you can spare the time.'

His humility made Freya faintly ashamed. Part of her longed for them to be together, but it wasn't that easy. She couldn't allow it to be that easy. She glanced back at the photograph of her father on his wedding day. He had chosen his life, and she had chosen hers. That's the way it was.

'Well, think about it.' Her father, suddenly brisk, hauled himself out of his chair. He peered long-sightedly at his watch. 'Ah. Just time to take Bedivere for a run.'

Freya noted the time with a fresh spasm of panic. The wedding was due to start in two hours. Where was Jack?

# 28

The tide was going out. Each wave slurped up a mouthful of shingle, then sprayed it back on to the beach in an undulating line. Jack had no idea how long he'd been sitting here: long enough for the sea to gurgle out of rockpools, leaving giant black noodles of seaweed whose ammoniac reek made him gag; long enough for the sun to rise over the far shore of the estuary and stab its brightening rays into his eyeballs; long enough for him to have reached a decision.

He was leaving. As soon as the wedding began, he would sneak back up to the house, gather his belongings and go. Freya would make up some kind of story to cover his departure; she was good at deceit.

He didn't want to think about last night. He wasn't particularly proud of his antics in the library with Tash. But he'd been drinking, and she had come on strong. Anyway, what did it matter? In a couple of hours she'd be married. As for Freya . . . If she didn't want him – and last night she had made it painfully clear that she didn't – she could do without him altogether. It was too painful to continue with this absurd charade as her partner, especially during the festivities of a wedding. He felt wrung out, hung over, pushed about, let down and fed up. He was going home.

Jack let his collection of stones trickle through his fingers and struggled unsteadily to his feet. Even this small effort brought beads of sweat to his forehead. His legs were leaden. His stomach felt as if it had been suction-pumped, then washed out with vinegar. 'A man shouldn't fool with booze until he's fifty': thank you, William Faulkner. Jack looked about for a shady spot where he could lie low and recover. Behind him rose the lush greenery of the garden through which he'd plunged, on a steep zig-zag path, to escape the waking household. The house was invisible from here; he could no longer remember where exactly the path had emerged. Trudging back across the shingle, he took the first opening he saw.

The narrow track climbed steeply. Jack could see that it had once been much wider, with broad steps carved out of the soil and shored up with logs. But the logs had rotted; the vegetation pressed close, closer, until he could barely discern the path. Jungly leaves batted his face; brambles scratched at his trousers. Tiny insects rose in clouds and settled on his skin. He was wondering whether to retrace his steps when he heard a crashing noise in the undergrowth, like the sound of a heavy beast. He paused. It was coming nearer. Were there wild boar in England? Jack quickened his pace. The crashing got louder; he could hear fierce panting. The path ended abruptly, and he found himself teetering on the brink of a ten-foot drop, overlooking some kind of sunken pit. Then a black labrador burst out of a thicket and cantered towards him, tail waving, and a voice called, 'Ah, well done. You've found Lethe's Leap.'

Jack turned to see Freya's father striding towards him, swinging a stout stick. The tilt of his head and his amused half-smile were so like Freya's that Jack suffered a wrench of recognition.

'Named, of course, after the river of forgetfulness in the Greek underworld,' Guy continued. 'One leapt in and forgot all one's responsibilities and the conventions of decent behaviour. Where you're standing is effectively the diving-board.'

Jack stared down at the rough rectangle of weeds edged with broken stone slabs. Comprehension dawned. 'It's a swimming-pool!'

'"Was" is the operative word. I shouldn't think it's been used since the Fifties. No doubt Freya's told you the colourful story of Annabelle's inheritance?'

Jack frowned. 'Freya tells me nothing.'

'I know the feeling.' Guy gave a wistful sigh. 'Never mind. I'll fill you in while we walk back.' He paused, and added courteously, 'Unless you have other plans?'

Jack was suddenly conscious of his dishevelled appearance and the oddity of his presence here, alone. 'No, I was just – '

'Splendid.'

Guy set off at a brisk pace along a curving track that took them out of the garden and up into wilder woodland. Jack loped alongside him, only half-listening to Guy's history of the house and the Ashleigh family who had owned it for centuries. He was trying to figure out how to avoid being shepherded back to the house and into a confrontation with Freya. But gradually the story claimed his attention.

It seemed that in the 1920s the house had passed into the ownership of Frederick 'Fruity' Ashleigh, a 'confirmed bachelor' with a taste for lithe young men, whom he imported in droves for house-parties of legendary debauchery. 'He's the one who had the swimming-pool built,' said Guy, 'presumably as an excuse to get his young friends to take their clothes off. The locals claim that the sounds of gramophone music and popping champagne corks could be heard on the other side of the estuary.'

Fruity's particular friend was a young man twenty years his junior, known as Bunny – 'one of these eccentric chaps, liked to paint the doves in rainbow colours and serve his horse tea in the drawing room, that sort of thing'. Guy's tone seemed to imply that every English family contained such a figure as a matter of course. 'The two of them set up house together, spending half the year in Cornwall and half in London. Despite spectacular quarrels and rampant infidelity on Bunny's part they were a devoted pair, and when Fruity died childless he willed the house to Bunny. *Stop that, Bedivere!*' Jack winced as Guy roared at the dog, who was rolling luxuriously in a gooey mess of feathers. Bedivere slunk over to them apologetically. Jack's stomach heaved at the ripe smell. Guy carried on blithely. 'After Fruity's death Bunny promptly took himself off to London, where he behaved very badly in Soho, by all accounts, and left the house to crumble. In due course he died himself – keeled over in a pub. Not being the most practical of men, he had failed to make a will. After a great many months and an extortionate legal bill, it transpired that his nearest living relative was Annabelle.'

'I see.' Jack's head was pounding. He wanted to lie down. He didn't care dick about the Ashleigh family, but it seemed polite to make a contribution to this conversation. 'So, uh, Annabelle is no relation at all to the Ashleighs?'

'None whatsoever. She's an army captain's daughter from Suffolk, and I'm a vicar's son from Berkshire: not a drop of blue blood between us. We met shortly after she inherited the house. Her husband was dead, she'd a small child to look after and hardly any money. She'd tried putting the house on the market, but no one would touch it. So in the end we decided to take it on together.'

They had now arrived at a stile leading into an open meadow that sloped steeply upwards. Guy looked a little wobbly as he climbed over; Jack stood unobtrusively close, anxious that he might fall. But he seemed very fit for his age, capable of walking uphill and talking fluently at the same time. Jack sweated his way after him, making interested noises as Guy recounted their struggles to renovate the property. Most of their achievements, he insisted, were due to Annabelle; his own work had kept him in London and abroad for long periods. It was she who had fought for grants, badgered local craftsmen, learned about lime mortar and roof-slates, researched the history of the gardens and laboured to restore them until she could open them to the fee-paying public. There was a plant shop and small café, which now brought a trickle of income. They rented fields to campers, wings of the house to Buddhists and writing groups, the chapel for weddings, outbuildings for parties. 'I'm afraid we're dreadful tarts. Have to be. The house is still a bit of a muddle, as I expect you've noticed.'

'No, no. It's very . . .' Jack trailed off as he saw Guy's eyebrows rise in a sceptical expression that was extremely familiar to him. He gave a sheepish smile. He liked this man. 'It's delightful,' he said firmly.

At last they reached the top of the hill and paused to catch their breath. A magnificent view unrolled in all directions. Behind them, the sea was now visible in a shimmering strip beyond the trees. Across the valley, the house lay tranquilly in a green pool of mown lawns. Immediately below them, snug in a wooded dip, was a small stone chapel in a neat enclosure of iron fencing. Jack could see figures bustling in and out, carrying flowers and cardboard boxes. He remembered the wedding, and turned back to catch the freshness of the sea breeze in his nostrils.

'Yes,' Guy mused, 'the house should see us out.' He paused. 'Goodness knows what Tash will do with it.'

The mention of Tash sharpened Jack's attention. He wondered if Guy's inconsequential ramblings masked a subtle intelligence at work. He had the sense of being drawn along by an invisible thread. 'So all this goes to Tash,' he said slowly, 'not Freya.'

'Yes. That's a bit of a problem.'

Jack scuffed the grass with his shoe. In what way was it a problem? Did Guy suspect him of being a fortune hunter – after Freya for her inheritance – and was trying to warn him off? The thought made him angry. His Madison pride rebelled at the implication that he could covet someone else's money. Or was Guy suggesting that Freya was envious of Tash? Jack felt a flash of indignation. Surely Guy knew his own daughter better than that.

'I don't think Freya's interested in the house,' he said coolly.

'Good Lord! Neither do I. I only mean that I don't like her to feel excluded. She's not, of course. In fact, the boot's on the other foot. She's the one who stays away.' Guy sighed. 'I don't know if you've noticed, but Freya is rather an independent sort of person.' Jack's mouth twisted. Yes, he had noticed. 'She doesn't like to be helped. She wouldn't take any money from us when she went to New York – insisted on making her own way. She's made herself very tough. It's as if she fears things will be taken away from her unless she controls them herself.'

'Mm.' Jack was beginning to feel uncomfortable.

He was here on false pretences and didn't deserve Guy's confidence.

'Unfortunately, things *have* been taken away. It's a terrible thing for a girl to lose her mother. One tries to compensate but . . .' Guy jabbed at the ground with his stick. 'I don't think she's ever forgiven me for marrying Annabelle. She doesn't seem to understand that Annabelle isn't a substitute for her – nor could Freya ever be a substitute for Annabelle.' He looked up at Jack. 'I sometimes think that's why she hasn't settled into a relationship of her own.'

Jack avoided his glance. He wasn't playing this game. 'I guess she hasn't found the right man.' He shrugged carelessly.

'Very probably. It would take someone of special qualities to make Freya happy. Shall we walk down?'

Jack stomped after him, feeling disconcerted and irritable. Freya wasn't his concern. She didn't want to be his concern. They weren't really a couple, so it was irrelevant whether he possessed 'special qualities' or not. He glowered at Guy's boots, trying not to think of all the ways in which he had abused this man's hospitality. He should never have allowed Freya to tempt him into coming here.

'I'm very pleased Freya brought you over,' said Guy, turning to him with a friendly smile. 'We don't often get to meet her men friends. She likes to keep her life compartmentalized. Still, I expect you know that all too well, since you're living together.'

*What?* Jack's head snapped up. He tripped over a tussock of grass and nearly fell.

'She was telling me about it this morning.'

*This morning?*

'She said you didn't bore her. I must say I was impressed.'

'But – '

'Oh, don't worry. It's not for me to approve or disapprove. In fact, I'm glad she has someone to care for her.'

'Yes . . .' Jack pictured her face when he'd shouted at her last night.

'Someone to stop her doing silly things.'

'Right . . .' Like going on dates with Professor Parkenrider and that little squirt Brett. Like losing hundreds of dollars at poker and shortening people's trousers.

'She reminds me of those cats who climb out on a limb and can't get back. You see, I'm not there to rescue her.'

Guy's face was so sad and tender that Jack was moved. To distract himself he pointed at a small enclosure to the side of the chapel and asked, 'What's that?'

'Come along and I'll show you.'

They passed through a rusty gate and entered an area of rough grass and weeds studded with gravestones. Some were of normal size, lying flush with the ground, but most were upright and unusually small, barely a foot high.

'Are those – children's?' Jack was shocked. He'd no

idea that infant mortality had been as severe as this.

Guy chuckled. 'Pets,' he said. 'Pets and servants – probably in that order.'

Jack's head swam as he bent down to peer at the worn lettering. Xeno the tortoise. Echo the parrot. 'Mabel Cruttwell 1820–1910, nanny to the Ashleigh Family: In grateful memory of ninety years of faithful service.' Harold the cat. Swithun the butler. An entire row was devoted to dogs: Arthur, Guinevere, Gawain, Lancelot, Morgana, Kay, Merlin, Galahad, Iseult.

'We thought we'd carry on the Ashleigh tradition with this fellow.' Guy waved his stick at Bedivere, who galloped over and cocked his leg on poor Sir Kay. Jack slumped down on to one of the headstones, feeling suddenly light-headed. And something funny had happened to his arm. He'd been aware of a prickle of pain as he'd pushed some weeds away from one of the graves; now he noticed with alarm that a cluster of red bumps had formed on his skin. He hoped this wasn't an English version of poison ivy.

'Don't worry, it's only a stinging nettle.' Guy showed him a patch of dark green plants with hairy leaves. 'The trick is not to brush past them. If you grasp the leaf firmly' – he demonstrated with forefinger and thumb – 'it doesn't hurt at all. Rather like some women.' He grinned.

'Thanks,' Jack said drily, rubbing his arm. He pictured Freya alone at the wedding, chin in the air, eyes watchful, alert to any slight. *Oh, Freya . . .* She was so stubborn, so mistrustful. How could she have thought he was 'pretending' last night?

'I'd better get a move on,' said Guy. 'Annabelle will be flapping. It's a man's job to stay out of the way until the last moment, then lend a calming presence, wouldn't you agree?'

Jack didn't answer. He sat on top of Nanny Cruttwell, watching a distant car winding its way up the drive. There would be plenty of cars dropping people off and going away again. It shouldn't be hard to get a ride to the station.

'Well, I'll see you up at the house. Come along, Bedivere. By the way . . .' Guy thwacked a bramble into submission. 'I don't wish to be personal, but I do happen to know an excellent cure for a hangover.'

# 29

The chapel was filling up. Above the dogged drone of the organ came the rustling, flapping, chattering, cawing sounds of gathering guests: stately great-aunts adorned with brooches as big as sheriffs' badges; jolly uncles buttoned tight into the waistcoats of svelter days; hair-tossing young women in skimpy dresses and off-the-shoulder pashminas; guileless-looking toddlers warming up their vocal cords. Jamie was on duty at the door, dashing in striped trousers and black tailcoat, handing out service sheets. At the front of the chapel Reverend Thwacker, an elderly rubicund gnome swamped by his surplice, pottered about the altar, ensuring that all was in order, and beamed short-sightedly at the congregation. Roland and Sponge huddled close on wooden Sunday School chairs, observing his every move as if he were the Grand Inquisitor laying out instruments of torture. Roughly every thirty seconds Sponge's hand crept to his waistcoat pocket, checking that the ring was still there.

Freya looked at her watch: three minutes to go. In her heart, she had not seriously believed that Jack would stand her up. But he had. Here she was, sitting in the front pew with a ringside view of the event she had dreaded for months. On her right sat Annabelle, a vision in peach silk; on her left, an empty expanse of woodwormy elm planking proclaimed her solitary status and isolated her from a clique of Tash's Huffington relations, all strangers. Her father was outside, preoccupied with Tash. Apart from Vicky's family and a few old friends of her father's, she knew nobody. At her back, she felt the pinpricks of curious eyes. '*Who is that woman in the extraordinary hat?*' '*That's the stepsister. All alone, poor thing.*'

Freya flared her nostrils and stared straight ahead, as if facing a firing squad. 'Land of ho-ope and glory . . .' How depressing all this was: the smell of damp plaster and mildewed hymnals, the chill stealing up her legs from the stone floor, the sheaves of garish gladioli flanking the altar, the artless designs of lambs and crosses and sunbeams hand-stitched on to hassock covers by the good women of the parish. She bent her head to the service sheet. 'Jerusalem' was not an obvious choice for a wedding-hymn, but at least everyone knew the tune. Hardly anyone in England attended church for religious purposes any more. Weddings, funerals, christenings, Christmas: these were the occasions that, like dinner-gongs, summoned guests into the house of God for a spot of spiritual sustenance. It was best not to be too inventive with the menu.

His suit still hung in the closet; his shaving kit and toothbrush were in the bathroom: she had checked. But Jack himself had disappeared. Where was he?

What if he had gone for good? She clamped her jaw tight.

The organ music broke off. A roar of chatter rose briefly to fill the void, then hushed to an expectant whisper. Roland stood up, his features rigid with bravery. Sponge put his hand once more to his pocket. Reverend Thwacker took his place at the head of the aisle, glasses flashing fiercely in a stray sunbeam. Annabelle slipped a hankie out of her sleeve, preparing for a gush of maternal joy. The organ gave an asthmatic wheeze, gearing itself up for the entrance march. Freya turned her head and caught a distant glimpse of Tash, deceptively virginal in off-the-shoulder ivory, adjusting her floral head-dress with the help of Polly (or possibly Lulu). She became vaguely aware of a commotion nearer to hand – the shuffle of people rising to their feet, a murmured tut-tutting, a voice saying 'Excuse me, ma'am . . . Thank you, sir'. She whirled around to look. It was Jack.

For a moment she couldn't think of anything to say. He looked wonderful. His suit was perfection. His shirt was crisp. His tie dazzled. His hair gleamed like old gold. Relief pumped through her; her spirits soared.

'What kept you?' she said.

Before he could answer the organ erupted into the triumphant peals of the 'Entrance of the Queen of Sheba'. There was a rumble as everyone stood up and turned to admire the bride. Freya rose, too, shoulder to shoulder with Jack, inhaling his masculine smell of shaving soap and shirt starch. Her eyes slid sideways to search his face. He smiled his easy smile.

'Great hat.'

'A writer, eh?'

Barry Swindon-Smythe, father of the bridegroom, who had been giving Jack a lecture on Britain's privatized rail system, and his own pivotal role therein, did not seem impressed. He took a swig of champagne. His rapacious eyes darted about the crowded marquee, as if making a cost/value assessment of everyone and everything in it, and flitted back to Jack. 'Should I have heard of you? What name do you write under?'

'My own.'

Barry shook his head. 'Sorry. No time to read, myself. My wife's the intellectual in the family. Always got her nose in some wretched book. Matter of fact, she's reading something now by one of your compatriots. Got one of those funny American names. Clint or Carter or somesuch.'

Jack's eyes narrowed. 'Carson McGuire?'

'That's the one. Know him, do you?'

'Sure. I had lunch with him just the other day, at my club in New York.' Jack's conscience gave him a passing nip.

'Marilyn will be impressed. Let me see if I can find her.'

Jack watched him push through the crowd, sleek and self-important in his fat-cat suit, and decided not to wait. He had absolutely no desire to discuss the genius of Carson McGuire. Having decided to honour his promise to Freya, despite the way she had treated him, he intended to enjoy himself. His hangover had miraculously receded. Sunshine, champagne and a complacent awareness of his own noble behaviour had restored his good humour. He escaped from the muggy warmth and candlewax smell of the marquee and strolled out on to the bright lawn, pausing only to allow a pretty waitress to refill his glass.

So this was an English wedding. He must make some notes. The house rose in front of him, its curlicued gables sharply profiled against a serene blue sky. Guests assembled at the entrance archway to run the gauntlet of the reception line in the hall and emerged, a few yards along, from the French windows of the library, where the wedding gifts were on munificent display. There were flowers everywhere, spouting from urns by the front entrance, tumbling from pots placed by the guy ropes of the marquee, colourfully bunched on the damask-covered tables where, it seemed, lunch would shortly be served. Back home, wedding receptions were more like cocktail parties – a sit-down meal was regarded as a barbaric Northern custom; but as he saw platters of salmon being carried to the marquee Jack felt he could be open-minded on this point.

He began to circle the marquee, a pink-and-white striped affair like an outsized jousting pavilion, eaves-dropping on conversations and trying to sniff out the social nuances of the gathering. There were Guy's academic cronies, distinguished by their creased linen jackets, bold ties and obsolete hairstyles; locals in formal suits green with age or dresses billowing with cabbage-rose prints; the slicker Swindon-Smythe contingent, equipped with chunky gold jewellery and mobile phones; Roland and Tash's twentysomething friends with cigarettes poised, tongues and shirt-collars already loosening. Everyone seemed in high good humour, talking uninhibitedly at top volume.

'Absolutely riddled with dry rot . . .'

' . . . bonus last year was seven-and-a-half K.'

'St Ethelburg's may be the better school academically, but Nigel and I don't think they give sufficient consideration to the whole person. Orson's such a sensitive child.'

'Prada, actually.'

' . . . doesn't know his Canaletto from his *cannelloni*.'

'No, no, you haven't changed *a bit*. It's simply that people look so different in hats.'

Ah, the hats. Anybody who thought British women reserved should attend a traditional wedding to appreciate the flamboyance that smouldered beneath that dowdy exterior. Straw with ribbons, silk with buckles, gauze with flowers, velvet with feathers; shocking pink, military scarlet, daffodil yellow; hats shaped like bells, like stovepipes, like fountains and toadstools and flying saucers: they bobbed and fluttered above the crowd, exotic as migrating birds blown off course.

Jack recognized a bowed figure, smoothing out a paper napkin on the top of a plinth from which some statue or decorative urn had long ago toppled. 'Hey, Sponge. How's that speech?'

'Jack! Thank God. The ink's run. I can hardly read a thing.'

After sorting out the speech as best he could, Jack clapped Sponge on the shoulder. 'Keep it short. Speak up. Don't gabble. They'll love you.'

'Do you really think so?'

'I know it. Now, why not get yourself some champagne and go and talk to that pretty girl in blue? She's been staring at you for the last five minutes.'

Adjusting his cravat, Sponge prowled towards his quarry. Jack scanned the crowd again, looking for Freya. She had stayed behind after the ceremony to pose for photographs, and he hadn't seen her since. There had been no chance to talk, though he sensed an unspoken communication between them as they sat shoulder to shoulder in enforced silence, listening to the words of the service: ' . . . for better for worse, for richer for poorer, in sickness and in health, to love and to cherish . . .' Cheap sentiment, he had told himself. But he was glad that he hadn't deserted her.

Meanwhile, he did his duty. He talked to the vicar. He chatted to Annabelle. He complimented Polly and Lulu on their dresses – pink, tight to the knee, then fanning out into a kind of frill; truthfully they looked like a pair of cooked prawns. When Vicky waved him over, he allowed himself to be introduced to her mother, a plump woman with a smiling mouth and a sharp, inquisitive gaze, standing foursquare on thick ankles.

'So you're the new boyfriend?' Her eyes raked over him, as if she was judging 'best dog' at the local show. She gave a tiny sigh. '*Dear* Freya . . . I remember when she first came down here, trailing about the place like a little lost waif. "Boarding school," I said to Annabelle; "it's the only answer. Girls her own age, plenty of fresh air, and lots of stodge to build her up." Mind you, she still looks half starved. I expect it's living in New York. One reads about these single girls, all desperate to be married, heading for middle age and still trying to look like teenage models, wearing themselves to the bone with their "careers". One is so thankful that one's own daughter – '

'Desperate to be married?' Jack, who had been growing steadily angrier at this trickle of poison, threw back his head and gave a rich, dismissive laugh. 'My dear Mrs Carp, Freya wouldn't even think of tying herself down to some boring husband. She's having way too much fun. Even if someone persuaded her to get married, I can't imagine her giving up her job. She's too good at it. Did you hear how she sold a piece by one of her artists to Tom Cruise?'

Hilda Carp's eyes widened. 'The actor?'

'Or was it Dustin Hoffman? Serious collectors watch her like a hawk, you know.'

'Really?' Jack could see her swelling with the freight of this ingot of gossip.

At that moment Jack caught sight of Freya emerging

from the house and stepping across the lawn like a racehorse. She was looking sensational in some dress thing that was cut low at the top and high at the bottom: his favourite kind. Her hat was wonderfully ridiculous, in a defiant, so-whaddya-looking-at-buddy? way that seemed to him pure essence of Freya. He liked the way it emphasized her elegant neck and cast intriguing shadows on her face. He raised his hand to attract her attention and caught her smile of relief, quickly replaced by wariness when she saw who he was talking to. His protective instincts rose.

'Sweetheart, where have you been?' he called out, as she approached.

'There's been a flap about the cake. I was helping Annabelle.'

'That's nice of you.' He put his arm around her waist and gave her an approving squeeze. He felt her resistance, and tightened his grip. It gave him an ignoble thrill to know that, having brought him here for precisely such play-acting, she could hardly rebuff his intimacies in public. Besides, she smelt delicious.

'Excuse us, will you, Mrs Carp?' he said. 'I have got to get some champagne into this woman.'

'Oh – yes – I quite understand.' Vicky's mother moved respectfully out of their way, as if yielding to royalty. 'You look lovely, Freya,' she called after them in an ingratiating voice.

'What on earth have you been saying to the old cat?' Freya demanded, once they were out of earshot. 'She's practically purring.'

'Just telling her how wonderful you are.'

'Oh.'

'That all you can say?'

He felt her ribcage rise and fall under his hand. 'Thank you, Jack. You are marvellous. How's that?'

'It's a start.' He let go of her for a moment to swipe a glass of champagne off a passing tray, then handed it to her with a smile and clinked his glass to hers. Wedding guests were now flocking past them towards the marquee, intent on lunch; one or two gave them a benign glance.

Freya took a long, slow sip, eyeing him beneath her hat brim. 'No need to overact,' she told him. But she was smiling.

Freya put down her dessert spoon with a contented sigh. The lunch had been delicious, the wine plentiful, the company amusing. She felt soothed by the hum of conversation, and pleasantly lethargic in the warm air trapped inside the marquee. Jack was on cracking form – funny, attentive, equally adept at debating American politics with Toby or encouraging one of Tash's friends in her ambition to write a novel. It was relaxing to listen to the familiar cadences of his voice and feel the presence of his arm resting casually across the back of her chair.

She had misjudged him by thinking he would let her down. His disappearance had been perfectly understandable: his masculine pride was hurt, and it had taken him time to recover. She remembered what her father had said this morning about forgiveness and compassion, and decided to be especially nice to him. Jack had recently suffered two major blows: first the loss of financial support from his father, then the cancellation of his book contract. Then he had made a pass at her – probably out of some psychological need to assert himself – and she had rejected him. Quite rightly, of course, but that wasn't the point. What was the point . . .? For a moment Freya pictured his face in the moonlight when he had kissed her – when she had kissed him. She straightened in her chair and crossed her legs. A woman could hardly be held responsible for the way her body behaved, especially under the influence of alcohol. Probably she had still been suffering from some kind of purely physical frustration after her disappointment with Brett – was it really only a week ago? The point was . . . Freya's eyes rested on Jack's profile, as he talked about agents and publishers and advances. The haircut emphasized the rounded shape of his head and his strong masculine features. He really looked quite – *The point was*, she reminded herself, that she and Jack were friends again. Yes, that was it.

Her thoughts were interrupted by a peremptory clinking of cutlery on glass, a signal for silence.

Jack turned to her. 'What's happening?'

'Speeches,' she said curtly. This was a moment she had been dreading. She moved her chair to face the wedding table and watched her father rise to his feet, swallowing her jealousy as she prepared to listen to him praise the bride.

He looked very handsome, tall and straight in a dove-grey tailcoat teamed with a wildly unauthentic pink tie. 'Ladies and gentlemen,' he began, surveying his guests with a benign smile. 'I am a lucky man.' There was a warm ripple of appreciation. 'I have had the joy of watching Natasha grow up from a beguiling three-year-old into the beautiful and charming young woman you see today. I remember . . .'

Freya twisted her hands in her lap and stared at the coconut matting. It was a good speech – affectionate and urbane, with an edge of that self-deprecating humour she loved. He was welcoming to Roland. He praised Annabelle. He paid tribute to Tash's real father, who had died so young and whose relatives he was delighted to welcome today. He was graceful and courteous. Freya could not help feeling proud.

' . . . and another way in which I am lucky is that I do, of course, have *two* daughters.'

Freya looked up, startled.

'I am particularly pleased that my daughter Freya is able to be with us today, along with her friend Jack. For those of you who don't know, Freya leads a very successful and fulfilled life in New York – in fact, I am relying on her to keep me in my old age. She is the best of companions as well as a beautiful young woman – thanks to her mother, I may say. I love her, and I am proud of her. This event would not be

426

complete without her presence. Thank you for coming, darling.'

Freya bent her head to hide her face. Her heart was full. He had not forgotten her. He was still her daddy.

His speech came to an end; now Roland stood up to embark on his long list of thank-yous. As Freya's father sat down, he misjudged the position of his chair and stumbled slightly. It was nothing – nobody else seemed to notice – but Freya saw with a kind of panic that he was indeed getting old. One day, not too far from now, she would lose him for ever. Instinctively she turned to Jack, and found that he was watching her. He smiled reassuringly, as though he could read her mind.

The audience was laughing now. Roland had sat down. Heavens, it was good old Sponge! She must pay attention. 'Marriage is a field of battle,' he was saying, 'not a bed of roses.'

How strange. That was just what her father had been trying to tell her this morning, about his marriage to her mother. Perhaps she'd been pursuing quite the wrong idea of relationships all these years, expecting them to meet some ideal of perfection and destroying them when they didn't. Now she thought about it, a bed of roses sounded rather insipid. For a moment she glimpsed an alternative view of men and women as sparring partners, continually testing each other's strengths and discovering their own weaknesses – combative but not destructive, giving as good as they got, knocking each other into shape. It sounded

427

a lot less boring than lying around on smelly old flowers. It sounded exciting – an adventure.

'. . . to Roland and Tash!' Damn, she had missed Sponge's speech, though his huge grin indicated that it had been a hit. Freya raised her glass in a toast and took a sip of champagne, enjoying the fizz on her tongue. Impulsively she turned to Jack and clinked glasses with him. 'Thanks for coming, Jack. It's made all the difference.' Her words surprised them both.

The mood relaxed. Cigarettes were lit. The chatter resumed. Everyone started to get up from their tables and spill out into the fresh air. Freya was about to do the same when Hilda Carp's voice swooped close to her ear. 'Freya, *dearest*. Could you spare a mo? I have a favour to ask. The thing is: do you think you could possibly get me Tom Cruise's autograph?'

'We could show him our old haunts in Brooklyn – take him to Ambrosio's to say "hi",' Jack said persuasively.

'I don't know . . .'

'And that Japanese place with the live shrimp.'

'Mmm . . .'

'What about a football game?'

'The thing is, I don't have a place for him to stay.'

'He won't care where he stays. It's you he wants to see. He's your father. He loves you.'

Freya bent her head. 'I know.'

'So do it! In fact, why not go the whole hog and

428

get yourself a decent, permanent apartment. Then you can throw a party for him.'

'A party?' This was a daunting idea.

'Sure. I'd help you.'

'Would you really?'

Jack and Freya were sitting together in a saggy old swing-seat half-hidden in a cave of yew, lazily watching the guests criss-cross the lawn. The cake had been cut. Roland and Tash had gone upstairs to change. The sunshine still held, bestowing a mellow glow on the proceedings. After the speeches Freya had mentioned to Jack that she was thinking of inviting her father to New York for a visit, and was surprised by his immediate enthusiasm. 'He'd love it!' Freya still wasn't sure, but she felt comfortable and relaxed, and it was fun to be planning treats for him with Jack.

'What a happy day!' The vicar's wife had paused on the path in front of them and was beaming into their hideaway.

'Yes, it's been great.' Freya smiled.

'Don't they make a lovely couple?'

'Yes,' she repeated tranquilly.

'Who knows, perhaps it will be your turn next?' She gazed beadily at Jack.

'Who knows?' Freya could hear the amusement in Jack's voice. 'I love old ladies,' he said, when she was out of earshot. 'They're so subtle.'

Freya lay back in the seat with a sigh. 'Today,' she announced, 'I love everybody.'

'I say, Jack, do you know anything about cars?' It

was Sponge, holding the hand of a pretty girl in blue, and looking anxious. He and Jamie were titivating the going-away car with the usual 'Just Married' paraphernalia. It was a flash new Japanese sports car – the Swindon-Smythes' wedding present to their son. Jamie had somehow engaged the steering lock and no one knew how to free it. Jack said he'd see what he could do, and Freya waved him off.

She sat alone, idly swinging, and rested her head on the faded cushions. She closed her eyes. It was nearly over. She had survived. In fact, she had positively enjoyed herself. Having someone to accompany her had made all the difference. She wondered if she and Jack would be able to sneak off this evening for a walk to the pub and a quiet supper together. She pictured them in a wooden booth, hemmed in by a fug of beer and chips, or perhaps sitting outside with a candle twinkling between them in the darkness and the swish-swoosh of the sea. They could pick over the wedding and share their thoughts in the comfortable, argumentative way they had always done. Freya felt a spurt of happy excitement. Afterwards, they could walk back in the moonlight and –

The swing-seat squeaked protestingly as Freya sat upright, jolted by a shocking realization. How blind she had been! The issue of whether she had a companion for this wedding – an issue that had tormented her for so long – was, she suddenly saw, absurdly trivial. It was not *a* man who had made the difference. She wouldn't be feeling like this if she had brought

Michael, or Brett, or anyone else she could think of. What had made the difference was one particular man, a man who took care of her and made her laugh, a man she knew with the intimacy of long friendship, a man she liked – perhaps more than liked . . .?

A hubbub broke through her thoughts, and she noticed that all the guests were now milling towards the driveway at the side of the house, where Roland's snouted car gleamed like a freshly killed barracuda. Freya's lips curved in a small, secret smile. No doubt Jack was congratulating himself on his mechanical genius in getting the car moved, even if he'd done nothing more complex than flicking a switch. Men! She strolled over, looking out for him, though there was no hurry. She would have plenty of time, before they returned to New York, to examine this new, exciting idea that swelled within her.

Tash had changed into a summer dress splashed with poppies; she looked pretty and excited. Freya saw her hug Annabelle and step into the open-topped car. Roland sat importantly at the steering wheel, a cool dude in shades. Someone was passing around a basket of rose petals to throw; other people had bought their own confetti and were busy ripping open packets.

Roland sounded the horn and Tash stood up on the passenger seat, holding something high in the air: her wedding bouquet. There was a murmur of excitement from the crowd. Tash scanned the faces below her with a slow turn of the head. Her words floated across the air. 'Where's Freya? Where's my big sister?'

Freya felt a prickle of embarrassment, tinged with anger that Tash should draw attention to her in this manner: her 'big' sister, still unmarried. She wondered if this had been her father's idea – a mistaken 'nice' gesture urged upon his reluctant stepdaughter. Feeling foolish, she folded her arms, hoping not to be noticed. She had no wish to scramble for the trophy bouquet, even if it was tossed straight into her hands. But she was far too tall to hide; her hat was like a big green 'Go' sign. Already Tash had seen her. She had climbed down from the seat and was walking forward with a smile on her face. The crowd parted. There was a collective cooing.

'Aah, how sweet.'

'What a generous girl.'

Their words brought Freya to her senses. However they might each feel privately, this was Tash's version of an olive branch; she could at least accept it graciously. She raised her head, and stepped forward to meet Tash halfway. Tash pressed the bouquet into her hand, then pulled her into a sisterly embrace. Freya bent down to hug her back. She felt Tash's arm snake about her neck and the smack of breath in her ear as Tash whispered, 'Jack's a big boy, isn't he?'

Freya jerked with shock. Her head whipped back so that she could look into Tash's face, which radiated such malicious triumph that Freya was left in no doubt about her meaning. She tried to pull away, but Tash held tight, her fingernails vicious. 'Pity he's not your real boyfriend,' she spat.

Then her armlock loosened. There was a gleam of teeth, the glint of narrowed eyes and she had gone.

Freya rocked on her heels. Blood thumped in her ears, louder than the cheering voices around her. 'Good luck!' they called. 'Goodbye!' She saw a blur of waving hands. The air exploded into colour. There was the growl of an engine, the spatter of gravel, a clinking of tin cans. She was icy cold. If she moved, she feared she would fall over and splinter. Something was digging into her palm. It was the stiff wired handle of the bridal bouquet.

The crowd wheeled and dispersed, leaving her standing alone in an empty expanse of green strewn with petals. From a distance she saw Jack walking towards her. He was smiling.

Ah, there she was.

The last shreds of confetti spun and drifted to the ground. The crowd cleared. Jack saw Freya staring straight at him. Her hat turned her face into a Cubist portrait of fractured light and geometric shadows, and he thought with wonder and affection of all the different women hidden behind that single configuration of features: scornful goddess, brash poker-player, resentful little girl; the clever woman who kept her brain – and her tongue – sharply honed, the gorgeous creature running down the beach. He realized that he wanted to kiss her.

'Freya,' he called.

She turned and walked away in slow-motion, like a figure in a dream who cannot hear however loud you shout.

'*Freya!*' He loped after her.

'Excuse me.' A female voice shrilled in his ear. 'Aren't you Jack Madison?' He heard a tinkle of jewellery as a manicured claw gripped his arm. 'My husband tells me you know Carson McGuire. Our little reading circle in Totteridge – Totteridge *Common*, that is – would be so thrilled to know what he's really like.'

'I'm sorry.' He was conscious of musky scent and a confection of tinted hair. 'There's something I have to do. I'll catch you later.' He pushed past, ignoring Marilyn Swindon-Smythe's gasp of pique.

But Freya had disappeared. He'd lost her. He thought she'd been heading for the house, and hurried inside. It was cool and silent. He peered into the empty library, then retraced his steps to the kitchen. There was the slow drip-drip of a tap. Bedivere lay pressed to the Aga; he gave a civil thump of his tail. 'Where is she?' asked Jack.

He thought he heard a tiny sound from beyond the kitchen, and wandered down the cluttered passageway, looking through doorways. She was standing with her back to him in a kind of pantry-room, doing something at the sink.

He smiled with relief. 'Freya, I wanted to – '
'*Get out!*'
She spun round and something hit him low in the

stomach. Jack clutched it instinctively – something pulpy and damp – but it was Freya he was looking at. She had taken off her hat. Her face was grey, with witchy slits for eyes.

'What is it, sweetheart?' Jack was appalled. 'What's the matter?'

'How *could* you?' she shouted. 'After everything I told you. When you knew how I felt. How could you just – *fuck* my little bitch of a stepsister?'

Jack swallowed. This was bad. 'It just happened,' he said. 'It wasn't my idea. I was trying to get some sleep in the library and she – '

'Tash, of all people! What's wrong with you, Jack? You're like a dog that has to sniff at every lamp-post.'

'It wasn't like that! She practically seduced me.'

'Oh sure.'

'She did! She came right in and took off all her clothes – '

'Bollocks, Jack. Do you really expect me to believe that? On the night before her own wedding?'

'It's the truth.' He gestured helplessly. 'I'm sorry. I was mad at you.'

'So you thought, "I know, I'll go sleep with Tash. We'll have a good old snigger together about poor, sad Freya."'

'*No!*'

'*Yes!* She boasted to me about it. She wanted to prove that no one could like me enough to show me even the tiniest bit of loyalty – that my feelings are worth nothing, that *I* am worth nothing. And the terrible thing is, she was right.'

'That's not true!'

'You even told her that we weren't really a couple – that you were pretending. Imagine how great that makes me feel. Imagine how much fun it will be for her to stick the knife in for years to come. But hey – who cares? Jack Madison got his rocks off, and that's what matters, right?'

'It wasn't like that.' Jack felt as if he'd been caught by a sudden wave and was tumbling blindly in its murky turbulence. He struggled to find his footing. 'It didn't mean anything.'

'It does to *me*!' Freya slammed her own chest with her fist, so hard that he heard the thud of knuckle on breastbone. A sudden tenderness made him want to put his arms around her. But her teeth were bared. Her eyes blazed wide. 'What kind of a friend are you? I ask you to do *one thing* – pretend that we're a couple, for four lousy days. But you can't do it – one temptation, and you cave in. You're pathetic, Jack!'

'Now wait a minute. *You* were the one who pushed me away. It would never have happened if we'd – '

'Oh, for Christ's sake, grow up! "It didn't mean anything." "It wasn't my idea."' Her mimicry was savage. 'I don't give a shit who you have sex with. This isn't about Tash. It's about you. About what a useless human being you are.'

Her words poured over him – burning, un-stoppable.

'Everything's always someone else's fault – your dad, your publisher, Tash, me. You always take the easy way out. You want constant adulation without making any effort to earn it. All the advantages in the world have been showered on you, and you've squandered every one of them. You're too spineless to commit to *anything* – whether it's a woman, or a friend, or even your own writing.'

'That's not fair!'

'Isn't it?' Her face twisted with contempt. 'Let me tell you the truth, Jack. You're not a writer. You're a spoilt dilettante living on Daddy's money and wasting your time with people like Candace Twink and Leo Brannigan. You'll never finish your novel because you're too fucking lazy! You will never be a real writer, because you have absolutely no respect for the human heart.'

Freya let out a shuddering breath. There was a long silence. Something was hurting. Jack looked down and saw what she had thrown at him. It was a bunch of flowers – roses. A thorn had drawn a trickle of blood.

When she spoke again, it was with a quiet hopelessness that was more damning than her anger.

'I opened up my whole life to you, Jack. The house, my father, my stepmother, how I feel. I thought you were someone I could rely on. Someone I could trust. Someone I could respect. I thought we were *friends* . . .'

Her voice broke on the word. Her head drooped. Jack saw that she was crying. A cavity opened in his chest, as if a great stone had been rolled away.

She looked into his face. Her eyes were raw with tears. 'I keep trying to like you, Jack, but I *can't* . . .'

He stepped forward. 'Freya – '

'Get away from me!' She gave a violent swing of her arm, and nearly fell. She gripped the edge of the basin. 'Get out! Out of this house and out of my life. I never want to see you again.'

# 30

Because it was a weekend at the start of the summer season all the flights to New York were full. Jack had ended up spending the night in Heathrow airport, among grey-faced travellers slumped over their luggage and listless cleaners pushing brooms. The hours passed in a fog of jumpy dreams, echoing announcements and relentless internal voices that pursued him round and round.

Finally, mid-morning on Sunday, he had been offered a last-minute seat on some Middle Eastern airline, and had handed over his credit card without even bothering to ask the price. He was eager to escape home. He wanted to be out of the airport before Freya turned up for her own flight – the one he would have accompanied her on if everything hadn't gone wrong.

Now he was in that strange no-man's-land in the sky, numbed by the drone of the engines, sluggish from poor ventilation, dazed by the flickering images that played out some Arab drama on a screen by the bulkhead. His seat was in a central bank of five, between two voluminous Kuwaiti ladies swathed in shawls. Everyone but himself was Arab or Indian. All the announcements were in Arabic. Thanks to the

Muslim code of behaviour, the flight would be dry. That meant no alcohol. Great.

He felt tired and sick at heart. Though he longed for oblivion, sleep was impossible. Random scenes from the last few days played over and over in his head. He saw Freya bouncing on the four-poster gleefully hurling pillows; he heard Guy's dry voice saying, 'I'm glad she has someone to care for her.' Most insistently of all, Freya's words festered and stung. Maybe he deserved her censure; he had made a big mistake. But did he really deserve such ferocious, all-consuming contempt?

She hadn't given him a chance to answer back. Reeling with shock, he'd packed his bag, propped an adequately brief thank-you note to Guy and Annabelle on the kitchen table, and slunk out of the house like a thief. But now answers and explanations clamoured in his head, demanding expression. Jack shifted this way and that on his seat, edgy with frustration. Finally, he reached down for the rucksack he had stowed under his seat, and drew out a pen and his writer's notebook. He flipped down the tiny plastic table from the seat in front of him, gathered his thoughts and began to write.

Dear Freya
I know you'll want to scrunch up this letter when you see who it's from – but <u>don't</u>. Just for once, listen to what someone else has to say.
Yes, I slept with Tash. It was an incredibly stupid

thing to do, and I wish I hadn't. Maybe it's not an excuse to say that I was angry and drunk, or that she deliberately set out to seduce me, but that's the truth. I'm not proud of myself. I don't regard Tash as a 'conquest'. I'm sorry it happened.

But Freya — let's be honest. Can you give me any good reason why I <u>shouldn't</u> sleep with Tash, or with any other woman? You don't want me: that's crystal clear. <u>You</u> threw <u>me</u> out of the bedroom — remember? So why the big melodrama?

Jack paused, and frowned at the words he had just written. A niggle of conscience told him that something about this was not quite right. But Freya's words were now flooding back to him in a strong, stinging tide, filling him with rage. For the last few days he had jumped through every crazy hoop she had held up for him, eager and obedient as a show dog, and all she could do was call him a 'useless human being'.

The real truth is, your pride is hurt. You don't want me, but you wanted everyone at that wedding to <u>think</u> that I wanted you. Doesn't that strike you as a little unfair? Even, dare I say, immature? This age thing is in your head, Freya. The truth is that you're beautiful and successful and you don't happen to be 'attached' at this exact moment. End of story. The idea that everyone in Cornwall is going around sneering at you shows how self-obsessed you have become.

Why don't you think about other people, for a change? Your poor father, for example, who obviously adores you and gets the cool Freya brush-off like the rest of us. Are you still blaming him for marrying another woman <u>twenty years</u> ago? What was the poor guy to do – wait until his darling daughter gave him permission to have a life?

It's tough that your mother died, but it was tough on him, too. He and Annabelle have tried to give you a home – a home most people would envy. But oh no, it's not <u>your</u> home so you're not going to enjoy it. Ever since I've known you, you've lived in crappy apartments. What's that about? You're not homeless; you've <u>made</u> yourself homeless; you <u>want</u> to be homeless so you can go on feeling sorry for yourself and let everyone see what a tragic victim you are.

Again Jack paused. Freya wasn't a victim; she was the bravest woman he knew. But he didn't want to stop and think. Now he'd opened the floodgates, he needed to let his resentment rush and roar.

And what about me?

He wrote, with a fierce, audible scratch of pen on paper.

We've been friends for so long. I let you stay in my apartment. I came to England with you as a favour, because you were desperate. I thought we were having a good time. Obviously, I was wrong. Your wild overreaction to the Tash episode shows that you were just waiting for an excuse to tell me how very little you think of me.

I know I'm not perfect. But at least I'm human; at least I reach out to people – in my lazy, wastrel, dilettante way. Whereas you, at the first whiff of imperfection, reject the very people who love you best. Including me.

Okay, I stand rejected. Throw away ten years of friendship if you want. I have other things to think about.

Like what? Jack asked himself, as he stabbed an emphatic, black full stop into the paper. His pen hovered, and then began to race again across the notepad.

I'm sorry you don't think much of me as a writer. It's good to know the truth after all these years. Your opinion will be a comfort as I try to finish my book with no income, no publisher and no apartment to write in. Fortunately, I have faith in myself.

Jack stopped again and bit the end of his pen. He could picture the dog-eared folder on his desk that contained the unsatisfactory, incomplete draft of his novel. Would he ever finish it? Perhaps if he switched agents to Leo, he could get a new – and bigger – advance from another publisher. Yes, a fat new contract with lots of zeros: that would show Freya. 'Dilettante', hunh? Not a 'real' writer. What did she know of the artistic struggle?

> You don't understand how hard it is to write a book
> – to reach right down into the depths of oneself
> and –

And in that moment Jack did reach down into the depths of himself. The seconds tolled past while his hand hovered, motionless. Then he slammed down his pen, so hard that the Kuwaiti women jumped in fright, and stared. Let them. He closed his eyes and sank his head back on the headrest.

All he could see was Freya's crumpled face and the tears in her eyes. He had hurt her. He had made her cry. Freya *never* cried. He could justify himself to kingdom come; he could even be right on every point. But nothing could eradicate the pain in her face, and the knowledge that he had inflicted it. Trying to apportion blame in precise measures was as cruel and pointless as Solomon offering to cut the baby in two.

He picked up his notepad and read through what he had written. His mouth twisted with self-disgust. The half-truths leapt off the page. The real truth tore at his heart.

Freya was right. It wasn't the sex with Tash that mattered; it was his betrayal of Freya. She had trusted him, and he had delivered her into the hands of her bitterest enemy.

And she was right about his book. It was his own fault he hadn't finished it – not his father's, not his agent's, not the lack of money or time.

She might even be right about his talent. When had he last seriously tried to look into the depths of himself (whatever that meant)? Perhaps he didn't dare. Perhaps nothing was there.

Jack reached out his big hand to smother the page in front of him and crush it into a tight ball. He squeezed it in his fist, tighter and tighter, smaller and smaller.

*'I keep trying to like you, Jack, but I can't . . .'*

He didn't blame her. He was a failure. A bum. He had made her cry.

*'I never want to see you again.'*

Well, fine. She wouldn't.

Freya had only one thought in her head when she arrived back in New York, and that was to see Cat. Cat would understand. Cat would open a bottle of something and sit up late with her, listening for as long as it took. Cat would help Freya to tear Jack to shreds. Together they would denounce Tash as a slut and a snake. At last Freya would be able to give vent to the rage and misery that she had been forced to keep hidden, a smouldering, spitting, crackling furnace inside her.

She had told the family that Jack's father was seriously ill – a heart-attack – and that Jack had flown straight home to be with him. She was almost certain that her own father didn't believe her; there were too many holes in her story. (Why hadn't she gone with Jack, to comfort him? Why hadn't she at least driven him to the station? Why did she herself look so shaken?) Freya saw that he was wounded by her reticence, but she could do nothing. Tempting as it was to expose Tash as a trashy little bitch to her own mother – and her 'Daddy' – Freya could not bring herself to inflict such pain. Besides, it would be impossibly humiliating to admit what had happened. Though she ached for comfort, she was too enmeshed in her own lies to tell the truth. Pleading a headache, she had gone to her room and lain curled up in the big bed, reliving the moment of Tash's triumphant, vindictive revelation. She wanted to sleep, but her eyes remained wide and staring. In his hurry, Jack had missed his pyjamas, which were still hanging on the back of the door. Their presence tormented her to the point where she leapt out of bed, grabbed them off the hook and stuffed them into the wastebasket. They even smelled of Jack.

She had cried practically all the way back on the plane – hating herself for this display of weakness, embarrassed by the curious gaze of other passengers, but too tired and wretched to stop. In a daze, she had taken a cab into the city and let herself into her new home. It was a tiny, charmless apartment in an untrendy part of the Village: two boxy rooms and no view, overwhelmingly silent and empty. The belongings she had brought over from Jack's last week stood in a forlorn pile on the bedroom floor. There wasn't a scrap of food in the fridge. Outside, it was raining.

She stayed only long enough to take a lightning shower and change into clean jeans and a shirt. At the last minute she called Cat to make sure she was in – though where else would Cat be at nine o'clock on a rainy Sunday evening? The number was busy, and Freya was too impatient to wait. Besides, if Cat was talking on the telephone, that meant she was home. Freya threw on her raincoat and plunged out into the street, hands in her pockets, head bent against the rain.

Cat's apartment was only a few blocks away. Freya practically ran the whole way. Finally she pushed through the door to Cat's building, flipped a hand at her old friend the doorman and raced into the elevator. Sanctuary, at last! Fresh tears welled as she began to rehearse the story she was about to unfold. She longed to hear Cat's rousing denunciation of men. Freya felt that if only she could stay angry, then she wouldn't feel so sad.

Now she was outside Cat's door, ringing the bell. *Quick, Cat! Hurry!* But nothing happened. She rang a second time: still nothing. She leaned her cheek against the door and moaned in despair. *Where are you?* Then she sniffed – and sniffed again. Was that or was that not the pungent aroma of Cat's legendary *spaghetti alla putanesca*? Freya rang the bell again, and started to pound frantically on the door. 'It's me!' she yelled. 'Let me in!'

Almost at once she heard movements, then the click of the lock. The door opened, and there was Cat – familiar, wonderful Cat. Freya stumbled into the apartment and threw her arms around Cat's neck. 'Thank God you're here!'

Cat tottered backwards under her weight. 'What is it? What happened?' She steadied herself on Freya's shoulders. Her eyes swept over Freya's face and bedraggled hair, wide with concern. 'You haven't been attacked, have you?'

'Much worse.' Freya began pulling off her raincoat. 'You won't believe what happened to me in England.'

'But you're not hurt? I mean, physically.'

'Well, no.' Freya glanced at Cat, slightly perplexed to be taxed on this point. 'But I've had the most ghastly time.' She tossed the raincoat on to a chair and swept back her wet hair.

'Freya – ' Cat began urgently.

'I *hate* men, Cat. Don't you?'

'Well, that's just – '

'Let's get a drink, and I'll tell you what happened.' Freya brushed past Cat, leading the way round the corner of a tall bookcase that divided the entranceway from the rest of the living room.

'Freya, *wait*!'

Afterwards, Freya recognized that she had absorbed multiple impressions in a single second – the unusually dim, romantic lighting; Cat's small dining table set for two, lit by a flickering candle; the warm smell of cooking; a sound behind her that was part gasp, part guilty moan; the belated realization that Cat was far too stylishly dressed for a normal Sunday-night chill, and had deliberately not answered her door at the first ring. But at the time, all she felt was simple astonishment. There was a *man* in Cat's apartment. And that man was Michael.

He stood stiffly between her and the dining table from which he had obviously just risen, for he was still clutching a linen napkin. Yes, she noticed that, too: Cat's precious heirloom napkins.

Freya and Michael stared at one another in shocked silence. Freya could not make sense of his presence here. Cat had mentioned meeting Michael in the course of her work, but surely she wouldn't invite a colleague to her home. They must be discussing *her* – how humiliating! Then Michael's gaze slid to a point beyond her, and his expression subtly altered. Freya whirled round, just in time to catch the same expression on Cat's face. It was a look of complicity – of utter, naked intimacy. Freya's eyes darted from one to the other, her comprehension as swift and sharp as a blade slicing through a concealing curtain. Cat and Michael. Michael and Cat. Her best friend and her ex-lover: together.

'Whoops,' she said, attempting a laugh, though it sounded more like a sob.

Cat was coming towards her, reaching for her hands. 'Sweetie, don't be upset. Let me explain.'

'We were going to tell you as soon as you got back from England,' Michael added, stepping forward to stand beside Cat.

'The thing is, there was nothing to tell – not at first.'

'I only met Caterina a couple of weeks ago.'

*Caterina?*

'Everything's moved so fast.'

'It's a surprise even to us.'

The word 'us' gave Freya a piercing sense of exclusion.

'I've been almost crazy with guilt.' Cat stared up at her with pleading eyes. 'But I couldn't help it. These things happen. Please don't be upset.' She tugged at

Freya's hands, trying to get through to her. 'I couldn't stand it if you were upset.'

Freya drew herself up, tall and dignified. 'Why would I be upset?' she enquired, disengaging her hands. 'You're both free agents. It's nothing to do with me.'

Cat's eyes flickered desperately to Michael, and back again. 'Of course it's to do with you! You're my friend. I love you. *Please* don't be like this.'

'Like what?' Freya tried to smile, though her lips felt frozen. 'Look, I've had a long flight, and I'm tired. And your dinner's getting cold.'

'Fuck the dinner! (Excuse me, Michael.) Stay and talk with us,' Cat begged.

'Maybe another time, okay?' Freya took a step backwards and sketched a stiff wave. 'Have a nice evening,' she said carefully. Then she retreated swiftly round the bookcase. There were footsteps behind her, and a beseeching call from Cat, but now Freya had her palm pressed tight against her mouth and couldn't have answered even if she'd wanted to. She grabbed her raincoat from the chair, pulled open the door and ran to the elevator. Cat's front door was swinging shut. Behind it, she could hear Cat and Michael arguing in urgent whispers.

As soon as she reached the lobby, Freya bolted out into the dark street. But having got there, she stood stock still in the middle of the slick sidewalk, not knowing what to do or where to go. She felt utterly bereft. Her mind seethed with tormenting questions

– about how often Cat and Michael had met, where and when, whether Michael compared Cat to herself, what Cat said to him about her. She pictured the pair of them talking about her now, like concerned parents about a teenager at the 'difficult' stage. She imagined all the secrets they would keep from her. *Oops, don't tell Freya.*

People streamed past her as she stood in the rain. They scraped her with their umbrellas and buffeted her with their shoulders. They muttered and shouted at her to get out of the way. Freya looked around her in a daze – at the cars, the lights, the buildings that stretched out and out, up and up. This was a big city, full of people. If Cat abandoned her, she could find another friend.

Yet still she didn't move. She had a sudden, fearful vision of this whole, huge sea of humanity receding further and further until she was left standing quite alone, marooned on a desert island of her own making. She sensed that this was a turning point. Either she could retreat to her silent apartment and lock herself in, alone and safe; or she could go back up to Cat and Michael, dispel the shadow she had cast on their happiness, and re-admit herself into their lives. Freya hugged her coat tight as the rain spattered and bounced. Which was it to be?

# 32

Jack slowed the car on the rutted track, braked to a halt, and reached for the piece of paper on which he had scrawled directions to the cabin. This was the third time he had stopped in the last hour: once to fix a flat tyre, once to move a sunbathing turtle gently out of his path, and now to check if he was as lost as he felt.

He'd been to the mountains before, naturally. The Madisons had a place down near Asheville, the summer playground for moneyed Carolinians where Jack had spent vacations swimming and rafting with his brother Lane, while their Dad played golf and held cocktail parties. As a student, he'd come roistering up here with friends, to ski in winter and hang out in summer, listening to bluegrass and country bands. But he'd never been so far north before, practically within hiking distance of Virginia and Tennessee. And he'd never come alone. This part of his home state was known as the High Country, the Lost Provinces, or simply 'out there'. He was beginning to see why.

Jack gazed out across the scene with a flicker of misgiving. Blue afternoon shadows lay on the steep, wooded hillsides. Down in the valley the grass looked smooth and soft as billiard-table baize. A dark, snaking line of pine and dogwood marked the course of the New River, and far in the distance he caught the greenish gleam of its rushing passage. The country was beautiful, but wild and lonely. The comfortable, cutesy resort towns had petered out. For the last several miles he'd climbed steadily along winding dirt-and-gravel roads, past apple orchards and Christmas-tree plantations, past tiny white-steepled churches and lonely farmsteads with their big red barns and grazing cattle. There didn't seem to be a lot of holiday cabins, as Jack understood the phrase. Still, he'd burned his boats now. His apartment was in the hands of a realtor; his belongings were in storage – all except the things in the trunk of his car. The car itself he had hired at the airport in Charlotte, and would return to the nearest drop-off point as soon as he found an old jalopy to buy. Studying the map again, Jack concluded that he was on the right road, unpromising as it looked. He pulled on a battered fishing hat to shade his eyes from the sun, and pressed on.

It hadn't taken him more than twelve hours back in New York to realize that he had to get out of the city. After Cornwall, Manhattan's frenetic pace jarred; everyone, it seemed, had a purpose except himself. The double-whammy of losing his allowance and his book contract meant that he couldn't afford to stay anyway. Most tormenting of all was the knowledge that Freya was on the same island, only a mile or two away, despising him. He could almost sniff her corrosive contempt in the grimy air. *Lazy . . . spoilt . . . dilettante.*

What he needed, he decided, was a writer's retreat – nothing fancy, just somewhere peaceful so he could shut himself away with his computer and concentrate on his novel, free of city distractions and mundane household responsibilities. His stepmother Lauren lived in Virginia now, in a very pleasant, comfortable house which she left each day to work as head of an outreach program for disadvantaged and 'problem' children; it occurred to Jack that her guest room might be the perfect place, and he called her up to suggest it. To his chagrin, Lauren did not share his enthusiasm for this plan. In fact, her questions about his sudden desperation to leave New York and devote himself to his writing were uncomfortably probing. That was the trouble with intelligent women: they could never accept a simple statement at face value; they always had to read their own meanings into the smallest nuance.

'Don't tell me someone's got under your skin at last, Jack,' she'd drawled affectionately, as Jack's explanations became increasingly tortuous. 'I can't wait to meet her.'

'I don't know what you're talking about,' he had responded gruffly.

Still, Lauren had come up with the goods. Within twenty-four hours she'd called him back with an offer, which she strongly recommended he accept. A friend of hers owned an old vacation place up in the mountains that had been in the family for generations. Last year the cabin had been broken into by survivalists on the run from the police, and no one had got around to fixing it up. There was no electricity, and her friend wasn't sure exactly what state it was in, but Jack was welcome to stay there rent-free so long as he repaired the house and made it secure. Jack had accepted eagerly, fantasizing himself into the role of a latterday Thoreau, Southern-style – at one with nature, free to let his imagination roam unfettered, the epitome of rugged American individualism. His novel would flow. At one bound he would be free.

There was a hand-painted sign coming up on the left. Jack pushed his glasses into position and ducked his head to peer through the windshield. 'Feed Store,' he read. Good. According to his directions, he was to drive a further mile, then turn right by the twin pines and keep going until he reached the cabin. He felt a surge of excitement; the adventure was about to begin. And here at last was the private track, so overgrown that he almost missed it. He heard the whisper of long grass and the crunch of pine needles under the tyres. Overhead, the trees grew close, admitting random shafts of deep golden light. He gunned the car up a sudden incline, rounded one bend, then another, then coasted to a stop as his foot slid off the accelerator in shock. Ahead of him was a miniature forest of shoulder-high hogweed, above which he could just discern a sloping tin roof swathed in creepers and the upper half of rough log walls, with the outline of a window crudely barricaded by criss-cross planking. Jack stared. This wasn't a place where one could spend a vacation. It was barely a cabin. It was a shack, a wreck.

Switching off the car engine, he swung the car door open and climbed out. Silence enveloped him like a shroud, and for a moment he experienced something akin to panic. Then he pulled himself together, excavated the carjack from the back of the car, and used it to beat a path to the narrow raised porch and lever off the defensive planks from the front door opening. Behind, the door itself hung ajar off broken hinges. Jack took a step inside, ducking in alarm as a bird swooped out of the gloom and flew past his head.

He was now standing in a biggish room, maybe fifteen feet by twenty, with a roughly sawn floor and walls. At one end was a square pine table and a rickety gas stove; at the other, pulled close to the stone fireplace, were two chairs and a couch with the stuffing half torn out of them. Either the survivalists had had a fight, or small creatures had found a very cosy spot to make their nests. There were mouse droppings everywhere, as well as drifts of dead leaves and a choking layer of dust. Jack discovered two small windows, covered by makeshift shutters, and a further door that led into a tiny back room, furnished with a bare bedstead, a plain country chair, and a splintered rail that must once have been used for hanging clothes. That was it.

Jack went back outside and sat on the porch steps, fighting down his dismay. He wondered about trying to find an inn or a hotel, just for tonight, but it would be dark in an hour and the likelihood was that he would get lost first. Anyway, that would merely postpone the problem, and he didn't have money to squander. The key question was whether he was going to stick this out, or give up now. A rustle in the bushes made him look up. A groundhog had emerged from the undergrowth and was sitting up on its hindlegs, front paws hanging limp, pot-bellied and inquisitive as an old man. It stared at Jack, and Jack stared back. In his head he heard his own voice explaining, *You see, I was going to finish my book, but unfortunately the cabin was uninhabitable. I always wanted to be a writer, but unfortunately I ran out of time. I was going to do something different from my father, but it didn't work out. There was this woman I always liked, but . . .* Woodland noises resumed as he sat for a long time, thinking. Finally he gave the groundhog a comradely nod. 'You and me, pal,' he said, and rose purposefully to his feet.

He used the remaining span of daylight to gather a stack of brushwood, reconnoitre a source of water, and sweep out the cabin with a surprisingly serviceable broom located in a lean-to shed. When the mosquitoes began to bite and the bats to swoop, he exchanged his shorts for jeans, pulled on an old sweater and carried a selection of items from the car to the cabin. By the time he had finally wedged the broken door shut, the sky was black as pitch. Clouds had drifted in on the evening breeze, obscuring the stars and a fingernail of moon. Jack built himself a fire, more for light and comfort than warmth, and sat on his sleeping bag in front of it, munching his way through a mega-sandwich, two apples and a package of Krispy Kreme doughnuts, while he made a list of all the things he would need to buy tomorrow. Outside, the temperature dropped and the wind rose. Unknown creatures crashed in the woods outside (deer? possums? skunks? *black bear?*). Around ten o'clock it began to rain. Raindrops pinged on the tin roof and dripped through multiple leaks. The chimney smoked ferociously. Jack took off his shoes and slid fully clothed into the sleeping bag, resting his head on his folded jacket and staring into the flickering flames. Arthur Miller, he remembered, had built his own cabin with his own hands before moving into it to write *Death of a Salesman*. Jack conceded that he was not Arthur Miller; he would never get to marry Marilyn Monroe, for one. But his Madison pride was seeping back. He would not be beaten.

It took him five days to make the cabin habitable. He fixed the small generator that pumped water up from a hillside spring, scythed the hogweed flat and piled it in the woods, patched up the roof and re-hung the door. He replaced the mosquito screens and cleared the chimney of birds' nests. In the small, sleepy local town he bought a second-hand stove and fridge plus the gas canisters to fuel them, and invested in three brand-new kerosene lamps. He got himself a fishing licence and a stack of local maps with the hiking trails marked. He solved the problem of a bed by slinging a hammock across one corner of the cabin, and was almost getting used to sleeping in it. The small back room he turned into his study, with a desk made from an old door propped on sawn rounds of pine-logs, securely nailed. Parked outside under the trees stood his new vehicle, a wheezy pick-up bought cheap on account of the way it had been painted by its previous hippie-girl owners – screaming pink decorated with flowers. Farm boys on tractors honked their scorn as he passed. Jack just grinned back, and turned up the *yingle-dangle-doo* music on his radio.

Finally he was ready to start writing. His portable typewriter sat square and neat on the makeshift desk, alongside a high stack of virgin paper and several folders containing his notes and unfinished script. Jack made a ceremony of his first day of real work. He got up early, shaved in front of the mirror he had hung on a tree outside, fixed himself coffee and a ham-and-eggs breakfast, dressed in shorts and a clean T-shirt and seated himself in his bare wooden cell. Pumped full of hope and determination, he reached for a folder and took out the familiar script. Ah yes. 'The ship lumbered into harbour . . .'

Five hours later, Jack slammed his hand on the desk in frustration and strode outside to the front porch, glowering at the magnificent view. He was still stuck. The story was there, but it was dead on the page; he could not breathe life into it. For the rest of that day and the next two days Jack wrestled with the problem, scribbling phrases, typing paragraphs, rolling paper into his typewriter and tearing it out again, to screw up and toss away. He wondered if he should change the ending – or the beginning – or rewrite the whole book in the first person. Sweat poured off him as the July sun beat on the tin roof and turned his study into an oven. He cursed himself for all the hours he'd wasted back in New York when he could have been writing in comfort, with all the conveniences of air-conditioning and a computer. Yet he craved distraction, and had to practically tie himself to the chair to stop himself from jumping in the truck and driving into town for a beer and companionship. Time was ticking by. On a stringent budget of fifty dollars a week, his money might just last for three months. This time, his deadline was immovable.

On the fourth day he rose at first light, pulled on his hiking boots and slung a rucksack over his shoulders, and set off into the woods. Morning cloud hung thick and damp over the trees. The pine-spiced air was alive with the whistle of birds and gurgle of cold, clear streams. Once he surprised a herd of deer, who bounded off in a flurry of white rumps. His eyes absorbed the scenery, as a strengthening sun turned it from misty sepia to vibrant colour, but his mind was focused on the story he was trying to write. It hung there like a hologram: he could see it, but he couldn't feel it. As the miles passed and the path wound upwards, Jack's thoughts began to drift – childhood memories, scenes from movies, whether he had enough bread to last the week, and then – without warning – Freya. He had been trying to shut her out of his thoughts, but suddenly she was achingly close. He could feel the bouquet in his hands, the prick of thorns; he could see the twist of her body as she clutched the sink. '*You have no respect for the human heart.*' The memory brought shame and tenderness, regret and self-doubt in a powerful, swirling mix.

He climbed on automatically towards the bald pate of granite mountain-top that was his goal. Finally he reached the summit, panting a little, and stood to admire the landscape that unrolled beneath him to a hazy horizon. He was struck by its ordered perfection. Seen from this vantage point, the terrain that seemed so confusing at ground level now assumed an irresistible logic. He could see how streams connected with rivers, why farmers had shaped their fields to certain precise patterns, how the interlocking hills created a mirror-image of interlocking valleys, and that the maze of dirt-tracks where he had so often got lost were merely man-made copies of the natural contours of the landscape. He wished he could discern the structure of his novel this clearly. An author should have authority.

In that instant, Jack's thoughts about writing and his feelings about Freya connected, striking a spark of insight that flamed into life and illuminated his whole book. He saw that in worrying over structure and theme he had forgotten the human heart of his story – forgotten it because he had refused to look into his own heart for so long. No writer could produce even a hundred words without revealing something of himself – without committing to a viewpoint; Jack understood that it was his obstinacy in this matter that had blocked him for so long. He sat down on the bare rock, overwhelmed by a sense of release and excitement. Instead of stifling all these unwelcome emotions – guilt, envy, pride, doubt – he would face them, and harness the insights they brought to drive his narrative forward. This was *his* book, and no one else's. He wouldn't worry about what the reviewers might say, or what his father thought, or listen to the doubting self inside him. Ideas, scenes, whole passages of dialogue began to race out of his brain, like fishing lines that had finally hooked on to something live.

It was late afternoon by the time Jack returned to the cabin. He washed hastily, throwing off his clothes and upending a bucket of spring water over his head. Then he dressed and hurried to his desk, grabbing a hunk of bread and cheese on the way. His muscles ached but his brain was jumping. He placed two lamps on either side of his typewriter, prepared to be as profligate as need be with the kerosene. Even as he was sitting down, connections snapped together in his head. Fleetingly he wondered where Freya was and what she was doing. Then the conscious thought of her was swept away under an intoxicating rush of words. Placing his work-scratched hands on the keys, he began to type.

Freya was in Chelsea, having spent the afternoon poking around disused garages and run-down warehouses. Two weeks ago Lola Preiss had announced her intention to move the downtown gallery out of SoHo, which was rapidly turning into designer-label heaven, with rents to match. Several of the cannier dealers were moving up to Chelsea, and Lola didn't want to be left behind. She had instructed Freya to draw up a shortlist of likely sites.

Now it was after five. There was no point going back to work. Freya hovered on a street corner, wondering whether to take a cab back to her mini-apartment. But the sun was shining, and today the temperature had dropped again into the pleasant mid-seventies. She wasn't ready to go home. Instead, she decided to have a little wander, nowhere in particular – just, you know, wandering.

She walked out to the end of one of the old shipping piers and stared at the river for a bit, then retraced her steps and began to thread her way through small leafy streets, aiming vaguely for the subway station. Everything looked very familiar – the decorative wrought-iron hoops around the trees, the pot-holed sidewalk she always used to trip on, that man practising baseball catches with his son, the sound of children screaming with delight as they ran in and out of a playground sprinkler. She did, in fact, seem to be in Jack's actual street. She hoped he wasn't looking out of his window. She did *not* wish to see him. But it would be silly to turn back now. So long as she stayed on the opposite side of the street from his apartment, she'd be safe.

Glancing across, she saw that there were builders at work on something, cluttering the kerbside with their usual paraphernalia of planks and cement mixers and bags of sand. Freya felt a pang of regret that yet another house was being renovated. Soon the neighbourhood would be full of bankers, and its character would change. But as she drew closer, her idle nostalgia sharpened to surprise. It was Jack's house that was under reconstruction; specifically, it was Jack's own apartment that was being gutted. What was going on?

Without pausing to think, Freya dashed across the street and asked the builders if they were working for Mr Madison. But nobody knew except the foreman, who they said had gone home early – as usual. They were pretty sure some new people were moving in, one of those hot-shot career couples to judge by the fancy fittings they'd ordered.

Freya gripped the front railings and stared into the empty shell of the apartment she had known so well. Now that the first shock had passed, she realized that there was nothing particularly strange in the fact that Jack had moved. He'd said himself he couldn't afford to stay. What surprised her was how swiftly he had acted. She wondered where he had gone.

She walked on, lost in thought, until a sound somewhere between a grunt and a greeting made her look up. It was the old Italian man in his undershirt, sitting on the stoop and tilting his beer bottle at her in greeting.

Freya waved back, then walked over to the bottom of the steps and looked up at him, shading her eyes from the sun. 'Do you remember my friend Jack?' she asked. 'A big blond guy, early thirties, who used to live in the apartment they're working on down there?' She pointed.

'Sure.'

'Well, do you know what's happened to him?'

'Gone,' said the man, swilling his beer. 'Moved out.'

'How long ago?'

'Maybe three . . . four weeks.'

'Do you happen to know where he went? Did you talk to him?'

'I say to him, "You moving out?" And he say to me, "I'm leaving the city."'

'*Leaving the city*?' Freya was stunned. 'But why? Where?'

The old man gave her a baleful look. 'What am I, psychic? People come. People go. That's New York.'

Freya thanked him politely, and walked on. She told herself that it was silly to feel unsettled. It was of no interest to her where Jack had gone. Jack was a bastard.

She could never forgive him. She never wanted to see him again, and had told him so.

*Never.* The word seemed to reverberate in her chest. She saw the long months stretching ahead – July, August, September ... Surely he'd come back in September, to start his teaching courses.

But what if he didn't? What if she had driven him away for good? Freya realized that she couldn't even remember the name of his home town. Oakville? Oakland?

Oh, what did it matter? She stepped straight off the kerb at Tenth Avenue and almost collided with a cyclist, who swerved wildly and gave her the finger. Freya wondered what Jack had done with Rosinante. *Where are you?* she shouted angrily in her head. But there was no answer.

Jack had settled into a routine now. Every day he got up with the birds at dawn, washed, dressed and did the necessary chores. Then he wrote right through the day until five, when he went out for a long evening hike or a swim in the stream, and sometimes caught himself a trout for supper. At night he'd settle by the fire and revise what he'd written that day and make notes for tomorrow. Then he'd climb into his hammock and be asleep by ten. It was sort of boring, but he felt healthy and energized and the routine kept him focused. Slowly the pages were building on his desk.

Saturday afternoons were the exceptions, when he

spruced himself up and jumped in the pick-up for a brief return to civilization. He'd got so used to solitude that the bustle of the small town seemed as exciting as a walk up Fifth Avenue. (Hey, a pizza place! Women! TV!) Everything took a long time because people liked to talk, and it seemed only friendly to talk back. First, Jack would check to see if he had any mail waiting at the post office, though there usually wasn't, because hardly anyone knew he was here. Then he'd shop for food and supplies. In the funny little super-market-cum-grocery store he resolutely ignored the rack stocked with wine and beer (hard liquor was forbidden by law), in the same way that he ignored a certain look the checkout girl had given him when she asked if he was new in town or just passing through. (Down, boy!) Once or twice, as he passed the display of postcards, he'd thought of sending one to Freya — just a one-liner, a signal. But what could he say? 'I'm here writing my book' — too boastful. 'Thinking of you' — she'd tear it up. After shopping, at the unfashionably early hour of six o'clock he'd go to the Barbecue and Pickin' Parlor, where he'd eat a mountain of chicken, ribs, beef and pork, served on a wooden, pig-shaped platter with creamed corn, biscuits and gravy. Then he'd stagger back to his truck and drive home to read *Remembrance of Things Past* by the fire. He had ploughed his way to book five and was almost beginning to see the point of Proust.

Today was a sizzler, even though a new bronze veil on the upper mountain slopes warned that autumn was already on its way. Jack parked the pick-up on the main street and headed quickly for the shade of the post office with its clanking fan. There was the usual stir, as people turned to check him out. Jack responded with a vague, genial smile. He had no premonition of what was to come.

'Looks like you're Mr Popular today,' said the man at the counter when Jack finally reached the small window, and he handed over three letters. Jack took them over to a corner, feeling curiously uneasy as he noted that his father, Lauren and Candace had all chosen to write to him at the same time. He decided to open Candace's letter first (pale lilac stationery, with her address written on the flap in swirly writing). He slit open the envelope, and took out what was evidently a long and important communication.

*Dear Jack*, he read. *I'm afraid that the news I have to tell you will come as a terrible shock . . .*

# 33

*Three months later*

'Don't be nervous.'

'*I am not nervous!* . . . How do I look?'

'I've told you before: you look fine.'

'*Fine?* Last time I asked, you said *beautiful*.'

'You look beautiful.'

'The time before, you said *fabulous*.'

'You look fabulous *and* beautiful – and radiant and serene and all the other things a bride's supposed to be.'

'What about my hair? I hate November: New York's always so windy.'

'Your hair is perfection. We're in a cab, remember?'

'What if he isn't there?'

'He'll be there. Stop fiddling with your bouquet.'

'But I was so mean to him!'

'And he was horrible to you. You've forgiven each other. That's what love means.'

'I think I'm going to faint.'

'You are not going to faint.'

'I really love him, you know.'

'I know.'

'Oh God, we're here! Did you bring the valium?'

\*

The church was stuffy and the bride late. This was the third time that the organist had played 'Jesu, Joy of Man's Desiring'. Jack fiddled with his cuff-link and stole a glance at the rows of guests dressed to kill, at all the faces familiar from childhood. Expensive perfumes clashed with the heavy fragrance of open-throated Madonna lilies. He felt hot and constricted in this ridiculous outfit. He could feel the stock around his neck pushing his chin into an aggressive tilt, as if he was about to lead the last Confederate charge against the damned Yankees.

Still, he'd promised Candace, and he'd promised his father. He had to go through with it.

'Okay: deep breath. Are you ready?'
'You go first.'
'Don't be silly.'
'Take a peek. Please. For me?'
The door to the church stood ajar. A modest aisle paved in coloured tiles led through rows of seats, packed with murmuring guests. At the far end a man waited, rigid with anxiety, staring at a particularly colourful representation of the crucifixion. Freya smiled. Michael turned his head, and his face flooded with such joy and relief that her eyes pricked with tears.

' . . . we are gathered together to join this man and this woman in holy matrimony, which is an honourable estate . . .'

Jack caught his stepmother's eye. She winked, and for an instant his tension relaxed. Lauren had been the last wife but two: his father had never taken marriage very seriously. Jack had often wondered if he would be the same.

Yet the solemnity of the service made it hard not to take marriage seriously. Love. Fidelity. Fortitude. Endurance. It felt quite different to be up here at the altar instead of sitting among the congregation.

'Do you, Candace Marie Twink, take this man to be your lawful wedded husband . . .'

Jack snapped to attention. His big moment was coming up. *Where was the ring?*

'Do you, Michael Josiah Petersen, take this woman to be your lawful wedded wife – to have and to hold from this day forward . . .?'

'I do.'

Freya looked at his face, so proud and excited. She had never seen his brown eyes glow like this, or such a tender curve to his smile. Love was truly amazing: powerful, irresistible, unpredictable. Who could have guessed that out of all the women in the world, the right one for Michael – the only one – would be her dear friend Cat, whose face shone with the same happy confidence as she repeated the marriage vows?

Freya felt humbled. How little she knew of human nature. Here were two people she could have sworn would dislike each other on sight; yet they had slotted together like a key in a lock, opening the door to a new future together. It looked so easy. If only –

'I now pronounce you man and wife.'

A chorus of uninhibited sobs broke out behind her. That would be Cat's mother and the other da Fillipo women. Italians were so emotional. A cascade of glorious, liquid music poured from the organ loft. Freya ducked her head and glared at the tips of her exquisite new shoes. Just for a moment, she was feeling rather Italian herself.

'Congratulations, *Mrs Madison*.' Jack bent to kiss the bride.

Candace smiled at him triumphantly. She was practically airborne on a waft of gauzy white material – veils and trains and other stuff he couldn't name. There was no sign of the tongue stud today.

Across the street half of Oaksboro – the half who hadn't been invited to the wedding – crowded the sidewalk in a scuffle of red and yellow leaves, and peered from the windows of red-brick storefronts. It was just late enough in the afternoon for the football game to be over, yet too early for Saturday night hijinks. What could be more interesting than to loiter in the last rays of a dying November sun, memorizing every last detail of the latest Madison bride? Jack wondered what they made of it all.

'Come on, everybody.' Jack winced at the commanding boom of his father's voice. 'Let's go back to the house and *celebrate*!'

'Sweetie, how can I ever thank you?' Cat threw her arms around Freya, high as a kite. 'You've been wonderful.'

'Don't be silly. I just – '

'No, she's right.' Michael gave Freya's elbow an appreciative squeeze. 'We'd never have got all this organized without you.' He gestured at the roomful of guests, already attacking the party food. 'You've done a great job.'

'Fantastic!' agreed Cat.

'Really incredible,' Michael added.

'Nonsense. Thank *you* for giving me the chance. I've loved doing it.' Freya smiled. She hadn't done this much smiling for months, and her cheeks ached.

They all stood beaming at each other until Freya pretended to remember that there was something vital she must check, and managed to shoo Michael and Cat away to join their guests. She watched them go with mingled affection and relief. It wasn't that she *minded* that Cat and Michael had fallen in love. She didn't mind that Cat had moved into Michael's apartment and was sleeping in the bed only recently vacated by herself. She didn't mind helping Cat to choose her outfit, compile her wedding-gift list, order the flowers, arrange the reception. She didn't even mind being a bridesmaid – at least they hadn't made her wear a stupid garland on her head. It was just a little . . . painful. There was still a slight awkwardness between the three of them, though they did their best to pretend otherwise. The story of the shortened trousers was now a hilarious joke. Ha, ha! Freya's bedroom revelations had been wiped from memory. They all agreed that it had been quite miraculously providential that Cat had been able to take advantage of Michael's spare ticket for the *Ring Cycle*.

Freya was glad now that she had gone back up to Cat's apartment that terrible, rainy night, though it had taken every scrap of courage she possessed to put her own misery aside, and absolve Cat and Michael of guilt. She was proud of herself for behaving so well. In fact, she had behaved bloody brilliantly for months and months. She had spent hours of overtime with Matt Rivera, encouraging him, bullying him, persuading him to think about his work and not the velvet mafia of critics – with the result his show had been a colossal success, both financially and critically, and Lola Preiss had finally stopped questioning Freya's every decision.

On the home front, she had finally signed a rental lease on a long-term apartment in TriBeCa and redecorated it herself. Last month she had christened it with a huge dinner-party for Cat and Michael and their separate groups of friends, though she nearly had a nervous breakdown over the cooking – not to mention re-encountering those friends of Michael who remembered *her* as the girlfriend. It was a lovely apartment with a proper doorman, a sunny aspect and heart-lifting views; there was even a small spare room for her father, who was coming to visit next month.

At a personal level, although Freya had told Cat about Jack and Tash – and Cat had denounced Jack in a very satisfying, robust manner – she hadn't gone on and on about it. It seemed selfish to wallow in misery when Cat was so happy; Freya had made a big effort to redirect her energies into showing how delighted she was for her friend.

And she *was* delighted. She'd loved being swept into the heart of the da Fillipo family, who were openly jubilant at having got Cat married at last. It was fun to be here at the centre of a party that had taken off with such a roar of good humour. Italians certainly knew how to enjoy themselves. A small band played brassily in one corner. Everywhere she looked there were cakes oozing with cream, dredged with sugar, soaked in marsala, studded with almonds and dried fruit. There were cratefuls of *Asti spumante*, emptying at a terrifying rate. The room was above a restaurant in Little Italy, owned by Cat's fourth cousin's brother-in-law's son. Already it was packed to capacity with wolfish uncles and dyed-blonde aunts, children in velveteen suits and frilled dresses, even a little dog that looked like a floor-mop and was called Pookie. The now-legendary Blumbergs were here, of course, beaming at everyone and holding hands, a walking advertisement for marriage. Fred Reinertson, Michael's boss, was here. Poor Fred, having spent several expensive weeks in hospital recovering from a bowel operation, had returned home to find his apartment stripped and a petition for divorce from his wife; though as he gazed at the magnificent cleavage of one of Cat's teenage nieces, he wasn't looking too inconsolable.

Whoops! There was Mrs Petersen, in navy blue. Freya changed direction smartly. It had been decided to skate over any connection between the deranged ex-girlfriend who had pretended to be a Spanish-speaking cleaner and the English woman acting as maid-of-honour to Michael's bride. As it was, Mrs Petersen had suffered one of her worst attacks ever on learning that her beloved Mikey was marrying a woman she hadn't even met, let alone approved: a career woman (feminist), a New Yorker (hard), in her thirties (after Mikey's sperm), from an Italian background (Catholic!). Even though Cat treated her like an empress, begged for permission to call her 'Mother' and lavished praise on her son, Mrs Petersen maintained an expression of noble martyrdom – that faltered into a quizzical frown every time she caught sight of her new daughter-in-law's best friend. So far Freya had resisted the temptation to click her fingers and shout '*Olé!*'

She lost herself in the crowd, drinking and chatting and trying to suppress memories of the last wedding she had attended. This was Cat and Michael's day, and she wanted it to be perfect. At one point she caught sight of the pair of them together: Cat talking animatedly, carving the air with her hands, while Michael watched mesmerized, as if a goddess had floated down on her cloud. Cat was carrying her nephew Tonito on one hip, his fat legs tucked comfortably around her waist. She glowed with happiness. Freya was prepared to bet good money that Cat would be pregnant within the year. She pictured Cat in the Chinese restaurant, only a few months ago, loftily insisting that she didn't *need* a man, and smiled at the tricks life played.

Freya kept herself busy, checking that the food and drink were circulating, that there were enough chairs for the older guests, and helping to fill glasses for the toasts. Then everybody gathered close, someone rapped on a table for silence and Cat's father stepped forward. His dark eyes raked the room. 'I have only one question,' he growled. 'Why did it take her so long?' Freya listened with affection as he talked about Cat's character and achievements – her big heart, her fighting spirit, her tiny forgivable flaws – until, with an old-fashioned formality that she found moving, he took his daughter's hand and placed it ceremonially in that of her husband's. Now it was Michael's turn. Freya nibbled at a thumbnail, wondering how he'd measure up, hoping he wouldn't be too ponderous and sentimental. When Cat confessed that she had first been attracted to Michael because of his wonderful sense of humour, Freya had only just managed to refrain from retorting 'his *what*?' But now, as he began to tell the story of how he and Cat had met as antagonists in the Blumberg divorce case, Freya saw that Cat was right. People were laughing. He was funny! Love had made him confident. He even looked different, his hair shinier, his eyes brighter. Freya was glad for him, but his happiness was also the gentlest of rebukes. She had seen Michael as dependable and 'nice', but ultimately boring; it had taken Cat to light that bonfire inside him.

Cat was hilarious. She interrupted Michael regularly – correcting his stories, chipping in with asides, once even smoothing his hair into place. He took it all with patient good humour, teasing her back, calming her down. Cat made her own short speech, naturally; this was, she announced, an equal opportunities marriage.

After the speeches, time seemed to hurtle forward. A car had been booked to take Cat and Michael to the airport; they were flying to the Caribbean for a week of sun. There were suitcases to be taken downstairs. Someone needed to pay the band. There was a minor diplomatic incident when, for no apparent reason, Pookie bit Mrs Petersen on the ankle. Cat and Michael slipped upstairs to change. While she waited for them to reappear, Freya noticed Cat's grandmother sitting alone, apparently overwhelmed by the noise and bustle. She must be well into her eighties, poor thing. Freya walked over and stooped low. 'May I bring you something?'

The old woman took her hand gratefully and drew her into the next chair, glad of someone to talk to. In her eccentrically accented English she told Freya what a marvellous party it was, how handsome she thought Michael, how lovely Cat looked in her wedding suit. Freya smiled and smiled. She retold the story of Cat's broken ankle and the tap-dancing class where they had met. She agreed that everything was quite, quite wonderful.

Mrs da Fillipo stroked Freya's hand while they talked. Her own were small and incredibly fragile, the skin soft as worn velvet.

'You are not married?' she asked.

The question took Freya by surprise. She looked down at her ringless fingers, suddenly jolted out of the comfortable mundanity of small talk. 'No,' she said shortly.

'Someone special?'

'No.'

'But why not? You are so pretty.'

Freya tossed her head. 'Men aren't everything.'

'That depends on the man.' The faded eyes peered shrewdly into her own. 'You have never been in love?'

Freya felt her lip tremble. *Please stop!* 'Oh, love,' she shrugged. 'It's such a silly word. I mean, how can you tell?'

Mrs da Fillipo smiled and patted her hand kindly, as if they both knew Freya was talking nonsense. 'The first time I saw my husband,' she said, 'was at his engagement party to someone else. But that didn't stop me.' She chuckled. 'A woman always knows. And when she knows, she must *act*.'

'But . . . it isn't always easy to know what to do.' Freya dropped her flippant tone and met the old lady's gaze frankly.

Mrs da Fillipo gripped her hand tight. 'You must follow your heart,' she urged. 'You *must*. Gianni and I were married for fifty-six years. I miss him every day.' Her kind, creased face clouded with sorrow. Freya swallowed hard.

'Oh, look!' she said brightly, pointing at Cat and Michael, who had reappeared in casual holiday clothes and were making their sentimental farewells. Cat came over to say goodbye to her grandmother, and Freya gave up her seat to allow them some privacy. She wandered aimlessly through the crowd, trying to regain her equilibrium, and found herself face to face with Michael.

'Great speech.' She smiled.

To her surprise he stretched out his arms and pulled her into a warm hug. 'Promise to invite me to *your* wedding.'

'Of course,' said Freya, rather stiffly. She knew he meant to be kind, but it was not his most well-chosen remark. 'Don't hold your breath,' she added, trying to make a joke of it.

Then it was time to say goodbye to Cat. Now that the moment had come, Freya was suddenly overwhelmed by a sense of loss and loneliness. Old friends who knew you through and through, good and bad, and loved you anyway, were hard to replace. She feared that their best-friends relationship would never be quite the same again. She hugged Cat tight. 'Have a wonderful, wonderful time,' she told her.

Cat pulled her close. 'Oh sweetie, I'm going to miss you so much!'

'Rubbish! You've got Michael now. And he's got you.' Freya smiled. 'I'm so happy.'

Finally the bride and groom were ready to leave. They stood together at the door to the stairs, with guests gathered around them in a tight circle to wish them well. 'Goodbye everybody!' shouted Cat. With a theatrical wave of her arm she tossed something into the air.

The bouquet sailed up to the ceiling high above Freya's head, where it seemed to hang for long seconds. Then it spun downwards in a whirl of cream and gold and bronze. Freya saw its tiny petals catch the light and turn into a shower of sparks. Down it came, faster and faster. Oh no! It was heading straight for her. How would it look if she let Cat's bouquet smash to the floor? Surely someone else would catch it? *Please*. But no one did. At the last moment she put out her hand and caught it. *Aaaah* . . . sighed the crowd. *Bravo!*

Freya stared into the tender open hearts of the flowers. They were so beautiful. Her fingers tightened on the stems. Then she burst into tears.

There was a ripple of consternation. Freya covered her face with her hand. *Please . . . no! Don't do this, Freya.* But she couldn't control the gasps that jerked her shoulders and tore at her chest.

'Sweetie, what is it?' Suddenly Cat's arms were around her.

'Nothing,' Freya sobbed. Everyone – *everyone* – was watching. She was ruining Cat's wedding. How could she?

'Tell me,' Cat asked gently. 'What's the matter.'

'I don't *know*,' wailed Freya. 'You go. Please.' She flapped her hand.

'I'm not leaving you like this.' Cat's voice was low but firm. 'Come on, we'll go somewhere quiet and talk.'

'You'll miss your plane, Mikey.' Mrs Petersen's chiding sing-song sliced through the silence.

Cat's head snapped up. 'The plane can wait!' she answered back. She put a protective arm around Freya's shoulders and shepherded her to the doorway, where Michael hovered anxiously. As the two of them stumbled past and headed for a door marked 'Ladies', Freya saw Cat and Michael exchange a look. Michael nodded. He'd wait.

Then Freya was in a small, tiled room that smelled of air-freshener. Cat sat her down on an upturned waste bin and crouched in front of her.

'What is it?' she demanded. 'Who upset you?'

'Nobody.' Freya wiped her nose with the back of her wrist.

'Here, let me get you a Kleenex.' Cat turned away for a moment and rummaged through her capacious handbag, discarding items on the floor until she found a travel-pack of tissues, which she tore open and passed to Freya. She waited until Freya had blown her nose, then grasped her hands.

'Oh baby, I thought you were okay about this.'

'I *am* okay.'

'Maybe we should have waited longer.'

'No, no.' Freya shook her head. 'It isn't anything to do with you and Michael.'

'Are you sure?'

She nodded.

'Then what is it?'

Freya thrashed her head from side to side. The wave of feeling that had been gathering inside her all day – for weeks – for months – finally broke. 'It's . . . *Jack*!' she burst out.

'Jack?' Cat rolled on to her heels. Her eyes were wide. Her hair practically crackled with shock. 'As in "that bastard Jack"?'

Freya's head jerked up. 'He's not a bastard!' She scowled through her tears.

'The one who slept with your stepsister?'

'He didn't mean to.' Freya blew her nose loudly.

'The spoilt, lazy good-for-nothing, living off his daddy's money?'

'He can't help having a rich father. Anyway, he's not any more.'

'The lousy writer?'

'He's a *wonderful* writer!'

'I don't get this.' Cat frowned. 'I thought you told him you never wanted to see him again.'

'I *know* . . .' Freya wailed. 'But I think he was *The One*.'

'Oh, sweetie . . .'

'And now he's *married*!'

'*What?*'

Freya ground the heels of her hands into her forehead. 'It's all my fault. I drove him away. And now I'll never see him again.'

Ever since that day in Chelsea, her fury and humiliation had begun to abate, to be replaced with a gnawing curiosity. Where was he? What was he doing? What was he thinking? She replayed the events in Cornwall over and over again. It hadn't been all bad. Some moments had been good. In fact, some had been *marvellous*. On painful reflection, she admitted that Jack might have told the truth when he said that Tash had seduced him. Tash didn't care about Jack; she'd wanted to hurt Freya – and had succeeded brilliantly. It tormented Freya that Tash had slept with Jack, while she had turned down the chance – twice – and now she never would. Her desire shamed her. Jack was no good. Jack was unreliable. Jack had no heart. And yet she missed him. She couldn't stop thinking about him. By September, she'd been desperate enough to call the Madison home in Oaksboro (Oaksboro! that was it) – not to talk to him, of course, just to see if he was there, maybe even hear his voice say 'hello'. But her call had been answered by a housekeeper. Freya asked tentatively if Jack happened to be there. *Not right now*, came the answer. *He's out to dinner with his fiancée ... Miss Twink*. Freya couldn't believe it. She refused to believe it. Pathetically, she had scrolled through the local papers on the internet until she'd found the announcement for herself. It was true.

There was an urgent rap at the door. 'Caterina! . . . *aeroporto!* . . . *subito!*'

Cat shot furiously to her feet. 'In a minute,' she yelled.

Freya made herself stand up, too. She caught sight of her blotched face in the mirror above the basin, and tried to pull herself together. 'You must go, Cat,' she said. 'It's your wedding day.'

'Fuck the wedding day! My best friend needs me.' Cat threw her arms around Freya and held her close.

'Oh, Cat . . .' Freya gave a weak hiccup of laughter and laid her head on Cat's shoulder, letting Cat stroke her hair. She stared bleakly into nothingness. 'What am I going to do?' she moaned.

Cat pulled back a little and looked Freya in the eye. 'Honey, *forget him.*' Her hand swiped through the air. 'There are lots of men out there – plenty of 'em. When I get back I'll find you a nice man, just the way you found Michael for me.'

'But I didn't find Michael for you,' Freya protested, laughing through her tears. They reached for each other's hands, smiling mistily.

There was another knock, gentler this time. The door squealed open. 'Uh, darling? The car's outside. When you're ready.'

'I'm coming.' Cat beamed at Freya. 'Isn't he wonderful? Now wash your face. You look terrible.'

While Freya obediently splashed water on her eyes and cheeks, Cat repacked her handbag: passport, paperbacks, mineral water, vitamin capsules. 'Oh look,' she said, 'I picked this up at the bookstore.'

'What?' Freya peered blearily at Cat's reflection. Cat had stood up now, bag slung over her shoulder, and was studying something in her hand. It looked like an invitation.

'Hmm,' said Cat, reading. 'Fifth Avenue . . . very upscale . . . November eighth . . . the day after tomorrow. *Perfect!*'

'What's perfect?' Freya turned to look more closely, and gave a cry of repugnance. 'No way!'

'Yes! Don't you see? It's a sign.'

'But that's my birthday! I don't want to go to a bloody singles evening on my birthday.'

'What else are you going to do?'

Freya opened her mouth and closed it again.

'Listen: here's the plan. Promise me, or I'm not leaving.' Cat looked so bossy that Freya couldn't help smiling.

'I promise,' she said.

'On Monday night you're going to get all dressed up. Buy something new. Do something with your hair. Think *fabulous.*'

Freya gave a pitiful mew.

'You're going to go to this singles evening.' Cat thrust the card into her hand. 'And you're going to meet a Nice Man.'

'Am I?' Freya sniffed.

'Oh, sweetie.' Cat's face softened. She drew Freya into a fierce hug. 'You never know. Look at Michael and me. Anything can happen.'

# 34

Jack stepped out of the office building and paused for a moment to flip up the collar of his overcoat. He'd forgotten how ferocious the wind could get here. While he'd been inside the sky had darkened from overcast grey to soiled black. Yellow lights blazed and blinked around him. There was the grind and screech of congested traffic. Figures blurred past, as if on a continuous loop. Jack savoured the tainted air while he considered what to do next. He allowed himself to look at his watch, though he knew almost to the minute what time it was. An inner clock had been ticking in his head for days, for months, getting louder and more urgent until now he could think of nothing else but what might – *might* – happen tonight.

He still had an hour to kill. If he took the subway he could be at his destination in twenty minutes – but then what? To sit alone in some coffee shop or bar, at the mercy of his giddying emotions, was unthinkable. He decided to walk. Shoving his gloveless hands into his pockets, he slotted himself into the pedestrian traffic and headed south at a New Yorker's implacable stride.

It was good to be back in the city. He felt energized by the rush of people on this ordinary Monday evening

– young and not so young, fashionably thin and grotesquely fat, black, white, brown, glamorous in fur coats, wretched in stained tracksuits. He was amused by the preposterous extravagance of the store-window displays – crocodile briefcases, cashmere slippers, thousand-dollar teddy bears, silver toothpicks – all tricked out with Thanksgiving motifs of turkeys and corncobs. He liked the feeling that he belonged, that he was one of this elite band of gutsy survivors.

For it seemed, from what Ella had said to him this afternoon, that he had succeeded on one front, at least. His agent had looked him in the eye, laid a reverent hand on the script he had mailed off from the little country post office two weeks ago, and pronounced it 'wonderful'. The best novel she'd read all year. 'Dramatic', 'moving', 'memorable', 'original'. She'd already slipped some pages to a couple of editors; one of them had tried to secure a pre-emptive offer, but she thought she might have a little fun with an auction. The guy at Knopf who never admitted to liking anything had called specially to yawn down the phone that he wouldn't mind taking a look. Even the publishers who had cancelled Jack's contract were backtracking wildly, after yet another new broom had taken over. Ella didn't care to put a figure on the probable advance, but she was confident that it would be 'substantial'.

Jack had spent a luxurious couple of hours asking her to remind him just one more time what it was she especially liked – which scene, what phrase, that joke on page 211 (great! wasn't it?). Hadn't she in fact, now he came to think of it, uttered the word 'masterpiece'? Well, no: in fact, she hadn't. Jack smiled at his own egotism. The book was good, and he had completed it. That was enough. No one could call him a 'dilettante'. Right at the end he worked practically night and day. He'd had to, in order to finish in time for the wedding.

His pace slowed as he reached a bookstore, one of those new palaces of literature and caffeine where you could get lost on your way from New Fiction to Travel, emerging hours later with crisp paperbacks on chaos theory or the Russian Revolution and a stomachful of cinnamon cake. The windows were brightly lit and artfully styled, spilling over with desirably packaged books on every subject. Jack hadn't seen a place like this for months; he paused to feast his eyes. One window was devoted to a single title, a first novel which had been rapturously praised and lavishly publicized. Copies were propped and piled in opulent heaps, flanked by giant review quotes with the usual superlatives. *The Times'* bestseller list, magnified to poster size, showed the title ringed at number four. Nestling among the books were blown-up photographs of the author, a young man with movie-star looks. Jack stared at the cocksure face, waiting for envy to kick in, but he felt only a swell of sympathy. *A great beginning, kid: make sure it's not the end.*

'Hey, man, watch your back!' He heard a shout and the clink of bottles as a delivery man trundled a handcart past his heels and swivelled it towards the glass entrance. The bookstore must be putting on some kind of shindig – a book reading or an author signing. Jack hitched up his trousers, wondering whether to go in and see. (Something funny had happened to his clothes. His jackets pinched at the shoulders, yet his trousers almost fell down unless he wore a belt notched on the last hole. Weird.)

He checked his watch again, feeling his ribs contract around his lungs. The long countdown was almost over. The bookstore might offer a welcome distraction for the twenty minutes still to go. But what if she was already waiting? No, that was crazily optimistic. Jack shifted from foot to foot, making up his mind, while his breath puffed miniature clouds into the frosty air.

# 35

'Retail is my life,' Mr Blue Suit was saying.

'Oh, me too!' agreed Ms Grey Suit.

'Maybe we could get together some time and really rap.'

'I'd like that. Here's my business card. You can call me at work.'

Mr Blue Suit pocketed the card and turned away, mission accomplished, to home in on another quarry. His questing glance skimmed the crowd and swept straight over Freya as if she was invisible. It wasn't surprising: Freya didn't fit. She had dressed up to signal unmistakably that she wasn't really a desperate thirtysomething. 'Think fabulous,' Cat had said. So she had. Her dress was sleeveless and severely cut, but made out of the softest possible leather, with buttons all the way down the back; she wore very high heels of a purply colour so sensational that it would have been criminal not to buy them. This was quite wrong. All the other women wore business suits with sensible hemlines and nice white blouses. They were so confident, so smiley, so bloody efficient! Chat, card, move on; chat, card, move on – as if they were harvesting a crop, on piece work. Did they then go on a dating binge, or hoard the cards as some kind of illusory insurance against loneliness?

Freya took another sip of her tepid white wine and gazed into the middle distance with a half-smile on her face, as if she wasn't really part of this sad, singles group – merely sightseeing, or perhaps gathering material for an amusing little feature on the women's page. This was turning into one of the worst evenings of her life. She thought of Cat, downing cocktails with the man she loved amid whispering palm trees, and wanted to strangle her.

The party, if that was the word, was taking place on the bookstore's cavernous first floor, in the Biology section (how witty!). The lights were bright, the temperature stifling. Freya wasn't in the mood for this. She didn't have the energy to start from scratch yet again. There seemed to be no learning curve to romance: all she knew was that every one of her relationships had failed.

Still, she had promised Cat. She must make an effort. Freya straightened her shoulders and braved the chattering hordes. Before too long she found herself talking to an okay-looking guy, about the right age. He was pleasant and polite, but she found it almost impossible to think of anything to say that didn't sound stupid or boring or both. This was all so banal! She could see him losing interest, his attention beginning to drift over her shoulder. Eventually, he made an excuse about refilling his glass; a few moments later she saw him laughing heartily with Ms

Grey Suit and accepting her card. Freya realized that she had not even got to first base in this ridiculous dating game. She circled the crowd, gathering the courage to try again, picking up snatches of conversation.

'I *adore* novels – especially the fictional ones.'

'No, but I saw the movie.'

'He said his favourite writer was Tom Clancy. I mean, *hello*?'

'Don't you feel that Shakespeare is, in a very real sense, with us here today?'

If only Jack was here. If only she hadn't said those terrible things to him. If only he wasn't *married*. Freya could think of no explanation of why Jack had married Candace Twink. Could she be pregnant? Had Jack's father forced him to marry her? Was there some Madison inheritance dependent on marriage? Had he just given up and decided that he might as well marry Candace as anyone else? Nothing made sense.

The touch of a hand on her elbow made her jump. 'Well, well,' said a familiar voice, 'if it isn't the woman who mistook a pocket calculator for her mobile phone.'

It was that literary agent, Leo Brannigan, smiling in his irritatingly superior way. He was wearing the cool-media-person's uniform of casual jacket and immaculate T-shirt. 'How's it going?' he asked with a leer. 'I hear these evenings are great for pick-ups.'

'Oh, I'm not with this lot.' Freya trilled with laughter at the very idea. 'I just, er, came in to buy a book and, er, decided to sneak a free glass of wine. It's my birthday,' she added, as if this were an explanation.

'Oh yeah?' Leo looked unconvinced.

'What about you?' she countered. 'Found any nice girls?'

'*Me?*' Leo's dark brows snapped together. 'Jesus Christ! I wouldn't be seen dead with these losers.' He had the perfect face for sneering, Freya thought. 'No, I've got one of my writers downstairs signing books. I'm just hanging out till he's finished.'

'It's not . . . Jack, is it?'

'Who? Oh – *Jack*. No. Wish it was. He decided to stay with Ella Fogarty.'

Freya nodded. *Good for you, Jack*, she thought.

'No, I missed a trick there.' Leo gave Freya a brooding look, as if it was her fault. 'I just hope Ella knows how to extract the right level of advance. These publishers are such tightwads.'

'Mmm.' What was he talking about?

'The word is, it's very good. Even better than *Big Sky*. Maybe bestseller material.'

Freya tried not to goggle. Jack had finished his book! She took a slurp of wine to cover her surprise, choked, and had to be patted on the back. 'I always knew he'd do it,' she croaked.

'It didn't look that way back in the summer,' said Leo. 'Even though I tried getting him on my list I wasn't sure he'd ever perform. It looked like he was heading nowhere. Then something happened to him, I don't know what.'

*I do*, Freya thought. Her heart sang.

'Maybe it was the marriage,' Leo suggested.

'Bollocks!' Freya exclaimed. Candace Twink could no more inspire Jack to write a novel than she could fly to the moon. The woman couldn't even see her own two feet! Catching Leo's startled glance, she added, 'I mean, I don't see why that should have any particular impact on his writing.'

'Well, I do. I'd say that was a real punch in the balls.'

'Would you?' Freya smiled brightly. *What* was a punch in the balls? Was he calling Candace a ball-buster? She didn't seem to be doing too well with conversations tonight.

'I mean, from the old man,' continued Leo helpfully.

Freya frowned. 'What, you mean cutting off his allowance?'

'The guy had an *allowance*! Jeez, these spoilt rich boys. No, I mean the business with the girlfriend.'

'What girlfriend?'

'The one he married, of course.' Leo's tone implied that she was a halfwit. 'I mean, what a great story. There's a novel right there.'

'You think so?' Freya cocked her head intelligently. She was utterly mystified.

'Well, sure! You introduce your girlfriend to your father, and the next thing you know they're getting married. It's your worst fucking nightmare.' He cackled maliciously.

Freya stared at him, open-mouthed. There was a strange noise in her head, like one of those complex

3-D puzzles clicking into place. The very week she'd left for England with Jack, Candace had gone out on the town with Jack's father. Jack's father liked women. Candace liked money. Candace wanted to *be* someone. Leo had said 'father'. Freya took a gasp of breath as the glorious, miraculous, obvious truth arrowed into her brain and finally hit the bull's-eye. Candace had married Jack Madison *senior*! Which meant . . . *which meant that Jack wasn't married after all!!!* She burst into hysterical laughter.

Leo was looking at her as if she'd finally flipped.

'I just think it's terribly funny,' she explained, raising her hand to hide a huge, foolish grin. He wasn't married!

'You women are so callous.' Leo shook his head in disgust. 'Just think how upset the poor guy must be about it.'

'Who? What?' Freya couldn't concentrate with all the voices jabbering in her head. Jack wasn't married! He was free! He'd even finished his book! How wonderful he was.

Leo rolled his eyes. 'Isn't Jack upset that his, i.e. Jack's, father has married his, i.e. Jack's, girlfriend?'

'Don't be daft!' Freya scoffed. 'Jack wouldn't care who married her. She's a bimbo, for heaven's sake. You could count her brain cells on the foot of a three-toed sloth. Jack's much too good for her. I mean, he's so . . . talented and so . . . funny . . . and nice and handsome and – ' Whoops! She was babbling. 'At least, some people seem to think so,' she ended feebly.

'Oh I get it . . .' Leo gave her a sly look. 'I heard you'd moved in with him for a while. But you couldn't get your hands on him because of this other girl, right? Now the field is clear, you can start chasing him again.'

Freya drew herself up tall. 'I was never chasing Jack,' she informed him with dignity. 'We were just friends.'

'Oh sure,' he said sceptically.

'We still are!' she insisted, stung.

'Really?' said Leo. 'Then how come you're not with him now instead of hounding poor single men?'

'What?' He'd lost her again.

He sighed at her stupidity. 'Didn't you say it was your birthday?'

'So?'

'You know: you and Jack – the bet?'

'What bed?' Freya blushed scarlet. She pictured the moonlit room in Cornwall, Jack smiling down at her, his hands tugging at the straps of her dress. But how on earth could Leo know about that?

'Bet,' Leo repeated, as if to a moron. 'B-e-t. Don't tell me you've forgotten.'

Freya stared at him. Her heart was beginning to pound. Of course she hadn't forgotten. The scene had replayed a thousand times in her mind. The hot night at Café Pisa, it seemed a lifetime ago – Jack saying, 'I'll be there' – and her making that stupid crack about marrying a lord. Only it was Jack who'd got married. Except he hadn't . . .

'*The bet!*' she shrieked, so loudly that the room hushed for a moment and everyone stared. Her mind whirled. The eighth at eight. *Today*. Oh God, he might be there now!

She grabbed Leo's wrist and looked at his watch, forgetting she had a perfectly good one of her own. Nine-fifteen. He'd think she wasn't coming – that she didn't care – that she'd meant it when she said she never wanted to see him again. *Oh Jack, wait!*

She started to sprint for the escalator, then turned back and slung an arm around Leo's neck. 'Come here, you bastard ten-percenter.' She gave him a smacking kiss.

Leo rubbed his cheek, a look of astonished recognition spreading across his face. 'You're in love with him!' But Freya was already gone.

# 36

The waiter pounced on Jack's empty glass and shot him a dirty look. Jack had lingered for almost an hour over two Bloody Marys; outside, there was a queue waiting for tables. Yet again the waiter asked if he should open the champagne; yet again Jack told him to wait.

How much longer? Jack had spent many hours of his life waiting for women. He still hadn't figured out exactly what they *did* all that time, but he knew that whatever-it-was took them twice as long as one could possibly imagine. In fact, in female terms, Freya was barely late at all. Candace, for example, had kept his poor father waiting in the Oaksboro church for forty-five minutes — and that was for her own wedding. But she had turned up in the end. They were on their honeymoon now in Candace's dream destination, Las Vegas. Candace Twink was a remarkable woman in her way.

Her note had been lying on the hallway floor of his apartment when he got back from Cornwall.

You bastard! Harry from upstairs told me where you've gone and who with. I always thought there was something between you and Her. Well, chacun a son goo, as they say in France. I have too much respect for myself as a woman to play 'second fiddle'. It is time for me to focus on my own life-goals and fulfil my potential as a human being. DON'T call me.

It had not immediately occurred to Jack that Candace's 'life-goal' might be to marry his own father. In fact, when he opened the letters from Candace, Lauren and his dad, all on the same subject (though Lauren's was much the funniest), he'd almost broken his no-drinking rule. Once he'd recovered from his surprise, the news of the marriage seemed entirely appropriate, though even he was struck by the single-mindedness with which Candace had embraced her destiny. Over-night, she had reinvented herself as Scarlett O'Hara. With a ruthlessness that inspired awe, if not admir-ation, she had repudiated her background, her friends, and very nearly her own family, eagerly agreeing to celebrate the wedding at the Madison home and admit-ting only a small group of terrified Twinks, who stood outside the church in an ostracized huddle wearing their best Macy's suits. Jack now suspected that, even as she'd composed her note of dismissal, Candace's eye had been firmly fixed on a prize infinitely more valuable than himself. He had no doubt that she would do her best to siphon off as much of the Madison fortune as she could; the swift production of a baby, proof of 'Old Jack's' undiminished virility, would speed the process. Jack's brother Lane had boycotted the wedding, and had tried to browbeat Jack into a joint lawsuit that might safeguard their interests in Madison Paper. Jack refused. Instead, he had accepted his father's offer of the role of best man, 'to show everybody we're still friends', as his father put it. 'Everybody' meant the whole of Oaksboro and practically everyone Jack had ever known. He was in no doubt that they all knew exactly how the happy couple had met. The story of how a man approaching seventy had stolen his own son's girlfriend was too good not to broadcast throughout every bar and hair-salon in the county.

Oddly, the potential humiliation of this situation had produced the opposite effect. Contemplating Candace in her wedding creation, her left hand locked tight into the crook of his father's arm and displaying several thousand dollars' worth of diamond ring, Jack had felt no jealousy at all, only a faint sadness that this was her narrow definition of happiness. He felt sorry for his father with this absurdly young trophy wife, who was unlikely to make him any happier than his previous four. Dad's cronies might josh about old dogs and lead in pencils, but the truth was that his father had not been up to the challenge of a real companion with a brain, like Lauren. Jack knew he wanted to do things differently.

It was a dramatic and liberating reversal. His father – God of creation, King of Madison Paper, exemplar of all masculine virtues, whose respect Jack had craved even while forging a different path – was suddenly just his father. Jack owed him his affection and his support; but he was no longer dependent, either for money or approval. He saw that he could win a hundred Pulitzers and his dad would still think no more and no less of him.

Still, it was going to take some getting used to, having Candace for a stepmother. Jack longed to tell Freya the whole story. He knew how hilarious she'd find it. But she wasn't here.

Jack looked at his watch: 9.15. She must come. *She must!* He had arrived with such excited expectancy, even while warning himself to expect nothing. Every time the door opened he had looked up, hoping it would be her. He'd secured one of the most desirable tables, in a quiet corner, romantically lit. He'd enjoyed choosing the champagne (dry? brut? *pink??*), and ordered it at once so that it would be waiting for her in its frosted bucket. He wanted to tell her about his book. He ached to see her face – her smile, her eyes, her lips.

Tonight had been his real deadline for months. Valhalla's, the eighth at eight. All summer and into the autumn, riding back and forth in the pick-up, listening to Country songs of love and loss and longing, of women whose men had done them wrong, of men who'd lost the only woman that mattered, he'd dreamed of this chance to tell her that he was sorry, and to prove to her that he had changed. Sometimes he thought of those dog-graves in Cornwall, carved with the names of King Arthur's Court, and imagined his own inscription: Sir Jack, not very chivalrous knight. Freya had banished him; and only Freya could recall him. If she chose to.

Jack gripped the edge of the table, so tight that his thumbnails whitened. He wanted her here – *now.* He missed her company and her laugh; he missed her cleverness and her fighting spirit; he even missed their arguments. Ever since Cornwall he'd been unable to think about any other woman: again and again he'd found himself waking from vivid erotic dreams; his mind full of her eyes, her breasts, her legs . . . He remembered how she had looked, lying on the bed beneath him. She'd once said to him, 'You don't want a woman like me.' But she was wrong. Freya was exactly the woman he wanted. She was the *only* woman.

Here was the waiter again. Jack waved him away and checked the time: 9.30. Once again he ran through the reasons that might explain her lateness. But he was kidding himself. She wasn't late; she had never intended to come. She wasn't sick or stuck in a meeting or stranded without a cab; she wasn't here because she didn't want to be. He couldn't help thinking of the final scene in the *The Third Man*, where Joseph Cotten waits for the girl as she walks towards him down a long avenue of winter-bare trees – towards him, and straight past, not even turning her head to look. The flame of hope that had been burning inside his heart flickered one last time and went out.

Well, that was it. He could take a hint. He wouldn't bother her again.

Could she have forgotten? No, he knew her too well to hope for that. Jack glanced again at the champagne resting in the bucket beside him, and the sheaf of flowers waiting on her chair. Then he signalled to the waiter to bring him the bill.

# 37

Where were they all? She couldn't believe it. Cars raced towards her, headlamps blazing, paintwork rippling with reflected light, but she couldn't see a single cab. Wait! There was one. Damn, its light was off. Freya strained her eyes down the avenue. She thought she could just make out another one, lined up at the traffic stop. The lights changed. Yes! She stepped off the kerb and waved wildly. The cab put its blinker on. Thank God! Then, to her fury, it stopped about ten yards before reaching her and someone else got in. Freya shook her fist as it shot past. Now the traffic lights had turned to red again, banking up another wave of cars. She pictured Jack in the restaurant, waiting for her, looking at his watch, wondering if she was coming. Frantic with impatience, Freya turned and began to walk.

Was she kidding herself? Would he really remember the bet after so many months? Even if he did, would he turn up after the terrible things she'd said to him? Jack probably wasn't even *in* New York. She knew now that he hadn't married Candace, but he might still be canoodling with some little sugarplum down under the ol' magnolia trees.

Still no cabs. She could see the criss-cross flash of

34th Street ahead of her. It was already 9.30. This was hopeless. Should she give up? She stopped dead, catching her breath, trying to decide. There was a ringing in her ears, drowning out the sounds of the street. Into the muffled hush, as clearly as if old Mrs da Fillipo were standing right next to her, came the words: *A woman always knows. And when she knows she must act.*

Freya broke into a run, long coat tangling in her legs, high heels stuttering on the sidewalk. She remembered the terrace in the moonlight, when the heel of her shoe had come off, how Jack had picked her up in his arms. A flame of desire licked through her. She had known then, but she hadn't trusted her heart. She had let fear of rejection and her own stupid pride stand in her way. But she knew now. And she was suddenly certain that, against all the odds, against reason or probability, Jack was waiting for her. She would race into the restaurant, breathless – she could see his incredulous smile. She'd be smiling too. She'd walk right up to him and say . . . What would she say? The words formed in her mind – words she had never allowed herself to speak aloud – like tight buds swelling, unfurling, bursting open to the light. *I love you.*

A cab! She waved at it desperately and it stopped. *Thank you, thank you, thank you.* Freya fell back against the seat, amazed at the idea she had just admitted into her mind. She loved him! Well, of course she loved him. Hadn't she been carrying him around in her heart for months? She missed his laugh. She missed his company. Some nights she couldn't sleep for wanting the touch of his body.

At last! Here was the long plate-glass curve of the restaurant. There was a queue outside, figures huddled into coats, stamping their feet. Freya squashed dollar bills into the cab driver's money tray, and raced to the door of the restaurant.

'Hey, you! Get in line!' called a belligerent voice.

'I'm meeting someone,' Freya tossed over her shoulder.

She pushed her way into the entrance, into the clatter and roar of a restaurant at peak hour. A crowd of people was clustered two and three deep around a long chromium bar: laughter, perfume, the brilliance of mirrors, the rattle of cocktail shakers. She barged her way through and walked straight into the sea of tables, head swivelling this way and that. Her heart slammed at her ribs. Where was he?

'Excuse me, Miss, do you have a reservation?'

Freya jerked her head impatiently at the polite male voice without looking round. 'I'm meeting someone,' she repeated, stepping further into the room. She felt a chill of panic. He *must* be here.

'May I have the name?'

Freya turned reluctantly, taking in the white shirt, black trousers, professional smile.

'Madison,' she told him, with a tiny thrill at saying the name aloud.

'If you'd just come with me . . .?'

Freya followed him to his smoothly sculpted lectern, and held her breath as she watched his forefinger skim down the open pages of his reservations book. He reached the end and began to backtrack slowly.

'He's here. I know he is,' Freya insisted, silencing an insidious whisper that told her he had never come, that she was a fool.

'Madison. Here we go,' said the man.

*Yes!* Freya could have kissed him.

'But that table was booked for eight o'clock.' He cocked his arm fussily to check his watch. 'I think he's gone.'

*No!* Aloud she said, 'Are you sure? Which table was it?'

The man put out his hand to stop a young woman who was passing, a slim blonde in a black dress. 'Suzie, this lady was supposed to be meeting Mr Madison, table twelve. Do you happen to remember if he left already? Suzie takes the coats,' he explained.

Suzie was looking curiously at Freya. 'I remember him all right. He gave me some flowers — absolutely gorgeous. Said he didn't need them any more. Then he left.'

Freya stared at her bleakly, not wanting to believe it.

'Tall, blond guy,' Suzie added. 'Handsome.'

'Did you see which way he went?' Freya demanded, looking from one to the other. 'Did he saying anything? When did he leave? How did he look?'

'He went maybe twenty minutes ago,' Suzie

answered. 'He looked pretty low.' Her expression suggested that *she* would not have kept such a man waiting.

Freya gave a sigh of defeat. 'Okay. Thanks.' She turned away.

She walked back past the bar and pushed her way outside. The queue was still there. Instinctively she swung away from the lights and laughter, and walked alone down the dark street, head down, hands pushed into her pockets.

Jack had come, and she'd missed him. How could she ever explain? *Sorry, Jack, I was at a singles evening.* She'd rejected him before. He would think that she'd done it again, deliberately – that she didn't care. Jack was a proud man. He'd given her one last chance, and she'd blown it.

Her own cruel words taunted her – 'useless', 'pathetic', 'too spineless to commit to anything'. But Jack had kept his promise. He had waited for her for almost two hours, conspicuously alone in a fashionable restaurant. He'd bought her flowers. She was the one who had doubted. This time she had disappointed him as bitterly as he had once disappointed her. Could the breach be mended? Could they even go back to being just friends? Freya's eyes squeezed tight at the thought of what she had thrown away. *Just* friends? What was so 'just' about it? What could be more exciting and intimate than being with someone who knew what you were thinking almost before you thought it, who caught your jokes and tossed them back in an instant, who knew all your likes and dislikes, who saw into the dark corners of your heart and liked you anyway – and who also happened to be wildly sexy. Freya had always fancied Jack – she could admit it now – but it was the *friendship* that was dazzling.

Freya gave a despairing sob. She didn't even know how to contact him. He could be anywhere – *anywhere!* – in this teeming city. She'd lost him, maybe for good.

Freya blinked, then blinked again. Something was bothering her at the extreme edge of her vision, an intermittent, flickering light. She turned her head. Across the street was a fluorescent sign. *North by N rthwest*, she read. The second 'o' had slipped and was dangling by a cable, spitting sparks. Freya stared. It was a cinema. *North by Northwest* was one of Jack's favourite films.

Before she knew it she had stepped off the kerb and was walking across the street. The place looked like an old fleapit, probably on the last lap of its lease before demolition. A ticket-lady – Chinese, maybe, or Korean – sat in a glass booth, watching a small portable TV and eating popcorn.

Freya bent her head to the narrow slot. 'Excuse me, has anyone bought a ticket in the last half hour or so? A man?'

The lady stared at her with bored eyes and chewed her popcorn. 'You want ticket?'

'Okay.' Freya took out her wallet and handed over a bill. What was she doing?

'Movie almost finished,' the woman said, sliding Freya's ticket across.

Freya ignored her. She crossed the dingy foyer, drawn by the music – panicky violins and the bang of drums.

She pushed through the doors and stopped, blind in the sudden dark. Onscreen, Cary Grant was clinging to a rock-face with one hand; the other gripped the hand of a blonde woman dangling in space, about to fall towards pine trees far, far below.

Freya scanned the audience as her eyes adjusted to the dark. There were perhaps a dozen figures scattered through the rows. None of them was Jack.

The agonized face of the blonde woman filled the screen. 'I can't make it!' she cried, raising despairing eyes to Cary Grant.

'Yes, you can. Come on.'

'I'm tired . . .'

Freya turned to go. She felt desolate. It had been stupid to think she could find her way to Jack, just because she loved him.

*Wait a minute!* There was a lone figure right over the other side, his legs propped on the seat in front. It was Jack. He was wearing those cute college-boy glasses. Freya felt her heart would burst. She hurried round the walkway behind the empty rows and down the far aisle.

On screen the couple were now in each other's arms on the upper bunk of a train compartment. The woman was wearing white pyjamas. 'This is silly,' she laughed.

'I know. I'm sentimental.'

Freya reached the row where Jack was sitting, one seat in from the end. He hadn't noticed her yet. His face was unguarded, his expression wistful. Freya melted with tenderness. She began to tremble.

But when she spoke, her voice was light, almost teasing. 'Is this seat taken?'

Jack looked up. His face flooded with astonishment and delight. He reached for her hand, holding it as if he would never let go, and flipped down the seat to draw her close. His eyes smiled into hers. 'I've been saving it for you,' he said.

# Acknowledgements

My thanks go to Susan Dull and Maureen Freely for allowing me to pick their brains; to Harriet Evans of Penguin for buoying me up with her effervescent phonecalls; and to my brilliant editor, Louise Moore, who demands the best and always gives it, too.

I owe a huge debt to my family: to my mother for her insight and encouragement; to my in-laws for unstinting moral and practical support; to my children for enduring a famine of holidays and maternal attention; and to my sister Tamie and her husband Paul for a wonderful visit at their Chelsea (NY) apartment.

Last, first and always is my husband Adam – my severest critic and most loyal champion.